# OTHER TITLES BY SUSIE BRIGHT

*The Best American Erotica, 1993–2003*

*How to Write a Dirty Story*

*Full Exposure*

*The Sexual State of the Union*

*Nothing But the Girl* (with Jill Posener)

*Herotica 1, 2, and 3*

*Susie Bright's Sexwise*

*Susie Bright's Sexual Reality:*
*A Virtual Sex World Reader*

*Susie Sexpert's Lesbian Sex World*

www.susiebright.com

# The BEST AMERICAN EROTICA 2003

## THE 10th ANNIVERSARY EDITION

### EDITED BY
# SUSIE BRIGHT

**A TOUCHSTONE BOOK**
PUBLISHED BY SIMON & SCHUSTER
New York  London  Toronto  Sydney  Singapore

*TOUCHSTONE*
*Rockefeller Center*
*1230 Avenue of the Americas*
*New York, NY 10020*

Touchstone *and colophon are registered trademarks*
*of Simon & Schuster Inc.*

*For information regarding special discounts for bulk purchases,*
*please contact Simon & Schuster Special Sales*
*at 1-800-456-6798 or business@simonandschuster.com*

*Designed by Michelle Blau*

*Manufactured in the United States of America*

*10  9  8  7  6  5  4  3  2*

*ISBN 0-7432-2261-X*

THE TENTH ANNIVERSARY EDITION IS DEDICATED TO THE
*BAE* AUTHORS WE MISS SO MUCH:

John Preston
Donald Rawley
Paul Reed
Bob Flanagan

# Contents

# Introduction

Happy anniversary, everyone. This is the tenth year of *The Best American Erotica,* and in the last decade we've enjoyed some of the most memorable erotica ever published in the English language. We've been on best-seller lists and shit lists; we've been hailed both as the decline of fine literature and as the end of hallowed traditions in mediocre smut. We are the only "Best of . . ." series, in any genre, to stay in print for all ten years we've published.

I suppose our dirtiest secret is that we've had an awful lot of fun.

This year, I decided to interview as many of our *BAE* author alumni as I could find, and discover a little about their writing lives and history—as well as their sexual opinions. Out of the 257 authors I've published in *BAE,* I spoke to 137, and researched another 50 or so from previous interview material, Web sites, and editors' notes. Four authors had passed away since we began the series, much to my sorrow. The ones I didn't get my hands on, as they say, "remain at large." If anyone is offended that they don't see themselves included, I can only say—we understand you're busy, but your mom says she wants to talk to you, and there's a check waiting for you at your last publisher's office.

In addition to interviewing our authors, I talked to hundreds of fans about their favorite stories of the past ten years. At the end of this edition you'll find "Readers' Choice: The Top 100 of the Past Ten Years," your favorite *BAE* fiction of the decade.

I loved tallying the results, and at the same time, I have a tender spot about any sort of contest—I wanna give a trophy to everyone. After all, fans voted on over 300 different stories, so virtually every *BAE* story was *somebody's* favorite. Hunter Thompson, who I had no idea was a BAE reader, called me at three in the morning to tell me that "The Queen of Exit 17" was his favorite *BAE* selection. And yet it didn't make the Top 100. Many superb stories didn't make the cut, but I'd never call this poll the final arbiter. My favorite part of *BAE* isn't any one story—I could never narrow it down—but rather the unprecedented variety of expression and sexuality we bring under one cover. It doesn't happen anyplace else.

Finally, in lieu of cutting a big enough cake for all to partake in, I'd like to thank a few people who have worked with me on *The Best American Erotica* since we first began the series in 1993.

My managers, Joanie Shoemaker and Jo-Lynne Worley (favorite stories: "Horse Heaven" and "Quiet Please"), are always the first to report that *BAE* is selling at a new small bookstore in a town ordinarily known for selling more Bibles than erotica. They've negotiated with six different editors and two publishers since the series began, and they've taken *BAE* to places as far-flung as Beijing (where I hear I have quite a following if I ever want to make an appearance). Their experience in every facet of publishing and the entertainment business has meant all the difference in how my editorial work has developed—and their loyalty and insight have kept me going through every political and artistic hurdle.

My father, Bill Bright (favorite story: "Sweating Profusely in Merida"), has been the best reader and editor this series ever had. I've never taken a formal writing course, but every time my father edits one of my books, I feel like I'm receiving a master class in the English language—as well as the many other languages that crop up in *BAE* storytelling! Bill has been a writer and editor in linguistics, anthropology, and poetry for decades now. When I was little, he would let me get into his big oak desk chair and look over his manuscripts with a red pencil, to see if I could find any typos. I remember the glee I felt when I found a mistake—even then, I was an editorial sadist. He said when I got good enough, I'd be able to use a red pen, but frankly, I've never let go of the pencil—it reminds me that he's still there, to look through the pages one more time.

Since I began *BAE,* my partner Jon Bailiff (favorite story: "Je t'aime, Batman, je t'adore") has had a thankless, and occasionally exhilarating, task—to live with a woman who takes every story so to heart that he never knows who's going to emerge from her writing studio at the end of the day. Jon's tastes in literature and smut are equally fine; he always has the right instincts. He nurtures this series every year by loving me well; and he is the one with whom I share the most laughs and curses along the way.

I'm sorry, but nostalgia makes me sentimental. There is one last piece of cake to honor, the piece with the hard bean hiding inside it—which will probably break the tooth of whoever bites down hard. That prize would go to the notorious and plentiful critics of erotica, the people who said:

"Literature and sex don't mix!"
"Women want romance, not smut!"
"Men want crotch shots, not stories!"
"Great writers don't write filth!"
"When it comes to erotica, people only want to read about themselves!"
"Why's a nice girl like you doing a dirty book like this?"
and,
"But you can't say *that!*"

Yet we did say it, and we wrote it, and we've lived to see a banquet of inspiration come out of it. Thanks to everybody, for making it taste so sweet.

# Talking with
## *The Best American Erotica* Authors

What do people think of erotic writers? The stereotype is that they are spectacled horndogs, nerdy nymphos, or the "A" students into kink. To a certain degree, *BAE* authors proved this to be true. Most of them confessed they were overeducated, and the National Merit scholars, grade grubbers, and stuffy literary award winners are too numerous to list here. They overachieved, and suffered the consequences.

What people *don't* know about erotic writers, according to my interviews, is how sexy, wholesome, daring, brave, strong, tough, and hilarious they are. What you'll find below are my ordinary questions to them, and their extraordinary answers in return.

Q. **Have you ever won an award for your writing? How about any sort of prize for your talents, no matter how silly or awful?**

I've led a remarkably award-free life, although, of course, I realize that virtue is its own reward.—*Marian Phillips*

I won "Best Mom" for an essay I wrote about my mother in 1972 and "Top Pop" for an essay about my father in 1973. And I won a $50 U.S. savings bond for my essay about "What America Means to Me" in 1975 (I cashed it last year and it was worth almost six hundred bucks).—*Chuck Palahniuk*

I am the reigning queen of our local hamburger chain's beauty pageant—I get free burgers and fries for life, plus my poster all over town.—*Ivy Topiary*

I am a Knight of the Garter of the Order of Mark Twain (a group in Hannibal, Missouri). I hasten to add that the Miss Universe Contest won by Carter Wilson, the contestant from Virginia, in 1973 was the *other* Carter Wilson and not me.—*Carter Wilson*

I have won boxes and boxes of awards for high school debate and made it to the state quarterfinals. Once a team forfeited when I walked in the room. ("Oh my God, it's her! Never mind. We give up.")—*Jess Wells*

I was one of the "50 Most Intriguing Women" in *Boston Magazine* in 1996. Hee hee hee.—*Amelia Copeland*

I came in second once in a competition for shortest hot pants. —*Nalo Hopkinson*

I have never won any awards, trophies, etc., unless you count, to my intense embarrassment, winning the Howdy Doody look-alike smile contest when I was ten. My mother sent my picture in. —*Tsaurah Litzky* (who has appeared in more *BAE*s than any other author—*ed.*)

### Martial Arts

Working on my third Dan, Shotokan Karate.—*Susan Volchok*

### Musical Achievement

I used to be a classical mezzo-soprano—I won the George Whitfield Chadwick Medal for contemporary music performance, and I was a fellow in voice performance at the Tanglewood Institute.—*Hanne Blank*

Twice won "Best Bassist in Boston," according to our local magazine, *The Noise.*—*Margaret Weigel*

I was a bassoon player, a double reed man, a player of Stravinsky's "Berceuse," from *The Firebird*. I wanted to be Brahms but I wasn't.—*Nicholson Baker*

## Special Awards
In the late seventies, I won the PIG award, from the National Organization of Women, for the most chauvinistic advertising of the year—I was the only woman to receive it that year. I was the one who created "The Maidenform Bra Woman: You never know where she'll turn up next."—*M. J. Rose*

I got a pair of engraved handcuffs for being the top academic graduate in my police academy.—*Mel Smith*

"Most Christian Day Student" award for my leadership of the Missionary Committee.—*Charles Flowers*

When I was twenty-two I won the Wormwood Award for "most neglected book of the year." Shit, that should have told me what the rest of my career would be like.—*Greg Boyd*

Have I ever won an award of any kind for my writing? Other than being worshiped by disenfranchised teenage girls, disturbed grown men, faded strippers, runaways, would-be presidential assassins, and volunteers for chemical castration—No, not that I remember.—*Maggie Estep*

I won an award in fourth grade for the "Best Arbor Day Essay." It went, "Trees are happy, trees are gay, if they could talk here's what they'd say . . ." My brother Buddy won the same award eight years before me, so I just copied his essay! Did you know my brother has never read a book cover-to-cover in his entire life, except for mine?—*Lisa Palac*

## School Daze

I won lots of baseball trophies, and many track and cross-country awards, all of which I threw away after I became a hippie. They were all won for years and years wasted running and running in the cold, dark nowhere day after day.—*Bart Plantenga*

I never won an award for anything, not even my beauty, which is surprising because in an unlit room I'm frequently mistaken for Juliet Prowse. In fact, one guy once looked at me naked and the only compliment he could come up with is "You have beautiful testicles." I did win a five-pound bag of sugar at a fair once.—*Brandon Judell*

### AWARDS

**Beauty Pageant Winners**
FIRST-RUNNER-UP FOR MINI-MISS OF CHELSEA, MASSACHUSETTS.
  Michelle Tea

MR. TEENAGE TWIN LAKES PHYSIQUE CONTEST, 1957.
  Jack Fritscher

THE KIWANIS CLUB "LITTLE MISS PEANUT" BEAUTY PAGEANT.
  Bernadette Bosky

AMATEUR STRIP CONTEST AT THE OLD GAY BAR QUEST IN BOSTON.
  Michael Lowenthal

**The Pulitzer Prize**
  Robert Olen Butler

  Jane Smiley

**The Bram Stoker Award (Horror)**
  Mike Ford

  Lucy Taylor

**The Lammie (Gay and Lesbian Lit)**
  Carol Queen

  Michael Bronski

  Michelle Tea

  Steven Saylor

  Mike Ford (two-time winner)

  Gerry Pearlberg

  Susie Bright

**The Herodotus (Historical Mysteries)**
  Steven Saylor

**Martial Arts**
TWO SILVER MEDALS FROM THE U.S. CUP TAE KWON DO CHAMPIONSHIP.
  Cecilia Tan

BLACK BELT IN SHORINJI KEMPO.
  Claire Tristram

TROPHY COLLECTION, TAE KWON DO.
  Wendy Minkoff

**New York Times *Best-seller Authors***
Nicholson Baker
Bret Easton Ellis
Susanna Kaysen
Chuck Palahniuk
Jane Smiley

***The Pushcart Prize***
Ed Falco
Lars Eighner
Jane Smiley
Jerry Stahl
Shay Youngblood
Donald Rawley
Nathan Englander
Marge Piercy
Stacey Richter

***The Wynner Award (Crossword Puzzles)***
Eric Albert (three-time winner)

***School Daze***
"PINKEST LIPS."
 Shay Youngblood
"EATS THE MOST."
 Paula Bomer
"EIGHTH-GRADE ATHLETE OF THE YEAR."
 David Shields
"BEST PERSONALITY."
 Elise D'Haene
"BOY OF THE YEAR."
 Wade Kreuger
"CLASS TOPPER."
 Ginu Kamani

***The Nebula (S/F)***
 Samuel R. Delany
 (four-time winner)
 Robert Silverberg
 (five-time winner)

***The Hugo (S/F)***
 Robert Silverberg
 (five-time winner)
 Samuel R. Delany
 (two-time winner)

Q. **How old are you?**

25–35: 26%, 36–49: 46%, 50+:21%, 60+: 7%

Next month I'll be a great-grandfather—so there!—*Bill Noble*

Q. **What sign are you?**

I asked about authors' astrological proclivities as an afterthought, thinking that some might be insulted, or shake their heads at me.

Some of them did just that, but out of the almost 200 people I interviewed, over 100 not only volunteered their sun sign, but also offered their rising sign and moon position.

Some interesting results: Pisces, Sagittarius, Libra, and Capricorn all scored in double digits. I was one of only six shocked Aries. Lowest scores went to Scorpio, known for her sex appeal, yet secretive nature, and also to Taurus, a terrifically sensual sign who sometimes just can't get off the couch.

Q. **What occupation do you hold, or have you held, besides being a writer?**

I was an attendant at the lunatic asylum for about ten years.
—*Lars Eighner*

**The Top Ten Professions**

| | | |
|---|---|---|
| 1. | Teacher | 56 |
| 2. | Editor | 39 |
| 3. | Waiter/Waitress | 36 |
| 4. | Secretary | 25 |
| 5. | Film/TV Production | 19 |
| 6. | Cook | 17 |
| 7. | Reporter | 16 |
| 8. | Retail | 15 |
| 9. | Publisher | 14 |
| 10. | Bookseller | 12 |

Some *BAE* authors were willing to admit to more unusual occupations, as long as their names were not used. Such discreet positions included one bill collector, an EPA inspector, a "notorious shoplifter," four drug dealers, and two stockbrokers.

Other authors were outspoken about their unique job history, like Mel Smith (former hot-air balloon artist), Shar Rednour (vice president, Girl Scout troop), and Thomas Roche (veteran soda jerk). Alison Smith was happy to reveal that she'd been a switchboard operator at a convent, but unfortunately, she didn't keep any tapes. Two authors confessed they had been go-go dancers, but wondered if such a job description dated them. Wendy Becker spoke for a lot of devoted spouses when she gave her occupation as "Butch girlfriend—hey, it's a full-time job sometimes . . ." Sometimes!—C'mon, Wendy, you needn't underestimate the task.

**Military Veterans**
  *Robert Olen Butler,* U.S. Army
  *Shaun Levin,* Israeli Defense Forces
  *Marc Levy,* U.S. Army
  *Bob Vickery,* U.S. Navy
  *Patricia Williams,* U.S. Navy

Q. Have you written and published in the following genres?

  Children's or Young Adult: 20, S/F: 33, Mystery/Crime: 26
  Romance: 6, Poetry: 60, Plays: 23

I have a total mobster fetish. I love the concept of having to be loyal and do the right thing or getting your thumbs taken off with a garden shears. I even drive a Lincoln Town Car—black with tinted windows, of course.—*Amelia G*

Q. Are you now, or have you ever been, a sex worker?

Most of the professions that *BAE* authors have pursued are either the sort of things that everyone does when they're young, or reflect their interests in working with words, whether as teacher or typist. They're the kind of jobs that any writer might take up, regardless of the genre they write in.

The one exception is sex work. Erotic writing is probably the only genre where you'll find writers who began to write because of their profession. Their work in the sex trade—as hookers, porn actors, phone sex voices, vibrator-peddlers, pornographers—often inspired them to write about what they saw. One inexplicable wrinkle: of the working prostitutes who are *BAE* authors, the ones who went to college were all graduates of an Ivy League school. Two from Yale, another from Barnard, Vassar, Harvard, etc. Go figure.

Twenty-six *BAE* authors said they work, or have worked, in the sex trade, which puts them below teachers in our profession poll, but way above cooks. About half are active in the business today, but many of them spoke with some hindsight.

Yes, I've been a sex worker. [Before my gender change] I appeared in an educational movie about female masturbation, and I made a movie for a fetishist's private collection (it featured two girls rubbing their stocking-clad legs together in mock wrestling poses), and I was briefly a professional dominatrix. I think sex work is a hard job; you earn every single damn dollar. My favorite client was a guy who kneeled down in front of me and followed my instructions to push his money under my spiked heel with his tongue. I had him straighten up, I cinched a dog collar around his neck, and he came in his pants. He was also visibly sweating. He said, "That's more than I can handle," and ran away. Poor thing. I hope he eventually managed to find a way to act out his fantasies so he could have more than a five-minute scene.—*Patrick Califia*

In publishing, the other side of literary erotic fiction is straight-ahead smut writing. What professional writers know is that the exact same story can be published in both venues—packaging and marketing are the only places where art becomes porn, and vice versa.

Forty *BAE* writers reported that they've written for unapologetic porn mags—'zines like *Juggs, Leg Show, Adam, Penthouse Letters*. Older writers like Robert Silverberg have dozens of pulp novels under their belt.

I'm the one who gets hired to write the "socially redeeming" material for porn magazines.—*Michael Bronski*

But the past ten years have seen the end of old-school porn, whose main benefit, aside from happy readers, was that it paid fairly well. The drawback of magazine writing was the insipid list of formula constructions every author had to follow—just as in the *nonerotic* magazine trade.

I'm becoming uncomfortably restricted in what fiction I can sell to people due to prior censorship. Publishers frequently say that they won't accept works of fiction that have any violence, nonconsensual sex, or underage people in them. What do you write, given these restrictions? "Today, I had consensual sex with someone who was over eighteen. The end." I wish we weren't doing the censors' work for them.—*Lauren Burka*

The Web, by comparison, has a virtually censor-free—as well as pay-free—environment for sex writing. Many new Web writers honestly don't know whether the sites they deal with are considered pornographic or erotic—that's old-school thinking, headed for the dustbin, along with movie ratings and nipple-counters.

"Porn"? I'm not sure what you mean by the characterization. I've never really bothered to separate out the smut I write into divisions of acceptability; it's all acceptable to me, and I don't worry too much what others think.—*Todd Belton*

Q. Who knows about your erotic writing? Your peers, friends, parents, children?

My mother, who passed away a few years ago, was incredibly supportive—although I don't think she really looked much at [my erotic magazine, *Libido*]. Still, she would send subscriptions to her friends, who would freak out . . . She'd just shrug and say, "If this bothers you, it tells me more about you than it does about my daughter."—*Marianna Beck*

When I asked *BAE* writers if their peers knew about their sex writing, only six people said it was a secret. Typically, these folks work in government jobs, where their social and creative lives are quite separate. It seems like the federal government is the last place where you cannot admit to being a sexual creature—at least until you get to higher posts where you can confess tabloid-style and possibly be redeemed.

Family relations were a different matter altogether. Forty-six authors reported that their parents would not want to know about their sexual writing. Mom and Dad are out of the loop, and everyone concerned is determined to keep it that way. Some gay writers say that their sexual preference, their professional life, and their erotic writing are seen as one and the same family scandal . . . the assumption being that if they were heterosexual, they would never think of writing about sex.

I don't think anybody in my family has ever read anything I've published. For the most part they are devout Mormons and small-town heterosexuals. They find me very scary. The most scary thing about me is that I am a therapist. After that, it's the writing, and at the bottom of the list goes my queerness.—*Patrick Califia*

More commonly, there was every variation in family reaction: mothers who know, fathers who don't, and vice versa. Bragging rights at one family get-together, and a cloak of silence at the next. The famous "knowing, but not knowing."

After she found out about my erotica, my mom told me my grandmother had supported the family during the Depression by writing for *True Confessions* and other confessionals. She was always a bit proud yet ashamed of that, too. It was kind of a family secret. —*Susan St. Aubin*

Most authors with children said their kids were too young to know anything beyond Winnie-the-Pooh. Interestingly, those with grown children found them to be discreetly more tolerant than they might find their own parents to be.

My twenty-six-year-old son knows about my erotic writing but has not read the porn books. The tacit assumption is that we don't want to share our sexual imaginations that closely, just like we don't smoke dope together and I don't tell him the kinds of anxieties I share with my girlfriends. He has read one of my romance novels, which has some steamy scenes, but no (well, almost no) S&M. He was a fine, fair, and generous critic.—*Molly Weatherfield*

Finally, we had the baker's dozen of authors who said their parents—or their grown children—were their biggest fans, the ones who throw them book-launch parties and offer them encouragement when the publishing world looks dim.

My parents not only know about it, when my mom threw a book party for me when *Black Feathers* came out; she invited all my relatives, godparents, high-school teachers, neighbors, etc. I sold about two cases of books that night, and toward the end of the evening she told me, "You know everyone is waiting to hear you read." So I had to get up and read an erotic story in front of them all. They loved it.—*Cecilia Tan*

## Q. How many books have you written and published?

A healthy minority (forty-five) of *BAE* authors have not published their own book—yet. What's more surprising is that it is even more rare to publish only once, and never return to commit the crime again.

A mere sixteen respondents have published one book and quit before the compulsion came over them twice. Most *BAE* writers did not have the good sense to stop bookmaking before it consumed them. The saddest cases, detailed below, were the compulsive book-doers, the authors who may be admired and worshiped by the out-side, but who are known to their family and friends as "out of their minds."

> **Over 20 Titles:** Cecilia Tan (39), Edo Van Belkom (22), Marge Piercy (35), Mike Ford (43), and Sam Delany (24+).
>
> **Over 100 Titles:** Robert Silverberg, who has written 186 major novels, 80 minor ones, 76 major nonfiction books, and 15 minor nonfiction ones.

Q. Did you attend college? If so, which one? What was your major?

*BAE* authors went to college—way too much, and for far too long, according to their reactions. They attended every sort of institution with no discernible pattern whatsoever except that nine of them graduated from Brown—the only school to have more than four *BAE* alumni (that honor goes to U.C. Santa Cruz). Both schools are known for their liberal traditions, but in that sense they are a minority, since most of the other authors who responded went to colleges where granola never really caught on.

> My alma mater no longer exists, so I'd prefer not to mention it except to say that it was an evangelical Christian college where, among other things, we were required to abstain from the use or possession of playing cards and "attending the theater as a way of life." My major was English literature, and I would describe myself with the phrase "least likely to attend my Bible classes."
> —*Mike Ford*

When it came to a course of studies, the group finally showed some predictability. Fifty-two of their diplomas are imprinted with a Bachelor's Degree in English Literature or Creative Writing. Psychology and Theater were next down the list, with six graduates, while Philosophy claimed five.

Q. **Has any of your work been produced in popular music, film, theater, or art?**

Authors today are not purists in any medium or genre—neither sexual
nor artistic labels stick to them easily. Nearly everyone I spoke to had
"crossed over" in some fashion with their words—as lyric, dialog, rant,
or performance. Their accomplishments were remarkable, and often a
surprising contrast to their erotic literary contributions.

*Permanent Midnight,* 1998. I also co-wrote two porn classics,
*Night Dreams* and *Cafe Flesh,* under the pseudonym Herbert W.
Day, which is known to anyone who admits they ever watched late-
eighties porn.—*Jerry Stahl*

I get royalties from Rhino records . . . and Bill Moyers made a
video of my poetry and interviewing me. Does that count? I didn't
dance or show my belly button.——*Marge Piercy*

*Rollerball,* 1975; *A Shining Season,* 1979; *Mountains of the Moon,*
1990.——*William Harrison*

A chair I made from seven hundred chocolate biscuits appeared
on the cover of *Australian Art Monthly.*——*Linda Jaivin*

*Fight Club,* 1999.——*Chuck Palahniuk*

I used to have a scandalous theater life—in the sense that I acted
in TV commercials and soap operas in my late teens and early
twenties.——*Dani Shapiro*

*A Thousand Acres,* 1997. But it wasn't popular—a bomb, actually.——*Jane Smiley*

I created *My Mother's Imaginary Husband* at the Knitting Factory, which relates the absolutely true story of how I helped my mother build a small altar to the actor Brian Dennehy.—*Martha Garvey writing as Nell Carberry*

*Girl, Interrupted,* 1999.—*Susanna Kaysen*

I co-wrote the narration for *The Times of Harvey Milk* and *Common Threads,* which both won the Oscar for Best Documentary. —*Carter Wilson*

My video documentary of New Orleans painter/photographer George Dureau is in the permanent collection of the Museé de Photographie et Vidéographie in Paris.—*Jack Fritscher*

I have a visual work hanging in a gallery in Oakland for what they call "The Orange Show." It is a row of images: a bottle of Orangina with the product's name written underneath, an orange vagina with the work *orangina* written underneath, an orange anus with the word *organus* written underneath, and an orange penis with the word *orangenis* underneath. It just sold.—*Robert Gluck*

Q. **Has your work ever been banned in another country, expelled from a local library, or seized at Customs?**

What a stupid question this was. Virtually every erotic writer—and even those who had no such intentions—during the eighties and much of the nineties had their work seized at the Canadian border during the heyday of "obscenity" busting by the Canadian Customs Department. They singled out anything from gay publishers, anything shipped from California, anything from a press whose size wasn't monolithic, and of course, anything that dared call itself sexual. This procedure continued unabated until Little Sisters Bookstore of Vancouver successfully sued the pants off them in the Canadian Supreme Court for unfairly prosecuting queer works of literature.

The funniest Canadian seizure was when a December issue of *On Our Backs* was stopped because of a photo that showed me wearing nothing but a strap-on dildo, draped in Christmas tree lights. They said I was in bondage, from a single strand of tree lights!—*Shar Rednour*

Small- and medium-press writers were the ones who suffered in the border wars—best-sellers reached their destination, regardless of the material. Famous writers in the States, by comparison, would usually realize just how controversial they'd become when their work was made an example of at a local library or school board.

*A Thousand Acres* was banned in a couple of school districts in Washington, not for the incest theme, but for the adulterous sex between consenting adults, which seems to have been less acceptable in those school districts than the incest.—*Jane Smiley*

What interested me in writers' reactions to my question was the weary or indifferent acceptance of this state of affairs. Writers know that they can expect to be censored, hidden, and airbrushed throughout their careers, with nary a First Amendment blush to betray its occurrence.

Once while touring as a poet with Lollapalooza I was told I would be arrested if I performed my poem "FUCK ME" in Detroit. So I did it again and again and again—alas, no one arrested me. —*Maggie Estep*

While controversy may sell books, it's a rare artist who rises to the taboo fame of a Robert Mapplethorpe

My story "Je t'aime, Batman, je t'adore" was made an example of by DC Comics and removed upon their legal protest, by Simon & Schuster, in subsequent printings of *BAE* '99—probably the worst, best, and most bizarre experience of my writing career.—*Kelly McQuain*

The short film I wrote and directed, *The White to Be Angry,* about a young neo-Nazi as refashioned by film homage to Woody Allen, Clive Barker, and auteur Bruce LaBruce, was held up at Customs in Toronto. On the night of the screening at the Pleasuredome Experimental Film Archive, two undercover cops came to see if this film directed by a black ghetto drag queen was white supremacy propaganda. The *über*-hunky young cops identified themselves after the Q&A and surprisingly told me they liked the film. The entire incident became a *cause célèbre,* written about all over La Canada. —*Vaginal Davis*

In truth, there's little chance of getting rich off a censorship scandal. Instead, the typical result is isolation for the author and ignorance on the part of the public. Being banned isn't fun, and it's more numbing than any of us admit.

### Best American Erotica Authors Who Are Really Canadian

*Michele Davidson, Barbara Gowdy, Nalo Hopkinson, Nancy Kilpatrick, Debra Martens, Susan Musgrave, Edo Van Belkom*

Q. Has your work ever been "made an example of" by various people with an agenda?

Erotic writers get tarred and feathered sometimes, that's part of the job description. In America, we have a very curious combination of forces who like to exploit every chance of sexual condemnation. First, there's the Church, which is predictable enough, but sexual literature has almost always been blasphemous.

The Catholic Church, currently embroiled in a priest-molestation scandal, has excommunicated me because of my 2001 novel, *What They Did to the Kid: Confessions of an Altar Boy.* And to think I attended seminary with Cardinal Law. —*Jack Fritscher*

Next comes the government, which has always taken a prurient interest in artists and activists whom they believe, however delusionally, are a threat to the state. Hoover and his black petticoats seem to have an unending lace ribbon of sleazy surveillance.

I finally received, via the Freedom of Information Act, my extensive files from the FBI and CIA, obscured with many black globs of ink.—*Marge Piercy*

The blows that hurt the most always come from your kin. The most intimate attacks against erotica have come from feminists, liberals, and radicals who created the monster called "politically correct."

In the mid-1980s, I published several text and image montages in a 'zine based in Northampton, Massachusetts. Their satirical subject was sexism and violence, but one bundle of the 'zine was burned on the publisher's doorstep, accompanied by a note stuffed into his mailbox that said something like "We don't need this sexist bullshit." This was in an era and in a town that measured its radicalism in degrees of crabbiness.—*Corwin Erickson*

A feminist publisher who wanted to reprint one of the books I was in required that all the overtly erotic poets be removed from the edition. I refused to grant the rights under those circumstances. Other than that, I have been fortunate in being spared nonsense of this kind.—*Gerry Pearlberg*

Q. Any interesting felonies or misdemeanors you'd like to mention?

Most authors replied, "I'd rather not mention." A goodly number of them rued the fact that they have been inexcusably well-mannered and law-abiding.

I believe I've engaged in oral sex in states where it's a felony—but really, who hasn't?—*Marian Phillips*

Just the usual boring shit that happens when you're a junkie. Nothing dramatic.—*Jerry Stahl*

I was court-martialed for refusing to get out of bed one morning on an officers' training course. (It was the only way to get chucked out of the course.) I was caned at school in South Africa for not having my hair cut, and forgetting my Afrikaans textbook at home.—*Shaun Levin*

I tried to be a burglar for a short while a long time ago, but I felt too guilty; I even went and put stuff back.—*Maggie Estep*

As an undergraduate I was arrested for "conspiracy to defame the flag" while filming a spoof of Captain America. One of the actors was using a flag for a cape. Must have been a slow news day, because the story was all over the New York news media. The *Newsday* headline was something like "Film Reel Reels Four." All charges were, of course, eventually dropped.—*Ed Falco*

Q. "When not writing, I am likely to be . . ."

What is the Great American Pastime? In our authors' poll, "reading" and "having sex" outscored baseball as favorite ways to waste a perfectly nice day.

"Being with my family" and "Cooking" tied for third place, but aren't those actually the same thing? After the tie came music, movies, dancing, gardening, and traveling. Walking the dog trounced petting the cat. Other popular pastimes included the following:

Attending AA meetings
Alphabetizing my porn.—*Thomas Roche*

Birdwatching
Breast-feeding
Canoeing

Researching. Meeting people and stealing their best stories. Paranormal ghost shit. Rock masonry. Spoiling my dogs. Weight lifting.—*Chuck Palahniuk*

Crying
Diving
Dogsledding
Doing errands with my husbands.—*Bernadette Bosky*
Doing yoga
Dressing up
Drinking

My hobbies are having people visit and cleaning while they read a magazine. I love to hang out with my five-year-old son, lay in a hammock, lay on the grass, lay in bed, lay on a big bed I have in front of the TV, etc. I also like to plant vegetables.—*Jill Soloway*

Eating out
Eavesdropping
Fishing
Fighting off psychological demons.—*Jack Murnighan*
Hiking and mountaineering
Horse racing

I just met a woman today who was telling me how her grandmother advised her to bet. I said, "You were really lucky to have a grandmother with a betting system." Some people get all the breaks.—*Jane Smiley*

Housework

Motorcycling
Mushroom hunting

In my free time, I enjoy reading, drinking martinis, and resting, usually in that order.—*Ivy Topiary*

Practicing Zazen
Procrastinating

Running around in the woods stark naked in a chamois loincloth while living with straight mountainmen on weekend buckskin rendezvous.—*Jack Fritscher*

Sewing, quilting, knitting
Shooting pool
Sleeping
Studying Sanskrit

I like to go on long vacations alone to Third World countries in which I try to spend less money progressively each day until I'm living like a homeless person.—*Claire Tristram*

Swimming
Reading Tarot cards

Q. **Do you have any collections we should know about?**

Accordions.—*Marian Phillips*
Antique costume jewelry and fabulous hats.—*Hanne Blank*
Harmonicas and Christian iconography.—*Bob Zordani*

I collect model horses and tack—but that's odd without being very interesting to most people. More interesting, perhaps, is my growing collection of Pervert Fashion Dolls physically augmented to be more than anatomically correct: Naughty French

Maid Boyfriend Doll; Naturally Blonde Fashion Doll (with crotchless panties to show it); Sex Goddess Fashion Doll; She-Male Fashion Doll (with broader shoulders & chin, added Adam's apple); Punk Fashion Doll (with tattoos, armpit hair, and nine piercings). I'm working on Sixteen But Trying Not to Show It Younger-Sister Doll; Masturbating Boyfriend Doll; Flasher Boyfriend Doll; and Dominatrix Fashion Doll.—*Bernadette Bosky*

Autographs.—*Kevin Killian*

Barbara Stanwyck films, fountain pens.—*Martha Garvey writing as Nell Carberry*

I collect Virgin Mary memorabilia. Still very hot to get a Polish Black Mary.—*Carol Queen*

Books about organized crime.—*Thomas Roche*

My hobby is my girl, my workout regime is with my girl, I pursue my girl, and I collect really cool fantasies with my girl. —*Adelina Anthony*

Bottom boys.—*Simon Sheppard*

My wife and I collect antique picture postcards, not so much for the images on the front but for the messages written on the back. We also collect old shoes, though not as erotic objects. They speak to our novelist selves of the lives that once were led in them. We have, for example, a lady's shoe from the 1780s, a Civil War boot, a Chinese foot-bound woman's shoe, a shoe with a rhinestone butterfly that Ella Fitzgerald performed in.—*Robert Olen Butler*

Boxer figurines, old nature books, vintage dog photographs. —*Gerry Pearlberg*

Jewish comedy albums from the late 1950s.—*Michael Bronski*
Encyclopedias.—*Joe Maynard*
Dinosaurs, dictionaries, furniture, glass-boxed vignettes of traditional Beijing life in which the people are created with pussy willow bodies and beetle heads, arms, and legs.—*Linda Jaivin*

Fire King dishes.—*Dodie Bellamy*

I share an interesting collection of fetish gear that includes various dental and surgical tools, a welding tool which makes funky tattoos, and an incredibly sexy rubber and vinyl wardrobe.
—*Name Withheld*

Lizards, matchbooks, pitchers, postcards.—*Vicki Hendricks*
Medicine bottles and yogurt cup caps.—*Estabrook*

I founded the American Newspaper Repository, a collection of original newspapers discarded from libraries.—*Nick Baker*

Miniature shoes.—*Marcy Sheiner*
Nepali art, religious extremist propaganda.—*Bonny Finberg*
Old Girl Scout manuals.—*Shar Rednour*
Old postcards of my neighborhood.—*Linda Rosewood Hooper*

My house looks like a library, with every wall lined with bookcases containing thousands of books. I have more than 1,200 LPs and CDs. I have around 5,000 porn videos, including Robert Rimmer's collection. I have a bottle of almost every brand of commercial sex lubricant that was available in the U.S. in 1998.
—*Eric Albert*

Police reports.—*Corwin Erickson*
Politically incorrect postcards.—*Carter Wilson*
Shell art.—*Michelle Tea*

Stamps.—*Paula Bomer*
Statehood quarters.—*Bill Brent*
Victorian mourning jewelry and hair wreaths.—*Poppy Z. Brite*

I collect little things, ostensibly because I have a sand tray in my therapy office. I am obsessed with Playmobil. I lean toward their medieval and magical lines of figurines, so I have a lot of knights, wizards, wicked queens, fairies, witches, and also an entire village of Native Americans, including a tepee. I like salt and pepper shakers in the shape of animals, and action figures like the Mystic Knights of Tir Na Nog. I'm also collecting The Realm of the Claw figures and Lady Death, and I have all of the Harry Potter Legos. Does anybody have a wolf from the Wade porcelain "endangered North American animals" series? (There is one figurine in each box of Red Rose Tea. Terrible tea. But the animals are fabulous.)

My other hobby is collecting enemies. I keep a running tally of who has done me wrong, so I can check them off the list either when I get even or when I have reached some sort of milestone in my life. There are certain key points at which some of my political prisoners will be freed and then invited to attend a public gathering. The subtext of just about any party that I have ever thrown is, who among the guests was recently liberated from my shit list?—*Patrick Califia*

**If you are interested in reading the complete interviews and comments of any of the *BAE* authors, contact the editor at BAE@susiebright.com**

Martha Miller

# THE BABY-SITTER

Dan had been fucking the baby-sitter all winter. Cory was suspicious the first time she met the blond-haired, blue-eyed graduate student from Kansas. Dan told Cory that Heather needed to supplement her income while she wrote her thesis, and that she loved children. Cory noticed that their nine-year-old, Jamey, didn't get along with Heather any better than he got along with his father. When Dan wouldn't offer an explanation for the time away from home and his lack of interest in their sex life, Cory made excuses for him. She decided he was depressed about his fortieth birthday, the new head of the English department, and Cory's recent five-pound weight gain. Then, on a Tuesday night in April, Cory returned early from a faculty wives' dinner. When she entered the living room, she discovered Dan on his knees in front of her favorite chair, his face buried between the baby-sitter's thighs.

Cory cleared her throat. "Um—excuse me?"

Heather looked at her and smiled weakly. Dan obviously hadn't heard. Heather tried to gently push his head away. Dan moaned and attacked his feast more vigorously. Heather lay her head back on the chair and shrugged, as if to say, *What can I do about it?*

"Dan!" Cory's voice had a strange high pitch. He didn't budge. Finally she sighed and asked Heather, "Where's Jamey?"

"He went to Michael's to play Nintendo," Heather answered in a slightly shaky voice. "I told him to be home by nine."

"Did you say something, sweet pea?" Dan finally raised his head and looked at Heather.

Heather pointed at Cory.

Dan's chin and cheeks were glistening in the light from the TV. "Home early?"

"I—I had a headache," Cory started to explain.

"Heather, maybe I should take you home," Dan said.

"I'll take her home," Cory interrupted.

Only then did Heather pull her legs together and stand. She brushed her skirt into place and gathered her things. The long drive back to the campus was tense, and thankfully silent. When they reached the sorority house, Heather turned to Cory and said, "Listen, no charge tonight, okay?"

Cory felt a weight on her chest. Her breathing was slow, labored. "How long has this been going on?"

Heather looked at the ground. "It started last January, I guess. I'm sorry. It's over now, honest."

During the drive home, with the headache buzzing between her ears, Cory weighed her options. A divorce right now was out of the question. She could go home to her mother for a few days, but then she'd have to listen to her I-told-you-so's. There were the payments on the bedroom furniture and the roof on the garage. She thought about Jamey. What would a separation do to him? This wasn't Dan's first infidelity. Actually, he'd been cheating on his first wife when he started dating Cory. Back then, she had been the enthralled student. . . .

That night, Dan begged her forgiveness. She cried. He held her, stroked her hair, then slowly and gently made love to her. His erection was huge. He was more excited than she'd seen him for a long time. Her headache dulled while the rest of her body responded intensely. As she came for the third time, she closed her eyes and saw Dan, on his knees in front of her favorite chair, eating the baby-sitter. It pushed her over the edge, then and in the months that followed, in a way none of her other fantasies could.

Cory used all her resources to find a new sitter. She placed an ad in the newspaper, checked agencies, put notes on Laundromat bulletin boards, and asked her friends.

Finally, Marsha Endeley said, "I know a student you might like better."

"Another student?" Cory sighed.

Marsha nodded. "She's nothing like Heather."

"What's her name?"

Lisa Monette was five foot ten, weighed close to two hundred pounds, had a Mohawk haircut, and wore six earrings in each ear. She owned a motorcycle, though it was broken-down most of the time. Her eyes were black, and her skin was dark. Dan smiled cordially when he met her, then he looked at Cory with a frown, and she knew she'd made the right choice.

Jamey loved Lisa. She owned her own joystick. Over the course of the summer she taught Jamey to catch a pop fly and to bat without closing his eyes. Eventually, she started showing up at his Little League games, at Jamey's invitation.

Cory was uncomfortable about it at first, but she pushed the feeling away. Every time Jamey was at bat, Lisa hollered and clapped. "Get 'em, Jamey. Knock it out of the park!"

One afternoon, Jamey connected with a ball that was high and outside. He hit it deep into center field. Lisa jumped up from her seat, yelling, "Go, Jamey, go!" Someone behind Cory took up the chant when he rounded first base and headed for second. Cory stood and hollered, "Go! Go!" Cory noticed that, thanks to Lisa's lead, the entire small bunch of uninterested moms were on their feet, yelling. Jamey ran across the dusty home plate and headed toward the crowd. Cory opened her arms with pride, but he ran to Lisa.

"That's my boy!" Lisa hugged him. "What a hit!"

"Good job, Jamey," Cory said.

"Oh, Mom." Jamey embraced Cory suddenly. "I did it, Mom."

Cory ran her fingers through Jamey's damp, sweaty hair. Later that afternoon at the Dairy Queen, Jamey would ask for a Mohawk haircut. And to her own surprise, Cory seriously considered it before she said no.

It was the self-esteem seminar that finally rocked the boat. Several of the faculty wives signed up for the all-day Saturday workshop. Most of the husbands were at a meeting in Chicago and would be away all weekend.

"All day? I have a thousand things to do." Cory hesitated when Marsha brought it up.

"Do something for yourself for a change!"

"I don't know, Jamey has a game. . . ."

"Let the baby-sitter take him. Come on."

It did turn out to be a nice Saturday, away from everything. After a long lecture, the women sat in a circle and talked about what they would change if they had higher self-esteem. That was when the woman next to Cory said softly, "If I felt better about myself, I would divorce my husband. He's been screwing around for years." The woman started to cry. Cory scooted closer and put her arm around her shoulders. She thought about the night she walked in on Dan eating the baby-sitter. She blinked back her own tears.

After the session, Cory refused a dinner invitation from Marsha, and slowly drove home.

Lisa's motorcycle was standing in the driveway. The house was quiet when Cory entered. "Anybody home?" Cory called.

"In here."

Lisa was reading in Cory's favorite chair. The image flashed. Heather. Her legs spread. "Where's Jamey?" she asked.

"His grandma came and got him for a movie and dinner," Lisa

answered. "They left about five o'clock. I just hung around to make sure you wouldn't worry about him."

"God, that was two hours ago. You could have left a note."

"Aw, it's all right. I'm as comfortable here as my place." Lisa smiled.

Cory's shoulders slumped.

"You look like hell, if you don't mind my saying so."

Cory's knees gave and she sat down hard on the couch. She could feel the tears starting.

Lisa came across the room and knelt beside her. "You don't look *that* bad, come on. I'm sorry."

"It's not you," Cory stammered. Lisa slid onto the couch beside her. Cory started talking. It all came out. The seminar. The woman beside her. Heather. Dan between her legs. Cory's favorite chair.

"That sucks," Lisa said softly. "Why, if I had a woman like you, I'd never look at another."

"You mean if you were a man and had a woman like me," Cory corrected her.

"No, I don't."

Cory realized that Lisa was stroking her arm. Goose bumps rose beneath her touch. "I've never cheated on Dan," Cory said softly.

Lisa whispered, "Maybe you should." Her lips were close to Cory's ear. Cory could feel Lisa's hot breath tickle her neck.

Cory leaned back, and Lisa was on her—unbuttoning her blouse and kissing her neck. Cory moaned, surrendering. Somewhere in the back of her mind she wondered who would do what and how. But her cunt was tingling. Her nipples were hard. Lisa pulled her blouse off and with one hand reached behind and unhooked her bra. Her breasts fell loose. Lisa gently clamped her mouth over one, then the other erect nipple.

"We shouldn't do it here," Cory protested.

"Why not?" Lisa slid her hand under Cory's skirt and squeezed the damp crotch of her panties.

Cory reached to help pull her panties down over her hips. She pulled one foot out and with the other kicked her underwear across the room. They landed draped across an expensive lampshade.

Lisa's hand worked slowly, sliding two fingers inside her. Cory rocked her hips, gently fucking. Each time she came down on the hand, Lisa's thumb pressed against her clit. Just as Cory thought she might come, Lisa pulled her hand away.

Cory whimpered.

Lisa replaced her fingers with her mouth.

Cory could feel the hot moist tongue wash her swollen vulva. She raised her knees, reached down, and pulled her wet lips open as far as she could.

Lisa slid two fingers back inside and fucked and sucked her slowly.

"I'm going to come!"

"Don't."

"I've got to!" Cory tried to distract herself. She thought about the housework. She thought about Jamey. She thought about the home run, the crowd cheering. A white-hot flash, like a jolt of electricity, went through her. Tingling spread through her body to the tips of her fingers and toes. Her pussy started to convulse. "Oh— oh!" she cried, pulling Lisa's head to her. She ran her fingers through the stiff Mohawk and rubbed her cunt in the woman's face as she experienced the most intense orgasm of her life. At last, gently and reluctantly, she pushed Lisa away.

"Well." Lisa smiled broadly up at Cory from between her legs. "If you've got to, you've got to."

Cory laughed. She was breathing hard. Her body felt weak, like she couldn't move. Lisa was laughing softly, too. Then they were both quiet.

It seemed like hours had passed when Lisa said, "Right there in that chair, huh?"

"Yes," Cory said softly.

"He was on his knees?"

Cory looked at her. She hadn't sat in her favorite chair for months. She'd considered throwing it away. The whole family seemed to avoid it. From somewhere far away she heard her own voice saying, "Take off your pants and get over there in that chair."

# FROM CHOKE

It's dark and starting to rain when I get to the church, and Nico's waiting for somebody to unlock the side door, hugging herself in the cold.

"Hold on to these for me," she says and hands me a warm fistful of silk.

"Just for a couple hours," she says. "I don't have any pockets." She's wearing a jacket made of some fake orange suede with a bright orange fur collar. The skirt of her flower-print dress shows hanging out. No pantyhose. She climbs up the steps to the church door, her feet careful and turned sideways in black spike heels.

What she hands me is warm and damp.

It's her panties. And she smiles.

Inside the glass doors, a woman pushes a mop around. Nico knocks on the glass, then points at her wristwatch. The woman dunks the mop back in a bucket. She lifts the mop and squeezes it. She leans the mop handle near the doorway and then fishes a ring of keys out of her smock pocket. While she's unlocking the door, the woman shouts through the glass.

"You people are in Room 234 tonight," the woman says. "The Sunday school room."

By now, more people are in the parking lot. People walk up the steps, saying hi, and I stash Nico's panties in my pocket. Behind me, other people hustle the last few steps to catch the door before it swings shut. Believe it or not, you know everybody here.

These people are legends. Every single one of these men and women you've heard about for years.

In the 1950s a leading vacuum cleaner tried a little design improvement. It added a spinning propeller, a razor-sharp blade mounted a few inches inside the end of the vacuum hose. Inrushing air would spin the blade, and the blade would chop up any lint or string or pet hair that might clog the hose.

At least that was the plan.

What happened is a lot of these men raced to the hospital emergency room with their dicks mangled.

At least that's the myth.

That old urban legend about the surprise party for the pretty housewife, how all her friends and family hid in one room, and when they burst out and yelled "Happy birthday" they found her stretched out on the sofa with the family dog licking peanut butter from between her legs . . .

Well, she's real.

The legendary woman who gives head to guys who are driving, only the guy loses control of his car and hits the brakes so hard the woman bites him in half, I know them.

Those men and women, they're all here.

These people are the reason every emergency room has a diamond-tipped drill. For tapping a hole through the thick bottoms of champagne and soda bottles. To relieve the suction.

These are the people who come waddling in from the night, saying they tripped and fell on the zucchini, the lightbulb, the Barbie doll, the billiard balls, the struggling gerbil.

See also: The pool cue.

See also: The teddy bear hamster.

They slipped in the shower and fell, bull's-eye, on a greased shampoo bottle. They're always being attacked by a person or persons unknown and assaulted with candles, with baseballs, with hard-boiled eggs, flashlights, and screwdrivers that now need removing. Here are the guys who get stuck in the water inlet port of their whirlpool hot tub.

Halfway down the hallway to Room 234, Nico pulls me against the wall. She waits until some people have walked past us and says, "I know a place we can go."

Everybody else is going into the pastel Sunday school room, and Nico smiles after them. She twirls one finger next to her ear, the international sign language for crazy, and she says, "Losers." She pulls me the other way, toward a sign that says *Women*.

Among the folks in Room 234 is the bogus county health official who calls to quiz fourteen-year-old girls about the appearance of their vagina.

Here's the cheerleader who gets her stomach pumped and they find a pound of sperm. Her name is LouAnn.

The guy in the movie theater with his dick stuck through the bottom of a box of popcorn, you can call him Steve, and tonight his sorry ass is sitting around a paint-stained table, squeezed into a child's plastic Sunday school chair.

All these people you think are a big joke. Go ahead and frigging laugh your frigging head off.

These are sexual compulsives.

All these people you thought were urban legends, well, they're human. Complete with names and faces. Jobs and families. College degrees and arrest records.

In the women's room, Nico pulls me down onto the cold tile and squats over my hips, digging me out of my pants. With her other hand, Nico cups the back of my neck and pulls my face, my open mouth, into hers. Her tongue wrestling against my tongue, she's wetting the head of my dog with the pad of her thumb. She's pushing my jeans down off my hips. She lifts the hem of her dress in a curtsey with her eyes closed and her head tilted a little back.

She settles her pubes hard against my pubes and says something against the side of my neck.

I say, "God, you're so beautiful," because for the next few minutes I can.

And Nico pulls back to look at me and says, "What's that supposed to mean?"

And I say, "I don't know." I say, "Nothing, I guess." I say, "Never mind."

The tile smells disinfected and feels gritty under my butt. The walls go up to an acoustical tile ceiling and air vents furry with dust and crud. There's that blood smell from the rusty metal box for used napkins.

"Your release form," I say. I snap my fingers. "Did you bring it?"

Nico lifts her hips a little and then drops, lifts, and settles herself. Her head still back, her eyes still closed, she fishes inside the neckline of her dress and brings out a folded square of blue paper and drops it on my chest.

I say, "Good girl," and take the pen clipped on my shirt pocket.

A little higher each time, Nico lifts her hips and sits down hard. Grinding a little front to back. With a hand planted on the top of each thigh, she pushes herself up, then drops.

"Round the world," I say. "Round the world, Nico."

She opens her eyes maybe halfway and looks down at me, and I make a stirring motion with the pen, the way you'd stir a cup of coffee. Even through my clothes, I'm getting the grid of the tile engraved in my back.

"Round the world, now," I say. "Do it for me, baby."

And Nico closes her eyes and gathers her skirt around her waist with both hands. She settles all her weight on my hips and swings one foot over my belly. She swings the other foot around so she's still on me, but facing my feet.

"Good," I say and unfold the blue paper. I spread it flat against her round humped back and sign my name at the bottom, on the blank that says *sponsor.* Through her dress, you can feel the thick back of her bra, elastic with five or six little wire hooks. You can feel her rib bones under a thick layer of muscle.

Right now, down the hall in Room 234, is the girlfriend of your best friend's cousin, the girl who almost died banging herself on the stick shift of a Ford Pinto after she ate Spanish fly. Her name is Mandy.

There's the guy who snuck into a clinic in a white coat and gave pelvic exams.

There's the guy who always lies in his motel room, naked on top of the covers with his morning boner, pretending to sleep until the maid walks in.

All those rumored friends of friends of friends of friends . . . they're all here.

The man crippled by the automatic milking machine, his name is Howard.

The girl hanging naked from the shower curtain rod, half dead from autoerotic asphyxiation, she's Paula and she's a sexaholic.

Hello, Paula.

Give me your subway feelers. Your trench coat flashers.

The men mounting cameras inside the lip of some women's room toilet bowl.

The guy rubbing his semen on the flaps of deposit envelopes at automatic tellers.

All the peeping toms. The nymphos. The dirty old men. The restroom lurkers. The handballers.

All these sexual bogeymen and -women your mom warned you about. All those scary cautionary tales.

We're all here. Alive and unwell.

This is the twelve-step world of sexual addiction. Compulsive sexual behavior. Every night of the week, they meet in the back room of some church. In some community center conference room. Every night, in every city. You even have virtual meetings on the Internet.

My best friend, Denny, I met him at a sexaholics meeting. Denny had got up to the point where he needed to masturbate fifteen times a day just to break even. Anymore, he could barely make a fist, and he was worried about what all that petroleum jelly might do to him, long term.

He'd considered changing to some lotion, but anything made to soften skin seemed to be counterproductive.

Denny and all these men and women you think are so horrible or funny or pathetic, here's where they all let their hair down. This is where we all go to open up.

Here are prostitutes and sex criminals out on a three-hour release from their minimum-security jail, elbow to elbow with women who love gang bangs and men who give head in adult bookstores. The hooker reunites with the john here. The molester faces the molested.

Nico brings her big white ass almost to the top of my dog and bangs herself down. Up and then down. Riding her guts tight around the length of me. Pistoning up and then slamming down. Pushing off against my thighs, the muscles in her arms get bigger and bigger. My thighs under each of her hands go numb and white.

"Now that we know each other," I say, "Nico? Would you say you liked me?"

She turns to look back over her shoulder at me, "When you're a doctor, you'll be able to write prescriptions for anything, right?"

That's if I ever go back to school. Never underestimate the power of a medical degree for getting you laid. I bring my hands up, each hand open against the stretched smooth underside of each thigh. To help lift her, I figure, and she twines her cool soft fingers through mine.

Sleeved tight around my dog, without looking back, she says, "My friends bet me money that you're already married."

I hold her smooth white ass in my hands.

"How much?" I say.

I tell Nico that her friends might be right.

The truth is, every son raised by a single mom is pretty much born married. I don't know, but until your mom dies it seems like all the other women in your life can never be more than just your mistress.

In the modern Oedipal story, it's the mother who kills the father and then takes the son.

And it's not as if you can divorce your mother.

Or kill her.

And Nico says, "What do you mean *all the other women?* Jeez, how many are we talking about?" She says, "I'm glad we used a rubber."

For a complete list of sexual partners, I'd have to check my fourth step. My moral inventory notebook. The complete and relentless history of my addiction.

That's if I ever go back and complete the damn step.

For all those people in Room 234, working on their twelve steps in a sexaholics meeting is a valuable important tool for understanding and recovering from . . . well, you get the idea.

For me, it's a terrific how-to seminar. Tips. Techniques. Strategies for getting laid you never dreamed of. Personal contacts. When they tell their stories, these addict people are frigging brilliant. Plus there's the jail girls out for their three hours of sex addict talk therapy.

Nico included.

Wednesday nights mean Nico. Friday nights mean Tanya. Sundays mean Leeza. Leeza sweats yellow with nicotine. You can almost put your hands around her waist since her abs are rock-hard from coughing. Tanya always smuggles in some rubber sex toy, usually a dildo or a string of latex beads. Some sexual equivalent of the prize in a box of cereal.

The old rule about how a thing of beauty is a joy forever, in my experience, even the most beauteous thing is only a joy for about three hours, tops. After that, she'll want to tell you all about her childhood traumas. Part of meeting these jail girls is it's so sweet to look at your watch and know she'll be behind bars in half an hour.

It's a Cinderella story, only at midnight she turns back into a fugitive.

It's not that I don't love these women. I love them just as much as you'd love a magazine centerfold, a fuck video, an adult website, and for sure, for a sexaholic that can be buckets of love. And it's not that Nico loves me much, either.

This isn't so much romance as it is opportunity. You put twenty sexaholics around a table, night after night, and don't be surprised.

Plus the sexaholic recovery books they sell here, it's every way you always wanted to get laid but didn't know how. Of course, all this is to help you realize you're a sex junkie. It's delivered in a kind of "if you do any of the following things, you may be an alcoholic" checklist. Their helpful hints include:

Do you cut the lining out of your bathing suit so your genitals show through?

Do you leave your fly or blouse open and pretend to hold conversations in glass telephone booths, standing so your clothes gap open with no underwear inside?

Do you jog without a bra or athletic supporter in order to attract sexual partners?

My answer to all the above is, *Well, I do now!*

Plus, being a pervert here is not your fault. Compulsive sexual behavior is not about always getting your dick sucked. It's a disease. It's a physical addiction just waiting for the *Diagnostic Statistical Manual* to give it a code of its own so treatment can be billed to medical insurance.

The story is even Bill Wilson, a founder of Alcoholics Anonymous, couldn't overcome the sex monkey on his back, and spent his sober life cheating on his wife and filled with guilt.

The story is that sex addicts become dependent on a body chemistry created by constant sex. Orgasms flood the body with endorphins that kill pain and tranquilize you. Sex addicts are really addicted to the endorphins, not the sex. Sex addicts have lower natural levels of monoamine oxidase. Sex addicts really crave the peptide phenylethylamine that might be triggered by danger, by infatuation, by risk and fear.

For a sex addict, your tits, your dick, your clit or tongue or asshole is a shot of heroin, always there, always ready to use. Nico and I love each other as much as any junkie loves his fix.

Nico bears down hard, bucking my dog against the front wall of her insides, using two wet fingers on herself.

I say, "What if that cleaning woman walks in?"

And Nico stirs me around inside herself, saying, "Oh yeah. That would be so hot."

Me, I can't help imagining what kind of a big shining butt print we're going to polish into the waxed tile. A row of sinks look down. Fluorescent lights flicker, and reflected in the chrome pipes under each sink you can see Nico's throat is one long straight tube, her head thrown back, eyes closed, her breath panting out at the ceiling. Her big flower-print breasts. Her tongue hangs off to one side. The juice coming off her is scalding hot.

To keep from triggering I say, "What all did you tell your folks about us?"

And Nico says, "They want to meet you."

I think about the perfect thing to say next, but it doesn't really matter. You can say anything here. Enemas, orgies, animals, admit to any obscenity, and nobody is ever surprised.

In Room 234, everybody compares war stories. Everybody takes their turn. That's the first part of the meeting, the check-in part.

After that they'll read the readings, the prayer things, they'll discuss the topic for the night. They'll each work on one of the twelve steps. The first step is to admit you're powerless. You have an addiction, and you can't stop. The first step is to tell your story, all the worst parts. Your lowest lows.

The problem with sex is the same as with any addiction. You're always recovering. You're always backsliding. Acting out. Until you find something to fight for, you settle for something to fight against. All these people who say they want a life free from sexual compulsion, I mean forget it. I mean, what could ever be better than sex?

For sure, even the worst blow job is better than, say, sniffing the best rose . . . watching the greatest sunset. Hearing children laugh.

I think that I shall never see a poem as lovely as a hot-gushing, butt-cramping, gut-hosing orgasm.

Painting a picture, composing an opera, that's just something you do until you find the next willing piece of ass.

The minute something better than sex comes along, you call me. Have me paged.

None of these people in Room 234 are Romeos or Casanovas or Don Juans. These aren't Mata Haris or Salomes. These are people you shake hands with every day. Not ugly, not beautiful. You stand next to these legends on the elevator. They serve you coffee. These mythological creatures tear your ticket stub. They cash your paycheck. They put the Communion wafer on your tongue.

In the women's room, inside Nico, I cross my arms behind my head.

For the next I don't know how long, I've got no problems in the world. No mother. No medical bills. No shitty museum job. No jerk-off best friend. Nothing.

I feel nothing.

To make it last, to keep from triggering, I tell Nico's flowered backside how beautiful she is, how sweet she is and how much I need her. Her skin and hair. To make it last. Because this is the only time I can say it. Because the moment this is over, we'll hate each other. The moment we find ourselves cold and sweating on the bathroom floor, the moment after we both come, we won't want to even look at each other.

The only person we'll hate more than each other is ourselves.

These are the only few minutes I can be human.

Just for these minutes, I don't feel lonely.

And riding me up and down, Nico says, "So when do I get to meet your mom?"

And, "Never," I say. "That's impossible, I mean."

And Nico, her whole body clenched and jacking me with her boiling wet insides, she says, "She in prison or a loony bin or something?"

Yeah, for a lot of her life.

Ask any guy about his mom during sex, and you can delay the big blast forever.

And Nico says, "So is she dead now?"

And I say, "Sort of."

Susan St. Aubin

# THE MAN IN THE GRAY
# FLANNEL TIGHTS

All day at work, Hal fantasized about change, even though he was
continually changing jobs, moving from company to company as
they went out of business, or reorganized their computer divisions,
or bought new software he scorned, or tried to impose dress codes
on him. The minute a boss said ties on Mondays, jeans only on Fri-
days, Hal was ready to move on. There was always a friend who
knew of an opening or was starting up something new. His life was
change, yet change made it the same.

Evelyn was still his wife, even though neither of them spent
much time at home and often saw each other only in passing. As he
left for an early-morning run, she would be coming in from a night
of baking for the restaurant where she worked, or maybe a night
with the boyfriend he knew about or one of the girlfriends he didn't
want to know about, whose images flickered at the place where his
mind froze. Marian was still his girlfriend but didn't have much
time for him now that she'd switched from teaching kindergarten
part-time to a full-time job teaching art as well as heading the whole
arts program at the local high school. She'd become someone he saw
from a distance, like his wife, both of them spinning away from him.

As time passed and jobs changed, Friday attire slipped from jeans to loose T-shirts and baggy khakis or shorts. There *is* no style any more, thought Hal, by which he meant no sex—the women's clothes were as shapeless as the men's. T-shirts occasionally slipped to reveal the shadow of a breast, but hips remained hidden beneath shorts that bagged over their knees, or pants that dropped at the waist and bunched around the ankles.

He was shocked to realize that he was getting old enough to re-member a different style. Only a few years ago women had worn tights. Some still did—well-toned women in their early forties coming out of gyms—but not the women he worked with, not Evelyn, who now wore the loose white drawstring pants of restau-rant workers, and certainly not Marian, who had always favored long, shapeless dresses to hide the wonderfully full hips she seemed ashamed to show. It occurred to him that if he wore what he wanted to see, others might copy him, starting a trend more to his liking. He didn't think men had ever worn tights, except maybe bike riders. He went to sporting goods stores to try on bicycle pants, but they were rubbery and heavy, with stripes in lurid shades running down the legs. When Hal took them off, they crackled like shrink-wrap, an implied kinkiness that disturbed him.

"Did you ever wear tights?" he asked Marian one Tuesday night in May after dinner at her house. He knew what the answer would be, but he wanted to prod her.

She was standing at the sink in the kitchen area of her studio apartment, her back to him so that he could see her shoulders stiffen. "Not me, no, they never fit right. I don't have the figure for them," she said as she rinsed their plates.

He thought she was wrong, and his cock stirred as he pictured her full hips in tights, black tights with a tight white top. He had to cross his legs to compress his erection. They'd had sex before dinner, which was Marian's limit; anything more would be exces-sive. He thought fondly of Evelyn, whom he could lure into bed (or onto the floor or the kitchen table) anytime. The fact was, he had more fun with his wife, and often wondered, when he was with Marian, why he was there.

"Do men ever wear tights?" he asked. He expected a sensible answer guaranteed to put the idea of tights out of his head, but Marian surprised him.

"Dancers," she answered. "Ballet and modern. But then, dancers have the body. You have to have the right body, slender yet muscular."

She had a dreamy look he found promising, as though she were watching dancing men, but he knew bodies were just raw material to her, shapes to be arranged artistically in space—a line here, a curve there.

"Bike riders," she continued, looking out the window over her sink at the brick wall opposite. "But they're so sporty that what they wear doesn't seem like tights."

"They have legs like sticks," Hal agreed.

Marian turned around to say, "Shakespeare. Robin Hood." She began to laugh. "Men used to be the ones who wore tights."

"So how'd women get into them?" He liked the way this conversation was drifting. "How come women took over the tights?"

Marian shrugged as she turned back to the dishes.

"I want tights," Hal said, so abruptly he startled himself. He watched the muscles of her back jump beneath the thin T-shirt she wore over her long skirt. "I want to take back the tights!" he whooped, laughing.

Marian didn't turn around, because the thought of a man in tights made her blush and she didn't want Hal to take this as approval. His birthday was next week, and tights occurred to her as a good surprise for him. Such a gift seemed more like something Evelyn would come up with, and Marian wanted to unsettle her, maybe even alarm her. She often felt Evelyn didn't take her seriously enough to feel threatened. But tights! Who would ever suspect that Marian would think of men in tights? She savored the thought of Evelyn's jealousy. She imagined dancers again; she liked ballet, and, more secretly, she admired the muscular legs, the intriguing bulges, of male dancers, whose discreetly bound genitals seemed no more than an extra muscle tamed beneath the fabric of their tights.

Marian ran more hot water into the sink, plunging her hands in steaming suds. Her ears, she knew, were now bright red. If Hal noticed, she wanted the heat of the water as an excuse, but to her relief, he lounged on her bed with the newspaper and began reading an article to her about the stock market.

"Technology, that's where the real future is. Forget everything else," he said.

Marian wondered whom she could ask about tights, and realized that Evelyn was probably the only person who might know where men's tights could be found. Only Evelyn would understand her attraction to tights, and the thought that she had possibly already bought him a pair made Marian angry enough to drop a glass against the sink's rim, where it shattered into the water in hundreds of slivers. Hal leaped off the bed and ran to her, holding her in his arms while she sucked a spot of blood off a small cut at the tip of her left index finger.

"You'd better drain this water," said practical Hal. "Then I can get all the glass out."

His jeans, when he bent over the sink, were tight as a dancer's leotards. *Ballet ass,* she thought. *I'm inventing sexual terms. Ballet ass.* Delighted, she put her hands over her mouth. This was a secret she could keep from Hal and Evelyn both. She liked the double meaning of *ass,* especially appropriate now because Hal was being such an ass, warning her to be more careful when she washed dishes. He was like a scolding mother, cautiously picking glittering slivers from the sink's trap as though he were plucking diamonds from mud, and setting them carefully on the counter.

Now that Marian was an art teacher, people made assumptions about her, often telling her things she'd rather not know concerning their sex lives and drug habits. They shared suspicions with her about who might be gay, or having an affair, as well as envious comments about what they thought of as her bohemian lifestyle. Sometimes Marian wanted to be deaf, to be able to nod politely in response to mouthings she couldn't understand and to communicate with others like herself in a secret language of signs.

On Wednesday as she sat in the teachers' break room, Marian thought of someone else she could ask about tights—Ed, who taught journalism and was gay, though no one suspected, not with his deep voice and dominant manner. Ed made assumptions about Marian, too, and when no one was around, he would tell her about the guys in the gym where he worked out, and about Sunday afternoons in the bushes of the local park, behind the playground there, and he'd say she'd never guess what went on there. One day, he'd even brought up the subject of women's dress sizes.

"I'm sure you've noticed," he'd said as he raised his arms to flex his well-developed muscles, "the more expensive the dress, the smaller the size. A boy just can't tell what size will fit! It's so confusing, because men's clothes run just the opposite. Men want to be big."

While waiting for Ed to come in, Marian unwrapped her cheese sandwich and listened to Jill, the home economics teacher.

"Ed just exudes masculinity," she whispered. "I can't believe he's still single."

"I don't think he is, exactly," Marian muttered to her bread. Jill looked at her, waiting for the wisdom Marian was too discreet to impart. Charm run amok was Ed's defense. With his narrow, deep-blue eyes, short well-styled hair, and the tight dark turtleneck sweaters that set off his muscles, he couldn't possibly be that object of Jill's frequently expressed frustration, the gay man. Marian also knew he dyed his hair, though this was the one thing he hadn't confessed to her, because she recognized the color as the exact shade of brown her mother used.

"It's hard to meet men these days," Jill lamented. "It seems like everyone's gay or married, except Ed."

Marian mumbled, "I haven't noticed," while smoothing her long skirt. She pictured herself as a nun, her black wimple falling in folds over her body, like the teachers she'd had in Catholic grade school, an image that stayed with her as she got off the couch to talk to Ed when he came in.

"Do you know," she asked softly as they sat side by side in two hard teachers' chairs, "where a man could buy tights?"

"Anyone we know?" He looked around the room. Jill tried to catch his eye, but he turned his glance back to Marian. "Is he a dancer?"

"No, just a man who wants to wear tights."

Ed's eyebrows shot up. "A small man?" He leaned forward, chin on his knuckles.

"Tall," replied Marian. "Not big, but very tall."

"Let me think. I could suggest a theatrical costume store, but they're expensive, especially tall sizes. What he needs is large women's sizes."

"Large?"

"Yes, sizes for *big* women. You know, 1X, 2X, 3X. Many men find these sizes fit them very well. With a tall man, the legs might be a bit short, but with tights, it's all in how you stretch the fabric."

Marian covered her mouth and smiled. "I can't believe we're talking about men in women's tights right here in the teachers' lounge," she whispered.

"It's not unheard of, in drama classes," he said. In addition to journalism, Ed taught an occasional drama course because the school didn't have a drama teacher yet. "We bought some X-size tights for the guys just last year, when we did *Romeo and Juliet*."

Marian's heart pounded and her ears burned. Jill winked and waved at her. Ed patted her knee before he stood up, stretched, and moved to the couch.

"What am I going to do, surrounded as I am all day by so many beautiful ladies?" He sat down beside Jill. "What if I lose control? What kind of example would that be for the boys?"

The store Ed recommended was one that everyone called the Fat Lady Store in the mall, though it was really Splendid Fantasy: Clothes for Women. Over the entrance was a picture of a not so very large woman in harem pants and a bangled headdress holding a golden oil lamp in both hands. Marian hummed along with the piano player under the dome at the center of the mall as she strolled inside on Saturday morning, armed with her new knowledge of X sizes. She half expected to see Evelyn, who surely knew how to clothe men in large women's tights, beating her to the surprise gift—but the shop was empty, with only one saleswoman, possibly a size 14, standing behind a counter shuffling price tags like cards.

"May I help you?" she asked without raising her head.

Marian looked around at the racks of dresses and loose jackets, at shelves of hats and wide-sized shoes. She picked up the sleeve of one dress, size 12, and dropped it as though it burned her fingers. The price was $350. Was it made of silk? Cashmere? Woven gold? Marian was a size 12. All along, this store she never went to had been for her, because she was beginning to be fat, she and the woman behind the counter, who now raised her eyes to look at her. Marian's eyes were fixed on a row of her favorite long, loose dresses.

"Tights," she murmured. "Where would I find tights?"

The saleswoman sniffed. "Oh, we're not wearing those this year." Her voice lowered with the confidential tones of fashion expertise. "Last year, yes, we did carry them. But now. . . ." She turned to a rack of clothes so new they didn't have price tags yet. "These are what we're wearing these days. I think this would be your size."

She spread a pair of baggy drawstring pants, size 12, in beige raw silk, on the counter.

Marian's fingers reached out to stroke the fabric. "Actually, I'm

looking for something for a friend," she said. "A friend who wears a
larger size." The saleswoman sucked in her breath as she pulled the
silk pants away from Marian. "What size?" she asked.

"X," answered Marian, who found herself not quite remembering what Ed had told her. "I think—2X?"

"Yes, we carry that size," said the woman, as her hands emerged
from under the counter with another pile of beige silk to spread out
before Marian, who tried to picture Hal swathed in this material,
perhaps drowned in it. The clerk smoothed the pants with her
hands while Marian reached out a forefinger. She didn't own anything silk; it was a luxury she couldn't allow herself as long as there
were people in the world who didn't have enough to eat.

"How much?" she asked.

"Two fifty," the woman answered, a price that took Marian a
moment to digest. Dollars? Hundreds? She pulled her finger back.

"I really was looking for tights," she said.

The clerk sighed. "As I said, we don't carry those." She began
putting the silk pants on hangers. "You could try Macy's. Or even
the Emporium might . . ." Her voice trailed off as she looked away
from Marian, who felt herself condemned to fashion hopelessness.
The clerk's silence followed her out the door.

In the Women's Department in a dark corner of the Emporium's
basement, Marian stood by a rack of tights. 1X, 2X, 3X: She held
each size up to compare it to the others. Size 2X seemed to have the
longest legs, size 3X the widest waist. 1X didn't seem much larger
than her own size 12, though it was hard to tell with tights, which
would stretch much more than her size 12 jeans. Here in the
Women's Department there were no size 12s, or even 14s or 16s.
This was X territory, filled with dresses Marian could wrap around
herself three times, as well as piles of tights and racks of enormous
shirts with sleeves that hung to Marian's knees when she held them
in front of her.

She wondered why whoever designed these clothes figured

heavy women would also have longer legs and arms. Did they conceive of large women's sizes as being for women who were in all senses large, rather than just overweight? Did they in fact design these things with men in mind? She found a blue-and-gray striped shirt that would look good on Hal, and held it up against a pair of tights, size 2X, in gray cotton that was soft and napped like flannel. If he wanted tights, he'd need something to wear with them that would cover his crotch. She looked at the floor, feeling her face flush at the thought of Hal's prick bulging under the tights, barely contained by the thinly stretched gray flannel. He'd wear a jock-strap, of course, thought Marian, pulling away from the fantasy. Surely he already had one; she wouldn't want to buy *that* for him. She imagined everything pushed into a neat bundle, like a purse, covered by the blue-and-gray striped shirt, hidden but available to those who knew what was there.

She carried her finds to the cashier, a small, bored high school girl whom she recognized, who took them out of her hands and pulled off the price tags. $14.99 for the tights, $15.99 for the shirt, two bargains that together came to about a tenth of the price of those silk drawstring pants Marian still coveted for herself. The cashier stuffed them into a bag without looking at Marian, and then, perhaps remembering some part of her training, smiled at the bag as she said, "Have a nice day."

When Hal looked out the small window on his front door, he saw Marian standing there clutching a package to her breast. It was a Friday, the restaurant's busiest night, so Evelyn wouldn't be home for hours. As he opened the door, Marian stepped back, hiding her gift behind her. He blinked at the light from the setting sun, which he found intense after working at his computer in the windowless closet he used for a study.

"Is this a bad time?" she asked.

"No, no, I just wasn't expecting you. Come in, come in." He'd read somewhere that when people don't mean what they say, they tend to repeat themselves, which made him conscious of his words. In fact, he wasn't sure what he meant, since in spite of his desire for change, he often had trouble adjusting to the unexpected.

He felt a moment of something like fear pass through him when he noticed the package. Marian had never before dared to give him a gift—in fact, on her birthday, she'd told him it wasn't right for him, a married man, to give her a present that wasn't also from Evelyn—a notion that struck him as so odd, but at the same time sweetly innocent, that he'd declared they didn't need to give gifts because they were each other's gift. Now he felt like hugging her and patting her hips in the jeans she wore so rarely that he got excited whenever he saw them, but instead he pointed at the thing she held in front of her, muttering, "What's that?"

She held out her crushed package, wrapped in white paper she'd painted herself with a design of candles and sparklers.

"Happy birthday," she said, with a smile that began with a reluctant twitching at the corners of her mouth. "How does it feel to be 42?"

"I don't know," he replied. "Just like 41, I suppose, but it's only been two days." He backed into his dark hallway, repeating, "Come in, come in. It's OK, Evelyn's at work."

She followed him down the long hall, a dark living room on the left, a dining room connected to it with sliding doors, and on the right the bedroom and, further back, a kitchen and the large hall closet that was Hal's study. Hal went to the living room, drew the blinds, then switched on a floor lamp. Marian trailed behind him holding his gift, until he turned around and took it from her. He sat on the couch, patting the cushion beside him, urging Marian to sit; and when she did, he patted her knee with his left hand while opening the package one-handed, being careful not to tear the paper. When the clothes spilled onto the floor, he bent to retrieve them.

"Tights!" He held them up, letting the legs fall to the floor. "Honest to God! Tights." He squeezed her shoulders and kissed her lightly on the lips. "And what—a shirt?" He unfurled that, too.

"Something to wear with the tights," she explained.

"I'll try them on right now." He stripped off his jeans, underwear, and T-shirt.

"Shouldn't you wear something underneath?" she asked as she watched him pull on the tights.

He stopped. "Should I? I thought tights were underwear. Do women wear anything underneath?"

"Of course," answered Marian, who always wore underpants beneath her pantyhose.

"They don't look like they do, at least not the women I've seen." Hal pulled the tights up to his waist, watching Marian's face as she looked him up and down, her lips pressing together while a blush spread over her cheeks.

The fit was perfect—a bit loose in the legs, perhaps, compared to the way tights fit women, but long enough, and snug enough through the pelvis to nicely contain his bulging crotch. He jumped up and down, laughing as she turned away.

"I like them, I've never felt anything so comfortable," he said, raising a leg to prove his point. He unfolded the shirt and slipped it on, but hesitated when he began to button it. "The buttons are on the wrong side. This is a women's shirt."

"They're women's tights, too," said Marian.

"That's different. They don't make tights for men. But why buy me a women's blouse?"

She shrugged. "I didn't know it would matter. It was there, and it matched the tights."

"I still think I'd rather wear a man's shirt. Wait." He ran across the hall to the bedroom and came back wearing a black T-shirt that didn't quite cover his crotch.

"How about this?" he asked, prancing before her, his penis wobbling inside the tights, which were beginning to stretch out more.

She put both hands over her reddening ears as she laughed. "But that shirt doesn't cover you. You look, you look—"

"Obscene?" he asked hopefully. "Yes! That's my ambition, to be an obscene old man. I'm looking forward to being *sixty*-two in tights!" He was delighted that demure Marian had unexpectedly given him tights. What next? Anything seemed possible. He slid onto the couch beside her, squeezed her shoulders again, then began unbuttoning her blouse.

"No," she said. "This is your house. Evelyn's house. I couldn't."

"Evelyn's at work." He went on unbuttoning her blouse. "Evelyn wouldn't object. You know we both have lovers, but you've never accepted that about Evelyn and me. Evelyn won't mind, she won't know."

Marian sat still as he undid the last button.

"I want you in my house," he whispered in her ear, sucking the lobe while his fingers began working at the button on her jeans.

She breathed rapidly as she wrapped her arms around her open blouse, but she didn't protest when he unzipped her jeans and pulled them off her hips, or when he lowered his lips to the clit protruding pink from a weave of soft brown hair, or when his wet and twisting tongue began its slow massage.

Were her hands on his head, in his hair? Her touch was so tentative he couldn't be sure this wasn't something he was imagining. His hands were kneading her thighs; her juices, mingled with his saliva, ran down his chin. Yes, her hands were fluttering in his hair. When he felt his prick lift the fabric of his tights, he had an image of an enormous stretch, an Aubrey Beardsley lithograph of a giant penis bursting out like a glorious flag, unfurling and waving at Marian.

When Marian's hips rose from the couch, he stuffed his nose into her cunt until she sighed and fell back again, her legs collapsing on either side of his head, her body immobilized with pleasure. Suddenly her hands were on his hair again, this time to push him away. He got up and sat beside her, licking his lips, then kissed her. She turned her head away.

"I never meant for this to happen." She was saying what he

knew she thought she should say, although he didn't think she sounded regretful. He missed Evelyn, who cried out as she came, and kicked her legs in the air. Already Marian was standing, pulling on her jeans, buttoning her blouse.

"Wait," he said.

"Oh, no, really, I should go. It's getting late."

"It's only nine. Evelyn won't be home for hours."

But she was leaving him hard beneath his tights, throbbing, congested—leaving him to his own hands, or to Evelyn if he could wait that long.

"So was this shirt a mistake? Would you wear it, or should I take it away?" She looked to the side rather than directly at him, not wanting to see the way his cock made a tent at the crotch of his tights.

"Take it." He looked down at that ridiculous penis pushing at his tights, refusing to either burst through or go away. Evelyn called it the Herald, for big Hal, she said. Herald of what? He willed it to collapse.

Marian picked up the paper from the floor, and wrapped it around the shirt.

"You could wear it," he suggested, but she shook her head.

"It's way too big. I'll have to take it back."

He followed her into the hall and turned on the light. Her hand was on the doorknob.

"Really, I should go."

As he approached her, his tent pole rising again beneath the tights, she stood on tiptoe, bending above the waist to kiss him on the lips, so light and nice that his heart and cock both softened, leaving him with a fatherly tenderness for her. He wanted her here, now, in his living room, and yet he would let her go because she'd brought him a gift, because she was so very nice. He kissed her again on the forehead, whispering, "Your place, a week from this Tuesday, OK?"

"Yes," she murmured, "of course," and was out the door as

though she'd never come. He watched her back, which was unexpectedly slender and vulnerable when set off by her sturdy hips in jeans that fit closely without being tight.

He had only the tights to prove she'd been there. He slipped one hand into the waistband, stroking himself as he walked into the living room and sat down on the couch. He pulled the tights down to his ankles, letting his cock free except for his confining hand, but, on the verge of coming, he stopped. She wasn't here, she'd left, why bother? He lay on his back on the couch and watched poor Herald fall in the diffuse light coming from the hall, then pulled up the tights. His eyes felt scratchy when he closed them, and all his muscles went limp.

When he opened his eyes again, Evelyn was tiptoeing around the room. She switched on the lamp by the couch.

"Are you awake? What's this? Tights? You have tights on!" She pulled the waistband, looked in, then let it snap against his stomach. "Where'd you find tights?" She bent over and kissed him, her tongue slowly swirling on his lips. "Hmmm," she murmured, "I sense you have not been alone."

He got up off the couch, saying nothing.

"You're always so mysterious." She laughed as she came up behind him, her hands moving over his ass. As soon as his pole stirred, Evelyn's fingers were on it.

"I've been saving them for you," he said.

She circled him, inspecting the tights. When she crouched in front of him and pulled them down, his cock jumped out.

"Come on, who gave you these tights? It couldn't have been Marian. Who else is there? Men don't just go out and find their own tights."

Her mouth was on him, sucking him into her throat, blowing him out, then sucking him in again. He was tempted to spill sperm and information together, to surprise her with the fact that it *was* Marian who'd bought them, but he didn't, holding back without a word while she worked on him, sucking and squeezing his balls, then his prick, then his balls again until he burst into her mouth and she drank him down. He felt like a good host worrying about the guest who'd left without dessert. Poor Marian, she'd gotten nothing.

Evelyn was chuckling. "My, that was enough for two women, at least. Come on, tell me." She sniffed the tights. "These are brand-new. Unused. You got them tonight, didn't you?"

He leaned against the wall, saying nothing.

"A dancer!" Evelyn pulled his tights up. "She's an exotic dancer and she found these for you backstage, in a bin, new tights for the chorus of boys who dance behind her in her act." She was making up a story for him, as she often did.

"Dance!" she ordered, pulling him away from the wall. "Dance for me."

When she released his arm he spun like a puppet, then put one foot awkwardly up in the air, toes curled. With both feet together on the ground he bounced in place, first springing to the right, then to the left.

Evelyn applauded. "Dance, dance!" she chanted. His cock bobbed up and down beneath the tights as he jigged in time to Evelyn's clapping hands. This was the real thing, he thought, as he felt another tent form in the crotch of his tights. Evelyn, he knew, had just begun with him—so why was he still thinking of Marian's back as she walked down the front steps?

# NASTY

I looked up and he was staring at me from across the walkway. He was one of those smoldering straight boys whose blatant contempt for queers undoubtedly harbors a need to have his ass plowed until the cows come home.

His eyes never left me. The sneer never left his face. He wanted to hurt me.

Well, he was about to learn that this queer wouldn't sit and wait to be bashed.

"What the fuck are you staring at?"

"I'm staring at you." The voice matched the look. As much as I hated to admit it, he was hot. Thick brown hair, a couple of days' worth of beard, black eyes that ripped through flesh, a body as sleek and powerful as a Harley-Davidson, and a mouth that would look incredible with a cock crammed down it.

I hated him. I hated his repressed, hypocritical, breeding ass. I wanted to pound that ass with my cock, then pound his face with my fists. Or vice versa. Either way, the asshole needed to know that not all queers are easy targets.

I sat up straight on the bench. I knew my six feet, two inches of iron-pumped muscle would be intimidating, even to a shithead like him.

"You want a piece of me?"

He moved toward me, very slowly. He had no fear. This was going to be nasty.

I stood when he was about three feet away. I only topped him by about an inch. Up close, he was even hotter.

He put his face in mine. It dripped with loathing.

My hands balled into fists.

"Yeah, I want a piece of you." I could almost taste his hate. "My ass eats cock for breakfast and I'm wonderin' if you're man enough to feed it."

Okay. Now that is not what I expected him to say.

I almost flinched, he caught me so off-guard, but I held it together and grabbed a handful of that thick, brown hair. I yanked his head back. He snarled.

"I already stuffed five sluts like you this morning, and it ain't even ten o'clock yet."

He licked his lips. I never saw anyone do it nastier.

I pulled his head back farther. "You want to do it here, pig, or does the little girl need some privacy?"

He dropped to his knees in the park in broad daylight and started chewing on my denim-covered cock. He sounded exactly like a fucking dog, panting and growling as he soaked my crotch with slobber. I pushed his head roughly against my straining rod. He chewed even harder.

I pulled him to his feet by his hair. I grabbed his crotch and squeezed. He snarled again, his eyes shooting sparks at me.

His dick felt like a fucking bazooka. It took everything I had not to let him see me sweat. There was nothing I liked better than to tear up a big-dicked bottom. The bigger they are, the harder they cum.

"You're coming home with me, fuck boy, and when I'm done with your ass, it won't be able to eat for a week."

"You better hope that's true, because it gets awful ugly when it's hungry."

"Boy, you couldn't get much uglier."

The corner of his mouth curled up. He knew I was lying, but I couldn't let him get the upper hand.

I yanked his hair and squeezed his cock harder. He flinched and the sparks became rockets.

"I want to see what I'm getting before I waste my fucking time on a whore like you."

Without a second's hesitation, he undid his fly and pulled down his pants. He wasn't wearing any underwear and nine inches of un-cut meat sprang free, wedging itself between my legs.

I was going to fucking lose it before we even left the park.

I took hold of that meat and it throbbed in my hand like some living being. I lifted it and pushed it back against his stomach. I hefted his nuts with my other hand and tried not to let him see me giving thanks. They were huge and heavy, dangling like a bull's. I could see his loads of spunk hosing down my carpet as I fucked the shit out of him.

"I want to see the rest."

He turned away from me and bent over. I took the opportunity to catch my breath.

I lost it again as soon as I looked.

His ass was a fucking trampoline, tight and bouncy. If I slapped it with my cock, my cock would slap me right back. The cheeks were solid, meaty mounds that could be used like handles to steer while plowing.

I took hold of those cheeks and dug my fingers into the flesh. My thumbs spread them wide and I said a silent prayer.

My prayer was answered.

A tasty, tight hole puckered and unpuckered at my thumbtips. It wasn't begging me to fuck it, it was daring me to.

I slapped his ass hard.

He yelped, then spit onto the ground. Still bent over, he looked back and up at me. "Think you can fill it up?"

"Fill it? Asshole, I'm going to fucking burst it."

He stood and pulled up his pants. He left the top three buttons undone. A ripe mushroom poked straight up, peeking out of his foreskin.

This is the one, I thought to myself. I'd finally found a bottom nasty enough to survive my abusive monster. I was sure of it. This one wasn't going to be tamed.

Those eyes of his challenged me, while he slipped his finger and thumb inside his foreskin and teased the mushroom until honey oozed out of the slit.

My tongue almost came out, it looked so fucking tasty, but I stopped it just in time.

"I want to see what you got, too, before I waste the trip."

I put one hand around his throat and slapped his cock-teasing hand away with the other. I yanked his foreskin out as far as it would stretch. The mushroom bloomed inside.

"I don't fucking show you anything unless I want to. Is that understood?"

He smiled, but the cockiness had slipped a bit. A chink in the armor. I yanked harder on his skin. "Is that understood?"

"Yes, sir." It was still a snarl. Not even a hint of submissiveness. God, he was perfect.

I took my key ring out of my pocket. It was big and loaded with keys. I pulled out his pants and slid the ring down onto his cock. I buttoned up his fly and could picture the keys digging into his balls. The tip of his mushroom was still visible over the waistband, oozing pre-cum like a leaky faucet.

I walked to my car and he followed. I got my extra car key out and I made him ride in the back seat. "You touch yourself and I'm booting your slutty little ass out of this car."

"Afraid you can't keep your hands off of me?"

He was pushing it. "When we get to my place, it will be more than my hands I'll have on you." I started the car. "Open your mouth again and I'm climbing back there and shutting it for you."

There was silence.

I looked in the rearview mirror. He was staring at me, wearing the smuggest grin I'd ever seen.

He held my stare for a couple of beats more, then he slid down in his seat. His knees opened wide and his fingers spread across his thighs. His T-shirt was bunched up and I could see fluid from his cock filling up his bellybutton. The outline of my keys was visible through his jeans.

While he watched me watching him, he started pulling and arranging the seatbelts. I thought, at first, that I had flustered him so much that he wasn't able to put his belt on correctly. Then I saw what he had managed to do.

His crotch was tied in a harness created by the seatbelts. I could only imagine the kind of pressure it and my keys were placing on his boner.

He licked his lips again, in that slow, tantalizing, shit-eating way he'd done before, then he began to rock rhythmically, strangling his basket with every move forward. His head laid back and a low growl vibrated from his throat. The bastard was masturbating.

I had to give him credit. He wasn't touching himself.

I looked at the road and fought the need to squirm in my seat.

Could this be love?

We reached my house and he followed me in. When I turned around, he was on his knees, pulling at my fly.

I slapped his hands away. "I didn't give you permission to do that."

He looked up at me through long, dark lashes, his eyes still smoldering.

"Stand up."

He stood.

"Take off everything except my key ring."

He did it slowly, his eyes rarely leaving mine. My keys jangled with his every move.

He was giving me time to look. He knew a man would have to

be dead not to like what he was seeing. His skin glowed like highly polished wood. His nipples were exactly the way I liked them—familiar with abuse but still young and tender. They stood at attention, their shiny gold hoops twitching with every beat of his heart. His abs were carved into his flesh. I could've done my laundry on them. His thighs were powerful without bulging, and his arms and legs were highlighted by the blackest hair I'd ever seen, giving his skin an even higher gloss.

I looked and I liked—God, did I like—but I wouldn't give him the satisfaction of showing it.

When he was done, he started to put his boots back on.

"I said, just my key ring."

He stopped and looked at me, missing half a beat. Then he smiled, and rose to his full six feet plus.

I liked my bottoms completely bare. It made them look more vulnerable. But, as my eyes traveled over him one more time, I realized it only made this one look more incredible, like some natural beast, raw and wild.

I led him by my keys to a straight-backed chair sitting against the living room wall. A small table with a drawer stood a few feet away from it.

"Sit and put your hands behind you."

He obeyed.

"I don't want to see your hands in front. I don't want you to touch me. Is that understood?"

He gave me that look up through his lashes again. God, he was a tease. A nasty, slutty, fucking tease.

"Yes, sir."

I stood back, about a foot in front of him. I opened my fly and set the monster free. It thrust forward, like a lance, and hit him in the face.

His eyes grew huge and the smirk disappeared.

I thought, for a moment, that I'd lost him; that it was fear I saw in his eyes.

Then those smoldering eyes burst into flames and he whispered, "Chow time."

I watched my pre-cum inch down his cheek. "Does just your ass eat cock, or does your face get hungry, too?"

The smug smile was back. "It's just all one, long chute to me."

The image of my snake sliding down his throat and poking out his asshole made my legs shake. There was no way to hide it.

His smile grew bigger.

I was going to have to make him pay for that.

His hands were behind his back, gripping the rungs of the chair. I grabbed a handful of his hair with one hand and my cock with the other. His mouth opened wide and I shoved my way in with one long stroke.

He retched hard once and phlegm oozed out around my meat. His hands came forward, then stopped, and gripped the seat of his chair.

I felt the back of his throat convulsing against my cock. His knuckles were white and the fire in his eyes shimmered with moisture.

I was about to back off, when I felt his throat open up and my cock slide forward some more. His hands released the chair and returned to their place behind his back. The smirk was gone from his lips, of course, but now I saw it in his eyes. They twinkled at me.

I couldn't help but smile back.

As his lips disappeared into the hairy darkness of my crotch, I realized how right I had been. His mouth did look incredible with a cock crammed down it.

I held his hair and his ears and I fed him a feast. I fucked his face hard, slamming it with my body, over and over. The corners of his mouth started to tear and a trickle of blood came out of one of his nostrils. His hands, for the most part, stayed behind, occasionally getting knocked loose by my ramming.

I looked into his eyes, sweat blurring my vision, and I saw them glaze over. Then, unbelievably, he winked at me.

I almost lost it before reaching the main course.

I pulled out quickly and shoved his head in his lap. I closed my eyes and took some deep breaths, trying to keep it under control.

Still holding his head down, my legs started to quiver. His labored breathing and twitching hands, still valiantly held behind his back, were pushing me over the edge. I wasn't going to make it.

Then his body suddenly relaxed under my touch and I wondered—had he surrendered or had he gotten a second wind?

Not knowing gave me the strength that I needed and I knew I was going to be able to dole out the punishment he so dearly deserved.

I yanked him off of the chair and he landed, face first, on the carpet. My key ring went flying. He was on his knees, his ass sticking straight up in the air like the anxious little whore that it was. With effort, he tucked his arms under his head, covering his face.

Still I didn't know if he'd given in, or if he was just waiting for more.

I grabbed the chair and threw it across the room. I opened the drawer and took out a tube. I shoved the end in his ass and filled his hole with lube. The empty container followed the chair.

I rolled two condoms onto my cock; I'd had too many tear on me from the strain.

I looked down on his body, feeling pumped and voracious. Then everything came to a stop. His ass suddenly looked too vulnerable, too perfect. It was plump and full and pink. He couldn't control the tiny shivers that shook it.

No matter how much he asked for it, did anything so perfect really deserve such brutal treatment?

As if he could read my hesitation, his voice rose up to me.

"Don't worry. Guys with monster dicks like yours often suffer from performance anxiety."

That was all I needed.

I drove my jackhammer straight down into him. He howled like a dog, and I pulled all the way out just so I could plunge it right back in again. My body slammed him into the floor with every ram of my cock.

He soon began making animal noises. All kinds of animal noises. Pig grunts, dog whimpers, rabbit screams. Did you ever hear a rabbit scream? It makes your skin crawl.

Still, I wouldn't let up. His hands were clawing at the carpet, but he couldn't get a grip. His knees gave out and he started to fall to the side, but I held him by the hips and kept him in place.

Every time I thought I would come, I'd picture that smug smirk or hear one of those cocky statements and I'd find the strength to hold on for a few more thrusts.

Suddenly, his body began to jerk and I heard those loads of spunk splattering onto my carpet. He let loose with several screaming sobs, his hands still searching for a hold. I pulled him up onto his knees as I dropped onto mine. I held him tight as I continued to pound his ass, watching in amazement as rope after rope of cum rocketed into the air.

Then I heard him gagging and I wondered if maybe he was right; that it was one long chute and my cock had reached up into his throat.

With that, my balls could take it no more. I pulled out and he fell forward. I ripped off the condoms and he rolled onto his back. I stood up and held on to my hose, draining every ounce of fluid from my body onto his stomach, chest, and face.

I bucked with the power of an orgasm the likes of which I had never felt. I had devolved into something less than human, grunting and shouting and shaking as if possessed.

When I had squeezed the last remaining drop onto his twitching body, my brain started to function again.

The fog lifted and I looked down on him. He seemed barely conscious.

I knelt beside him and realized, with regret, that I had ruined another one. Like all the others, when he came round he would either run for the door, frightened and damaged, or he would become an obsessive puppy dog, shadowing me like I was its master.

Neither one was the reaction I wanted.

His face had dried blood and rug burns on it, and it was sprayed with cum. Looking at him, almost comatose, he no longer looked hot and nasty. He looked only, quite simply, beautiful. I realized with a shock that beneath the sneer and the growth of beard, he couldn't have been much older than twenty.

How could I ever have believed that he truly understood what he had been asking for?

I did my best to mask the concern in my voice. "Well, slut, did you get your fill?"

The eyes opened and embers flew out at me. His voice was weak but the sneer was still there. "I guess this can last me until dinner-time."

I smiled. It was definitely love.

Damn, this was going to be nasty.

# A LIVE ONE

What an asshole, Sheila thinks as she plays with her pussy. He's been popping quarters into the booth like they were rock candy. A smile wouldn't cost anything extra.

She smiles down at the customer through the glass, a sugary, seductive smile full of bubble and promise. He responds with a blank stare, the same blank stare he's been giving her for the past five minutes. His face is flat and listless, a cheap cement statue of a gloomy frog, with a trickle of hostility leaking through the stone set of his mouth.

She sighs and spins around, giving up, turning her face away. She sticks her butt in the window, bends at the waist, and runs her hand slowly over her ass. *The flicking brick-wall men,* she thinks, as she rocks her hips slowly from side to side. *I've never understood why they come here. I mean, I can give them the sight of a dancing naked woman, but I can't give them the joy of watching a naked woman dance. Don't they understand that they have to bring that themselves?*

She licks her forefinger and runs it up and down her pussy as she gyrates to the thumping music. She catches Tanisha's eye, and gives her the contemptuous look she can't give the customer. Tanisha rolls her eyes, gives a quick nod of sympathy, and turns back to Danielle. The younger girl is sprawled over Tanisha's lap; she squirms and rolls her hips dramatically, putting on an extravagant show for the two drunken sailors in the corner booth. Tanisha scowls ferociously and slaps Danielle's tight, round rump; Danielle gives a theatrical squeal of pain and fear and wriggles in delight.

*I like a girl who enjoys her work,* Sheila says to herself. She knows these two; they'll be doing the real thing later on tonight. They get a kick out of faking it for the guys, but they never do it for real for money.

She hears the window panel slide down behind her, and glances over her shoulder. Yup, he's gone. What a tragic loss to the human race. She arches her back, aching from bending over, and looks around dutifully for a new customer.

Sure enough, just as she finishes stretching, the panel in the other corner booth slides up. Sheila glances at Lorelei, who's on her hands and knees, busily spreading her pussy for a middle-aged man with a briefcase in one hand and his dick in the other. Guess the new one's mine, Sheila concludes. Conscientious as always, she shimmies over, squats in front of the guy, and smiles. "Hi," she hollers over the deafening synth-pop din. "I'm Chloe."

In response he pulls a pad and pen out of his pocket and begins scribbling. He holds it up to the window and smiles back. *Hi Chloe,* it reads. *I'm Henry.*

Her eyebrows shoot up, surprised and impressed. *Smart guy,* she thinks. *Inventive. And he actually wants to talk to me. Maybe this will be a live one.*

She tucks her legs under her like a cheesecake model and runs an exploring hand over her torso. "So, Henry, you come here often?"

He writes furiously for a minute and holds the pad up to the window. *Yes,* it says. *That's why I brought this. I know it's too loud in there for you to hear me. . . .*

He flips to another page and scribbles some more. *But I want to be able to talk. This is the best I could come up with.*

He reaches into his pocket and quickly inserts a handful of quarters into the slot. She ducks her head and blushes; she knows she should know better, but she's always a little surprised when guys drop their money just to look at her. She licks her finger and runs it over her nipple, pinching it lightly. "So, you like me?"

*Yes,* he writes. *You seem . . . friendly.*

She leans back, spreads her pussy lips open for a teasing moment, then lets them close again. "I try," she answers. "So what would you like to talk about?"

*You,* he writes.

"Sure thing," she smiles. "What would you like to know?"

He thinks for a moment, then scribbles again. *What part of your body do you like best?*

Her eyebrows shoot up again. "Interesting question. No one's asked me that before."

*Really? Nobody?*

"Well, nobody in here, anyway," she says with a shrug. "But to answer your question, I'd have to say . . . my ass. I really like my ass a lot. Would you like to see it?"

He scribbles hastily. *Sure, I'd like to see your ass. . . .*

He flips to a new page. *But I want to see your face too.*

"You got it, bub," she says cheerfully. She leaps to her feet, spins around, flops over at the waist, and gapes at him between her legs. "How's this?" she grins.

He laughs and shakes his head. *That's really silly,* he writes.

"You're right," she answers. "I never understood that one either. Okay, let's try this."

She gets on hands and knees, putting her body in profile. She gives him a smoky look over her shoulder, tousles her hair, and growls. Tiger woman, she thinks. Queen of the Jungle. She shifts her leg to show him her soft, round ass, arches her hips into the air and grinds them around in slow circles. "How's that?" she asks.

*Much better,* he writes. *So what do you like doing with your ass, Chloe?*

She doesn't hesitate. "I like to get it fucked," she replies crudely.

*Show me.*

She puts her finger in her mouth and draws it out slowly, getting it nice and wet. An unexpected shudder goes through her body as she raises her eyes to meet his. His gaze trails down her back like gentle fingers, and she squirms and wriggles, pleased and flattered and oddly bashful. She reaches back with one hand, opens her ass cheek invitingly, and runs her wet finger up and down the crack. He gazes back at her face, solemn and anxious; she gives him a small, coy smile and waits.

*Please?*

She grins and licks her lips. She wets her finger again, teases her crack for a moment, then slowly slides her finger into her asshole.

A sudden rush of warmth and pleasure rolls into her head. She moans and slumps and closes her eyes, almost against her will, as she slowly pumps her finger into her ass. A small, tight spot in her throat begins to dissolve, melts down into her breasts and stomach; she bucks her hips up hard, bites her lip, and begins to whimper quietly. Her ass clenches tight around her finger, pulling it in deeper.

She opens her eyes suddenly, remembering where she is, and gives Henry a wild, intent look. His hands are pressed against the glass, clutching the notebook; his eyes are open wide, shining with lechery and delight. She shoves a second finger into her asshole and begins to fuck herself in earnest, hard and crude and a little rough, just the way she likes it. Her asshole grabs her fingers like a vise, demanding and insistent. She moans louder, throws her head back, and lets out a sharp little cry of bliss.

She collapses onto the floor, panting dramatically. She rolls onto her back, pulls out her fingers, and surreptitiously wipes them on the grimy carpet. "Oh, my God," she whispers.

He takes a deep breath and pulls away from the glass. *Jesus, you're beautiful,* he writes. *Thank you. That was wonderful.*

She stretches out and props herself up on her elbow. "You're welcome," she says.

*Was it real?* he writes.

"Mmmmmmm," she murmurs. "You bet."

*Really?*

She hesitates. "Well . . . yeah," she says uncomfortably. "More or less. I mean, it felt good. Felt real good, actually. But no, I didn't come, if that's what you're asking."

He smiles, nods, and writes for a long moment. *Thanks for being honest. I appreciate that.*

A softer song comes on the jukebox, a sweet, slow-dance love song with a low female voice. *So, do you like working here?* Henry writes.

The lie springs to Sheila's lips, the automatic lie hammered into her by months of unspoken training. She gives him a long, serious look, closes her lips tight, looks around to make sure nobody is listening, and speaks.

"The truth?" she asks, leaning into the glass.

*Of course,* he writes.

"Well . . . here's the deal," she murmurs as softly as she can and still have him hear her, as loudly as she can without being overheard. "Yeah, I do like it. The money's good and the hours are flexible. I don't have to work forty hours to pay the rent, so I have time to do my own stuff. And the dancing itself is fun. I like to dance and I like my body . . . and I like sex, I like being sexy." He grins and waggles his eyebrows. "And the other women are amazing. They're smart and sexy and funny, and they really take care of each other. I just love them to pieces."

*But . . .* he writes.

It all comes out in a rush. "The flicking men," she says bitterly. "They want it all spoon-fed to them. Pussy and pleasure and all the rest of it. They think sex should be like TV, but with hotter babes and no commercials. They just wanna sit back and suck it down like baby birds. They don't smile, they don't say hi, they don't say, 'Thank you' or 'You're pretty' or even 'Nice tits, baby.' They just stare like dead fish. Not all of them . . . but a flicking lot of them." She takes a deep breath, startled by her own anger.

He nods. *Men are assholes,* he scribbles.

She laughs heartily, her bitterness broken for the moment. "Thank you," she says. "So . . . what would you like to see now? Anything special?"

*What would you like?* he writes.

She chuckles. "Why don't you take your clothes off and dance for me?" she jokes. "Just for a change."

He scribbles seriously for a long minute: *Okay, I'll do that. But I'd better warn you, I'm not a very good dancer.*

He sets the pad on the bench, runs his hand through his hair, and slowly begins to unbutton his shirt. She stretches out like a cat and watches in awe, amazed that he took her seriously.

He unbuttons his shirt slowly, caressing his chest as he uncovers it bit by bit. She plays with her own body in response, moving her hand in slow circles over her belly as he strips off his shirt and shows her his thin chest. He begins to roll his torso in slow, hesitant, snakelike ripples. She can smell herself—the sharp, salty smell her pussy gives off when it wants something really badly. She watches hungrily as he runs his hands over his chest and slides them down over his hips. He begins to rub his dick through his jeans, squeezing it in rhythm with the slow music, and she draws a sudden, ragged breath. Her pulse beats hard inside her clit; she shoves her hand between her thighs and squeezes tight.

Suddenly he stops dancing and snatches up the pad and pen. *I feel silly,* he writes. *I feel like a dork.*

She shakes her head. "You shouldn't," she replies. "You look great. I'm getting totally wet watching you." She stares meaningfully at his crotch. "Now show me more."

He drops pad and pen, slumps against the wall, hooks his thumb into his waistband, and gives her a moody, smoldering stare like a model for designer jeans. She laughs and nods approvingly. He begins to move again, squirming and writhing against the wall. Slowly, teasingly, he unbuckles his belt, unzips his fly, tugs his swollen dick out of his pants and into the open air. He cradles it in his hand and gives her a wide-open look, proud and fearful and eager for approval.

She ogles his cock and licks her lips, drinking in his eagerness like water. "Very pretty," she says. "Very nice indeed. But I wanna see more. Turn around and pull them all the way down. Show me your ass."

He complies immediately; turns to face the wall, arches his back, and slowly pulls his jeans down over his slim hips. She whistles appreciatively as the fabric drops down to his thighs and his bare ass is revealed. He blushes bright red, presses his hands against the wall, and slowly bends over to give her a better look. She stares intently at his smooth, tight ass, relishing his exposure, sucking in the view like a starving woman. Her clit thumps hard, demanding attention; she begins to caress it in earnest, moving her finger in slow, tight circles. *I love a boy who does what I tell him,* she thinks.

"Now turn around again," she commands. "Let me see your dick. Let me see you jerk off."

He spins around to face her, jeans around his knees, face flushed, his dick twitching of its own accord. He jams his back against the wall, licks his hand, and begins to slide it up and down the shaft of his cock.

A sudden flash of longing stabs into her cunt, and she whimpers and spreads her legs wider. She opens her pussy lips with her fingers and thrusts her hips toward the glass, frantically and insistently, forcing her hole into the open, trying to show him as much of herself as she can. His eyes widen as they take in her sopping-wet cunt; he grips his cock with a trembling hand as she spreads herself apart and furiously rubs her swollen clit. Their eyes connect; they stare intently, flushed, shivering, mouths hanging open, eyes wide. His hand moves faster and faster; a shudder travels through his body, and he bites his lip, throws his head back, and squirts into his hand. She sees his face contort. She cries out hard, and comes.

They both take a deep breath and slump backward. Sheila stretches back on the grimy carpet and clamps her thighs around her hand; Henry collapses against the wall, lost in quiet bliss.

Finally he pulls his pants up, takes a handkerchief out of his pocket, and wipes the come off his dick and his hand. Shoving the hanky back in his pocket, he picks up the pad and pen.

*Thank you thank you thank you,* he writes.

"Jesus," she gasps. "You're welcome. Thank *you.*"

*That was real . . . right?*

She nods. "Yeah," she answers. "That was real."

The window panel starts to slide down. Henry scrabbles through his pockets and quickly drops another quarter in the slot. The panel slides up again; he spreads his hand and shows her the contents with a sad, wistful smile. One more quarter. He drops it in and shrugs. *How much time do we have left?* he writes.

"About a minute," she answers. "A little less actually. Shit. You'd better get dressed."

He pulls his shirt on and quickly zips his pants. *So is your name really Chloe?* he writes.

"No," she replies. "Of course not."

*What is it really?*

She gives him a long, clear look. *Maybe I should make up a fake real name,* she thinks. She likes this guy a lot; it'd make him happy to think she'd confided in him. She gazes at the floor, thinks carefully for a moment, then looks back at his face and shakes her head.

"I'm not going to tell you that," she says. "I'm sorry."

*Quite all right,* he scribbles. *I understand. Thanks for not lying to me.*

"You're welcome," she replies.

They stare at each other awkwardly, somewhat at a loss for words. "That was wonderful," she says at last. "Really. You made my day."

He kisses his hand and reaches out to touch the glass. The panel drops down, sliding over his hand, clicking shut. "Come back sometime," she calls into the metal plate. She presses her hands against the window, drained and dazed and a bit forlorn, hoping that he heard her.

She feels a light touch on her shoulder. "Hey, Chloe," Tanisha says. "It's time for your break." She gives Sheila a light slap on the rump. "Nice show, girl," she adds. "Hell, you even got me going."

"Thanks." Sheila sighs. "Me, too. Sometimes I really like this job."

"I know what you mean, babe," Tanisha says as Sheila walks off the stage. "I know what you mean."

# Ponyboy

## I.

"Mr. Benson?" I said. "I don't know any Benson."

"No, sir," Clyde answered over the intercom, "not Benson—Benten, B-E-N-T-E-N. He says he's here to talk to you about horses."

"Oh! Benten! Yes, I can see Benten."

I punched off the intercom and spun my chair around. Today was going to be a high point in a most miraculous year. I stood up and walked to the window, and made sure my shirt was well-tucked, my cuffs shot to the ruby links, my tie knot settled. Twenty-eight floors below, San Francisco was spread out before me like a virgin eager to get laid. I could see great mountains of fog re-treating back over the Marin headlands to the Pacific like ethereal, white-whale ghosts. We'd have clear air everywhere by dinnertime. I took it all as a good omen.

October 29. One year ago I was still a married man, a slave in principle to a gorgeous wife who didn't turn me on in a marriage of convenience I could not afford to leave. I had the old family name her daddy wanted, she had all the money I wanted—and then she had all the money, period. When my picture showed up in a local gay paper the week before the Folsom Street Fair, I was summarily escorted out of the family business: Oops, so sorry. It had all been such a joke! Except, of course, the joke was on me. I'd been to the Fair a few years before in shades and cap and vest with my buffed chest and biceps bulging and Richard on my leash wearing the littlest excuse for a codpiece I thought we could get away with. He'd been a big hit at Mark I. Chester's annual photo show, and we even got invited in to Dr. Tech's private bash across the way so people could eyeball Dick up close. I never saw anyone take our picture, but obviously someone did: with Richard bent over a barrel sucking Charlie's Angel while I pumped him with my fist halfway up to the elbow.

Credit where credit is due: The paper didn't run the picture for three years, and when they did the photo was set as part of a nostalgia collage they had the good sense (or taste) to crop. But anyone who knew me knew it was me, anyone who knew Richard knew he was Gloria's brother, anyone who knew cock-sucking and fist-fucking knew what we were doing, and whoever sent the clipping from the paper to my father, my wife, and my father-in-law knew *all* of the above.

Shit, you might say, hit the fan. Shit happened. Shit fell on Alabama like stars. I was up shit creek without a paddle. I was in deep shit. In less than three days I was legally disowned, and everything but everything was in Gloria's name. I couldn't buy a newspaper without begging for a dime. For two years I suffered in silence, or my best whining imitation of it. I even fucked Glory from time to time. I thought I needed her forgiveness, and a hole's a hole for all of that.

October 30 last year, Glory died in an auto accident. Bye-bye.

Sorry. I don't mean to make light of this: family tragedy, personal tragedy, successful youngish woman with still lots to live for, and so forth.

But you have to understand: It changed my life.

A week later, November 6, four days after the funeral, I was sitting in the house on Broadway wondering what I was going to do with my life when the lawyer called, and the rest, as they say, is mystery. My story.

What everyone had overlooked was that Glory hadn't changed her will, so I was still the beneficiary and heir unapparent to the last dregs of the Robber Barons' ungodly bank accounts. No trillions, no billions, but many many many millions: enough for me to roll happily in spare change for the rest of my self-indulgent life. And the house, of course—30 rooms with a lot of history. I sat down in my leather chair in the library off the formal dining room and put my feet on my leather ottoman. I stared out the window down the hill to the Marina and the Bay. I rang for Chives—his name is Larry, but I've always called him Chives—and had him pour me some of the better calvados.

The intercom buzzed, and Clyde opened the door for Mr. Benten. I let Clyde close the door, then took two steps in the direction of my guest with my hand stuck out.

"Mr. Benten, a pleasure."

"Mr. Townsend." His voice was quiet, soft, and low as a slow cat's-purr. "Call me Preston. Please."

"Edgar. Refreshment, Preston? It's nearly evening."

"Thank you, Edgar." He rapped his leather portfolio twice with his knuckles and smiled as if deferentially. "Yes. One is for 'no,' two is for 'yes.' A cognac?"

I buzzed, two hots and a trot. Clyde came in with the tray, poured, and left. Preston said, "No need for small talk?" I smiled and shook my head. He sat on the couch and opened his portfolio, and spread some photos out. I sat down beside him, picked one up, and felt a rush go through me like the days of wine and poppers. The boy was stunning on his hands and knees: naked, smooth, well-built, and well-hung, wearing a full head harness complete with bits, reins, and bridle, and a big fluffy ponytail just

the soft brown color of his hair arching like a fountain out of his
ass. The next boy was saddled, with very short stirrups, and the
standing man holding him close on reins was wearing shiny lizard
cowboy boots with rowels on his spurs. There were saddled boys
standing up with hoof-shaped boots, standing boys harnessed in
traces pulling sulkies and carts, ponyboys in poses, ponyboys at
ease. They all seemed to be five or ten years younger than I, as Preston was probably that much older.

"When?" I asked Preston.

"Saturday. Come for the afternoon, stay for dinner. You'll enjoy
the company."

After Preston left I buzzed for Clyde again. "Close the door," I
said when he entered, "and take off your clothes."

"Sir?" he asked.

"Take off your clothes. Don't make me repeat myself."

"Yes, sir."

I never understood why people are obedient, but Clyde did as he
was told. Not bad: he could use a gym, but he was young yet. I
said, "Get me some ties."

"Ties, sir? Yes, sir."

"And a harness."

"Yes, sir."

Clyde was clearly puzzled, but his naked ass shimmied as he
stepped to the closet and brought me a leather harness dotted with
cone studs and a handful of Monday-go-to-Meetin' ties. I cinched
the harness tight around Clyde's chest, put his back to the side of
my desk, strung four of the ties together with bowlines, and ran the
thousand-dollar rope I'd made through the O-rings in the back.
Then I climbed up on the desk holding the two ends of the rope
like reins.

"Now: pull," I said. "Lean into the harness and pull. Strain,
damn it, let me see your muscles work."

And he did strain, pulling at my huge, landlocked mahogany
desk as if it were a lightweight cart on wheels.

Clyde is such a good boy. His shoulders bunched, his rib cage heaved, his back bulged, his thighs and ass cheeks crimped, and he set his jaw so firmly I thought the desk might even move.

I like to see naked men at work. I leapt right down on top of him and threw him to the floor. Before he could say a thing I had my pants open and was fucking him right there without condoms, lube, or anything. I came very quickly, and almost immediately felt his sphincters clamp around my dick a half dozen times. Clyde turned his head around to try to see me over his shoulder.

"Edgar!" he whispered.

One is for "no." I rapped his skull once with my knuckle. "Shush," I told him. "Relax. It's only lust."

2.

Saturday I left home earlier than necessary and made a slow drive up into the wine country, consulting the map Preston had given me. I had to get off the Silverado Trail and follow the country road a little less than three miles. A quick right, an obscure left, look for the orange Road Work sign, turn left, and the rest would be apparent.

And it was. Two private guards who were decked out to look like Royal Canadian Mounted Police sat their exquisitely turned-out horses—real ones—before a rustic wooden gate. I had the top down on the Quattro, so over my windshield I sang out the word Preston had advised. The Mounties parted like a bright red sea, and the gate swung open like an obedient boy's mouth. I drove in and followed the trail to a tree-shaded parking area full of Boxsters and Benzes and Lexi and one bubble-gum pink Bentley convertible, where more RCMP look-alikes were stationed in front of a huge burgundy velvet curtain. The velvet was artfully suspended between the tops of a couple of telephone poles and draped with old gold ribbon. It had to be thirty feet high and twice as wide, and was perfectly designed to block from sight whatever was on the other side of it. I heard distant music as one attendant took the keys to my car and another passed me through the curtain. On the other side, the world was altogether different.

Beneath the shade of a white canvas tent-top big enough for a modest circus, a lawn party was in full swing, composed of well-turned-out men of a certain age, dressed in casual silks and linens, who would not have been uncomfortable one way or another with my bank account. Sculpted, undressed, and scrupulously shaved rather younger men about my age, wearing bright chrome collars with understated locks, circulated among the guests with trays of food and drink, while a small clutch of strolling musicians played gentle melodies. I took a flute of bubbly off a passing tray and cruised the lawn, taking its measure. I was curious to see a politician I would not have expected to be so bold, and a publicly conspicuous neighbor of mine whose hands on the help appeared to be as forward as his magazine tongue. But a different kind of movement at the lawn's far side caught my eye, so that was where I went, and that was where I found what I had come for.

Beyond the backs of a couple dozen serious connoisseurs, the stock was being put through its paces. Lawn chairs were strewn here and there and some were free, but I found a comfortable tree to lean against and watched the show from the shade that it provided.

Among several ponies, each with his own handler, the boy who took my eye completely was the very definition of horse-dick, cut by Michelangelo from warm Sienna marble and hanging lower than the five-pound disk of lead weight swinging from balls so swollen they looked like a bulging pair of chestnuts sheathed in fascia shells. He was got up with silver, blue, and white streamers pinned to his silver bridle, and his arms were locked behind him with his elbows stretched around a chrome bar that matched his collar and pushed his shoulders high and forced his chest forward. He lifted his knees one after the other and brought his feet down with great precision so his fat cock looked like a third leg, while his handler held the owner's end of a ten-foot lead and paced him in a circle where the wide swath of lawn was just beginning to show dark stains of hoofwear. He didn't even glance to the sides, though he was wearing no blinders. He really knew how to prance.

The boy had started to perspire, and the weight kept bouncing up and down just above his knees. Even though it had to be causing him some kind of pain every time he took a step, his handler made him jump a couple of bars, which he did very gingerly, then stopped him, whispered in his ear, removed the arm bar, and led him away. Everyone else was engaged by a couple other show ponies, but I was so attracted to this boy I wanted to know more about him. I pushed off my tree to follow where his handler led him.

Almost immediately beyond the tent-top they passed a big yellow sign that said No Entry, walked through a gate with automatic locks, then passed a second, similar sign. I slipped my wallet into the gate latch so it couldn't close completely, and when the handler and boy had disappeared I pushed the gate open, retrieved my wallet, and went on after them while the gate closed behind me.

Handler and boy had gone past a structure that looked as if it had once been a small barn, but now seemed like something from a surreal 1960s movie. The wind had torn the roof off long ago, some of the walls had gone with the roof, and what remained was irregular anyway because whole boards and slabs of wood had fallen off, holes had been ripped out here and there, and whatever glass had once stood in the large window frames must have turned to dust long before the ponyboy was born. Inside the remaining weather-whitened fragments a dozen men lounged on leather furniture much too fine for the ruins and watched two well-muscled boys Greek wrestle. The handler had taken his ponyboy behind the structure, and I could see at my distance where a split-rail paddock held a dozen other ponyboys more or less like the first who all stood nearly motionless in the shade of a stand of black oaks. I watched from beside a small thicket of madrone.

Inside the corral the handler bent the ponyboy over a sawhorse and pulled out his tail, stuffing it dildo-end down into an obvious bucket of disinfectant. He rubbed the pony from head to hoof with a towel soaked in so much witch hazel I could smell it where I lurked, gave him a pail and let him drink, then chained his hands behind a smaller elbow bar. He lifted the weight suspended from the boy's dark balls, slid it into a narrow slot in the fence in front of the boy, and closed it, then took up the reins of two other boys. He bent first one and then the other over the same sawhorse, and tailed them with ponytails that matched their own hair, then led them out toward the lawn with the same kinds of big weights swaying from their balls.

I waited until the handler had taken the boys away, then moved closer to the fence. The boys saw me, but none of them moved and none of them talked. All their hands were locked behind them and they all wore the same kinds of weights that were pushed through slots to rest on shelves at about thigh level in a way that was designed to relieve the ponies and still secure them. In effect, I had before me a dozen pretty ponyboys, hobbled in the paddock by their balls. None of them could move. No one was going anywhere.

I took a bag of chocolates from my jacket and approached the fence, closing in on the ponyboy I'd first seen prance. I admired his companions, and admired him in particular. I opened the bag and nibbled at a little mint.

"You pranced very well on the lawn. Are you hungry?"

It was a little like talking to a real horse. Some of the other boys snickered and one cleared his throat with a kind of luffing warning sound that horses make with their cheeks, but my ponyboy said nothing. Why would a young stud show off his muscle this way? I figured maybe he got off on all the attention, so I gave him some.

"I'd like to see you really run," I said. "I'd like to see you straining at a cart that I was riding in. I'd like to drive you, see your muscles growing taut, see you pulling on the harness, see your veins bulge out, see the sweat run down your back and in between the cheeks of your ass. You have such gorgeous legs, I'd like to see how fast you run. Do you like buggy whips? They feel so elegant in the hand, they sound so vicious in the air, they really sting, they hurt like hell, but the marks they leave are gone in a day. Unless you cut the skin with them. Draw blood. You could really mark a ponyboy with one, you know. Do you like to pull a cart?"

I held a chocolate out to him the way you'd hold a piece of sugar toward a horse, but he was having none of it. He didn't come and lip it up the way real horses do. He couldn't turn or move because of the hobble, but his eyes seemed to widen as he leaned away from me and turned his head. I moved closer to the fence and made the chocolate last.

"So I guess you're not supposed to talk with the buyers, is that right? To let us make our minds up on our own? But how can a man know what property he wants unless he has the chance to get to know it? Can I count your teeth at least?"

I finished the chocolate finally, reached out and took his hair in my hand, and tried to turn his face toward me. I don't know now if I really wanted to count his teeth or if I was just goofing around with him, but he held his head back with a kind of stubborn equine pride. I shook his head by the hair.

"Don't make me angry, boy. I might just buy you."

"Edgar," I heard Preston's soft voice behind me, "let go of my pony, please."

### 3.

I dropped the boy's hair as if I'd been shocked, and turned around. "Preston! Well, hello! I didn't know he was your pony. He's such a handsome lad, and he prances so well—you must be an excellent trainer."

"Thank you," he said in a cool, matter-of-fact tone. He wore jodhpurs and a riding blouse, and slapped at his bootleg with a crop. "I've had experience."

"And you give excellent directions, too. I found the place first try."

"How good," Preston said. The voice I had thought was as warm as a cat's-purr just a couple of days ago now sounded feline in a different way: Deep in his throat it was almost predatory. "Edgar, how do you come to be back here in the paddock area?"

"Here? I just followed the handler when he brought your boy back from show."

As if on cue the handler appeared from around the Fellini barn, but this time he had no ponyboys in tow. Instead he had a handful of tack, and was accompanied by a couple of Mounties. Preston turned to the handler.

"Gardiner, did you bring Mr. Townsend back here?"

The handler looked at me and back at Preston. "Mr. Townsend? Why, no, sir, I don't bring anyone. That would be against the strictest rules."

Edgar turned back to me.

"I didn't say he brought me, Preston. I said I followed him."

"Past the No Entry signs? Through the locked gate?"

"Well, yes. I was just so enchanted with the pony that turns out to be yours."

Preston closed his eyes and seemed to meditate on his feet, and time slowed down for me, the moment stretching out so I felt I filled an hour just taking and releasing a single breath. When Preston opened his eyes he was already walking toward the paddock, but when I turned as if to follow I found myself hemmed in by Gardiner and the Mounties. For the first time I felt a wave of apprehension.

Preston went directly to the ponyboy, who was clearly glad to see him: He smiled and bent his head to nuzzle at Preston's touch. Preston spoke a few words to him and actually kissed his pony, then he turned and rejoined me.

"I think, Edgar, you have misunderstood my invitation."

"Excuse me?"

"I think you expected to enjoy the flesh of other ponyboys."

"Of *course* I did. What else would I expect here?" Suddenly I felt hollow. "What do you mean, 'other' ponyboys?"

Preston nodded, and I could not have counted to "one" before I felt Gardiner pinning my elbows from behind and a Mountie slipping a halter over my head.

"Do not cause trouble, Edgar, and I think you will not be unhappy with the outcome. Or, of course, you can rebel and pay the price."

Gardiner was enormously powerful: If I were to judge by this one encounter, he could have wrestled genuine horses and won. Over my protests he held me gently but firmly as the Mounties lifted, twisted, and handled me bodily until they had stripped me naked and set me on the ground among them. To my horror I found myself extremely hard, a fact that Preston did not miss.

"You respond to discipline quite favorably, Edgar. That's a good sign. Get down on your knees. The time has come for a little change."

"Preston!"

"Do not cause trouble, Edgar. I can be very patient, but I am not always." Preston slid his crop across his thigh. I heard blue jays squabble. The first Mountie returned from leaving my folded clothes in a neat pile well outside the circle the four men made. Reluctant and peevish but confused by my combination of growing alarm and mounting excitement (because by now I was sporting a raging hard-on), I knelt facing my host, which gave me a chance to notice the delectable bulge in his cavalry twill jodhpurs. Apparently Preston too responded quite favorably to discipline.

"Good boy," Preston said to me. Good boy? "Now, kiss my boot."

"Preston!"

"Kiss my boot, Edgar." He moved so quickly I did not even see the crop slash through space, and the stick whipped the back of my thigh in exactly the spot that allowed the crop to keep on flying and slap hard against my balls. "Now."

With the fresh sting racing around my tingling nerves, I nearly fell on my face to obey his command, and as I did I felt rough hands take me from behind. I tried to sit up, but Preston's crop on my other thigh stopped me cold.

"Not a peck, Edgar. Not a little buss. A kiss. You know, with your mouth open, and your tongue wet. Kiss my boots, Edgar. Both of them. Wash them nice and clean."

I tried to comply. Really I did. But those rough hands worked my ass and started to open me with a slick, smooth, relentless pressure. For an instant I felt sharply stretched and I cried out as if I were being torn, then the dildo sank home and I knew that I'd been tailed. One of those same rough hands worked the dildo until I felt that deep-down need for release that has nothing at all to do with cumming, then the other grabbed my balls and stretched them back like salt water taffy, making me ache so that I started to buck.

"Kiss my boot, Edgar," Preston said again, and I felt his crop land fast on one cheek and then the other, back and forth even while the dildo pumped my ass and the big hand that squeezed my balls now like Silly Putty punched them into the deep root of my cock and I tried to say, "Yessir," but it sounded to me as if I were drowning in a grilled cheese sandwich until I suddenly realized it was Preston's fine, supple, well-grained, tawny, casual riding boot I was sucking off as if I could get the whole toe of it in between my lips and down my gullet.

Gardiner took my head in his strong hands and pulled me away from Preston's boot. I smelled the thick aroma of deeply soaped tack-leather, very different from the soft, fragrant scent of a well-kept boot. With consummate smoothness he slid a full bridle over my face, cinched it tight, and locked it into place. It braced me across the forehead and held my jaw in a soft pocket sewn to straps that ran up the sides of my face and met at the crown of my head. There, one cross-strap ran down in front and split in two around my nose, and became one again at the jaw pocket. The other continued down the back of my neck and locked on a collarpiece that extended from the bottom of the jaw pocket and closed at the back of my neck.

Complete as the bridle was, it was designed to keep my mouth accessible. Now Gardiner forced my mouth apart and pressed a hard, narrow, rubber bit between my teeth. Then he kissed me, right over the bit, and while Preston and the Mounties laughed I finally stopped struggling. I was ready to do whatever Preston said. I felt defeated and I didn't like this feeling, but at the same time I felt thrilled in a way I had never felt before. Naked, on my knees, bridled, a little bit worked over, and helpless at the command of these four big men, my cock so hard it ached, and I wanted to kiss Preston's boots, and Gardiner's, and the Mounties'. I fell forward, but a hard tug on the bridle kept my head suspended.

"Follow," Preston said, and I scrambled to follow the measured movement of his boots as he strolled around the area outside the paddock. He used the reins to keep my head exactly at the height and angle that would make my bearing appear proud, if "proud" is a word I could apply to crawling around in the dirt and praying I would have a chance to grovel for this man's pleasure. He used the slightest pressure to let me know I was to turn to the left or right, and when he wanted me to stop he just tightened his fist on the reins so I felt the thin rubber bit against my cheeks. With every step I felt that dildo rubbing deep in my bowels, filling the cavity, and teaching my asshole to be hungry, as my hips and knees and shoulders and hands moved me along with greater and greater certainty, and the long horsehair tail brushed the backs of my welted thighs all the way past the insides of my knees to tickle my calves.

I had completely lost track of time when Preston brought me up before Gardiner and the Mounties. A pail of water was waiting, and when I tried to direct my head toward it, Preston pulled me up short and took the bit out of my mouth.

"I believe this new pony is thirsty, gentlemen. Does anyone have something for him to drink? Why, here's something now."

Preston pulled my head up sharply and turned my face to the

side at once so that my mouth was at just the right height for a very long, slender Mountie cock with beautiful veins that looked like wide blue rivers laid out on a map of heaven. The lines and ridges and marks on its head were the intricate byways God had set up to make the sinner's journey entertaining. I wanted to travel each little one-way street so slowly that I could come to a full stop at every twist and turn, but the Mountie with the open fly interrupted my reverie. He took my hair in one hand and his cock in the other, and jerked my mouth open and jammed himself straight past my gag reflex and out, and in and out, and he never even stopped to find out if I could handle meat that long, and by the time I could cough for the first time he was cumming so far down my throat I never even tasted him till he pulled out gradually, like a hungry snake reluctantly leaving the warmth of its sun-spotted burrow, wiping the head of his dick on my tongue as he passed.

I was gasping more than the Mountie, but I was getting the hang of it: If this was going to be the future, I started to see how I could have some unexpected fun, and I was ready for Mountie number two. He was thick as a plug, but I clamped him in my lips like a hose in an O-ring and sucked up a vacuum that must have yanked his balls straight up into his body and shot them out into my mouth, which is how he came, one-two. His mouth fell open but mine stayed shut, and I did not meet his eyes as I smiled to myself. I expected Gardiner next, but Preston put me in front of the bucket and I drank what ponies are supposed to drink.

While I drank I smelled something hot, as if a little piece of air was burning, and when I was through one of the Mounties threw a small piece of meat to the ground in front of me. Was I supposed to eat it? Preston stabbed it with a tiny iron, and it crackled and sizzled and smoked. He pulled the iron away and there was an arrow branded into the meat.

"I like the way you work, Edgar. That is a pleasant surprise. If you continue to please me, this meat might be you someday. If you continue. But today we have a different task. Stand up."

Beyond the paddock was a hedge. As Preston led me toward it I could see the hedge was made entirely of holly maybe two feet thick and dense with hard, curled leaves that were so pointed that the hedge was effectively made of thorns. From closer up the hedge seemed curved, and in a few more steps I saw that its curve hid a gap perhaps twice the width of a real, large horse. Preston led me inside the hedge, and then I could see that it was completely circular, containing a grassy area half the size of a soccer field, with a second gap about the same size set directly across from the first.

Preston removed the reins from the bridle on my face. "You will wear the bridle and you will wear the tail," he said, "but otherwise you will be free to run. If you can escape the enclosure through either opening before I capture you, I will bring you the ponyboy you seemed to admire so much, and put you out to stud with him for the weekend. If I capture you, however, you will join my stable and maybe pull a race cart that I will let him drive."

Gardiner appeared in the gap behind us, leading an English-saddled roan that had to be eighteen hands tall.

"I'll give you a little head-start," Preston said, "but I have never yet lost this contest. Enjoy yourself. Run!"

I made the same mistake I suppose anyone would make just then: I ran. But instead of maneuvering for position at close range and plunging through the gap we'd just come through, where I might have really had a chance, I ran for the far gap, supposing sort of automatically that with the little head-start I might outrun him. Outrun a horse. A big horse.

The dildo stretched my asshole and wallowed in my rectum and almost brought me to my knees all by itself. The bridle cramped my face and restricted my breathing. My bare feet were exquisitely sensitive to the nuances of little divots and pebbles and gopher holes, and the searing points of dry grasses and nettle seeds nearly threw me to the ground repeatedly. My unsupported balls bounced more heavily than I would have imagined, and hurt surprisingly. Maybe this wasn't going to be quite as much fun as I'd thought a little while ago. And only then did I realize I was a naked man with a bridle on my head and a horsetail dildo up my ass, running beneath the sky as if my life depended on it across an open, empty field. I turned my head to look behind me and saw Preston sitting in the saddle, leaning forward with his arms folded against the horse's neck, laughing. Now he was the one having fun. Fuck him. Preston reined his horse and started it in to walk, and then to trot, and then to canter. I turned for the far gap and bolted as fast as I could.

Preston never meant me harm, I know: This was just a game for him, and I was learning to play. But I had never been so terrified in my entire life as when I heard the rapid beat of horse hooves pounding on the ground behind me, closer with every set of steps. My eyes were blurred with sweat the first time he swept past me and sliced the skin of my ass with some kind of whip. I'm sure I screamed, but I kept on running. He scribed a wide arc in front of me, swept around behind me again, and I felt the terror again as I heard him coming up on me at a dead run when the whip cut my ass again. The breath was rasping in my throat and I'd forgotten all my pain, keeping my eyes on the gap that now seemed miles away. I heard Preston shouting from behind, "Run! Run! *Run!*" and then a lasso settled over me and pinned my arms to my sides and the horse just stopped, jerking me to the ground.

Preston was on me as if I were a steer, tying my wrists behind me, binding my ankles, and trussing me up in record seconds. I was panting hoarsely, trying to catch some breath, and Preston's shirt wasn't even ruffled. That made me mad.

"If you were me I bet you'd fuck me now, wouldn't you?" he whispered in my ear. At first I didn't have the strength to reply, but he took my balls in one of his hands. "Shall I geld you, Edgar?" And then I found my voice.

"Please, Preston, no. Please, no."

"Well then, what shall I do with you?"

Suddenly I had caught my breath. I was exhausted more from

the adrenaline that had been coursing through me than from the run itself, and I knew that I would ache by morning. But I realized that Preston was lying almost completely on top of me, holding my balls in his hand, and looking into my eyes.

Lying beneath him naked and bound, bridled and tailed, I got coy and almost smiled. I made music with my voice as if I were an old-time sweater queen batting my eyelashes at a butch. "Will you please brand me, Preston?"

Hah! I thought. He wasn't expecting that.

But he didn't miss a beat. "In time, perhaps, but you haven't earned that honor yet, Edgar. This is just the first day of your training. Perhaps I'll keep you or perhaps you'll fetch a pretty price when I get through with you, but you're an orphan for the moment. You're in my keeping but you don't belong to anyone just now, and you have a great deal yet to learn. And by the way, to you my name is Mr. Benten. But of course, ponies don't talk, and you are not allowed to speak again. Do you understand me?"

I wanted to spit in his face and I wanted to kiss him, I wanted to rip myself out of my bonds and destroy him and I wanted him to beat my rebellion out of me with his whip, I wanted him to make love to me and I wanted him to crush my balls in his warm, soft, exceptionally certain hand. It was difficult, hog-tied as I was, but this was going to be even more fun than I'd thought. I lifted my legs together and let them drop on the ground—one, two: yes.

# Robert Irwin

# IN THE GIRAFFE HOUSE

from *Prayer-Cushions of the Flesh*

The sounds of lamentation increased briefly, then died away. Orkhan did not move, but sat in pitch darkness. Where, after all, should he go? Passionate, brightly colored images chased one another about in his head—he had witnessed so many unfamiliar sights, so many curious tableaux, all in the matter of a few hours. Some of the things he had seen he did not even have a name for. Other things were as yet only names. The Rapture was still only a name. At least he had saved himself from that. Eventually his eyelids fluttered and drooped and he slumped back onto the stone floor and slept where he had been sitting. Even while he slept, the viper in his mouth flicked restlessly from side to side.

He was woken by the sounds of rustling, scratching, and muttering. He opened his eyes and beheld the daylight streaming in from a lantern in the roof of the pit. He looked into the cage expecting to see Mihrimah, but there, where Mihrimah had stood on the previous evening, was an old woman in a coarse brown robe. The woman's head was sunk so low that it hardly rose above her shoulders. On reflection, it was more like a skull than a head, for the thin hair did not cover it, skin stretched over angular bones and the eyes were set deep within the bones. A thin wispy beard sprouted from the woman's jaw, the jut of which was accentuated by her toothlessness. Orkhan toyed with the notion that he was indeed gazing at Mihrimah, that he had just been asleep for seventy years and that it was to this that the discipline of the Dolorous Gaze had brought him. The woman looked down on him briefly before resuming her work, scattering straw over the floor of the cage.

Then, when she had finished this task, she shuffled out through the door at the back of the cage. There were muffled shouts. Then the door opened again and a panther padded in. The panther was followed by a muscular girl with close-cropped red hair. She was dressed in black leather—skirt, laced bodice and gloves. Her feet were bare and she carried a whip. She did not notice Orkhan, for all her attention was on the panther, which she baited with her whip, lightly flicking at the creature's nose and muzzle. The panther, like a kitten confronted with a ball of string, snarled, lashed its tail, and sought to catch at the thong with its talons. At last the girl tired of this game and cast the whip away. The panther leapt toward her and together they rolled over the straw. Orkhan cried out, but he was ignored, as the girl and the panther tumbled over one another. She was momentarily astride the supple, rippling, velvety back of the beast, before he slipped out from under her and in a moment she was lying under him. Her skirt had ridden up and she was wearing nothing underneath. The creature stood over her, dripping saliva onto her body, seeming to devour her with his stony green eyes, before inclining his head to lash her face with his rough tongue. She reached up to clasp his neck and together they rolled over once more. The panther began to purr as she stroked his stomach.

Suddenly she cried out. She had just noticed that her game with the beast was being observed by Orkhan. She leapt up, as if embarrassed to be discovered at play. She strode over to the bars of the cage, with the panther slinking close beside her. Orkhan, who remained sitting, caught a blast of the creature's breath, which was both sweet and foul.

"Who are you?" said the girl, looking down on Orkhan.

"My name is Orkhan. I am your Sultan."

The girl seemed neither surprised nor impressed.

"I am Roxelana," she said, as she fumbled in her bodice, before producing a key at the end of a chain. "Roxelana means 'the Russian.'" And she gave the panther a final stroke before picking up her whip, unlocking the cage door, and joining Orkhan on the other side. The trapped and abandoned panther gazed balefully up at Orkhan.

"I call him Babur," said Roxelana. She stood close beside Orkhan and gazed down on her former playmate. Her face was smudged and there was a scratch of blood on her shoulders. She smelled of sweat and the panther. Her voice was husky as she had not yet recovered from her exertions, and her breasts rose and fell as she struggled to regain her breath. Those breasts seemed to Orkhan to more closely resemble extra muscles than any conventional feature of a woman's body. Roxelana was, like her panther, a mass of sinew and muscle.

"Are you one of the concubines of the Harem?" he asked doubtfully.

She let out a laugh that was half delighted, half scornful.

"Ha! I could not bear to have anything to do with the Harem women. No, I am one of the animal girls who work in the Imperial Zoo. I would much rather serve animals than the ninnies of the Harem."

"There is an Imperial Zoo? Where is it?"

She gave him a curious look.

"It is here. You are in it. Why else should you be talking to an animal girl and standing in front of a cage containing a panther? This is Babur's cage." And she pointed to a brass plaque attached to the bars at the top of the cage. The inscription in swirls of decora-

tive calligraphy announced: THIS IS THE PANTHER, MARVELOUS IN
HIS BEAUTY, WHOSE BREATH IS SWEET AS THE SPICES OF JAVA.

"But last night there was no panther," said Orkhan, who was
wondering if he was going mad. "Last night I saw a woman who
said she was called Mihrimah stand behind those bars and start to
undress herself in front of me."

"Ah! So it was Mihrimah? That girl thinks that the sun shines
out of her arse, that moonlight issues from her cunt, and she be-
lieves that she is the mother of cosmic mysteries, that her body is
an orchard, a sea, a desert, a fountain, a mirror, a mystic robe and,
at the end of it all, a bloody Prayer-Cushion for man to kneel on as
he prays before the Holy of Holies. She's mad, quite mad . . . She
also thinks that she can walk into the Zoo and do what she likes,
take over its cages, turn out the animals, give orders to the staff.
The insolence of those courtesans and dancing girls takes my breath
away. The reality is that Mihrimah and the rest of the concubines
are good for nothing, except fucking—and doing embroidery. But
they lie about in the Harem and thoughts of sex rot away their soft
insides and eat up their little brains. All that Prayer-Cushion rub-
bish that they preach . . . it's only the product of not enough proper
sex. Cooped up in their cramped dormitories, they pleasure one another and fantasize about men, but all they ever see is eunuchs."
She paused to calm herself and get her breath back, before continuing, "But we are all prisoners here, women, eunuchs and animals.
Of course, the main zoo is over at the Hippodrome. This is only a
little zoo within the Harem for the pleasure of the Sultan's concubines. We have wild boars, gazelles, porcupines, a buffalo, a small
herd of giraffes . . . Two of the giraffes are homosexual and they use
their necks to court one another."

She placed her gloved hand in his. Her eyes sparkled.

"Come and see the homosexual giraffes."

She led him up out of the pit and down a roofed and cobbled
street that twisted between cages and storerooms. They came to a
low doorway over which was written, THESE ARE THE SULTAN'S

HUNTERS WHO SIT ON THE GLOVES OF LADIES AND WAIT TO BRING DEATH FROM THE SKIES. Roxelana ducked in and Orkhan followed her through the imperial mews. Hawks in plumed leather helmets stirred restlessly on their perches. Roxelana explained that this was a shortcut. Then they emerged out through another low door into the high-roofed and airy giraffe stable. HERE ARE THE HAPPY OFFSPRING OF THE MATING OF CAMELS AND LEOPARDS WHO ARE CALLED GIRAFFES.

"Everywhere in the Harem is so cramped," said Roxelana. "Apart from the hammam, I think this is the biggest building there is."

A giraffe lazily sought to entwine his neck round that of his neighbor. Hands on hips, Roxelana stood gazing up at the animals in rapt delight. Orkhan followed her gaze. The creatures did not resemble the giraffes in the bestiary which he used to study in the Cage. They were strange, but then everything was so strange to him, and surely Roxelana was the strangest creature in her zoo. She slapped the flank of one of the languid giraffes, seeking to urge it on in its seduction, then turned to Orkhan and smiled. He was certain that he had never seen such strong white teeth or such brilliant eyes before. Suddenly he realized that he was desperate for her—desperate to feed off her energy and drink from her overflowing life.

"Aren't they wonderful?" she said, pointing at the animals who had begun to nuzzle one another.

"Never mind the giraffes," he said. "What about me?"

He yanked at her arm and pulled her down onto a heap of straw. She pulled up her skirt, ready for him.

"Now, quickly. If you want me, it must be now, before the jinns come."

Those were the last words that it was possible to make sense of, as she started to moan noisily. She gestured to him to make haste as he struggled out of his robe. Even in the dung-scented air of the giraffe stable, he could smell Roxelana. Her skin, caked as it was with dried sweat and saliva, stank. Also, it seemed that she had used rancid butter to give her helmet of red hair more of a sheen. The insides of her thighs were moist and smelled of cat. Like Anadil, she was clean-shaven between the legs. Driven by the cravings of the viper, he tried to thrust his head down there, but she was impatient.

"Not like that. I want something bigger than your tongue inside me." She wrestled under him and pulled him up and grabbed at his cock. She reminded Orkhan of his brother princes with whom he used to wrestle. Powerfully aroused, he entered her. However, the sensation of mastery hardly lasted more than a moment, for she so fiercely bucked and thrashed under him. Her eyes rolled and her teeth were gritted. Finally, she made such a great heave that he was unable to stay inside her. He withdrew and lay beside her and waited for her frenzy to abate.

"I am accursed!" she wailed. "Forgive me, master, yet it is not my fault." Now she was weeping. "It is the fault of the jinns. Whenever I even think about sex, the jinns enter my body and possess it. It is the jinns who make me do such frightful things."

She buried her head in the straw and continued to weep. Then, as her sobbing subsided, she raised her tear-stained face to Orkhan and said,

"I need to be purified. You can purify me. You can whip the jinns out of me. Please, I need to have the jinns driven out of me. They cannot bear the pain, but I, Roxelana, can bear anything. If you flog me, O Sultan, I promise you that you will then be able to enjoy my body as is your right."

Now she was in a new fever of impatience. She stepped out of her black skirt and with trembling hands set to unlacing her bodice. The bodice fell to the ground, and as she turned away from him, Orkhan saw that her broad shoulders were already covered with a light tracery of scars. Then she turned to him again and presented him with the whip.

"Flog me now," she implored. "I am begging you for it. I need it." And she turned away and bent to present her back for chastisement.

Orkhan struck at her a couple of times, but she was not satisfied.

"Harder. It must be harder. You have to draw my blood, for the jinns are in my blood. You have to let them out."

Her broad bottom seemed made for whipping and he struck at it again and again. Ugly red weals began to break up its milky smoothness. For the first time since his release from the Cage, Orkhan felt himself to be truly a sultan, and as he continued to lash out at Roxelana, he began to fantasize about how he would deal with Anadil and the other ladies of the Harem. He worked a little way up her back before pausing for breath.

Then she said,

"You must be able to do better than this. Harem girls have whipped me harder than you have. Come on, I really want to feel it—your touch of mastery."

Her words had the effect she desired. Orkhan struck out at her in a frenzy. Now she was crying and calling out to him, but his rage was such that it was some time before he could hear that she was begging him to desist. He stopped and she turned to kneel in front of him and kiss the whip.

"Thank you, master. Now you may do with me what you wish," and she lay back once more on the straw. This time it was different. The devils having departed, she docilely lay back and allowed herself to be penetrated. She embraced him tenderly as he moved inside her.

She sighed as he came within her.

"Thank you, master," she said again and kissed him hungrily. "It has always been hard for me, for the jinns that come into my body will not allow me to acknowledge the supremacy of a man. Now at last I am at peace."

And Orkhan observed that her eyes were dulled, sated. Yet, it now occurred to him that, with her back such a bloody mess, she must have been moving on a bed of agony as she gave herself to him.

"Did I hurt you?" he asked foolishly.

"Of course you did—a little, but women are used to pain. They are better capable of bearing it than men," and she smiled patronizingly at him.

"I do not believe that. Everyone knows that men are stronger, tougher and better able to bear pain."

"With respect, O master, perhaps men think they know that, but I do not. Women are born equipped to face far more pain than men, for nature has prepared them in advance to suffer the travails of childbirth. And every month I experience such pain that you cannot imagine. Your whipping was a little nothing by comparison." The brightness was back in her eyes again and she looked at him mischievously. "You could never stand such a whipping as the one I received from your hands."

"You are being absurd, Roxelana. I should certainly be much better able to endure it than you were."

"Then let us try it, shall we?"

Orkhan hesitated. Why, after all, should he submit to being whipped by one of his animal girls?

Seeing him hesitate, she urged him on.

"Come on my lord! It is only a game, like my game with the panther. Such sports make us feel more alive, for though we may walk through life as if we walked in a dream, the flick of the whip can wake us up. Turn and turn about," she insisted. "You will enjoy it. Trust me." And she gave him a brilliant smile.

Tempted by the challenge, seduced by her smile, he agreed. Then she led him to a corner of the stables, and pointed to a pair of manacles which were attached by chains to the wall.

"Put these on," she said.

Once again, he balked. Now she was angry and stamped her foot.

"You have to wear these. Otherwise it is not fair. It will not be a real challenge, if you can cry off at any moment, or turn round and snatch the whip from me and start beating me again. You have to trust me. You have to trust me, as I trusted you. Believe me, you will find that half your delight comes from trusting the lady with the whip. Trust me, it will only be a gentle whipping—like a series of butterfly kisses on your body."

Orkhan offered his wrists to the manacles.

"We sometimes put an unruly monkey in these," she explained, as she snapped them shut.

"Now it's my turn!" she cried and the whip sang in the air.

Orkhan was unable to stop his body wincing as the thong made its first incision in his flesh. She was more skilled with the whip than he had been and the blows fell fast and accurately.

He heard her cry out.

"O my beloved, I swear to you that I am only marking your body because I desire it. My whip is making a map to guide my loving kisses."

Then suddenly the blows increased yet further in ferocity and she seemed to be talking to herself in a foreign language, in which guttural words mingled with groans and hisses. It was not long before Orkhan, half swooning, slumped against the floor. Then she was upon him, pressing herself against his back and licking his blood.

"You are mad," he groaned.

"So I am," she replied. "My jinns have come back and they want your blood. O my beloved master, forgive me, but I cannot hold back from this." And she resumed kissing and licking at his wounds.

At last she raised her face from his body and gave a deep sigh. When she next spoke, her voice was calm and gentle.

"Now the kiss of the whip has taught you a little about the strange delight of suffering. Even so, you still have no idea about the pain of being a woman. In order to really make love to a woman, you will have to learn what it feels like to be one and to be made love to as a woman." She ran a hand over his hair.

"Don't go away, will you?"

And she was gone, leaving Orkhan chained on the floor of the giraffe stable.

When she returned, she nudged him with her foot and used it to turn him as far over as his chains would allow. Looking up at Roxelana, he first noticed that her mouth was rimmed with blood. Then he saw a large, greased, and gleaming red thing attached by an intricate array of straps to the lower part of her belly and he moaned in dread.

"This dildo," she said, pointing to the thing, "consists of a unicorn's horn sheathed in red Cordovan leather. It is only used for the deflowering of virgins."

Then she briefly caressed his mouth with her foot, before kicking and turning him again, so that he was lying face down on the straw. She prodded him again with her foot.

"I want you kneeling."

"When I am free you will pay for this."

But, she struck at him with the butt of the whip and he did as he was told.

"How will I pay for it?" Roxelana demanded sarcastically. "Have me flogged, will you?"

As she spoke, she knelt over his bottom and spat on her hands before using the spittle to moisten the passage of her instrument in advance. Then she mounted him and rammed the dildo in, or rather, she attempted to, but Orkhan was very tight.

So she began to whisper hotly in his ear, begging him to relax and calling him her "handsome darling" and her "plaything." But all the while she continued to thrust with the horn between her legs. It felt like a great fist which, in beating its way upwards, was seeking to cleave Orkhan from bottom to top. It was as if he was being impaled on the shaft of the animal girl. It was as if he was carrying the woman inside him. It was as if he was being possessed by a dark demon who would not be denied entrance.

There was a final shudder as she at last succeeded in driving the horn into him. Pleasure and pain, exquisitely compounded, surged within him, overwhelming his will, so that he suffered orgasm.

Roxelana stroked his head. He could feel her breasts pressing against his back. He was in agony, and yet he longed for nothing more than to be able to turn to embrace his violator.

"Now, my Sultan, a door has been opened for the Holy Rapture," she whispered, and giving the dildo a final twist, she continued, "It is possible that you are now ready to yield to the total extinction which is perfect love."

She might have said more, but at that moment they heard the sound of women's voices outside the stables. Roxelana thereupon swiftly unstrapped herself from the dildo's harness and slipped away. Orkhan briefly fainted.

When he came to, he saw that Perizade was kneeling beside him and drawing gently on the harness of the dildo to extract it.

"Yeeugh, it's all bloody!" she exclaimed, "One of the animal girls has been sporting with you. Anadil is waiting outside, but she must not see you like this. Most of the concubines and their servants have been hunting for you. At first we feared that you might have tried to flee the Harem, but then we thought that you would not and could not leave the Harem, because you are already addicted to what is between our legs. Finally we realized that you must still be in the zoo and that one of the animal girls must have spirited you away for her pleasure."

She rolled Orkhan over carefully. He tried to speak, but could not. He tried to stand, but slumped forward with his head on Perizade's heavy breasts. She laid him back on the straw. Her heavy breasts swung low over his face.

"You see, you cannot escape me. I am your destiny."

"Perizade, please help me," he gasped in his chains.

"I think that I know what will revive you. Your viper must be thirsty, isn't it?" she asked solicitously, and, without waiting for an answer, she drew up her skirt and straddled him, lowering her plump fleshy thighs onto his face. Once more the thirsty viper slithered its way in to slake its thirst in the Tavern of the Perfume-Makers.

Then she rose from his face and cast about to find the key for the manacles and his robe. When Orkhan was dressed and on his feet, she took his hand.

"We will not say exactly what happened—even to Anadil. It would never do for the imperial concubines to hear of this. But you need to be cleaned up. It is time for the hammam."

# Susan Volchok

# How We Did It

We smoked a fat joint and took off all our clothes and sat back on your narrow camp bed, my spine curving against your chest and belly, my legs open, straddling your thighs so that you could touch me down there, deliberate strokes of an unexpectedly tender thumb, until I came, gasping, stunned; and you didn't need me to touch you, you were big and hard up against my back, all I would've had to do was lie down, open to you, and when I said I didn't want to, I was a you-know-what, I'd never—you-know . . . you just laughed, dark, musical laughter, and asked, *What* are *you doing here, girl?* and I smiled, shook my head hopelessly, tears starting in my eyes, and answered, *I don't really know.*

We went down on one another every Saturday night in the pitch darkness of your parents' chilly bedroom, getting ourselves off as many times as we could, smoking our favorite unfiltereds before and afterward, hour upon hour, until the inevitable ringing of the telephone, the conscientious call from your mother warning they were on their way home, none of you should be embarrassed by their stumbling upon whatever depravity your slut of a girlfriend might have drawn you into in the empty flat.

We held one another on the neatly made single bed, kissing a little, murmuring love nonsense, but both beginning to be impatient with the preliminaries, because we'd decided, this was it, and you were already wearing the first rubber I'd ever seen, on a man, I mean, its latexy smell distinguishable (or so I imagined) from the more familiar odors of your monkish cell in the seedy men's residence—roach spray, stale coffee, soap, the loamy soil of succulents massed on the windowsill—and it was surprisingly easy, your moving into me, if you hadn't known me so well you might have thought I was fooling about it being my first time, for this, anyway, last thing left undone (as I thought of it then), yes, it was really that easy, and if I didn't cry out at the moment you did, it was nice, anyway, very very nice, you inside me but lying still now, heavy in my arms while I stroked your hair, filled with a high happiness that was at least half relief, another initiation out of the way and not even a spot of blood on the blanket.

We did it abruptly, after not doing it for so long it didn't seem to matter anymore whether we did it or not, or maybe that was just how we wanted to assure ourselves we both felt, the way it happened, happening as accidents happen, a quick coming together in my dorm room at dusk, a quicker falling away, which—because it was the evening of Valentine's Day and I was thinking of the man back home I'd so casually betrayed—inspired me to try to hurt you too: *Is it always like this with you, over so fast?* I asked, to which you breezily replied, *Depends* . . . then rolled off me altogether, pulled on your shorts (boxers, which I'd never seen anyone my age wear before), lit up one of my Marlboros, blew smoke rings at the ceiling: it was perfect, really, exactly the answer I deserved.

We were talking quietly in your mother's airy, Irish lace boudoir, where you'd let me lie down to rest after the long ride out from my midwestern college, when you suddenly leaned over to kiss my breasts, one and the other, and my belly, then drew down the quilt and knelt between my knees on the wide four-poster, opening me frog-legged, pulling my silly white cotton underpants all the way to my ankles, thrusting your face between my legs to lick and suck and kiss me, and nothing I could do but hold you tight with my thighs and move against your mouth, higher and higher until I came, the dark splintering into patterns of light: and when I opened my eyes, there you were, your cheek resting against my hipbone, watching me with the proudest, pleasedest, most pussy-eatingest smile I've ever seen in my whole life.

We sat, sprawling on the soft bed of earth and pine needles between the air-raid ditch and the tumbledown shack the earliest settlers had left for foreigners, both of us drunk on too much beer, but you sick as a dog besides on shots of slivovitz, puking it all up once, twice, your head hanging into the black hole in the hillside, and in between raging at me to go away, get the hell away, only I wouldn't, I was waiting, wanting you, wondering would it happen tonight, and now you wiped your mouth against the sleeve of your famous blue sweater, crawled over the sloppy ground toward me, wrapped your arms around me, up under my work shirt, and cried, *You're so warm, so warm* . . . because you were cold as death, your hair sodden against your skull, your teeth chattering, your fingers and hands ice on my skin, your body shuddering with some inward chill as we rocked and rocked and rocked, until finally (though it was your first time ever touching me, though I would have stayed there, holding you like that, forever) I stood, pulling you up with me, your arm slung heavy over my neck, and walked you into my room to lay you down across the spare cot, where you slept, muttering, snoring, while I lit a fire, drank black coffee, smoked half a pack, watching you, crying a little, falling asleep myself only after you'd left, at first light, without another word, without a look.

We stood on the black deck of the ferry, the dirty white bandage over your forehead your most visible feature in the darkness, and we kissed until we couldn't stand up straight, then ran to our seats in second class, threw a blanket over the whole business, tried to do something, whatever we could, but the seat arm was in the way and the old man next to us woke up, and I wouldn't let you open my blouse, wouldn't take you in my hand, either, someone watching like that, and you said you could get us a cabin, a bed, and I went upstairs to get the diaphragm from my backpack (always the world's most careful girl, I was), tell the friend I was traveling with what was going on; the next moment, a Greek ship's mate was sneaking us into what they called a semi-private, curtains instead of a door, outside which he stood guard (I guessed you'd paid him off), while, on a bed no bigger or better than a doctor's examining table, you got on top of me and started right in, and I closed my eyes, thinking, So much for the legendary Latin lover, hoping you'd at least come quickly, not even caring when I opened them, saw over your shoulder that the Greek was peering through the parted drapes, stupid leering bastard, because, after all, it was your bare French ass in the air, and besides, he'd probably seen it all, a thousand times.

We woke together once in a strange bed in a strange house in Georgetown, our hosts a gay couple sympathetic to the student strike we'd hitched across three states to join, and, good friends that we were, we lay there awhile that bright early May morning, lazing in the warm sunlight pouring through gauzy white drapes, talking softly, you shaking the bed with your laughter, I still so sleepy I could feel myself drifting back into dreams when, without a word, you moved your big hand beneath the sheets, fitted it between my thighs, tight against those soft folds, two fingers strumming, and whispered *Hush* when I said *Don't,* cooed *Doesn't matter,* when I tried to explain I didn't want to do you too, which even now I can't explain to myself, because god, you were good, the best of morning lovers, besides being that good a friend, my best friend: in a perfect world, desire would have come of love that deep and true, and it should have, it's what I wanted with all my heart; but wishing couldn't make it so, for us, couldn't make it happen, not then, not ever.

Another time, we stayed overnight in the gloomy off-campus

room in which I had little by little begun to lose touch, with friends, with family, with reality (whatever that was), in which I lay sleepless and scared of I didn't know what most of every night; but this night, I fell instantly and soundly into sleep, imagining it was safe to let go so long as you were sitting in the armchair by my bed, rocking and rocking the way you did when you were most afraid yourself, like whistling in the dark, awake and watching over me.

We were so comfortable together, it was hard to believe this was only our first time (officially, since we'd done everything but for a whole year, two years before, as if rehearsing for this) and still . . . I sensed something was off (hadn't someone I never made love to once told me that the moment just after is a moment of truth?) and suddenly, I knew, I knew what it was, held you closer, kissed your forehead, whispered, *I'm your first, aren't I?* feeling strangely moved, your saving it for me, but . . . and you gave a glum, *Yes,* then stopped my next question with a long kiss before sighing, *Don't ask.*

We fell into another mood, spoiled, almost surfeited: what about some scenario using that weird leather recliner from your parents' old house? and you tipped yourself back in the chair (fully dressed down to your black engineer boots), watched me (stripped to black panties) bend over you, unbutton your 401's to take it out, then kneel on the cushion between your legs to suck your cock until you reached for, squeezed both my nipples, so hard I squealed and dropped you as you came, silently, smiling a thin-lipped, foxy sort of smile at me, who smiled too, pleased by my success, ready to put my clothes back on, try the chair myself, give you a chance to serve, which is how I happened to make the mistake of crowing *My turn!* maybe a little too fast, or maybe it didn't matter, maybe you would've said what you said no matter what, because you were mighty righteous with your *No way will I eat a woman sitting like some empress on her throne.*

We went Parking, a sort of joke, because I'd mentioned (that very session of our sexuality seminar) that I never had, not even as a

suburban teenager whose boyfriends drove her everywhere, and after we passed from Petting to Heavy Petting to having to find a
place (your tiny import lacking the traditional big old backseat), I
took you home with me, worked on you with my good right hand
until you were ready again, at least for those few minutes it took
you to fling yourself on me, stick it in, finish . . . after which you
announced you had to split, which was okay by me because, all
things considered, this was the nearest thing to a backseat boff two
people could do in bed, a useful addition to my continuing re-
searches, my life list.

We didn't, until the night before I was leaving town for a while,
just in case I wasn't going to want to get too involved or want to
see you when I got back, only the delay, the pressure now, proved
almost too much for you—discouraging, deflating—and even
emergency head for a half hour barely got you hard enough; but it
was worth the effort, seeing what I'd heard was true, so astonish-
ingly endowed (as they say) were you, like a larger-than-life sculp-
ture of some pagan god, beautiful and terrible: given the choice, I
thought I'd just as soon worship it this way, to which you seemed
to say amen, seemed as surprised as I was myself when I suddenly
stopped, this close to your climax, and somehow managed (sitting
in your lap with my legs around your impossibly narrow waist) to
fit myself onto that impressive shaft, rocking us to our first and final finish, if nothing else at least satisfying my curiosity.

We slipped into a spare bedroom of the co-op on lower Fifth your
father was letting you and two other recent grads share, locked the
door behind us against that night's crowd of drinkers and dancers,
turned the light on just to locate the bed, rolled around on it for a
while, did the deed, after which we exchanged names, swore we
never did this kind of thing, ruefully wondered if we'd respect one
another in the morning . . . by which time I was home, happy to see
the end of such a long dry spell, but even happier to be sleeping
alone, and hopeful I wouldn't have much trouble handling being re-
jected by a guy I didn't ever want to see again.

We were standing on the edge of a subway platform, can't recall which line or where we were going or anything but the way I couldn't keep my hands off you, even there in the grim underground, touching your face, your ass, your everything within reach, endlessly longing to feel the surge of that live current the least contact with your body created, as if you were somehow directly wired to the mythic third rail and I, stroking your smooth, resistless skin, connected to the power that made all of this go.

We woke up in my tiny bed early the morning after the night I let you crash at my place, and you turned to me and said (so earnest it was almost touching), *Y'know, if you had told me last night you still wanted to, I would have: maybe we should have done it, after all;* and I just lay there with my eyes shut, put on a big smile, and said, *Don't be ridiculous, I'm over that: it would've been one of the stupidest mistakes I ever made.*

We were lying awake—you in your flannel-lined Boy Scout sleeping bag unrolled on the hardwood floor next to me on my studio bed—and in the silence I imagined I could hear your wheels turning, wondering if and when you ought to suggest we pull out the high-rise for you, figuring one thing would lead to another . . . though we were not even that close since I'd left school under a cloud, settled back in the city, finished up the degree here, got a job, et cetera, in other words, moved into a whole new life, which was not necessarily a disadvantage, casual was all right, the prevailing current, a whole series of lovers had sailed through here on it already, you were only temporarily moored yourself; meanwhile, though, I began thinking about you eating my food all week without once going shopping, you leaving your man's messes in the kitchen and bathroom, you talking endlessly about your old girlfriends, obsessing over your same old problems, oh yes, I was working myself up all right, one fine little rage, thinking and fuming until the faintest glimmer of our getting it on was extinguished before you were even sure it existed: damned if I'd give you the satisfaction of knowing you'd had a better than decent chance.

We climbed into the fresh sheets I'd put on the convertible sofa bed in the ritzy East Side pied-à-terre I was borrowing while I tried to find a new apartment for myself: the owner was unexpectedly back for a night, had brought his new girlfriend, and you (maybe remembering all those early gay campus dances, other ambiguous occasions on which I passed as your date before you came out to everyone) had fondly offered to spend the night in bed with me, in the room next to theirs, making the appropriate noises even if we couldn't make love . . . even if (as I didn't tell you, lying next to you all night long, our bodies never once touching) there was no way you could possibly fool anyone, except maybe me, because after all, I still wanted you enough for that.

We sat facing one another on your unmade double mattress, slung on the cold linoleum floor of the sad basement room you took to save money before the acting jobs came, and something about the scene, your shy half-smile, the solemn concentration with which you unbuttoned all the pearly buttons of my blouse, touched me, took me back to another life, a younger-self-in-love, turned me strangely self-conscious, slightly shy too, a bit solemn, and I actually blushed hearing myself softly say, *You make me feel like I've never been with anyone before*—which (I couldn't say *this* even to myself, then) was sweeter than whatever would happen between us, a gift for which I wouldn't be properly grateful until you were long gone.

We would start on the crowded floor of the old Corso or one of the newer clubs farther uptown, improvising our own mating dance, moving closer and closer together, and when we got hot and high and happy enough, I'd edge off the dance floor, go into the dingy bathroom to fix my face: I loved the mascara going all raccoony around my eyes, mimicking the kohl the Latin girls wore, and I'd reapply the red, red lipstick I'd started wearing, spray on some extra Arpege, then come back out to you, let you nuzzle my neck, whisper *I adore you* in Spanish (which I didn't and don't speak), seize my hand, kiss it (my god, with such passion, though you were laughing your wonderful toothy laugh), and pull me down the steep staircase to the street along which we ran, me stumbling after you in my highest heels, to my little building on East Ninetieth Street, then up those stairs to my little apartment, where I bolted the door, set the chain, and tore off our dancing clothes, excited beyond words to be alone and naked with you at last, maybe just because you were as much a stranger to me as anyone the locks were meant to keep out.

We got together in between what I called my real love affairs, as if the outrageous fun we had took us out of the running, made us slightly unreal, though there was never anyone else with whom I ever spent so many hours doing it so well and truly, whole days and nights, no one whose enjoyment of me had been or would be so self-evident, yes, you were frankly, fearlessly, a fan of the actual female body, an authentic aficionado, fascinated by the particularity of this particular cunt, endlessly extolling all the beauties of my most unbeautiful feature, amazing and arousing me with descriptions of such intensity and tender regard—all the colors you wished I could see for myself! the changing shapes, the aromas!—ah, you could almost talk me over the top, though you wouldn't have wanted to forgo the singular pleasure of using your tongue to literally finish me off, nor would I have, your big loose-jointed body looming over me, becoming (I could scarcely believe it) beautiful to me too, as I was learning to tell you, though talking in bed, even crying out at my coming, was new to me then; yet always, afterward, still talking, postmortems on our performance—*the best, the best ever!*—we made sure we knew what it was we were talking about and what we were making: nothing less than great sex, and no more, no strings, nothing Serious: we were way too cool for that, fast-talking ourselves out of love, fools for the perfect friendship fuck.

We were messing around, maybe going to make it, maybe not, a little awkward, really, your being the ex-lover, still-good-friend of a good friend in another city—it was all teasing kisses and tentative touches until you made the deciding move, pushing my skirt up, pulling the crotch of my panties aside, plunging your tongue in, past giddy resistance or guilt, until I was panting *Please, please, please* and you rose to press your mouth tasting of me against my mouth, and pushed yourself all the way into me past the silky twist of fabric still caught between my legs, between us, an exquisite equilibrium of force and delicacy, such a powerful image of spontaneous pleasuring that even now, sometimes, I flash on that time-stopped instant, swollen with uncertainty, expectancy, that delicious moment before you stripped away the last vestige of modesty, leaving me exposed, offered up, open to anything.

We waited three whole weeks—which in the run of things isn't so long, anymore, but it was for me, then, felt like forever, twenty-odd days of groping in the darkness of two different foreign film festivals, in the library stacks, on my narrow couch because (I said) it would be better, hotter, if we held back as long as we could stand to, because (I didn't say) I was so scared of being burnt again by that heat: and you let me put you off, play a little harder to have than usual, until the day I knew I was falling for you, the night I finally didn't send you home with your hard-on, but (owning my desire, banked, all but unbearable) lay back on my bed, opened my arms, my legs, even knowing (as I suppose I did) that what would happen next—your moving inside me four or five times, then collapsing, wordlessly finishing—would be something of an anticlimax after weeks of waiting; lying belly to belly, I wasn't so very let down, even let go the chagrin of being left undone, because I was still young and dumb enough to think we had all the time in the world to get it right, and that we would.

We stopped on the sidewalk outside my apartment house, beneath my own second-story window, so that if I had been looking out at that moment, midnight, I might have watched us stop, fiercely embrace, begin to kiss not at all tentatively (watching, I would not have thought it the first time), for such a long while that you were hard enough to make me feel you through all our dinner party clothes, stiffened and insistent, forcing my legs apart, rocking tight up against me, so that I could almost imagine a literally

zipless one, and I pulled back slightly from the kissing, my breasts
still crushed against your chest, started talking, why it would be a
bad idea, going upstairs, going to bed, talking desperately, knowing how easy it would be to just go and do it, knowing how much
I wanted to forget your wife, your nice university life, your well-
known womanizing, yes why not just go, with my loneliness, my
lust, upstairs to my cozy room, all the inconvenient realities forgotten, until morning at least.

   We both knew why I'd called that late Friday night in late September, asked you to come downtown the minute I got home from
a godawful holiday dinner *en famille* to which I'd gone alone (things
being still too tentative between us, far too soon for such an ad-
vanced intimacy as family introductions), yet we sat, stiffly, a little
apart, on the couch for a good while, talking about the usual
things, not even holding hands, as I recall, wondering whether to
watch some TV (you couldn't at home, didn't dare *own* one if you
hoped to finish the Ph.D. in this lifetime), then actually switched it
on, channel surfing to cut the tension, divert attention from the ev-
idently imminent event, which would explain how we could so easily, as if without noticing, have made the transition to legs up off
the floor, me sitting between your knees, lying back against you,
both of us, then, turned toward the TV table in the corner of the
room to watch whatever it was between ten and eleven, Friday
Night at the Movies, maybe? and James Bond rings a bell, albeit
faintly, or am I only free-associating on the cool, the suavity with
which you kissed my neck from behind, while sliding one hand up
under my T-shirt and one down over my belly into my jeans,
smooth, surpassing smooth, timing and touch both, no one would
ever be readier than I was, which is why I had to laugh (having
turned to kiss you, to tell you what I didn't have to tell you) when
you suddenly reached around and under me, began to pull the
cushions away (to get to the magic foldaway mattress), and asked
(without pausing even for an instant, grabbing, flinging those upholstered obstacles) *Am I moving too fast for you?*—this slapshticky

moment (me still laughing, *No, it's fine, fine*) so undercut any sense
of the occasion that I wouldn't have said, that night, it would mean
anything at all; couldn't know you meant to stay.

We talked sex right away—what we'd done with other people:
you into numbers (five hundred guys, you claimed, including the
lover you lived with so long, so unhappily), me ticking off my
modest list of names, you into basics (how two of you could do it
face to face, how once a top, always a top), me offering more sub-
dued, romantic narratives—talked sex for years, without once ever
saying out loud what it was we wanted with one another, so that,
by the summer we went off alone, a week at your mother's empty
country house, working on a project you'd concocted for us, we
probably knew everything we needed to know on the subject except how to find a place for us to be between your bedroom at one
end of the big house and mine at the other, a place (the dark oak
floor, a chaise longue in the sunroom) where we could finally lie
down, silent, stripped of all our cool, counterfeited intimacy, of
everything false between us, and fuck ourselves into something like
the lovers we really were, instead of lying, each of us, night after
night after night, awake and alone in our own darkness, tortured by
the humid heat, the hideous cricket chorus—god how I wished you
would come to me or that I could go to you, wished something
would happen to stop us having to make love to ourselves in our
separate beds, knowing all along that it would take a miracle now,
and that no such miracle would happen there.

We were dancing with other people after dinner, our desserts
untouched on the table where we'd sat across from one another, eating very little though drinking quantities of wine, talking with determined animation to those same other people, or some others, the
point being our apparent unawareness of one another, we wanted
that established, didn't we (yet I saw your eyes darken when I
laughed at someone else's clever remark, and I was laughing a lot
that night, the wine, sheer nerves); I wonder if, even now, you
would acknowledge you were watching me too, admit you felt

what I felt when you finally stood in front of my chair, asking in your careless, bantering way for a dance, and I took the hand you held out in that ironical gesture of gallantry: a jolt of electricity from fingertips to heart, a shock of recognition that left me breathless, speechless, moving into your arms and across the floor, moving with you without willing my steps, without awareness of anything but the force field we made touching, simply touching skin to skin, our coming together so stunning, galvanizing, that I never slept all that night but wandered the hotel grounds like a somnambulist, wondering what I would do if I actually found you again before dawn.

We didn't quite decide to do it, didn't discuss it right beforehand: no, it's funny, and still affecting, to recall that finally, we went and did it without the endless analysis, critique of ambivalence, plain argument which I, anyway, bring to Issues: after nine years of never once neglecting to consider consequences, Use Something, we made love this late-summer night using nothing but our own bodies, easily familiar and utterly strange, our inward-most membranes meeting for the first time, the distinct sensation of going deeper and deeper, infinitely further, touching bottom, or the edge of the sky, I couldn't tell which, the flashes of light behind my eyes blinding, bursting into awesome fireworks toward the end, so that even after you lay still, finished, I was watching the colored flares rise and fall against the blue blackness, and though I didn't think of signs, then, I was aware we'd done more than make a certain choice (*I guess this means we're trying,* I murmured afterward; *Hmmm, I guess so,* you answered), we'd made something different happen, and not just the earth move either (though it had) but the whole cosmos shift slightly, almost imperceptibly: I tell you I already knew that—not thinking, not talking it over, not even really trying—we'd gone and *done* it.

We began with an awkward, unpremeditated kiss one afternoon that left us giddy, guilty as kids on the sneak, and like them wanting more, more, no stopping, whole afternoons spent kissing, endlessly kissing (rediscovering the kiss as a complex, if not quite complete, act in its own right): not ready to go to bed (though you dutifully suggested it once, as if it were expected of you), unwilling to accept the risks of an actual affair, we went on kissing as if that didn't count, went so far as we dared—your mouth on my bared breast, my hand slipped beneath your belt to briefly cradle you in my palm—and though we couldn't go backward, to friendship, we couldn't fast-forward to something else either, were stuck, so to speak, kissing, timidly touching, tangling more and more inventively with less and less satisfaction . . . not the unhappiest fate in the world, hopeless passion has its place, yet it was making you the crazier of us two, making you cry, *Ach, what's the use? Where can it go now? What's the bloody point?*

Poor boy, I didn't have the words, didn't know myself, then, that I was waiting, wanting, holding out for a kiss too impossible to believe in anymore, an embrace that would somehow shake me awake, quicken me again, to this story of love and longing that goes on and on and on (is its only point)—the real thing, not moist and rosy reminiscence; the unmistakably actual thing worth risking all for.

And see how we did, just starting out, starting over: our first kiss twenty-five years later (too late, some would say, did say) defying signed-and-sealedness, delivering us from certain solitude, leading me straight out of the known world across the wide sea to the small, sun-filled room at the top of the stairs, where we took off our clothes as unceremoniously as if we'd been living together forever, as awed as if we'd never seen, never made love to another human being (all of this just true, the way it was), full summer light streaming over what we'd dreamed in darkness, your patient, knowing fingers tracing an invisible geography across my arching body, breasts, belly, thighs—where I'd been, where you want me to go with you—your tenderness inspiring, opening me, fullblooming flower, all the way open for the first time in my life, no shame, nothing hidden or forbidden, my hungry eyes, hands, lips, tongue, free to want, to wander everywhere over you too—skin impossibly soft, sex uncut, unutterably lovely—until we fell into one another's arms (whispering *come inside me now,* I was somehow inside you too), and did it and did it and did it and did it and did it . . . that being our first day and night and day together, only the beginning of telling ourselves the endless story of how we did it.

And how we do:

*That's right,* you breathed, opening my blouse to caress one breast before kissing the other. *That's right,* you murmured, tongue darkening teat, aureole prickling in sudden arousal whispered *that's right,* unbuttoning your own shirt, silky mancurls against pale womanflesh; nipple to nipple moaned *that's right,* big, soft palms boldly sliding southward, gripping me, hard, harder . . . *That's right* . . . sweet love slaps blushing rosy backside, your hands fastening onto my small, squeezable haunches . . .

*That's right,* I smiled to myself, *That's right, baby, that's right, that's right: that's—just—exactly—right.*

Myriam Gurba

# HOMBRECITO

I didn't know what sex was until the year I turned eighteen. That was the year I bought my first car and got fitted for my first suit. It was also the year I met Magdalena Cruz, *La Nena Mala de Boyle Heights* (The Bad Girl of Boyle Heights). Before her, I didn't know anything. After her, I felt like I knew everything. I know now that wasn't true, but it was La Nena who turned me out and to this day, the smell of gardenias still takes me back to the Twin Terrace Hotel, Room B-12, where La Nena took my virginity and made me into a stone butch.

I grew up in East Los Angeles. My parents moved there during the war so that my dad could find a job at one of the new defense plants. He said he was gonna build airplanes and we were gonna live in a house with a view of the ocean. Instead, the war ended and all the jobs went too. We never saw the ocean. My dad couldn't take it. He skipped town. My mom went crazy.

By the time I was sixteen, I'd already spent six months in reform school. By the time I was seventeen, they'd already kicked me out. They were tired of me picking fights, and I got caught smoking dope in the bathroom. The nuns that ran the place called me *machetona,* manly girl, because I wore pants and held my cigarette like a boy. When they'd had the last straw, the head matron called me into her office and told me to pack my bags—I was going home. The day after I left, I found a letter in our mailbox addressed to my mom. It said that I had a "brain injury" that made me "violent." There was no cure for me. I had been permanently discharged from the reformatory.

After that, I became another Mexican kid with nothing to do but hang out on the streets. I couldn't get a square job and I couldn't hang out with the other kids in the neighborhood. Their moms told them to stay away from the *machetona.* My mom sat at home all day and talked to the wall for hours. The neighbors felt sorry for us and took care of my two little sisters.

The only place left for me to go was the bar down the street, *Las Tres Hermanas* (The Three Sisters). It opened at six in the morning and I could stay as long as I wanted. At first, the owner, Pepito, didn't want me hanging out in there. He was scared the cops would bust him for serving a minor. But I showed him that he could trust me, and the bar regulars liked me. One of them would usually buy me a beer and we would sit and eat peanuts and listen to the jukebox.

One day, a man wearing a bright red suit with a swinging gold pocket chain came into *Las Tres Hermanas.* His hair was slicked with grease and he carried a shiny walking stick. He sat at the best table in the bar and Pepito came running out with a rag in his hand and polished his table.

*"Qué quiere para tomar, Don Juárez?"* ("What would you like to drink, Mr. Juarez?")

*"Rompope, Pepito, Rompope."**

I had never seen Pepito move so fast. He brought Don Juarez his drink and then bowed. Don Juarez pressed a bill into Pepito's hand.

*Rompope: A Mexican liqueur prepared by nuns that consists of vanilla, egg, milk, cinnamon, spices, and brandy that is cooked until creamy.

*"Gracias, Don Juárez, gracias."*

Don Juarez scanned the bar and noticed me staring at him. He broke into a grin.

"Hey, *machetona*, aren't you a little bit young to be in here?"

"No. I'm gonna be twenty-one next month," I lied.

He smiled. "Oh, sure, sure," he said. He sized me up. "Come over here and sit with me."

I followed his orders. I went and sat with him.

"So what do you do, *machetona*? You got a job?"

"No. I—I mean, I just quit one."

He smiled again. "Is that right? I'd think a *machetona* like you would want a job. You look like a hard worker. Think about what you could do with the money. You could get a nice suit, like mine. Or make some pocket change and take the *nenas* to the show."

I thought about what it would be like to have money in my pocket. I thought about what it would be like to wear a bright red suit. And I thought about my hungry sisters and my crazy mom. I decided to sit and listen to Don Juarez.

"Are you fast, *machetona*? Can you keep secrets?"

I nodded my head to both questions.

"Well then, I have some work for you."

Soon after this meeting, I began working for Don Juarez. First, he mostly had me running errands and making deliveries. I picked up packages from a boardinghouse on Belvedere and delivered them all over the city. It didn't take me long to figure out what was inside and I started skimming some of the grass for myself. After I'd been with Don Juarez for three months, I had enough to buy a '39 Olds and started taking longer trips for him. Once I had a ride, he had me making trips as far as San Diego and Tijuana. Don Juarez taught me how to watch out for myself so I never got busted by the cops.

I got so quick at making the deliveries that I had time to think up other schemes. I started fencing after I pulled my first scam on Chato. Chato worked for Max Factor packaging makeup. He was a

kleptomaniac and he would boost all kinds of stuff. He had bags of
white pancake, lipstick, and rouge stacked to the ceiling of his
apartment. I went to the drugstore to find out how much people
actually paid for the stuff. Then I bought two bottles of Thunder-
bird wine and showed up at Chato's doorstep after he got home
from work. He let me in and drank the two bottles so fast that I
was afraid my plan wouldn't work. But pretty soon, he was crying
about his dead wife, Flaura, and how much he missed her. Drool
came out of his mouth while he sobbed about Flaura being in the
company of angels.

"Chato, do you want another drink? I think you'll feel better if
you have one."

"*Ay, machetona,* please. Would you hand me another?"

Of course, there was nothing left. "Chato, I don't have any
more. You drank it all."

"No . . ." He started to cry again.

"Here, I'll tell you what. If you sell me all this stuff," I pointed
to the bags of Max Factor, "I'll give you ten bucks."

"You mean it, *machetona?*"

"Sure."

"Okay, but first you gotta bring me another bottle of wine.
Then you got a deal."

I got Chato his third bottle, gave him ten dollars, and carried
all of the bags out to my car. I made over ten times what I paid for
it and started selling all kinds of stuff from the trunk of my car.
People came to me for the things you couldn't buy off the shelves.

That summer was busy. Between working for myself and Don
Juarez, I hardly ever went to Las Tres Hermanas anymore. Finally, one
hot July night, I went back. That was the night I met La Nena. I had
seen her before. From first sight, I knew she was like me. She hung
out on the streets at all hours. She never showed that she was scared
even though she must have been. She knew that she was different.
And when she saw me that night, she knew I was different too.

Nena was the kind of girl you could see coming a mile away. She had red hair that piled into a fancy hairdo and always wore a bright red flower tucked behind her ear. She was tall and wore Cuban heeled stockings with tight dresses. They were so tight that you could tell all she had on underneath was the belt that held up her stockings. Her mouth always seemed to be smiling, even when her eyes looked sad. I had noticed her many times but that was the first time I had ever seen her at the bar.

She sat on a torn leather stool, nursing a drink. The men whispered and pointed at her. She looked like she was waiting for someone. She looked up and caught my stare. She smiled.

"Hey, what's your name, *hombrecito* [little man]?"

"Sandi," I told her.

"Sandi, come here."

I got out of my seat and walked up to her. She smelled like flowers. Later, I would discover that was the scent of gardenias. She slid a few coins across the counter to me. "Go pick me out a song on the jukebox, Sandi."

"What do you want to hear?"

"I don't care. You pick."

I walked to the jukebox and dropped in a couple of coins. I chose some tunes by the Tommy Dorsey Orchestra and turned around to see if La Nena approved. I couldn't tell because a man had approached her. They were talking. She looked bored. He looked like a sick Walt Disney. She let her legs dangle over the sides of the stool, sliding them open as she listened. Disney looked like he was getting frustrated. He started arguing with her in whispers. She just stared back at him with the same bored face.

Finally she said, "Fine."

She turned to me. "Sandi, you got a car?"

I didn't understand what was going on. "*Sí.*"

"Get your keys. We're leaving."

"What about the song."

"Do you want to stay here instead?"

"No."

"Then let's go."

She walked out of the bar with skinny Walt following her. I got my keys and went too. I unlocked the back door and the two of them climbed into the backseat together. I got behind the wheel and started to drive. I had no idea where I was going. I just had a feeling that this was what I was supposed to do. Nena didn't say anything so I just kept driving.

I don't know how long it was before I began to hear slow moans. The moans gradually turned to whimpers and before long, I heard a zipper coming undone. There were rustling noises and when I looked in the rearview mirror, I saw Nena's hand jerking with a rhythmic motion, her pale arm between Walt's legs. I knew his pants were open but I couldn't see anything else.

I drove for a while longer as the streets emptied. Walt kept groaning until he let out a low animal moan. I looked in the rearview mirror again and couldn't see Nena. Walt's mouth was hanging open and his eyes were rolling back in his head. I could hear licking, breathing, a swallow, and the sound of an open belt buckle being jostled around. My imagination went crazy with all these sounds and I tried to focus on my driving while images of me in the backseat, burrowing between Nena's legs while the trick looked on, flooded my head.

I saw a shock of red hair and Nena's head bobbed up. Her cheeks were rosy and her lips were wet. Several wisps of hair had gotten free and her flower was crooked. She wiped the spit and wet from her lips and spoke to me.

"Sandi, do you know where Twin Terrace is?"

"Yeah."

"Drive us there."

I drove there in silence. I heard Nena whisper, "*Quieres más, papi?* [Do you want more, Daddy?] That was only a taste. Wait until you get my pussy." The little man whimpered in the backseat. He sounded like a small hungry dog. When we got there, I parked behind the main building. We all got out and followed Nena up the pink staircase to the second floor. Walt followed her so closely he almost had his nose up her round ass. We got to the second floor and waited in front of Room B-12 while Nena fumbled for her keys. The building was dirty white with yellow pineapples stenciled around the doorway.

She opened the door and we went in. It was a small efficiency unit separated into halves by a moth-eaten Chinese scrim. I sat down at a cracked Formica table. I listened.

Nena and Walt formed two shadows behind the scrim. I could see his hand reach out and grab her tit. She stopped him.

"I want my money."

"Relax, Nena. I'll give it to you as soon as we're done."

"No. That's my rule. You pay me first or you get out."

"Okay, don't be so pushy."

I could hear him reach for his wallet and he must have placed a few bills on her nightstand.

"Thirty dollars! What kind of pussy do you think I have, *pinche pendejo* [stupid idiot]? There may be girls out there who'll fuck for cheaper but I'm not stupid, I know what I'm worth. And you already got a blowjob. You think that was free?" Walt didn't want to lose his chance to fuck the best whore in Boyle Heights. I could hear him peeling more bills out of his wallet and they must have been enough because the two shadows stopped arguing and began undressing.

They climbed into her squeaky bed and Walt got on top.

I could hear everything crystal clear.

"*Ay papi,* fuck me. Fuck me hard. With everything you got." I could see her shadow reach up and grab his tiny nipples and tweak them as he rode her. I could see the silhouette of his dick pulling in and out of her. I felt my face turn hot and I started to sweat. Between my legs started to feel liquidy and I loosened my collar.

"Come on, *papi,* anything you wanna give me, I can take." I could hear him huffing and puffing and after about three minutes, he inhaled deeply and his shadow quaked.

"Aaaaaaaaaah."

"*Ay papi,* that was so good. You know how to fuck me, huh? Your *nenita* [little girl]. You know what's good for my pussy, don't you?" Walt didn't respond. He climbed off of her and his shadow gathered up his clothes in a hurry. He got dressed and in a couple of seconds was gone.

I sat at the table, waiting.

"Sandi, come here."

I got up and walked behind the scrim. Nena was on the bed. Her hair was down and she was wearing nothing but her high heels, garter belt, and stockings. I looked at her and part of me began to throb. I felt a quivering between my legs and a warmth spreading.

"You ever seen anything like this?" She smiled.

I was too embarrassed to say no.

"Come here," she said. And then, I knew what was going to happen.

I sat down next to her and she started to kiss me. Her lips were gentle but her tongue was hot. It darted around my mouth and licked the insides of my cheeks. She pulled my tongue into her mouth and sucked on it. Her mouth tasted like liquor, cigarettes, and her trick's cum. The warmth between my legs was slowly turning into a throbbing and I wondered if Nena could sense it.

She took my hand and put it on her breast. I took her nipple between my fingers and it turned almost rock-hard under my touch. I turned and pinched it like I had seen her do with her trick. It was her turn to moan. I wanted to put my mouth on her. My tongue slid down her neck and found her nipples. I took turns biting and tearing at each one until it seemed any more would make them bleed. They felt hot and Nena lay back on the bed and pulled me onto her. She led my hands between her legs to her pussy. I stroked her hair and then opened the lips. I slipped a finger in and almost came from the warmth and wetness alone. She was so wet that I slid more and more fingers in with such ease that I was soon inside her up to my fist. Her cunt clenched around my fist and she began to buck. I was scared and excited and started pumping with her.

I fucked her with my hand and fist until the muscles in my arm were raw. When I finally pulled out of her, my arm was coated with wet juices. I was gasping for breath and a tension was building in my body. She looked me in the eye and pulled me on top of her again, only this time forcing my legs apart. She pulled my shirt off and began bucking as she gripped my waist. I felt my clit harden into a tight bud and felt blood rushing into my pussy. It was about to explode. Finally, my body twitched and waves of pleasure splashed through my body—I came all over my pants. Nena and I passed out on her bed after fucking for hours and slept well into the next day.

When I did wake up, Nena was getting ready to leave.

"Good morning, *hombrecito*. Will I see you at the bar tonight?"

"Sure."

"Before I leave, I wanted to give you this." She handed me forty dollars.

"What's this for?" I didn't understand why she was giving me money.

"For last night."

"For what we did?" I asked.

She smiled at me. "No. Because what you did last night is something that a lot of men would like to do but is something I have chosen you for. You work for Don Juarez, right? He runs girls, Sandi. He helps us sell ourselves. Ask him about it. Ask him about how it's supposed to be done. He can teach you things. I've worked by myself for a long time now, but I think it's time that changed. I need someone to take care of me. I need protection. In return, you make part of my money. Will you meet me at the bar tonight?"

"Yes."

She became my first Nena.

To this day, when I smell gardenias, I still think of Room B-12 at the Twin Terrace Hotel.

Vaginal Davis

# THE EVERLASTING SECRET FIRST FAMILY OF FUCK: AN EXPOSÉ

Warning to mothers everywhere! Lock up your stinky-feet skateboard-sexy sons! The First Family of Fuck is hootchie for them, and they're a greedy gaggle of fat-titty bitches, whose oozing fuck mounds stir-fry trouble.

The First Family of Fuck, also known as The Everlasting Secret Family of Fuck, is a loose-knit ring of sex-crazed strumpets who terrorize young, dumb, and full-of-pimply-cum skatefucks with their ever-hungry double-barrel hatchet pussies.

Their New York City–born leader is Patty Childers—she insists on using her real name. She wants the world to know that her cooze is so drippy and fidgety that she needs it filled at all times, and is hoping this article will bring her more fucktees.

Patty is also known in the filthy underground sex world she inhabits as "Clamps." That's right, this selfish libertine can leap through the air with a single bound and clamp her raw-action pussy (like that in-utero monster in *Aliens*) on any unsuspecting face. She's proud that her cunty juices are acidic, burning sex scars on those she claims as helpless victims of her grifty lust.

Patty may look 22, with her touched-by-an-angel face, petite frame, voluptuous curves, and Jane Wiedlin of the Go-Go's voice, but this blond scrampa actually is a ripe and seasoned 37.

Is she a sexual predator? Eh, maybe. She's definitely a major cock trap.

Patty doesn't spend any fool time analyzing her desires. She has been into skater-thrash dudes since the skateboard was invented, not exclusively, mind you, skaters just happen to be her fav flavor treat, she says it's like mixing pesto sauce with splooge.

"What can I say?" she cackles, "I'm cuckoo for caucasian cock. White skater cock is hot! So I'm not being politically correct, I'm still an equal opportunity hose monster."

Patty started The First Family in Manhattan with a core group of her best girlfriends, who she also bumps bush with from time to time.

She and her friends all dig crunching on younger men. When they started comparing notes and exchanging e-mugs they found out that they shared the same obsession for skaters. Patty readily admits she was the first to tumble down the ramp.

"The Family isn't a cult, we're not that mysterious. Everything we do is out in the open. I'm the worse offender, I can really be shameless when it comes to sex with these schmucks. They taste good. I'll even pay for it."

Which is exactly what she did recently with one kid who was skating with his friends in Tompkins Square Park in New York's bohemian enclave of the East Village.

"I spent a half an hour sizing him up." Patty continues, "I could tell even though he was wearing baggy pants that he had a hefty floppy between his legs. Big-dick arrogance is a total turn-on. I marched up to the fledgling, and in front of his skate pack told him I'd give him 20 bucks if he dropped the board and came home with me right now. Back at my apartment he was really excited and couldn't believe his luck. He was trying hard to act cool. It sort of makes you want to giggle out loud, because at his age, they're not good at hiding how they feel. It's a big deal for a kid to have an older woman give him attention like that."

Patty wound up giving him more than attention, bathing him and drenching Kiehl products on his adolescent acne. She wrapped a supersize prophylactic on his peterfication and let him plug away.

"These young bucks are all rigor mortisy even when they're unconscious!" Patty screamed.

Her motto: If you're going to have something in you, it might as well be hard. That's never a worry with her skaters.

"They have switchblades for dicks," Patty whispered breathlessly.

After she properly drained her latest conquest of all possible emissions, she fixed him a sandwich, and sent him on his merry way.

Minka, 35, is a critical care nurse living in the San Gabriel Valley with a gigantic pet hedgehog that bites.

She has pre-Raphaelite skin, natural red hair, is buxom, and still gets carded at bars. She and Patty went to college together in their native Toronto, Canada. Minka was married for nine years and lived with another guy for six. She has always been a relationship person, never into casual sex. One day she e-mailed Patty seeking this cute box boy at Trader Joe's doing board tricks in the parking lot on his break. Patty told her she'd kick her ass if she didn't give him her number and make him fucking skateboard all the way to her house in La Crescenta. Now Minka is juggling several skateboarder lovers.

"When my last long relationship ended I just wanted to have some fun. My job at the hospital is very stressful. I'm like one of those nurses you see on *ER* that yell, "Clear!" and put 200 joules through somebody. I deal in high-trauma situations, I work with cardiac arrests and people on life support," she said.

Minka is the kind of Nurse Betty that takes care of you during and after an emergency. When she first started seeing Damian (the skater bad boy that also got her preggers), he introduced her to the rave party scene. She'd get into these intense party situations with Damian and his crew.

"I'd have a boy beauty on each tit nursing, and another one doing the puppy chow down under my dress," Minka recalled.

Suddenly someone overdoes the partying and Minka winds up giving him mouth-to-mouth when he ODs. It happened to her a week ago for the second time. One boy stopped breathing on her twice while she was sucking his dick on a crowded rave dance floor. She would have killed him if he had died without first giving her a pud facial. "Damian was laughing saying that the party promoters should be paying me for keeping their customers alive."

Don't tell Minka she's practicing community medicine. She's not having it. "Not to sound selfish or anything," she said, "but when I go out I've got my whole party action on, I'm soaking a very expensive high, I wanna get fucked at least six times by skaters or surfers, and I really hate it when I have to be in that space where I totally have to focus, and take care of somebody. I do that at the hospital. When I've got a killer buzz going, I'm on bone time, and I'm really there to dance and have fun."

"The skating phenomenon is something relatively new in Europe," says internationally acclaimed visual artist and long-time Family member Kitty Duchamp. This progressive Greek active beauty, who was born in Athens, teaches at the Kunstgewerbe-Schule in Zurich and keeps a stable of boy interns whom she mixes up potent coffee and frappuccino enemas for. "Not only do my young men ride skateboards but they also snowboard and are generally quite athletic with a healthy desire to sexually experiment with an older, nurturing lover. From my enema and high colonic sessions with my students I am able to mix incredible colors from their feces, urine, smegma, and semen. A wonderful series I created is in the permanent collection at the Whitney. These masterpieces hold special significance for me, of course."

Kitty is slightly versatile in that she is also French passive. She mentioned to me that the giddy abandon of the gang bang is merely a harmless rite of passage for young males and is a necessary and natural phenomenon. "I can either feign outrage or pretend to be helpless as these crazed, testosterone-infested boys work me into an ecstatic frenzy," she said. "If things get a little rough, like they start biting at my nipples so hard that they tear them open, or if ounces of blood are shed, that's par for the course, and should be expected. The rabid intensity of the sex is worth any discomfort and/or long-term pain associated with this form of expression. Sex is war, and the body is its natural battlefield. In Europe we don't equate violent sex play with abuse. We consider it foreplay."

"Those young skaters are so inexperienced that anything you come up with they say, 'OK!' They want to learn, so you can train them, and somewhere along the line you're turning them into better lovers." So sayeth Cuntry Camille, the midwest Family member looking a little long in the tooth. Camille has mousy brown hair, is a bit snaggletoothed, but has a nice hard body and natural double-D cups. She works as a waitress at the Uptown Cafe in Blooming-ton, Indiana. The small college town was made famous years ago by the movie *Breaking Away*.

"After you fuck them a few times, they start looking real puppy-dog and you want to bitch-slap them, because it's really not attractive," Camille said.

Whenever she has to work a double shift, she takes a sex break and walks down to People's Park in the town square where she has her pick of the humpiest heshen skaters. All the townies make their money selling Cat, which is the local 22-cent equivalent of Crystal Meth. When she's in the mood she'll let the boys pull a train on her right in the park bushes. When a boy is on Cat, he can fuck for hours without coming. It bums them out, but she loves it.

"The kids that are drug addicts try so hard to play it cool, but they are totally beside themselves getting hot free pussy, and the ones that aren't drug addicts are doing handstands in your living room," Patty revealed.

Patty started to get all psychological on me, saying that she likes the skaters that are drug messes.

"If they couldn't care less, and start to act like they're doing you a favor, that's the type that's usually better in bed," she said.

Patty prides herself for being the horndoggiest woman alive. She's beautiful, with large breasts that are real, not store-bought. She is even married to a famous rock star who has never been able to keep up with her sexual appetite. He doesn't even try, he just lets her do as she pleases, knowing that sometimes he'll get to join in. He's really pussywhipped and corn-knobbed. Last summer Patty accompanied him on tour in Europe, where he played big outdoor festivals. After one gig they picked up two young groupie girls and had a hot buttered fourgy. Patty art-directed. She said it was fun, with lots of pert pussy grazing, and playing jump rope with squiggly vulvas, but it wasn't nasty enough to get Patty off, so she had the girls round up their boyfriends, who were German skate-Nazis with cruel club endowments. She choreographed herself and her husband getting deep tissue melts by the Krauts. The scene ended with the girls urinating all over everything and everybody and making quite a mess. Patty made the German hooligans clean it up with their tongues.

Patty works as a stripper, not because she needs the money, but because she's a writer and it gives her plenty of fodder. She's also a low-maintenance nymphomaniac. "I could probably get $100 for lap dances every night from the skaters that come to the club in New Jersey where I work, but I'd feel weird if I took money from boys I'd rather fuck later."

Patty is a pioneer in the field of bagging skater rats; none of her girlfriends had gone this route before her not-so-subtle indoctrination. She had a lot of disasters in the early days, because her heart would be broken or she'd hang on some word or phrase like there was a deeper connection than sex. She hadn't figured out that these kids were just acting their age. Now she knows them and their age group so inside-out, she knows what to expect and she's always dead on. It makes the other girls in The Family crack up.

Patty let me in on a secret. "A guy can be as dumb as a brick, but if he fucks good, a girl will fall madly in love with him." She says she has statistics and graphs to back up all of her unorthodox theories.

Camille used to live in Orange County. That's where she first met Patty. They were both wild punk rock gals working the nudie bar circuit. She realized they were gnarly kindred spirits when Patty started talking about how she had itchy knuckles and loved fisting her boyfriends.

Until meeting Patty, Camille didn't know too many women who like to fist and get fisted. Of course she and Patty had sex—*a lot.* Patty even shrimp-fisted Camille's twittering pussy, making her pass out four times.

After a series of sordid relationships and substance abuse problems, Camille moved back home to Indiana. When she first arrived, she'd hang at the one disco in town, Bullwinkle's, or go to shows at the rock club above it, Second Story. That's where she'd meet a lot of randy frat boys and wound up giving them, as she calls it, "high skank sessions." She got bored doing fraternity brothers; they were too vanilla-extract. One day she was trolling the student union and met her first skater boy, who was also in a local band called The Erections.

"With young boys they never have problems getting it up, even if they're drunk. A guy in his thirties who is tired, his dick gets all spongy and he'll lose it halfway through. But with skaters, the first fuck, they come real quick, then they're hard again in as long as it takes to smoke a cigarette. That's when they titty fuck you, and leave you a reservoir-sized pearl necklace. Then you can get four or five more fucks from them in several different styles and positions. Why do doggie style when you can have Pomeranian or Papusa, and who needs the missionary position when you can get righteous in Grunion position—yahoo!" Camille screeched.

★

"I'm a Gemini," says Minka, "and we like to live a double life."

I'm here with her and two of her skater beaus, Baby Daddy Chips and Suffer, at this awful rave party in the high desert called Release. The music is too loud for me, and everyone is dancing with these silly colored light sticks, like fan dancing at discos in the '70s. I want to leave, but I'm stuck because I made the mistake of riding with them.

"It's like having a split personality!" shrieks Minka, who is wearing a macramé halter top and a see-through micro-mini. Her look is called "from coon to can't." "I was at work for twelve hours taking care of people who are dying, I came home, changed clothes, and we'll be here raving for fourteen hours. I'm all hardcore."

Baby Daddy Chips moved to L.A. from Florida, where he was part of the rave scene in Gainesville and Jacksonville. He met Minka at the Dunes in the Desert party. He's 18, still in high school, about six feet tall, and is Dominican, German, and French. He's attractive in a sort of dopey boy stoner way. When Minka first met him, he wanted to come back to her house, but he had a friend with him and couldn't sleep over because his mom needed her car back. When they first started to fuck, she made it clear to him that just because he can fuck her with no strings or grief doesn't mean he's allowed to treat her like a doormat. Her makeshift ground rules are: 1. Sex is replaceable, if you don't show the expected excitement (like wanting to spend some time with her as a pet/friend since romance is too ridiculous) you are easily replaced. 2. If you want to drop by, fuck, and leave, it has to be done before 4:00 A.M. 3. Calls after 4:00 A.M. must be sleepovers with plenty of time the next day for sex. 4. No bringing friends along to sleep on the couch unless said friend is cute, and all parties are going to have sex. Bottom line: These kids don't behave badly out of rudeness or lack of respect. They just don't know any better, and have to be taught.

★

"As an art project I orchestrated a live sex show with me and my students," brags Kitty.

"To participate, the boys needed my vaginal prerequisite," she laughs. "I called Patty to tell her about it, and she said I'd better have the show videotaped and transferred to NTSC so that she can masturbate to it."

Kitty borrowed special lighting from the school's film department. It was quite a production. It culminated with a coed circle jerk and everyone drinking each other's piss in these giant faux platinum goblets. One black American student who had recently given birth started lactating, and got the bright idea to mix her breast milk with the urine and Nestle's Quik—the chocolate not the strawberry.

"Some people are just not organically interested in sex. With them, penetration or a blow job is more than enough. They will never eat pussy, and come up with lame excuses why. Skater boys will do anything. When I'm sitting on their sweet faces, they are like Labrador retrievers. They have the energy, but not the focus," Patty reflects. "I guess that comes with age."

Patty has sex with a lot of different kinds of skater boys. Some are hustlers and others are FITs (Fags-In-Training). "Fags always want to fuck me, god knows why." She shrugs. "I guess because I'm a femme top. Those of us who came of age when punk rock formed, you had to make a choice to be gay or straight. I've been sleeping with girls since I've been having sex, yet lesbians wouldn't take me seriously, I would have to hear that I'm on the fence blah blah, and I'm sure it was the same for guys. But now with these skate kids, they listen to industrial music, disco, punk, it's all mixed together now, and everyone is openly bi. They are not forced to take a side."

"When I used to be a stripper," said Camille, "I slept with a lot of girls I worked with. My generation broke all the barriers and opened it up for these kids. When I visited Patty in New York she

took me to this big club with all these cute 18-year-old boys. So
much eye candy. They had gay and straight entrances and all the
Guidos were holding hands so they could have access to all the
cool parts of the club. And I met two redheaded twins who are big
dick thickerous and I went home with them. They take turns
fucking my pussy to death with brutal accuracy for hours, then
getting bashful when I tell them I want to watch them do each
other. I accidentally-on-purpose shove my fist up one. Semen is flying everywhere, both twins are still hard and keep finding new
holes to fuck me in, and just when the ultra seriousness of the
brother-to-brother shit hits the fan, we start busting up laughing,
and it's morning. They have to go to school, so I meet their parents
(who are my age) at the breakfast table, and I'm getting moist again
wondering if their hot dad has a dick as succulent as his sons'."

"You have to come home and fuck me," Patty said to this skater at
Curfew, the big rave club in downtown Manhattan. He couldn't say
no because she caught him by surprise. Patty's famous DJ friends
had procured a bevy of young and very good-looking boys for her
pleasure, but for whatever reason, she wasn't into any of them.

"I'm not one of those li'l girls in the pop tops with no hips,"
Patty says, pointing a finger. "I'm working a mighty voluptuous
woman thing. I strip at this club in Jersey, and it's one-stop shopping for me there. Suburban boys are so cute, and people don't believe me when I tell them that. Hard, tight bodies and a
willingness to please. What more could you want?"

Patty's all-time favorite type of skater boys are the ones who
have melon-shaped bubble butts you can set a champagne glass on.
Patty loves to rim. She goes crazy feasting on little nappy dugouts
(as it's referred to on the East Coast). "One night this kid named
Nelson brought up anal sex, and I ask him, 'Me or you?'" she says.
He goes, 'Whatever.' So I finger him, and he sits on my face as I
scarf a pink loaf."

Patty grabs some lube and covers her hand in it and sticks it up his hole. "Not bad for a straight boy," she said to him. She then shoved both hands in him until it made a whooshing sound. Patty creamed right on the spot. Then she whips out a Ghidrah (triple-headed black dildo) and starts fucking him with all three heads. He gets into it, and asks for something bigger. With a John Wayne Gacy grin, she showcases this dildo that is so big that she can sit it on the floor and fuck it, which she does as a warmup. Then she fucks Nelson for 45 minutes and he's quietly hunching, letting her do whatever she wants, and not complaining. His penis is unlike any other. It's big and has a weird velvet-smooth texture like a camel's nose. Finally he goes, "Ow!" and Patty says, "Stop because I'm hurting you, or because you've had enough?" And he says, "A bit of both."

Patty figures that if she was a real guy, she would have come so long ago, that this scene must be a *Last Exit to Brooklyn*–style gang bang and that she is number seven in line. Then he says something that was like icing on the cake: "Imagine you were in jail and some-one with a cock that big wanted to fuck you all the time, wouldn't that be awful?"

Patty is crazy for this boy, even though he's catatonic. She rolls her eyes and says to him, "Yeah, motherfucker, it would be so awful you'd never let anyone with a small cock near you again."

I asked Patty if Nelson was a sloppy bottom, prone to mud-slides, and she said that he was meticulously clean. "At that age all they do is eat and shit." He's not much fun to have around when you're not fucking him, though, she said, adding that he's now in some lockdown, court-ordered rehab.

Patty fucked another boy who was a little dirty on the inside, and she asked him if he'd like a daiquiri enema. Patty is the queen of ex-otic enemas. And he says, "Why don't I just go to the bathroom?" And she looked at him and said, "You can do that on cue?" and he goes, "Yeah, can't you?" And frowning she says, "No, that stops after thirty. I'm lucky if I have a bowel movement every day." Then she pissed on him because she was not sure if he was being a smart-ass.

"Not every young boy will let me plow him, but skaters are more into it than anyone else," Patty testified with religious fervor in her voice.

"I spent all of last year sowing my wild oats with teenage skater boys," sighed Minka. "Now I'm taking a hiatus from it. I'm casually dating a guy who is a little older at twenty-two. He designs Web pages for Disney and is working on his Ph.D. in philosophy. He's set the new standard for any man who wants to see me on a more serious level, and he enjoys drinking my urine."

Minka may feel like she has slowed down a bit, but as of last week she went to a party called BurnAss and picked up two 19-year-old tweekers. They took turns jackhammering her twatkin. The tweek with the overzealous thrombone wound up scraping the walls of her uterus. After fixing some mushroom tea, Minka DP-ed, leaving them gagging on the lovely extravaganza of it all. "One of the boys, with a pecan-stubbied dick, had a bigger chest than me," she exclaimed. "He sure got a kick out of me calling him a dirty faggot bitch with Lee's Press On Tits. They sure took their sweet time in drinking the remainder of my piss, and my ego couldn't take that so I made them go home. The next day I felt funny and discovered that one of them had ripped the lining of my rectum and inflamed my hemorrhoids!"

Minka started having sex again with her original skater boy Damian, though she swore not to after he got her pregnant for the second time. "Damien's semen really tastes good," she admitted. "I guess I'm nothing but a pathetic dick pig. He churned that nasty cob down my throat so fiercely, I was coughing up blood. But I got my revenge when I raped his crater-faced ass with a garlic press as our fat neighbor watched through an open window beating off. Thank god I used my leather sheets, I easily wiped off the mess from Damien's two bloody stools with some Armor All."

★

"I can really turn boys out in a way nobody can," Patty proclaims. "Even if they're lame in bed like Louis, a professional skater and surfer with Quicksilver. He's twenty with a perfect face and body. He's a premature ejaculator, but is so serene that I know after being with me he feels a little robbed. I don't care, I like his energy and he smells all shiny and new, his skin is like butter, his breath is always fresh, and he has this delightful body odor and dewy jiss that brings back memories of the first blow jobs I gave in the fifth grade. I don't want to get all smarmy and sentimental but I just realized that I'm twenty years older than these guys I have sex with, and it's weird because I've lived more of a life than these kids ever live.

"Before I was in middle school I was hanging out at drag clubs, taking tons of drugs and staying out all night, and then I quit school altogether, went to Amsterdam and London, became a concubine doing the Shah of Iran, then I got hooked up with The Clash when they made *London Calling,* went to the States, started hanging out with Johnny Thunders. Moved back to Canada with this huge heroin problem. Got my shit together and finished school, and married a rock star. I lived through all this. So as doe-eyed as these kids get over me, I know it's not going to be lasting because there just isn't anything to build from. But when I get one that can fuck me from behind and slaps my ass just the way I like, and he climbs on me and gets epileptic when he's cumming, and I'm covered in so much of it that I can't move from the bed, I know that as the czarina of the First Family of Fuck I've done a good job."

# THE EROTIC ADVENTURES OF JIM AND LOUELLA PARSONS

It all started when Jim couldn't get it up. I guess I should find another way to say it, but we just country folks. That's how we put it. That was two months ago, and he been 'fraid to try ever since. Anyway, we been married for twenty-six years and have had more than our share in the love department. We youngish still; both in our fifties, and we got a lot of love left. I told Jim just that, but it didn't help none. In all our years of marriage ahead and three before, I have never seen him so upset. Jim has a lot of pride. He don't like the idea of not being able to do his business. I stopped trying to talk sense into him and did the next best thing.

Now, I had learned years before not to take stock in none of those women's magazines. Their sex tips usually included some food or Saran Wrap. Jim didn't like nothing too messy. He said the only thing he wants wet is me. Anyway, whenever things were tough with me and Jim, I pray that God will give me strength, make me humble, and show me where I'm wrong. Then I talk to the ancestors. I talk to them like they still alive, too. I just do it in my sleep. They always know the answers. This time I call on the women: my mama, Aunt T, and Grandma Sadie. They a hoot.

Mama say, "Hey, girl. Don't say a word. We know just why we here."

"Uh huh," Aunt T say. "Jim can't do the do."

Grandma Sadie tell them to hush. She say, "*They* men weren't too good *no* time." She say it's better to have a man who have it but lose it all the way once, than one who never lose it but only halfway does it the rest of the time.

Now I laugh. Grandma Sadie tell me that our problem is that we done got way too comfortable with each other. She say we hit it every Wednesday and sometimes on Sunday (depending on how good my fried chicken is). Until then, I didn't know about that connection, but I vow to take more time with Sunday dinner from that point on.

Mama say, "Girl, you need to spice things up a bit, fix your hair and put on a little makeup."

Mama know that I ain't into nothing too fancy, but I remind her anyway. Aunt Sadie say I need to learn some other positions. She say I got the wife and the mother part down pat, but I need to be a bit more whorish in the bedroom.

Grandma Sadie say, "Hush. Good loving ain't in no makeup, and it certainly ain't in no slutty ways. If the man want a whore, he pay one."

Grandma Sadie say the loving in the bedroom is in all the things you do before you get there. She also say me and Jim are real good to each other, better than most, but we need to find each another all over again.

I ask her what she mean, and she say, "Girl, when the last time you rubbed that man's behind?" Before I can act shocked or tell her "Never," she say, "Uh huh, that's what I'm talking about. Jim knows what he got, and he thinks he knows how he likes it. What makes a man hot is making his woman hot. He thinks he knows just what to touch and how to touch it. In all the years you've been married and all the time you were sneaking before, Jim ain't had to figure out too much. He made you happy in bed because he made you happy in life. But girl, there's a lot more you should be doing."

At that point, I want to ask what, but I hear Jim getting up so I do too. I roll over and see Jim lying on his stomach. I can tell that he's feeling bad because it's Wednesday, and in the morning he's usually feeling like he want it. Most times, but not always, he gets it too. Usually, I wait for him to come to me, but this time I go to him. I rubbed Jim's behind slow and soft at first. I hear him moaning real low.

"Mmm, baby, that feels good," he say.

I rub it some more and he turn over. And I see what I haven't seen in a long time. Mr. Jim, that's what I call him, is standing at full attention. Jim so excited he can't wait to say hello to Miss Lou. That's what he call me down there, on account of my name is Louella. Jim open my legs quicker than he usually do. He ain't wait to see if I'm ready, but I don't care, seeing his joy make me too happy to say anything. As soon as Jim try to get in Miss Lou, he loses himself.

"Dammit, God dammit," he say.

"Take your time, baby," I tell him.

I start rubbing his behind some more, but Jim too shamed to try again. He mumble "sorry" and get dressed and go on to the job he has had for as long as we been married. I pray that he don't lose that too.

After he leave, I go back to sleep so I can ask Grandma Sadie what I need to do. As soon as I get there, they're waiting.

"Girl, I told you. You need to be more seductive," Aunt T was saying.

"Hush up, girl," my mama told her. "Can't you see she feels bad enough?"

"Look like to me she ain't feeling nothing at all," Aunt T said, laughing.

"Be quiet, y'all," Grandma Sadie told them. "Baby, listen and listen good. I'm gonna give you the magic you need, but you got to add the spice to it. Like I said before, you've been doing the same thing the same way for years. You need to get to know every inch of that man's body and what really makes him feel good."

I tell her I thought I did. She say Jim and me don't know what we like 'cause we ain't had it. I don't say nothing 'cause I figure she on the other side. She got to know more than I do.

She say, "Baby, what I'm gonna tell you take patience and your 'bility to follow through. You got to do just what I tell you. How you do it is up to you, though.

"Tonight," she say, looking me right in the eyes, "you and Jim sit on this bed and talk about everything you think you want to do or have done to you. It's gonna be hard, but all you can do is talk. Don't touch no matter how hard he get. Tomorrow night you can touch each other, but you can't touch it. Then, the next night you can touch it, but don't taste. Next night, taste but don't enter. Then, on the last night, get ready to go in."

That night, Jim came home tired as always. I cook him his Sunday chicken dinner, and it ain't even Sunday. Jim smile at me real sweet, but say, "Baby, I don't want to try . . . let's give it some time."

I tell him, "Fine. I don't want to, but I do want to talk."

I take Jim into the bedroom that I had cleaned real good. I had the bed linens changed and sprinkled my best perfume on them.

"Sit down, Jim," I say. "Now, Jim," I say, "for years we've been doing things the same, but we gonna try something new."

Jim start to tell me how tired he is, but I tell him to listen. He ain't really seen me like that, but I know he like it. I sit him on the bed and undress him real slow. I never did that before either. When I take off his pants, I let my fingers touch him real lightly, but I remember what my grandma say so I stop myself. Then I undress. Now you got to believe me when I say this. I don't think I've ever been naked in front of my man with the lights on, so all this is making him crazy. I'm not as fine as I used to be, but he didn't see with the lights on then so all he knows is now. I sit on the other side of the bed, and Jim thinks I'm asking for some.

I tell him, "Tonight, baby, we just gonna talk. Tell me what you like, and I'll tell you. Tomorrow you get to touch me, but you can't touch me now. Friday you can touch, and Saturday you can touch it and taste it. Sunday, after church, if you still want to, I'll let you in."

With that, Mr. Jim came right to attention, and I was so wet I coulda slid right off my bed. Just that little bit of talk done got us hot and ready, but I know that I gotta do just what Grandma Sadie say. So I start.

"Jim," I tell him, "I love the way you moan. It's telling me that it's good. I love the way you pull my knees apart, but I wish you would stroke my thighs and play with my breasts more and my nipples. I know they ain't like they used to be, but I still got feelings. I love your kisses too, but I wish . . ."

This takes me a while to say, but Jim jump up and say, "What, baby? Just tell me."

Finally, I get to it. "I wish you would kiss Miss Lou. I want you to put those big lips of yours right down there. I want you to kiss it and put your tongue on it."

I was shamed to say all that, but Jim says, "All right, baby." He was about to do it right then, but I tell him it gotta wait.

Then I say, "Jim, I need you to touch me more. I want you to put your hand on my head like you used to. And Jim, years ago you used to smack me on the behind a little. I won't mind if you do that too."

Jim sure enough was grinning. So was I. Talking about it made me want to climb on top of him and ride him to kingdom come.

"Jim," I say, "it's your turn."

Jim ain't say nothing, but I open my eyes to see his hand is holding Mr. Jim and giving himself some good love.

"Jim!" I say. "You gotta wait." I declare. I have to call him three times before he comes to.

"Oh, yeah. Okay. Sorry, babe. Seem like I kind of got lost."

"It's your turn," I say.

Jim say okay and tell me things that make me want to lose my mind. "Baby," he say in his deep voice, "I want you to act like you can't wait to get it."

"I can't," I almost yell.

"Well, sometimes it seem like you just doing your duty."

I don't say nothing 'cause I know I got something to learn. I want to talk back too.

"Tell me what you want. Say it right in my ear. I want you to tell me it's good, that it's always good. I want you to put your mouth all over me."

I'm blushing now, but I try not to show it.

"Everywhere. My chest. I got nipples too, and I want your mouth on them. Baby, I want you to put Mr. Jim in your mouth too. I want you to suck him and lick him good. I been scared to ask you for it, but we talking, ain't we?"

Jim stood up and started fondling himself again. "We gotta wait, baby?"

I say, "Yes."

"I know. I just want to show you how I want it. Is that okay?" Jim ask. He hold Mr. Jim up with one hand and start stroking slowly with the other. "Take your mouth up and down like this, baby," he say. "Start slow and then suck harder and faster. You can touch my balls, too."

That make me want to laugh, but something tell me not to. Jim tell me to suck it 'til he say he want to come. Then he want me to stand up and bend over. He say he loves taking me from behind, but he don't do it too often because it seem like I don't like it. Now I know my grandma was right because I only remember Jim doing it twice, and both times it was so good I commence to crying. Jim must've thought I was sad, and I was too old-fashioned to tell him otherwise. I'm thinking all of this and look over to find Jim done come all over himself.

"Jim, we s'posed to wait," I say. Jim kiss me like he ain't never kiss me before and goes to sleep right there in my arms.

The next day Jim wake up singing, and so do I. He calls me three times from work, something he used to do back when we just got married.

"Can't wait to touch you," he say.

"Me neither," I whisper.

That night, I undress Jim again, but this time I lay him on his stomach. I open up some baby oil I found in the back of my cupboard and pour it all over his back.

"Mmm, that's nice," he say.

I rub his shoulders and back and down to his waist. I knead his strong back like I'm making bread.

"Yes, woman," he says between strokes.

Then I pour baby oil on his behind and down between his legs. I rub his behind and slip my oily fingers between his cheeks. It must feel good because he snatches my hands and tries to take me right then.

"Not yet," I whisper in his ear.

"Oh, woman, you driving me crazy," he say.

"You don't know the half," I whisper back.

"Who are you and what have you done with my wife?" he say, laughing.

"Lay down, man, and let me finish my business."

I oil his legs and rub them hard, front and back. I touch everything but Mr. Jim. Jim trying to get me to, but he know we gotta wait.

"All right, woman," he say, "your turn."

He lay me down and pour oil right in the crack of my behind. He rub my behind until I think I can see Jesus. I moan, and Jim moans with me. He rub everything but Miss Lou. I gotta tell the truth and shame the devil. Jim rub my feet so good I think I will die. I didn't know feet could get you so wet. He start at my feet and work his way back up. When he get to my breasts, he could have asked me to run down the street buck-naked, and I mighta done it! He rub my breasts in a way that lets me know he has done it before, but not with me. I forgive him right when the thought comes to me. I know that he wasn't getting this from me, and part of that is my fault. Besides, we been too far not to know how to forgive. Jim must've somehow felt my thoughts because he starts to cry. I tell him it's okay and hold him. We rock each other 'til we fall asleep, oily and wet.

The next day was my grocery shopping day. I got up and took a long, hot shower, fixed my hair, and put on a little makeup. Dora, who works down at the market, say, "Girl, you look like you been getting some on the side." I want to tell her to hush and that she needs salvation, but I just grin. I couldn't help it, but something about what she said makes me feel kinda proud. I push my pride back 'cause I wasn't looking to fall and say "Thank you." That got folks whispering and I let them. We live in a small town. I know folks gonna think and say whatever they want anyway.

That night, Jim came in smiling, holding flowers, and it ain't even my birthday. This our night to touch Mr. Jim and Miss Lou, and neither one of us can wait. Now, I have always had my husband's dinner on the table for him when he gets home. With the exception of the birth of two of our five children, his meal has always been waiting. This time though, I meet him on the porch. I give him some cold, tart lemonade and kiss him right on the mouth. Miss Brown from across the street is looking, but I don't care and neither do Jim.

"We better go in," he say.

"Let her go in if she don't like what she see."

Miss Brown must've heard me 'cause she did go in, but I saw her curtain pull back and her eye peeping through. Jim sit next to me on the porch step.

"I get to touch it tonight, don't I?" he say right up next to my ear.

His hot, sticky breath on my neck make my nipples stand out at attention and my behind got real hot. Before I could answer, Jim shock me by slipping his hand up under my dress. Now it was already dark so I know Miss Brown couldn't see nothing, but all of this is new to me. I was sure surprised, but I had one for Mr. Jim too. He reach under my dress and find me naked as the day I was born. I didn't have on a stitch of underwear.

"Louella Givens," he say, calling me by my maiden name.

I grin, and Jim commence to laugh like I ain't heard in years. He pull me by the hand and take me in. We didn't make it to the bedroom though. Good thing the children are grown and moved out of town 'cause otherwise, they'd seen more than they ever wanted to know. Jim lay me down right on the living room carpet and pull my dress up over my head. He start to kiss my breasts, and I remind him that he couldn't use his mouth 'til the next day. He shook his head but said he wasn't going to argue. He grab my breast with one hand and start playing with my nipple with the other. It feel too good to be true. I didn't know my nipple had that much life left in it. Then I take one of his hands and put it down on Miss Lou.

"You full of all kinds of surprises, ain't you, woman?" Jim say.

He rub across my thighs real light for what seemed like hours. I want to scream, "Touch it, man!" but I learned the importance of patience. By the time Jim stroke the hairs on Miss Lou, how I want to skip over the next few days and get right to it. Jim stroked the inside and whispered in my ear, "I love this pussy. This is my pussy."

My husband had never talked like this to me before. Three days before I would have been shamed to hear this kind of talk coming from him, but that night I couldn't get enough. He stroked the inside of my kitty until it was hard as him. I was moaning and hollering like I was crazy. Then, when Jim stroked my spot, which by the way I wasn't aware of before then, I squirted all over the place like a man. I was shaking so hard, Jim came right through his pants.

"Woman," he said, "what have we been missing?"

I was panting hard and smiling like a madwoman. Jim carried me to bed. I felt too weak to touch anything he had, but it was okay. I slept until twelve midnight exactly and awoke to find Jim sleeping like a baby. I waited until one minute past and pulled Mr. Jim out of the slit of his PJs and commenced to sucking him the way Jim showed me. Jim must've done thought he was dreaming 'cause he was moaning something 'bout, "No, I'm married. Please don't."

He opened his eyes and saw my mouth on him. I was looking right in his eyes. His head rolled back and he let out a moan that probably made Miss Brown across the street come to attention.

"I'm coming, baby." When he said that, I climbed on top of him and rocked slowly, allowing him to come inside me. Jim arched his back and yelled, "Sweet Lord, thank you."

"Yes," I said, "I'm coming with you."

We must've both passed out 'cause when I came to, Jim was lying next to me, grinning in his sleep. He woke up and smiled and started kissing me all over. He kissed as high as possible, and as low as possible. I stood up and bent over, and we did what we both like. We made love all day long. I fell asleep in between lovemaking and I saw my ancestors.

"Girl, you was supposed to wait," Aunt T said. "You never did know how to wait."

My grandma smiled. "Girl, hush. Sometimes rules are made to be broken. Besides," she added, "y'all been waiting over twenty years to get it right."

"Thank you," I told them.

Jim must've thought I was talking to him 'cause I heard him say, "You wait—you ain't had nothin' to thank me for yet. Come here, woman. Let me taste you."

# WHAT SHE DID WITH HER HANDS

For years I didn't really understand it—the way women would look at each other's hands across the bar, the way some women's glances would trail up from the fingers to the swell of the knuckles, past the wrist to the forearm, and then turn away suddenly if they saw me watching them. I used to hang out at the only gay bar in Tallahassee, Florida, and watch women stare as the tall, slim-lipped bartender would lift four beer bottles together, their pupils reflecting the cable-like tightening of the muscles from her wrist to elbow. I watched the other women lick their lips, look away, and inevitably look back again, and I knew by their manner that it was about *sex*.

I'd look back myself, admire the bartender's jaw, black eyes, and the curling short hair on her neck. I loved the way her hips moved, the way her tongue would peek out between her lips when she was counting change, but I didn't really see the power of her hands. They were small, finely shaped, and the nails were trimmed down and filed, but then most lesbians wore their nails that way. It was nothing special as far as I could see. I would look back to see what all the women were watching, but I couldn't quite figure it out.

There was a whole language in the subtle movements of women's hands on a shot glass, but for me it was like hearing someone speak French. Even what I thought I understood turned out to be mostly misunderstanding. A raised eyebrow, a direct glance, or a shy tongue appearing suddenly on a full lip were all obvious evidence of erotic interest, and I knew how to respond. But a woman who cracked her knuckles while looking into my eyes confused me. I suspected she might want something of me I might not want to give.

The older butchy women I liked best seemed to think that I would surely catch fire if they held me down and fucked me. I responded powerfully to being held down but not so well to fucking. Years of severe and persistent endometriosis had convinced me that nobody could possibly enjoy fucking. Well, one or two fingers perhaps, during that time of the month when you want to howl at the moon anyway, but not more than that, and certainly not with any kind of sudden or forceful movement. The kind of sustained and forceful fucking that made women with big powerful forearms so attractive was unimaginable to me. I was a master at coming by rocking on my partner's thigh or pulling my thigh muscles tighter and tighter while I sucked and tongued at my partner's clit. But fucking hurt me, and I'd only do it if my partner insisted, biting my lips and giving it up like a gift too costly to offer often. It wasn't until my mid 20s, well on in my life as a lesbian, that I finally had the surgery for what had plagued me since my adolescence.

Curing my endometriosis changed my life. After that, when the moon came on me, and a woman pushed three fingers into my wet and aching vagina, I got the shock of my life. There was no pain; there was a heated rush of desire. I wanted that hand. I wanted it hard. I wanted it fast. I wanted it as long as she could keep giving it to me. I remembered every bartender I had ever seen pick up a handful of cold bottles, and in the middle of an orgasm I laughed out loud. I had acquired the language.

"Speak to me," I told my lover. Without knowing what the hell I was talking about, she did just the right thing. She slipped another finger inside me and started all over again.

In the movie in my head, fisting is as savage as big cats rolling over each other in a jungle clearing. The instant of being entered is as abrupt and shuddering as a flying kick. In my bed, however, fisting is neither savage nor abrupt. It is slow, measured, enticed, and enticing. My women take their time, sometimes to my great frustration. When I beg them to move faster and harder, they just go on taking their time, putting in only as many fingers as the drumring entrance to my vagina will allow. They work me up slow, making sure that I am as open and aroused as possible. It is slow, teasing work, getting a whole hand in my cunt. But if it were easy, I don't think I would enjoy it half so much. Part of the charge is the excess of the act.

If we have to work on it, then it's about submission. If it's easy, then it's more about the physical sensation. It's the overwhelming aspect of it, the being totally carried away, shouting demands, shrieking to be fucked. The fact that it's hard makes it better, more satisfying.

I don't react to fucking like a character in a jack-off manual. My women almost never get their fists going in and out the way it's described in cheap pornography. Once the fist is fully inside, the motion is a slow, sliding, back-and-forth movement with the wrist sometimes swiveling enough to turn the knuckles up, pushing toward that mythological G-spot where all the nerves leading to the clit seem to cross.

I don't spurt the way some women do. Push me hard there, though, and I might pee. That's excessive too, the idea that we are fucking so hard and so furiously that I will just pee all over us. I like that. I like the idea of being that far out of control. Even the moment when I am shocked and embarrassed has its enjoyable aspect. Just so long as we don't stop, and especially if I am told that she wants it, wants me to let myself go like that, the thought turns around and I'm proud of myself. We are bad girls together, enjoying ourselves.

The first woman I ever really fisted was a big butch girl—a tall muscly woman who left working on her motorcycle to polish my belt buckle, get me a cup of tea, and blush when I hooked my fingers in her belt. She had been flirting with me and my girlfriend, and we were both enjoying her enormously. It was my girlfriend who checked it out with her girlfriend and got us all together at a party later.

"What do you want?" I kept teasing that girl, enjoying the size of her, the stretch of her shoulders and the slow, gliding way she moved.

"What can you do?" she replied, looking down at us. We were both so much smaller than her. Well, what? I wondered, but my pride wouldn't let me show her any uncertainty. I squeezed her, pinched her, and ran my hands over her body as firmly as possible, enjoying every little sigh and quiver she made. I was looking forward to watching my girlfriend fuck her, but somehow when we had her lying back and her jeans off and her legs spread, it was my fingers that were teasing at her slippery labia. I slid my thumb inside her and felt around. It was smooth and open and welcoming. I pulled back and slipped two fingers in and looked up into her half-closed eyes. There was lots of room. I pulled back and went in again with three fingers, then four. Her next sigh was deeper, and she shuddered slightly in our arms.

I looked at my girlfriend. She was smiling and nodding, watching my fingers closely. I laughed and pulled back, cupping my fingers. I was going to push, slowly, feel my way tenderly, but the big girl had other ideas. It felt almost as if she reached for me with her whole body. My hand disappeared, sucked into the warm, enclosing glove of her. I gasped, and my girlfriend laughed. I wiggled my fingers and felt the walls of the surrounding vagina balloon out and in on my hand. I closed my hand inside her, and the big girl rocked on my wrist.

"Goddamn!" Everybody around me laughed. I had never felt anything so extraordinary in my life. I tried to remember everything anybody had ever done to me that I liked. All right, I told myself and started moving my hand, the motion flowing from my elbow while I watched her face. When she started moaning and rocking with excitement, I let the muscles in my upper arm go to work. I felt my whole arm working. I wanted to do it right. All of my senses came alive. I needed to feel every motion she made, smell her as she got hotter, hear her guttural cries and slow grunting. "Please," I wanted to shout, but that would have distracted me. I tried instead to speak the language of her body. I felt a hot sweat break out all over me, and every time I looked to the side I saw a proud, happy smile on my girlfriend's face.

"This role reversal stuff," I told her, "I like it a lot."

"Uh-huh," she laughed back at me. "I can see that."

I know remarkably few women who enjoy anal fisting. But there was a time in my life when I became quite accomplished at it. Not that I listed being fisted up the ass as a goal—I just had lots of fantasies about anal sex, and I told a woman I was seeing at the time about those fantasies. Natalia was much older than me, and we had been playing schoolgirl and governess. When I was the governess, Natalia was my toddler who needed to be washed tenderly, powdered down, sometimes have her temperature taken—"Turn over, baby"—and invariably be nuzzled gently until she orgasmed in my arms. When I was the schoolgirl, I was a stubborn adolescent who accumulated countless demerits and had to be taught how to wash behind her ears and between her thighs. After weeks of this play and lots of talk about our mutual fantasies, Natalia decided she would like to play out one of hers and see if she couldn't train her schoolgirl to enjoy having her ass used.

"For me," she begged, feeding me warm baklava and cold dry wine. I didn't know if the butterflies in my tummy were from her suggestion or the snack, but I agreed. Thus began a period of about three months in which I spent at least two nights a week lying belly-down on her big oak bed stand while she whispered threatening enticements into my ears and slipped magic greasy fingers up my butt. She took her time getting me used to her manipulations and refused to tell me just how many fingers had done what at any one time. Regardless, it didn't seem to take very long until I was comfortable enough with what she was doing to climb up on my knees and start pushing back at her thrusts.

"That's my girl," Natalia would purr, and reward me with the fast, slippery swipes at my clit that always made me come.

Finally, one evening Natalia asked me to come early and have dinner. She served raw oysters, lots of wine, and a big salad, and after dinner sent me off to clean myself out and lie for a while in a hot bubble bath with a glass of cognac while she did some tidying up. When Natalia came for me later I was pink all over, giggly, and very tipsy. She was wearing her highest heels and the black jacket with the high collar and the tight-fitting sleeves. Without a word she wrapped me in a big towel, bundled me into the bedroom, and plopped me facedown on an enormous pillow on the floor. Before I could hiccup in confusion she had my wrists tied to a ring in the floor.

"Ma'am?" I tried, unsure which game we were going to play.

"Be still," she said sternly. "Don't think, just relax. I want something from you, and tonight I'm going to get it." She poured a pool of thick, creamy lotion into her palm and began to massage my ass, her blunt fingers pushing dollops of cream up into my butt. I hiccuped, giggled, and after a moment wiggled my ass at her. She laughed, slapped my thighs, and, leaning forward, placed a small, silver, bullet-shaped object in my hand.

"Take a deep breath of that," she told me, still pushing at my ass. I did, and was rewarded with a slow spiral of pin lights that rose from the base of my nose up to my brain. The room got hot. I got dizzy, and a beehive started buzzing in my ears. I had never done poppers before, didn't know that was what I was doing. I just knew I was suddenly high and horny and desperate to push back at her pushing hands.

"Ma'am," I wailed, and she purred back at me, "That's my girl," while her hand worked its way steadily into my butt. She hurt me, and I screamed at her. She laughed at me, and I howled at her. But she'd had all that practice and knew every crevice, every rudimentary panic, every movement I would make in response to every movement of hers, and nothing I did or said or cried stopped her. After a while she wasn't hurting me, she was guiding me, whispering soft words while her fingers played tickle-touch so deep inside me I wanted to burp. I was gasping and begging and coming every little while as easily as a big sponge choo-choo train would fall off a cartoon trestle. Everything was slow-motion, overwhelming and marvelous.

"Fuck me, ma'am. Oh, fuck me," I kept begging her.

"Oh, I am," she kept telling me. "I am. I am. I am."

The sun was coming up when she slid her hand out of me finally and completely. I burst into tears and tried to grab her with my thighs. I wanted it back, that full, marvelous, scary, wonderful feeling. She had pulled the slipknot loose on my hands hours before, and I was free to be coaxed up into the bed to wrap around her and fall asleep, but groggy as I was, I didn't want to sleep. Even if I couldn't move, I wanted to do it again. I pulled her hand up, cradled it to my cheek, and ran my fingers along her forearm. I dreamed of bartenders; slow-eyed, grinning butch girls; and big cats rolling over the jungle floor—big cats with wide, wide mouths, great hanging wet labia, and muscly, tapered forepaws. That woman spoke my language; what she could do with those hands. Oh!

Susanna Kaysen

# How This Story Should End

from *The Camera My Mother Gave Me*

This is what I want, I say to him. I want you to come to me completely naked. Take out your earrings, take off that silver ring on your index finger, take the watch and the bracelet off your arm, undo that string around your neck, take off your clothes, and come to me with nothing at all between us. That's how I want you, I say to him. Absolutely naked is how I want you.

We're in the kitchen. He looks at me and doesn't say anything. Then he takes the ring off. It clatters onto the counter. The watch and the bracelet, and the leather string from around his neck, follow the ring with a clink and a soft thud. He starts to fiddle with the earrings. I never take these out, he says. You're taking them out now, I tell him. I have the impulse to help him—it's difficult to remove earrings without a mirror—but I don't want to touch him yet.

I have a navel ring, he says. Shall I take that out too?

Let me see it, I say.

He pulls his T-shirt up an inch. It's a tiny hoop. His navel is also tiny, a flat half-moon on his belly.

Take it out, I say. All these decorations, you don't need them.

I like them, he says. He puts the navel ring on the counter, on top of the pile he's made there. Then he says, You like them too.

He's right about that. The idea that he knows I like them makes me shiver with pleasure, because it means he knows things about me that I don't tell him, which could include all sorts of things we're going to do.

Okay, he says. He points at me. You too.

I take my earrings out. I take my two rings off. I add them to the pile. My things are gold; his are silver. It's quite a trove of jewelry we've got there.

Without my rings, my hands feel new and exposed.

I feel stripped, I say. I feel—

I'm in his arms. I don't know how this happened. I don't remember moving there. He smells clean, and his body is so warm that I flush from being near it. I've forgotten the warmth that comes off another human being. His blood is beating in his neck under my cheek, slamming against his veins. I put my hands around his rib cage and the force of life, the heat and noise of it, assaults me. We don't kiss. I am too overwhelmed to kiss him. I will faint if I kiss him. I wonder if he feels the same.

He pushes me away a little.

He's sitting on the kitchen stool and I'm standing in front of him. In these positions, we are almost the same height. He looks younger without all his geegaws.

What was the rest of the plan? he asks. Take off my clothes?

Eventually, I say. My voice is weak.

His knee is propped on the rung of the stool, level with my hips. He knocks it into my thigh several times, gently, reeling me in toward him until I'm standing between his legs. He puts one of his hands, the one that no longer has a ring on it, under my shirt onto my back and presses his palm against my spine.

I can barely keep standing up. On the other hand, I don't really need to stand up, because I am floating or pivoting around my vagina, which has become the fulcrum of my existence. I am suspended on it, on the heat and wetness of it, and I no longer feel my legs or my feet or the kitchen floor.

Aren't you going to kiss me? he says.

My mouth is so dry I can't imagine kissing him with it. There's another reason I hesitate. The moment before you kiss someone is the best moment of all, and I want to extend it. Once you've kissed, once you've tasted each other, entered each other's bodies, the entire business has been concluded in some way. This is why a kiss equals an infidelity. A fuck is just a full-body kiss. The kiss is what breaches the separation between two people. Nothing is ever the same after a kiss.

I run my tongue over my lips, but everything is like sandpaper. I don't understand how I can be so dry above and so wet below. I feel that I cannot breathe and that in fact I am not breathing. He's only two inches away from me. I can't seem to close the gap between us, though.

I manage to put my mouth against his mouth. He opens his mouth and breathes into me, and then he starts talking to me, with his lips moving against me.

Are you afraid? he asks. I'm afraid, I guess, he goes on, but while he's talking, he's licking my lips and biting them a little, and my mouth is no longer like sandpaper at all but as soft and wet as the rest of me.

Why are you afraid? I ask him.

Now everything will change, he says, and we stop talking and everything changes.

Jack Fritscher

# THREE BEARS IN A TUB

Listen here, boy, there'll be no hibernatin till after I finish tellin you this bedtime story about Big Daddy when he was himself hardly more than a boy and how he turned into a six-foot-five man and what he done to earn that reputation he got that famous summer on Bear Lake when the canoe overturned late around midnight and Big Daddy on his thirty-fifth birthday saw them two young hairy fishermen floppin like bears in the water next to drownin with their rubber boots suckin them down to the clear rock bottom and them able to stand just barely with their chins on the surface of the moonlit water cuz Bear Lake as you know ain't that deep but deep enough that Griz and Cub was standin so chin deep both their beards was floatin around their heads and all of Big Daddy's two hundred and fifty fucky pounds standin spread-legged on the dock though even if it was the funniest gutbuster sight he ever saw he better climb on into his rowboat without so much as puttin on a stitch of clothes to cover his hide he was always so proud was so well upholstered that way with a coat of thick fur that grew out of his toes and wrapped up his foot to his ankle and grew up his calves like somethin you could curry with a brush especially near his pair of big thighs that made his powerful packed legs a sight to see especially if you caught a lordly eyeful of him come strollin butt naked out of the two-hole outhouse he had downwind from his log cabin up on Bear Lake which could happen since Big Daddy always walked around like a big built hairy man is God's gift which I suppose is true with no supposin after all us seein Big Daddy standin lathered up next to his cabin under that shower with the tub of hot rainwater he tied up on the roof where the sun could always shine so he could scrub up his hairy crack he said where the sun never shined except I know different but that's another story about harvestin dingleberries if you fudgin know what they are and I do appreciate Big Daddy's hairy butt cheeks and sweet sweaty hairy crack where there never was one of those little ingrown hairs cuz Big Daddy always rough-buffed his fur with a big ol towel which them two handsome boys Griz and Cub could have used while they was waitin still sinkin in the middle of Bear Lake next to drownin with the little waves lappin around their mouths and their beards and long hair floatin in the water cuz of Big Daddy sittin naked in his wood rowboat in the moonlight lookin down and laughin at the two heads floatin on the water and them yellin *Keerist, Big Daddy* cuz everybody always called Big Daddy *Big Daddy* ever since he done sired Griz when he was seventeen out of that sweet Kathleen Jones over the other side of Bear Lake and never bothered to marry cuz her father was one of them shaggy men who takes a sidewise shine at life and don't care if a young man rolls his daughter in the hay as long as he gets to roll the fucker himself the way he tried everyone knows to roll over on Big Daddy but Big Daddy rolled over on him and shagged him holdin him by his hair and forcin his mouth open and then his ass all the time shoutin that there was room on Bear Lake for only one Big Daddy and the cum was rollin down Kathleen's legs at the same time it was rollin out the hairy butt and down the hairy legs of her pa and they both was screamin for Big Daddy at first to stop fuckin them and then not to stop

fuckin them and that night was a night everyone heard about and
no one forgot mostly because nine months later little Griz popped
out of Kathleen and some months later out popped Cub makin Big
Daddy a real big daddy twice which he said was enough for him so
he gave up screwin Kathleen and just kept on screwin her pa who
by the way is famous for his moonshine still which he drinks from
frequently always namin the praises of Big Daddy who he calls his
son-in-law except no preacher hitched the unhitchable Big Daddy
to anybody so Kathleen's pa who's less than a dozen years older than
Big Daddy kept lit the torch Kathleen and just about everybody
else carried at Bear Lake after they saw Big Daddy layin naked on
those big rocks in the middle of Bear Lake where he always laid
sunnin his big burly belly and butt and exhibitin his famous foreskin dick right out there on the water in almost the same spot Griz
and Cub were sunk drunk as a skunk in their rubber chest waders
unable to move watchin Big Daddy five feet away kickin back in
his rowboat gettin a boner watchin them struggle in the bubbles
burblin up their own hairy bellies and up their fuzzball chests
floatin in the cool dark water on a moonlit night so bright people
sat on their docks under the big trees around the lake rockin in
chairs and watchin out on the still water those two curly heads spit-
tin lakewater out of their mouths like fountains in the middle of
their beards and shoutin to their pa *Big Daddy come on and rescue us*
and under the moon like exposin himself to some spotlight Big
Daddy leaned back in the boat and rubbed his big hands up his
naked thighs fingercombin his fur and runnin his palms into the
dark swirls of fur on his big chest with wet nipples that stood out
lit by night stars in the clear night like a constellation over the
risin sign of Big Daddy's hardenin cock that made all the voices on
the shore go silent out of respect except for the crickets and a loon
or two whoopin at the powerful sight of two men caught neck deep
wantin for all the world to be saved by a bear god in a rowboat rub-
bin his big woolly belly and scratchin his most beautiful beard in
all of Bear County him never shavin ever even as a growin boy so

that his wavy long beard was as full as ever a beard could be and he could part it in two and wrap it around his starry nipples or lean over as he did that famous night and wrap his beard around his big uncut cock which if truth be known he could suck himself better than anyone else includin Kathleen or her pa or even Griz or little Cub who all had their turns by choice or by force which was one of the stern ways Big Daddy had of makin sure everyone who turned an admirin glance on his broad hairy shoulders and the hams of his furry forearms and the baseballs of his downy biceps got a taste of his dick first in the mouth and then sized up the ass which impressed one and all becuz of the bristly bush surroundin the root of Big Daddy's blue-veined ramdick with the uncut head slidin out so big and shiny even that night drownin out in the middle of Bear Lake Griz and Cub who was both themselves famously endowed thanks to their pa had to comment at the size of their Big Daddy's huge bear meat weighin itself maybe a pound or two and tentin up like a big white pole out of the hills of his thighs over his shaggy pair of bear balls bouncin against his sweet smellin butt crack and archin up the forest hills of his belly and mountains of his meaty chest all of him oiled with bear grease so he shined shined shined in the moonlight on the water while Cub started to sob in his curly beard floatin on the water cuz his big dick was gettin bigger and harder inside his rubber waders an he couldn't get at it and Griz was pleadin *Come on Big Daddy we need rescuin* and Big Daddy's only response was a big bellylaugh which growled like a roar echoin through the warm night makin all the busybody eyes watchin from shore all the more surprised when the two hundred and fifty fucky pounds of Big Daddy like the Lord of the Bears stood up in the rowboat stark naked and shinin with grizzly grease settin starlight tweakin off his nipples like lightnin rods takin a huge piss aimed right down into the mouths of first one and then the other of his two sons who opened their faces like two little bears hungry and thirsty for Big Daddy's big piss which was their regular drink anyway like I say about Big Daddy and the way he trained his two boys

Griz and Cub to waste not and want not by learnin to drink his piss and lick his hair and toothcomb his beard and tonguesuck out the sweat from his armpits and big hairy balls and even when they was all drunk enough which was not as often as they pretended because pretendin to be drunk gave them huntin permits even Bear Lake was not used to when both Griz and Cub would wrestle naked and hairy at night on the cabin floor in front of the fire so the winner could be the first one to crawl up to Big Daddy's big hard butthole and suck wind from the cave when Big Daddy hung his buttcheeks and balls over the edge of the bunk showin his big cock standin up hard with excitement and strokin it himself in anticipation of leanin forward and suckin his own big knob while Griz and Cub took turns feastin on the just desserts of his big bear belly pushin peanut butter and jelly out of his hole and them goin shit for brains nuts suckin and jackin themselves and chewin out Big Daddy's gifts of nature which of course made them see stars and howl at the moon like they was doin that famous summer night the boys thought they'd nearly drown with Big Daddy standin over them pissin down on them with them drinkin every drop and beggin Big Daddy to do with them what he wanted because he was their Big Daddy and they loved him so much and that's what Big Daddy wanted to hear so he saved them yes saved them both by cuttin them out of their rubber waders so they floated to the surface of Bear Lake and Big Daddy took ahold of them by their hair and beards and nipples and dicks and buttholes and pulled both them boys into his rowboat where they sat the rest of the night laughin and drinkin and shoutin through their beards at the moon while stars glistened between them nipple to nipple with comets shootin flume tails from their dicks and they floated ever so happy on the still surface of the water while the real constellation of the Bear rose and set over their heads and their fudgey fingers sticky from their buttholes were all entwined in the fur on their chests and the hair of their bellies and the carpet on their shoulders and the bush of their crotches and the hugeness of their beards and the curly sweep

of the hair on their heads and they were all three of them so satisfied that the summer night smiled and half asleep in each other's
big furry arms, Griz and Cub and Big Daddy drifted slowly across
the mirror of stars to their dock on Bear Lake as if the rowboat
knew their way home.

# Lisa Wolfe

# How to Make a Cake

I stood in line patiently. I considered turning around and running right out of there. But I figured I'd paid my money already and got myself down there, so I might as well do it. I strained to hear the tall, lanky woman at the head of the line, talking to the man behind the counter.

"Lady, I can't hear you, please speak up, what'll it be today?"

"Fucking," she said in a loud whisper.

"What kind?"

"*What kind?*" the woman hissed. "What do you mean?"

"Woman-to-woman, woman-to-man, finger, fist, anal-cock, anal-dildo, cunt-cock, cunt-dildo, combination, grand slam, or customer special," the man droned.

"Um—*mawompocuc.*"

"What, speak up please, people are waiting."

"Man to woman! Cunt-cock!" the woman blurted out, her face bright red.

"Thank you." The clerk handed her a ticket. "Gate 52. Next." The woman scurried off down a long hallway.

Now a black man in his sixties, wearing sunglasses and a beret, reached the counter.

"Oral sex," he said—at least I think that's what he said. OK, I can relate to that.

"What kind," the clerk asked, yawning.

"You know, man, oral sex," the man said.

The clerk sighed. "Man-to-man, man-to-woman, woman-to—"

"Eating pussy!" boomed the man in a resonant baritone. "Getting my dick sucked!"

"OK, OK, no problem. Here you go, sir. Gate 7. Next."

One more person to go. I took a few deep breaths. In-out. In-out. The deep breathing wasn't working, my stomach was in knots.

The sexy-looking babe in front of me had learned her lesson from the previous customers.

"Fucking. Man-to-man. Anal. Bottom," she said. I looked more closely at her. Hmmm. Pretty convincing-looking hot woman. All the sexiest women in San Francisco were men, apparently.

"Here you go," the clerk handed him/her a ticket. "Gate 20. Next." Ms. Hot Pants sashayed off in her high heels.

I was about to step up, my heart pounding, when a girl grabbed my arm. Her hair hung down in neatly braided plaits and her starched white shirt, plaid skirt, and kneesocks made me wonder if she was a bit underage to be here.

"Please, miss?" she began, and as I got a better look at her and heard the tone of her voice I realized that this was no child.

"Could I cut in front of you, pretty-please? I know I'm a bad girl, but if you let me in front of you, I promise I'll make it up to you. You can make me stay after and I'll do whatever you want, I'll do your bidding if you please, please, please let me cut in front of the line?" The young woman's eyes were wide and almost filling with tears as she bit her lower lip and looked into my eyes with such pleading.

"Oh sure, yeah—it's all right. No problem—go ahead."

"Come on, ladies, I don't have all day."

"Um—OK," the girl stepped up to the counter. "Discipline, please," she whispered.

"What kind?" the clerk said, half-asleep by now.

"Um—spanking."

"Giving or receiving, paddle, hand, belt, or Other?"

"Receiving. Hand," the girl squeaked. She turned to me then—"I have to be punished, you see."

"I see," I said, smiling encouragingly. Well, it isn't going to be me, honey. I am going to a different gate.

"Gate 14. Here's your ticket. Next."

Finally. I stepped up to the counter, my heart racing, my mouth dry.

"B-b-ugh," I subsided into a coughing fit. The clerk stared at me menacingly.

"Baking!" There, I got it out. I fished for the water bottle in my bag and took a long swig.

The clerk blinked. "Excuse me?" he said.

"Baking," I repeated, blushing. The whole line was suddenly silent. God, this was humiliating.

"Ma'am, I've seen a lot of things, but this takes the cake."

"Yes, that's it—cake. Cookies, pies, pastries, all that. Kitchen appliances. Just tell me what gate or room or whatever."

"We don't offer that kind of thing at this establishment," he said, busying himself with some papers.

"Look—I was told you had everything here, *everything*. If you don't have it, then that was false advertising."

"We do have everything here. You want to see a catalogue?"

"Listen. I paid my money. And I was told you do have a baking—gate. Can't you just look it up on your computer?"

He gave me a long, dry look. He sullenly clicked his keyboard and stared at the screen. In a moment his eyebrows rose slightly, before he returned to his seen-it-all expression. He handed me a ticket without making eye contact. "Gate 11. Next."

I hurried down the hall, in the direction everyone else had gone, and followed the signs for Gates 1–15. It was just like an airport, but without baggage. The ads had promised to provide all the necessary paraphernalia. "Bring nothing with you, walk away with the experience of a lifetime." I hoped they would deliver, it certainly was a big chunk of change. The nerve of that man, acting like I'm a weirdo. It's true I'd never *met* anyone who was into baking, but then—face it—who would actually admit it? But the fact that they actually had a baking gate here confirmed my dreams. Of course there were other people out there like me. I was not alone.

And suddenly I was there—Gate 11. I stood at the door, wondering whether to knock or just open it. Just then it opened and a Donna Reed look-alike stood in front of me, beaming. She was wearing a light blue gingham dress with a big puffy skirt and a tight bodice. Over that she had a lacy white cotton half-apron, tied at the waist, that still accentuated the curves of her ample figure.

"Welcome," she said as she led me into a waiting room/dinette area, circa 1952. We sat down and she flipped through some index cards in a red tin recipe box.

"I'm here to help you with your menu for today. Now—group or one-on-one?" she said.

I looked at her, trying to adjust to the combination of homemaker and sex party organizer.

"Uh. What kind of group—I mean—who's here?"

She nodded briskly and flipped through her cards, all efficiency. "Today, we are expecting two gay men and one straight woman. And you are," again she flipped through her cards. "Bi. Correct? My records, I mean, my recipes show you're bisexual. Right?"

"Right."

"You know, you can start with group and go private, or vice versa," she said.

I was doing the math. Two gay men, plus one straight woman, plus me did not look promising. "I think I'll go with private today."

"Okey-dokey," Donna Reed said. Behind her were three doors. She led me to the middle one and opened it into a kitchen that was unlike any I had ever seen before. I felt my nipples get hard. The kitchen had a commercial stove, two Cuisinarts, a Magic Mixer, a blender, a coffee grinder, coffeemaker, slicer/dicer, juicer, toaster oven, and several other appliances I had never seen before. Seated at a round Formica table with a red marbleized pattern was a dark Cleopatra type wearing a black stretch lace bodysuit, a chef's hat, and high heels.

"This is Isis, your chef for today." Donna Reed left us in peace. I ran my hand along the miles-long countertop of the biggest kitchen island on the planet, eyeing Isis and making my way toward the Magic Mixer. Isis devoured me with her coal-black eyes.

"Wanna make a cake?" she purred.

"Yes, a cake," I said, running my hands along the Magic Mixer with desire.

"Lie down," she said.

"Where?" I asked demurely, staring at her nipples through the lace spandex.

"On the counter," she commanded. I felt my clit stand at attention. I jumped up on the counter and laid down, lickety-split (so to speak).

She unwrapped me slowly, like a Christmas present, unbuttoning my blouse and taking it off carefully, then my pants, socks, shoes. I was lying there on the cool tiled countertop in my bra and panties. I saw her open a drawer and get out a pair of kitchen shears.

"What—what are those for?" I gasped. I didn't sign up for that gate.

She calmly cut off my bra and threw it aside. I liked that bra but I didn't care, I wanted her to cut away anything that might stand between me, her, and the kitchen appliances in this room. She started in on my panties, cutting slowly and carefully. Then she slid the remnants all the way down my legs and off the edges of my toes. She licked my toes, briefly, with her snake tongue. She came up to my face and smiled, flicking her tongue around my mouth and between my lips quickly. I felt the heat in my face, the prickling in my nipples, and the slow hum in my clit that generally presages something good.

"Mmmm," Isis said, her voice like deep, dark honey. "Let's make a cake, baby."

I nodded my agreement.

"First," she said, "we need to *cream* the butter and sugar." I wanted to say I'm there, I'm creaming already, but by now the mechanism I normally use for forming words had become unhooked.

She reached into a cupboard below the counter and brought out the biggest brick of butter I had ever seen, and a jumbo size package of brown sugar. "I have everything at room temp," she said, in her phone-sex voice.

"Erg," I responded.

She unwrapped the butter and savagely jammed it in the Cuisinart. She turned the machine on and I felt the vibrations all through my body. My clitoris was buzzing right along with it, humming Broadway tunes, vibrating to the sound of the great cosmos, moving down the path of least resistance, finding the way to enlightenment, the Milky Way, the Cuisinart way.

"After I cream the butter in the Cuisinart I'm going to cream you," Isis whispered in my ear, lightly tonguing it for good measure, causing a few more jolts down to my nether regions. Then she slathered the creamed butter over my entire body. She made peaks of butter on my breasts, then pulled and twisted my nipples, kneading and turning and flicking them until I was moaning. I was a butterball, a butterfly, a butterdream, a butter slut. I was impatient and aching—down, down, down, you butter mistress you, I was thinking. As if she read my mind, she slid her tongue down my body and lazily circled my pussy.

"We need more butter for a really rich cake," she said in her Betty Crocker voice. She took another cube from the cabinet and rubbed it all around my labia, side to side to side, avoiding the main pleasure knob and *what was she doing?* she rammed the butter up inside me as she (finally) flicked her tongue on my clit. My body

took over, told my mind to shut up. I'm on my way, I'm on the
wild road, up the slope, on the plateau, rivers of honey are un-
leashed as I skate down toward paradise. But—wait—what was she
doing? Why was she stopping?

"No!" I protested.

"We haven't finished creaming yet," she said.

"I know, I know—keep going."

"No, I mean—for the cake," she said, and with that she dumped
a pile of brown sugar between my breasts and got on top of me. We
began seriously grinding against each other like it was the last time
we would ever be able to do this with anyone on this earth. The
sugar felt like sweet silken sand and her body was like a free gift, a
bonus, a mass of breasts and thighs and hips and curves. She was
like a voluptuous, vanilla-scented cat, humping and kneading and
purring and pressing, leading me toward—toward what? I still
wanted to get back to the creamery of the south, to her majestic
tongue and butterball technique. We rolled around on the gargan-
tuan kitchen island. I saw her chef's hat sail off her head.

Suddenly she pulled herself off me and stood beside the counter.
"And now we need to add the other ingredients," she announced,
all business. She placed her hand on the Magic Mixer and grinned
her wicked grin.

The Magic Mixer gleamed white and cool and hard. When I
looked at it my nipples tingled and my clit resonated with affirma-
tion.

"What are you going to do with that?" I asked.

"The Magic Mixer gives you what you want and need. Everything to bring you total satisfaction. So smooth, so cool, so powerful, the Magic Mixer can do anything! It's portable, it's powerful,
it's a woman's dream come true." With that, she lifted it off its base
and pressed a button. Cordless. It looked like no mixer I'd ever
seen. It had several rubberized beaters and each one had a different
shape. One was shaped like a finger, one like a small doughnut, one
like a cock, and one like a hand.

I closed my eyes and fell into a dreamy vibratory massage as she traversed every inch of my body with the Magic Mixer. When she moved down my aching form to my crotch I let out a sigh of relief. She snapped off the motor. Oh, not again. What was she doing now. I opened my eyes.

"Flour," she said. "We need flour and eggs to make a proper cake." Fuck the cake, I'm over the cake. She took out a giant package of flour and spilled it all over me. It was cool and silky. I looked at her. She had flour in her hair and on her nose. Her bodysuit was covered with butter and sugar and she looked good enough to eat.

I ran my hands down her body. "How long is this going to take?" I panted.

"We're still preheating the oven, baby, take your time," she said, and broke an egg onto my bellybutton, where it slid around until she spread the slick liquid north and south.

"One more crucial ingredient," she said. She got out a small pitcher and poured warm, melted chocolate over my coated body. She used her tongue to spread it around, then stuck her finger in the chocolate and into my mouth. I sucked the heavenly chocolate from her finger. Meanwhile, Clit Central was sending urgent radio messages. Preparing for Code O. Are you there? Are you coming?

Isis carefully wiped her hands clean on a towel and gently stuck a finger inside me. I gasped.

She pulled her finger out. "Actually, the oven is now preheated to the proper temperature. The time is right," she said.

"Yes, perfect, time is right," I agreed quickly.

Isis smiled impishly. Something told me she had other plans. "Turn over," she said. I complied. She coated my back body with batter until I felt as mixed as I could ever be.

Then I heard the motor of the Magic Mixer starting up again. My heart was pounding. She moved the many-fingered beast up and down, up and down. She ran it all around my butt cheeks and gently around the crack. I wanted to tell her I don't like that, stay away from there, but it was too late and I was too far gone. I felt her rubbing butter into my cheeks and crack and then her buttery finger slipping inside the opening. The vibration of the Magic Mixer resonated with her finger in such a way that all was forgotten in a haze of butterscotch delight.

Isis whispered in my ear, "Just relax. Tell me if you want me to stop doing anything." By now my mind was unhooked from any kind of instructional capability. Just keep making that cake, baby.

Again, as if she could read my mind, Isis asked me, "Ready to be baked?"

"Ready," I moaned.

She flipped me over, still with her butterfingers ensconced in my newly found pleasure center. Her tongue began its flicking dance on my clit, and yet another finger/apparatus—I didn't know *what* it was—entered my creamy tunnel. I lost track, my brain was mush, I was one mass of conflicting and colluding sensations—"too much, too much!" I wanted to say.

But I was heating up and congealing into something different—a something so sweet and formed and moist and light—I was—I realized, in a flash of enlightenment—I am—a cake! I am a cake! And then I came like a goddamn sunrise, like a Technicolor volcano, like a chocolate Disneyland.

Isis turned the motor off, her finger still inside me, and licked her lips as she smiled at me, with her butterscotch-flecked hair, and the flour on her nose. I lay there, registering little orgasmic aftershocks, my juices dripping on the counter.

Finally, I was still. I closed my eyes. It was quiet. Peaceful. I heard Isis moving around the kitchen. It sounded like she was getting something ready—if she had some other appliance for me, I didn't think I could take it. Soon I heard the sound of Mr. Coffee dripping and the rich dark roast smell entered my nostrils. Then I heard water sloshing. Water sloshing? I opened my eyes to Isis, standing close by, next to a big Japanese soaking tub. It looked inviting.

"Come on, get in."

She lowered my batter-coated body into the delicious warm water. She sponged me down, soaped and shampooed me, and poured buckets of water over me until I thought I'd died and gone to heaven.

I smelled something. Something different from coffee. Something sacred. I smelled—cake! I smelled chocolate cake!

She wrapped me in a big soft towel, dried me off, and put me in a black silk robe.

"Come," she said. The Formica table was set for two, with delicate china coffee cups and plates.

She opened the oven and pulled out the cake. It was a cake from the gods. It was beautiful, it was perfect. And—miraculously—it was already frosted! She sliced through the buttercream frosting and put big pieces of the deep, dark chocolate cake onto our plates.

We looked into each other's eyes as we simultaneously bit into the luscious cake. It melted in our mouths.

"Oh, Isis, you shouldn't have," I said.

She just smiled her trickster smile and purred, "My pleasure."

And I realized that—once in a while—you really *can* have your cake and eat it too.

# MERGERS AND ACQUISITIONS

Three months. Three long cruel months of migraine-inducing meetings and sleepless nights spent doing research. I don't know what compelled me to even agree to the madness in the first place. I take that back. I know exactly why I agreed. I did it for the recognition. I did it for the promotion. I did it for the money.

When I first started at Jones, Baker, and Kibblehouse five years ago in the Mergers and Acquisitions Department, I was the only black face anywhere in sight. Since then, a few others have started but none of them have attained my level of success.

When Charles Baker came to me and implored me to negotiate the merger with Hammonton Enterprises, my first reaction was to ask him if he had lost his damn mind. Once he assured me that a positive result would undoubtedly get me considered for the vice-president position in the department, my entire attitude changed. Michael Young had recently left to start his own e-commerce company, trying to get in on the Internet craze, so the position was wide open. Frankly, I felt I deserved it without having to prove my-self any further, but you can't knock the hustle, so I accepted the challenge.

I knew the merger wouldn't be easy. Roy Hammonton was infamous for his shrewd business practices. The mere thought of losing the controlling reins of his corporation probably made him age ten years overnight. I spent five days reading articles and other readily available information about the man, determined to step into the initial meeting and tantalize him so much that he would hand over the keys to the kingdom without any drama. I should have known better.

As it turned out, Roy Hammonton wasn't the problem. His son Martin was the real thorn in my side. I despised him from the moment I laid eyes on him. He looked so sure of himself, so determined, so much like me. I don't like it when the playing field is even. If I can't win, then I don't want to play. That's the Lourdes Mitchell way.

The first meeting was horrid. I left the office that night and headed straight to the closest bar I could find. After four Cosmopolitans and far too many sick and totally unfunny jokes from the bartender, I dragged myself outside, took a cab, went home, and passed out as soon as my head hit the pillow.

I woke up the next morning rejuvenated, focused, and more determined than ever. I set my sights on Martin and learned everything from the name of his tailor to his favorite cologne. Not because I had a personal interest in him. I'm just an avid believer that one should always know the habits of one's enemies.

The second meeting a week later was just as bad, but I refused to turn to the bottle again. Instead, I went to the gym and took three cardio-karate classes in a row. I had to limp up out of that bitch, go home, and soak in a tub of ice water. After I got out of the tub, I called on the services of my former lover Dawson. He wasn't the best lover but he gave the most hellified massages. He came over and rubbed my ass to sleep.

Three months later the agony was still in full swing. Martin had taken over the negotiations completely. Charles and the rest of the people on my side had given up as well. It was down to the two of us. The stubborn ones.

★

"You do realize I'll never agree to these terms?" he asked me, pacing around the conference room table for the fifty-eleventh time.

I decided to get up and stretch my legs as well. "I'll never agree to your terms either. They're ludicrous."

"I'm so sick of this."

I leered at him and issued a comeback. "I'm sick of you."

"This can't go on forever," he stated, as if I didn't already know that shit.

"Well then, agree to our terms so I can go home and get some sleep for a change."

He laughed at me, the bastard. "You really think I'm a fool, don't you?"

"If the shoe fits." I sat back down, took a manila folder off the increasingly larger stack, and opened it. "If you come down by 5 percent, I'll convince the partners to go for it."

"You need to stop taking those ginseng tablets, Lourdes," he responded. "They're clouding your common sense. Maybe if you come up 10 percent, we can do some business."

I don't like it when people, men in particular, try to step to me like that. "I don't need the ginseng tablets to realize that I'm more of a man than you'll ever be."

"But you're a woman."

"Exactly," I replied snidely. "I'm a woman and still more of a man than you'll ever be."

He sat down across from me at the table. "Let's cut the bullshit, why don't we?"

"I was never bullshitting, Martin. I sincerely hope you haven't been wasting my time with bullshit for the past three months."

He glanced down at his watch. "It's after eight. Want to grab some dinner?"

It was my time to laugh at him. "You're not seriously asking me to have dinner with you?"

"Why not? We both have to eat."

As much as I hated to admit it, my stomach had been belting out "The Battle Hymn of the Republic" for about an hour. "Okay, but on one condition."

"What's that?"

"I don't like—no, scratch that—I *refuse* to discuss business while I'm eating."

He stood up and started putting on his suit jacket. "Fine. We'll discuss something else then."

I put on my blazer and headed toward the door. "Fine by me."

Martin took me to the most elegant restaurant in town, Fratelli and Sons. I was shocked when they gave us a table without a reservation. I guess the Hammonton name still held a little clout. Once the waiter took our orders, Martin wasted no time getting into my business.

"So what's your real name?"

I almost choked on my cognac. "What do you mean by that?"

"You know good and damn well your name isn't Lourdes. Sounds like something you made up, probably in law school."

He grinned at me and I wanted to puke. Not because he wasn't attractive, because he was. Six-foot-two with caramel, smooth-as-a-baby's-ass skin, long curly eyelashes, and a cinematic smile. I wanted to puke because he read my ass like a book. Until I started Harvard Law, my name was Shanika Brown. I didn't think the name sounded professional so I legally changed it.

I tried to change the subject. "You're so damn arrogant."

"And you're so damn pretty."

I almost choked again. He was up to something and I didn't like it. The next sentence out of his mouth proved me right.

"Let's play a game, Lourdes."

I chuckled. "What type of game?"

"I intimidate you, don't I?" he asked confidently.

"Intimidate?" I adjusted the napkin in my lap and took another sip of my cognac. "Nothing and nobody ever intimidates me. I know I'm the shit, I've always been the shit, and I'm always going to be the shit."

He threw his head back in laughter. "Your conceit is somewhat attractive."

"I'm not conceited. I'm simply convinced."

He reached over that table and took my hand. "So convince me to come down by 5 percent."

I yanked my hand away. "That's what I've been trying to do for the last ninety days."

"Maybe you need to consider another approach," he stated sarcastically.

My curiosity was piqued. "Another approach like what?"

He looked at me seductively and the desire in his eyes was unmistakable, almost scary. "You said before that you're more of a man than I am. Well, I'm man enough to tell you I've wanted to take you to bed since day one. That's part of the reason I've let this whole thing drag out this long."

I was speechless. I was taken off guard. I was instantly wet.

"Everyone calls you the bitch in heels but I admire your determination and aggressiveness. It mirrors my own."

"Bitch in heels?" I giggled, trying to save face. "Sounds like some of those young bucks down in the trenches have a problem with a woman of authority."

"Forget them," he said, taking my hand again. "Let's talk about me and you. I'm wondering if a woman full of so much passion about her career is just as passionate in the bedroom. Are you?"

I yanked my hand away again. "None of your damn business, Martin Hammonton. Maybe this dinner wasn't such a good idea."

"Just like I figured. I intimidate the hell out of you."

I rolled my eyes and picked up a breadstick out of the basket, wondering how long my blackened chicken over fettuccine was going to take.

"Okay, Lourdes, if I don't intimidate you, prove it."

"I don't have to prove jack shit to you," I snarled back at him.

"What kind of panties are you wearing?"

I couldn't believe his audacity, even if it was turning me on. "What do my panties have to do with anything?"

"Tell me what kind," he insisted.

I decided what the hell and answered. "Red lace with a thong back."

"Damn!" he exclaimed. "I knew you were a sexy lingerie kind of woman."

"I just like to feel feminine, that's all."

"That's amazing, since you're more of a man than me."

We shared a good laugh.

"Maybe I was a bit out of line," I readily admitted. "I was just frustrated with your tactics."

"Let me see them."

"See what?"

"Your panties."

"Are you out of your damn . . ."

"Your food will be out in a few moments," our waiter said, preempting the rest of my sentence. "Can I get you another round of drinks while you're waiting?"

Martin answered, "No thanks."

The waiter walked away just as I was appreciating being saved by the bell.

"So let me see them."

"Do you really expect me to stand up and show you my panties?" I asked, stunned beyond disbelief.

"No. Take them off and give them to me."

Now, normally a woman would be highly offended by such a comment, but Shanika reared her freaky head and it was on.

"Fine," I said, getting up from the table. "I'll go to the ladies' lounge and remove them."

He pulled my arm. "No, do it right here."

"Right here?"

"Yes, sit down and take them off."

I sat back down and started surveying the situation. The restaurant was packed. It was dimly lit and a long white linen tablecloth covered our table. I inched my skirt up and shimmied out of my panties. I reached down, picked them up, and then slid them across the table beside his salad fork.

Martin held them up to his nose, whiffed them like they were roses, and then put them in his inside jacket pocket.

"Satisfied now?" I asked, proud of myself for proving that he didn't intimidate me.

"Not quite."

I frowned.

"Finger yourself."

"Excuse me?" I couldn't believe that he even went there. But once again, it was turning me on big-time.

"Finger yourself and then give me your hand."

I looked around and everyone appeared to be chowing down or engrossed in intimate conversation. I rubbed my clit with the forefinger of my left hand and then held it out to Martin. He drew my entire finger into his mouth, sucked on it like a vacuum, and then expressed his approval. "Very tasty. Just like I knew you would be."

I blushed. "You've really thought about it a lot, huh?"

"Every damn night." He flashed that cinematic smile at me and I melted like chocolate. "I have an idea. Why don't I just pay the bill so we can get out of here?"

"But we haven't eaten," I protested. "I'm starving."

"I'll feed you," he quickly replied. "We can feed each other."

Martin never gave me a chance to respond. He threw a fifty on top of the breadbasket, stood up, and pulled me up from the table. We walked out of the restaurant in silence. When we got out to the curb, through the picturesque window I saw our waiter standing in front of our table holding a tray of food.

Martin unlocked the car and opened the passenger-side door for me. As I watched him walk around the front of the car, I contemplated my next move. The repercussions of my impending actions on my career could be catastrophic. By the time he got in, I had made my final decision. I wanted the dick.

He turned on some jazz music and we engaged in minimal conversation for the next twenty minutes. The next thing I knew we were pulling up to the front gates of Broadmore Hills, the Hammontons' estate.

I was a nervous wreck. "I'm not sure this is such a good idea. I thought we were going someplace else. You live with your parents?"

"No," he chuckled. "I live in the guest cottage." He took ahold of my trembling hand. "Relax. No one is going to bother us."

Images of his father walking in on us while I had a mouthful of dick ran through my mind. "Are you sure?"

"I'm positive."

He pulled up to the guardhouse. I held my head down and curtained my face with my hand while the gigantic security gates rolled open. We drove up the long, winding driveway past the main house to the guest cottage in the rear.

I jumped out of the car and made a mad dash for the front door before Martin was even out of the car. "What's your rush? You don't have a key."

"I'm just ready to get inside."

"Do I sense some intimidation?" he chided.

I didn't respond. I just zeroed in on his key going into the lock. He couldn't get the door open fast enough for me.

"Come on in," he said after the door was open and the light in the foyer was switched on. "Make yourself at home."

I walked in and was completely in awe. His place was laid the hell out. Italian leather furniture, exquisite lamps, walls covered with originals from famous African-American artists like Wak and Vanderzee. What fascinated me the most was the greenhouse attached to the back of the cottage.

"You have a green thumb?" I asked in genuine shock. "You

don't seem like a plant enthusiast to me."

He looked offended. "It's relaxing. I need to do something peaceful after dealing with bitches in heels all day."

He laughed but I didn't see a damn thing funny. "You have one more time to call me out of my name."

"I have the feeling you get called out of your name a lot, *Lourdes*." The not-so-subtle reference to my name told me everything I needed to know. Martin had obviously done an equal amount of research on me and knew my birth name was Shanika.

I went out in the greenhouse to resist the urge to slap the shit out of him. He followed me and started giving me an express course on exotic plants from around the world, pointing them out individually and giving me a brief overview of their history.

I was beginning to think the desire he professed for me at the restaurant had subsided. Until . . .

He grabbed my breasts from behind and started grinding his dick on my ass. I turned around and grabbed him by the neck, pulling his face down to mine so I could explore his mouth with my tongue. I had subconsciously been yearning for that tongue action for months.

He picked me up and placed me on one of the wooden tables, knocking a couple of plants to the ground. I guess they weren't as rare as he claimed them to be. Either that or my pussy was a greater priority.

It was steamy and humid in the greenhouse, which only added to my intense horniness. He lifted the bottom of my dress up and took advantage of my easily accessible, already bare crotch. Before I knew it, he was eating the living daylights out of me.

I don't think I've ever cum so quick in my life, even when I've used my twelve-inch dildo. Damn, damn, damn! When I came, my feet hit something and we were bathed in warm water from the sprinkler system overhead. It was so incredible. It was so sensual.

Martin lifted me up in the air, my legs straddled around his shoulders and his head still buried between my thighs. He carried me back into his house and laid me down on a plush rug by the gas fireplace. He must've turned it on when I was already in the greenhouse. It was blazing when we came back in.

"I'll be right back," he whispered, getting up and heading into the kitchen.

I gazed into the flames and pondered over the situation. I knew I had absolutely no business there, but dick is like oxygen. You don't miss it until it's gone, and it had been out of my life for quite some time.

One thing was sure. Whatever was about to go down between Martin and me wouldn't be a one-shot deal. I think we both realized that. I wanted to confirm it, though.

When he returned from the kitchen, carrying a tray filled with a bowl of strawberries, a bottle of champagne, and two flutes, I asked him, "Where do you see this going?"

He sat the tray on the coffee table and joined me on the floor. I propped myself up on my elbows so I could stare him in the eyes. I like to read people's eyes. You can always tell if they're lying.

"Honestly?" he replied.

"Yes, honestly."

"Lourdes Mitchell or Shanika Brown or whomever you choose to be today, part of me hates the ground you walk on and the other part admires the hell out of you. All I really want is to see if you're as wild in the sack as you are out of the sack."

I took a restorative breath and searched for the right words to say. "So you know my real name?"

"Of course. You underestimated me and that was a mistake. I knew I would conquer you from the first day I stepped foot in Jones, Baker, and Kibblehouse and you smirked at me like you owned the world."

"Conquer me? Man, please! I'm doing you a favor by gracing you with my presence. Not the other way around."

Martin took my hand and kissed it. "So, are you staying or going?"

"This is crazy," I blurted out. "We can't."

"Why can't we?" Martin started pulling my damp dress up over my head and I didn't resist. "Give me one logical reason why we can't be together tonight and start arguing over the merger again tomorrow."

"Like it never happened?" I asked.

He unbuttoned his shirt and let it fall off of his shoulders while he undid the buttons on his sleeves. "Yes, like it never happened."

"Listen, Martin. As long as you know this is just about sex, then . . ."

"Shhhhh," Martin whispered, covering my mouth with his index finger. "Don't say another word. Just fuck me. We'll worry about the repercussions tomorrow."

Martin slipped his tongue in my mouth. I could taste my essence on his tongue. That excited me and our kiss grew deeper until we were both moaning uncontrollably. We didn't come up for air for ten minutes.

Martin stood up and unzipped his pants. I got on my knees and helped him take them off. There it was, staring me right in the face. His dick was such a scrumptious-looking specimen.

I sucked on the head of it until he threw his head back in ecstasy. Then I went for it and deep-throated the entire thing. Even when he sat back down on the floor, I wouldn't release him from my oral stronghold. Not until he exploded in my mouth and gave me the liquid candy I'd been craving.

We smeared each other with the juice from the strawberries and took turns licking it off. I figured out he was ticklish and lingered around his belly button until he couldn't take it anymore.

I climbed on top of him and contracted my pussy muscles on the shaft of his dick, taking more and more of it in until I could feel his thighs slapping up against mine as I went up and down. He poured the chilled champagne down my back and it trickled down between my ass cheeks. We both came and took a little break, basking in the glow of the fire.

We took it to the bedroom and went at each other in several different positions until the sun peeked its head over the horizon the following morning.

Martin served me breakfast in bed. Turkey bacon, grits, and scrambled eggs. The only thing a man had ever served me for breakfast was a bowl of cold cereal. I ate every drop on my plate. I was still starving from the night before.

Martin asked me to join him in the shower and I eagerly complied. He had me place my foot on the rim of the tub and spread my pussy lips so he could eat me out under the steady stream of warm water. Then he had me face the wall so he could take me from behind. I came so hard that I cried. Nothing like that had ever happened to me before.

We spent the rest of the day in bed, getting to know each other in three ways: mentally, physically, and orally. We found out that we had a hell of a lot in common. Everything from our favorite foods to our favorite music to our favorite athletes. It was a match made in heaven—or hell, depending on how you looked at it.

Our intention was to just end it right there, to go back to being enemies. But things didn't turn out like that. The sex between us was so addictive that we both knew we couldn't let it go. We ended up fucking on the conference table just about every evening before walking out of there like we despised each other. It was adventurous at first, but both of us started craving the real thing. We needed to get the merger out of the way so we could have guilt-free sex.

Martin and I decided to get together his father and the partners from my corporation for a night of beer and karaoke. Somewhere between Charles singing "Bad to the Bone," and Mr. Hammonton singing "What's Going On," they came to an agreement on the merger all by themselves.

That let Martin and me off of the hook. We didn't want to look like coconspirators because we were sleeping together. Yes, the word got out big time. It was probably the biggest water-cooler story of the decade. It didn't matter though. We were proud to announce that we were together.

In fact, Martin and I did a little merger and acquisition of our own. We got married last fall and two months ago we acquired our beautiful son, Caleb. The most stressful situation of my life ended up netting me a vice presidency *and* the man of my dreams. What more could a sistah possibly ask for?

Scott

# SEMEN IN A BULLET

I first saw Hank the day he got to our unit at Fort Riley, Kansas. He was being initiated. My unit is made up of Rangers and Special Forces and infantry from the regular army. But it's basically a Ranger unit. It's not something they send just anybody to.

I was 175 pounds. Five eleven, blond, blue eyes. Very chiseled, very well defined. I was in good shape, especially after joining that unit.

I became the supply sergeant. I loved that position. It was a position of power. Everyone would come to me to get stuff.

Whenever we got new soldiers, we sent them through this initiation. Basically it was just doing push-ups, but vertically, with your feet up against the wall. Like a hand stand. The new guys would have to stay in that position for fifteen or twenty minutes, to the point where they would be crying because they were in such pain. The whole company would be standing around watching and yelling. It would be a frenzy. Like sharks on chum. They would descend on these new guys, trying to break them down, almost like basic training. They would rip people apart. They were nuts. They were Rangers.

Our unit would go out drinking together, all seventy of us. My sergeant was big on camaraderie. We fight together; we stick together. Do everything together. Usually we'd go out to a strip club. We'd all get drunk, and we'd come back together. One time in particular everybody actually fought. With fists. We weren't fighting because we hated each other; we were fighting because it was a fun thing to do. We were fighting in the parking lots, in the barracks. It was crazy. It was fun. People would get hurt, but nothing too serious.

I did really good because I ended up fighting a staff sergeant. He was a country boy. The biggest, dumbest Ranger in our unit. And I whipped him. For a couple of months that gave me even more power.

I don't think the group fighting was sexual, although if I was fighting with Hank it could be. We used to rough around a little bit. We had great foreplay.

We used to box. We had these boxing gloves, and Hank would hit me. Like five or six times before I could even hit him once. He had a lot of speed, but not a lot of wallop behind his punches. So the only way I'd be able to box him would be to put my head down, and I'd come charging in there and whack him one. I could send him across the room and end the fight with one punch, *if* I could get to him. I had to learn how to run in there and—WHACK!

So anyway, he was one of the three newbies being initiated that day. Hank was by far the one with the most endurance. You can't be the first one to give up, because that shows that you're weak and that you're not going to be able to hang. Hank was a pig-headed, wacko, wiry guy, so he was up there for quite a while. He put on a good show. But you could tell he was getting smoked.

The next time that I saw him he was in my supply room. My clerk was giving him all the Gore-Tex gear and other special stuff you get issued in that unit, things that they don't give the regular army troops.

Hank was kneeling, adjusting something on the floor. I walked up on him from behind. I was looking at the back of his neck, the form of his butt in the BDU (Battle Dress Uniform) pants, and his high-and-tight haircut. I was like, holy shit.

Hank was about five-foot-eight, 160 pounds. He wasn't especially muscular, but he was toned. Just my type. A beautiful man. He was twenty-two. I was about the same. And he had this wonderful North Carolina drawl.

He was sweating; once again they were giving him a hard time because he was new. Right away I wanted to make things better for him. I went to the first sergeant. I told him, "Give me a couple of these new guys. I got stuff I gotta move around. I'll keep 'em busy." I made it sound like I was gonna dog them. The first sergeant was all happy about that. So he gave me Hank and one of the other guys. I don't even remember who the other guy was.

I gave him a break. I told him, man, take it easy. Don't worry about this. I'll keep you here as long as I can. He was very thankful. Both of them were. And then of course I had them do little jobs. But basically it was me just talking to Hank, finding out who he was, where he was from. So, I started to protect him immediately, and I befriended him.

One night we were getting trashed in my room. I was in a three-man room. Me, a specialist, and a PFC. The specialist was my clerk and he was already asleep. I don't remember if the PFC was there or not. We had the room cordoned off into three sections. It was pretty private. The wall lockers made it so that you couldn't see into my space.

We were pretty well lit. Hank liked to inhale aerosol cleaning stuff. He would get high from that. We would sit there and drink beer, and he would do this aerosol shit.

I had some blank greeting cards. One of them had a puppy dog on it. I can't remember what it said. Something mushy. Hank could tell that something was up. I could see that he was getting a little uneasy. I handed him the card. He asked me, "Do you want to give me this card?"

Just like that, a direct question. I was overwhelmed. I said, "Yes." He told me he was straight; he wasn't into that. I practically begged him to let me touch his face. Just let me touch him. And he did. I caressed the side of his face. He grabbed my hand. He pulled it down and put it right on his dick. He had this humongous hard on.

He never touched my dick, so sexually, it was pretty one-sided. But I didn't just give him a blow job. We made out. We were hugging and kissing. Hank's a great kisser.

The next day, he was standoffish. He didn't want to talk about it. It was like it never happened. But after a couple of days, he came to my room after PT (physical training). And it happened again.

It became a pretty regular thing. In the morning we'd go out and do our runs. We'd end up back at the unit. Hank would be all sweaty in the little gray army shorts and T-shirt. It would sexually arouse me, and I'd blow him.

Eventually he moved into my room. With me and my supply clerk Eric.

Eric was a bum. He was out of shape. He was a big dopey boy from Oregon. He had his hang-ups too. He liked to rough women up. He had fantasies about raping them. He talked to me for long hours at night about that. And he knew that I was gay. He liked to play psychoanalyst with me. I'd talk to him about being gay, and he was cool with it, and he'd talk to me about his rape shit. I wasn't too cool with that, but I dealt with it.

There was another soldier that was a friend of ours. He was from the Bronx. Little short guy. And he liked Jimi Hendrix. Hank was sitting on a bean-bag chair. I was sitting on my bed, and we were listening to this music. And all of a sudden, this other guy jumped up to get some other CD from his room. He lived right down the hallway. The second he left I dropped down on the floor and, without even asking Hank, I started blowing him. Hank was sitting on this bean-bag chair, with his hands up in the air, looking at me in disbelief. "What the hell are you doing? He's gonna be right back! He's gonna catch us!" And I was like, shut the fuck up. I went back to sucking him. He said, "You better hurry."

It had to have been under a minute. He came, pulled his pants up, and in walked the other guy. It was like this thrill that we might get caught.

Hank got an apartment. He was getting married to a German woman he'd met when he was stationed over there, before he got to Kansas.

I ended up moving in with him and his fiancée. They had a two-bedroom trailer. I got one room, and they had the big room at the end. If Gerta wasn't putting out for Hank, Hank would come to me. I would either be angry as hell because she had him, or he would come in and visit me.

She wouldn't blow him.

I remember one time she was in the living room with the baby. He called me into their bedroom. He laid down on his bed, and he pulled down his pants. I was looking through the crack in the door down the hallway and there she was. I could *see* her! I was like, oh my God, I can't believe we're doing this. But did I care? Fuck no. So many times I'd been sitting in my bed thinking about him, or listening to them fucking. No, I got right down on that boy.

We never got caught in the barracks, and we never got caught by her, but we did get caught.

Hank and I got sent to Saudi Arabia for Operation Desert Storm.

On January 16, 1991, we were staying in Khobar Towers when the first SCUD missile that was fired into Saudi Arabia blew up approximately 500 meters from us. It was a very scary day.

For the rest of the war, we were pretty far away from the fighting. Our mission was to send out teams of six or seven soldiers behind enemy lines to report back to division headquarters on whatever they could find out about troop movements. So, because

Hank and I weren't part of the crews that went on the actual missions, we were right there with the division general almost the whole time.

After we'd been over there a few months, I had my sister send a package from the States to make Hank happy. It made a lot of guys happy. I had two large bottles of mouthwash. One of them was rum and the other was vodka, with green food coloring added to make it look like Scope. We had gone at least two months without any alcohol, so it was a very welcome package. I shared it with a select few.

Somehow, the marijuana got through too. Hank liked to smoke pot. I ended up getting a good little quantity. It got a bunch of us stoned, more than once.

One of the times we left our base camp for a walk. It was probably about ten of us from the unit. And about a mile away there was a berm, a buildup of sand made for an encampment. Nobody was in it at the time. We all got stoned there, Hank included. And we drank some of the alcohol. We were all so lit that, walking back from this berm, we ended up all over the frigging desert. Picture this little gaggle of enlisted soldiers, bouncing into each other at one point, and then a few minutes later almost a quarter mile apart, then back again. Like an accordion.

Back at our encampment we were all shot. Everybody went their own way. Me and Hank were sitting on some sandbags outside our tent. Hank was so lit, he fell backwards off of the sandbag. I started touching him.

"No, no, no. I wanna go to bed."

I didn't want him to go in the tent. But he elected to go in anyway, so I followed him.

So there we were, fucked up off our gourds, walking into this GP medium tent that a staff sergeant, a specialist, and some other corporals were all sleeping in. There were probably eight to ten cots. Two of those bunks were mine and Hank's. Hank had mosquito netting over his cot.

Hank got into his bunk. I was sitting on the floor beside him, looking up at him. He'd taken off his pants and was in his underwear. I wanted him in a big way. I raised up the net and started caressing him. He grabbed my head and pushed me forcefully into him. I sort of giggled to myself, I was so fucked up. I started sucking on his dick. He got his hands around my head and forced it down my throat. But I couldn't stop giggling. All of a sudden he yelled out, "Suck my dick, bitch!"

"Shhh!" I got off his dick, whispering, "Hank, shut up!"

"Suck my dick *hard!*"

So needless to say, I climbed my happy ass right the hell out of his netting and went over to my bunk, because Hank was obviously bugging out.

Nobody ever said anything about that night to me. At least not directly. For one thing, I was not a pushover. From all the fighting and stuff, everybody knew that I was formidable. And there was the power that I had there because of my job. Everybody needed me to supply them. I was like frigging Klinger from *M\*A\*S\*H*. I would get shit from all over the place. I had eleven cases of soda in front of every tent in my unit when other units couldn't even get one soda.

But they did make a few comments to Hank. The next day everybody was playing volleyball. Hank was sitting on the sidelines; he didn't want to play. I was off somewhere else. Somebody started dogging Hank for not playing. Then somebody else said, "No, he'd rather go play with his *boyfriend.*" Everybody who was in our tent laughed. But that was pretty much the extent of it.

Like I said, from the minute I first saw Hank I was protecting him.

I don't think these guys were more tolerant because of the war. Because I think they were pretty tolerant back in the unit also. I think everybody knew. I couldn't have hid the fact that I was head-over-heels in love with Hank. Maybe the Rangers are more tolerant of that kind of thing because they bond more than other army guys. Like I said, everything in that unit was buddies. You had a buddy, and you took care of that fucking buddy. But I don't know if there was any other homosexuality in that unit.

After the war, I went back to the trailer with Hank and his wife, but only for a little while. My enlistment was up. I was getting out of the army.

My last night in Kansas, I was lying in bed. In came Hank, unannounced and unprovoked. He told me, "This one's for you." The next thing I knew he was on top of me, making out with *me*.

He actually blew me. And fucked me. It was wonderful. It was so wonderful that it was overwhelming; I could hardly comprehend that it was happening.

By the way, Hank had to have had a nine-inch dick. It was thick. He had big nuts, too. And a beautiful tight ass.

Whenever Hank came, after he was done ejaculating, he would have like a remnant left that you could actually pull out of his dick. Like fishing line. I can't remember how long it was, but it was amazing. It was a solid piece of orgasm. It was a hardened piece of come that was fresh.

One time I put it into a 22 shell casing. I don't remember exactly why I did that. I guess it was a "I'm gonna save his come forever" thing. It dried up, but it stayed there. It stayed solid. I held on to it for quite some period of time.

# Jill Soloway

# COURTENEY COX'S ASSHOLE

I can't come anymore.

I also can't stand my pink nail polish. It's called Baby. I got it at the Vietnamese place, Crazy Lady Nails, but it's fuckin' frosty and I hate fuckin' frosty. I also hate when I get the ugly old lady manicurist. It's bad enough to pay someone to work their hands through the vile parts of your feet. At least if she's young you can pretend she's your Asian bi-curious girlfriend.

I used to be able to come. I figured out how when I was eighteen, in the bathtub, under running water, and that was that. Then I went out with Adam somebody Jew in college for like, ever, and we lived in the patchouli-and-lentil-scented hippie co-op and made love on his futon every day, right after Food Science 134. But he was a big believer in feminism and all soft in the middle, so I never really got turned on when we'd do it. He did have a nice rag wool sweater though.

That's when I started making up these stories in my head, like little index cards I could flip through until I found one that would make me come. You know, your grade school principal is taking pictures of the whole thing for the Internet, or there's a hundred fat Armenian men watching. The usual stuff.

It's very common. My friend Donna Lazarus has to think of being tied to a tree and she's the daughter of a slave owner and a big oily naked black man is doing her and her dad is running toward them to capture the slave, but the slave is so turned on that fucking her is even more important than his freedom. I forget what else, something involving a woman in a kerchief yelling about cornbread burning on the stove.

Anyway, the second I was out the door from the manicure place, I drove home, rubbed the polish off with remover, and checked my voice mail. There were four messages about Courteney Cox's asshole.

I'm Courteney Cox's personal assistant. Or I guess I should say Courteney Cox-Arquette. That's all I've been doing lately, trying to get her stationery and rubber stamps caught up with her recent fabulous wedding and new name. She totally freaks when a piece of mail comes marked to Courteney Cox instead of Courteney Cox-Arquette, like it's my fault, and didn't I send these people godforsaken change of address cards. I tried to explain to her about mailing lists, how they grow and snake through computers all over the world. But she just cries and cries.

Anyway, she's out of town at this retreat called Tree of Life where, for twenty thousand dollars, you totally definitely for sure get to see God. They also give you enemas. So I was finally supposed to get a little me-time, but now this whole ass debacle has taken over. I don't know how it started, but there's a rumor going around Hollywood that Courteney Cox bleaches her asshole.

Let me clarify. The idea is that she goes to some Russki waxing bitch in Beverly Hills, and they swab bleach on the tiny, puckered door to her back room, and slowly, the skin there turns a delightful light pink, like the girls in the magazines, instead of doo-doo brown, as most assholes are, from years of misuse. Something tells me I could use a good bleaching myself. Luckily, I'm not that kind of person.

Anyway, the phone calls are beyond insane. *The Enquirer, The Star, Cosmopolitan.* They all want to know where this thing can be done, if it's safe, and if it's fair to attribute it to Courteney the way the landing-strip bikini wax has always been Pamela Lee's. I guess genital grooming trends need a star's endorsement if they're really gonna take off.

Now normally, I don't deal with press. I'm usually all about dry cleaning drop-offs, or I go to Neddy Crocker, the guy who bakes marijuana cookies, and pick up three dozen for David, who is basically high from the second he wakes up. I even know for a fact that sometimes he gets up in the middle of the night for a bong hit. Courteney told me once when she couldn't find anyone else to talk to.

Courteney's PR lady, who usually would deal with this, went to Guangzhou to buy a Chinese daughter. I tried to call her to find out what I'm supposed to say to the press, but it's like they don't have phones there or something. So I have to wait till she comes back. Courteney told me they kill girl babies in China. So they're pretty easy to adopt. That thought should depress me, but it doesn't. That depresses me.

Plus the whole thing about not coming.

Anyway, I'm too fat to come in L.A. In any other city, I'd be fine, I might even be the pretty girl, but in L.A., I'm so huge I'm invisible. I'm only talking like ten pounds overweight, but standing next to Courteney, I'm the white Nell Carter. Seriously, I'm Florida Evans, and I'm just riddled with necks.

I mean, when I was only working for her part-time, I could come and come aplenty, but ever since I went full-time and the ass issue ensued, it's like, *nada.* It's like I'm all out of Rolodex cards. I keep trying to use the old ones from before, but none of them work. Even the people in my fantasies look bored. All the fat Armenian men just shrug at me (eh), their soft cocks all in a row.

It's been two months and I still haven't had an orgasm. Courteney came back and she didn't find God. She did have a three-day-long diarrhea bout because she had written tofu-intolerant on her intake card but they got her confused with Lara Flynn Boyle, who happened to be there the same week and has a wicked egg allergy. So now Courteney's suing the Tree of Life and she's got me on the Internet looking for people who were burned by Coyote, the charismatic culty dude who runs the place.

I found a lady in Pacoima who says that when Coyote was a literary agent and his name was Marc Weinrib, he had sex with her twelve-year-old daughter. But that's all there was. Courteney yelled at me and told me I should learn how to use the Internet. I told her I would go to the library.

Instead, I went to Fancy Lady Nails and chose Bubble, but it was way too magenta. I'm all about a trend, but please, the '80s? I mean, Hall and Oates? "Maneater"?

After the manicure, I bought remover and cotton balls and wiped everything off in my car. Then I went to my twelve-step meeting for celebrity personal assistants. Step one is admitting to yourself that you are powerless over your celebrity.

I met a guy there. His name is Grant and he's Jackie the Joke Man's West Coast assistant. After the meeting we went out for Iced Blendeds. He told me he'd been thinking about what my pussy tasted like ever since I shared on the topic of shanger during the meeting. For those who've never been to a Personal Assistants in Recovery meeting, shanger is that nasty place between shame and anger.

So he said that thing at the Coffee Bean and then we were in his West Hollywood studio in like, minutes. I know you're supposed to make a guy wait, hell, get a real date out of him, maybe get a fucking balloon bouquet. Come to think of it he didn't even pay for my Ice Blended. But it didn't matter. I needed to touch some human flesh . . . and get my fingers through some of that crispy gel in his hair to break it up.

Before I knew it, I really got into it. Sure, I needed to supplement the action with some of my Rolodex cards. I stumbled upon one of my old classics—pretending in my head like it was the 1800s and women didn't have the right to vote. It usually worked wonders for me to concentrate on not voting and not being allowed to vote and listening to all the men talk about their votes and knowing I was too stupid to vote.

And then, Deedle-eedle-ee-ee-ee-ee.

It was the sound of my cell phone, Oriental, which I chose to be original, but then it turned out everyone in my peer group had programmed Oriental. I guess it's kind of zeitgeisty to think Orientals are funny. The same thing happened when I got an orange face for my phone. I had to go all the way back to the phone store the very next day and exchange it for kelly green. Oh no! I was thinking about the color of Nokia phone faces instead of my orgasm! Poor Grant was down there working away like a gopher and my brain had gotten away from me again.

"Just relax," Grant said, but his face was still in me, so I couldn't hear him, so I said, "What?" which is always a mood killer. That's one I gotta remember—never say "What?" during sex. Always better to guess wrong than to say "What?"

Grant kept going at it, but then Grant's phone rang, and without even looking up, he murmured "Fuckin' Joke Man" into my pussy. He pulled his Nokia out of his back pocket. Silver. How embarrassingly last year. He turned it off, but no matter. The incoming waves were now heading back out to sea.

I knew she was going to be mad, and boy, was I right. The second she heard the key in the door, she started yelling. It had something to do with, why did I have to pick the most expensive dry cleaner in the Palisades, and that if I was a decent assistant I would learn how to use the Dryel home dry cleaning system of products, and goddamn, it was written in the contract that I was only to use the downstairs guest bathroom, and that she knew I had been in her bathroom, because the toilet seat was still hot, and then she stormed out.

And in that moment, it was so clear that standing alone in her foyer, I spoke the words aloud: *I* am Courteney Cox's asshole.

It was time to leave. For good measure, I waited for David to get home, and let him fuck me from behind for like, fifteen minutes. He had been telling me forever that Courteney didn't like sex, and that he was so hot for me, and that if I would let him he'd love to ride me like a horse. This seemed as good a time as any.

I still didn't come. I mean, duh. When he was finished, he took a bong hit before he even pulled out. Then I went to Lovely Lady Nails. I picked out Cherries on Fire. It's like the color of the last day of your period.

Oh my God. I just found this. I can't believe who I was in L.A. I live in Eugene, Oregon, now. In Oregon I am pretty again. In Oregon I am considered on the slender side, even though I lost no weight.

In Oregon I met a man, a few days after getting here. His name is Frank Shankman and he's an industrial engineer.

I told him I hadn't had an orgasm in eight months, and he was happy to help me try. When we first had sex, I told him that I was imagining that he was some guy my parents left in charge of me, and I was like, fifteen, and they put all their trust in him, and so on, and blah blah.

Then he told me sh-sh-sh, and not to think of any stories and just to think about him loving me and see if I could come. So I tried and I tried not to think of any stories and just be. I tried so hard I turned myself inside out. Every time I almost came the orgasm ended up disappearing before I even got to it, like a bubble popping. He said we'd try again later. And we did. And finally, about a month later, I came.

I wish the end of this story could be that I came like a gentle flower, opening to the light of the love of Frank Shankman in a little green house in Eugene. But the end of the story is that I finally came up with a new one, starring Dennis Pickens, my high school gym teacher, and he's wearing gray polyester Sansabelt shorts and we're in the equipment closet and some cheerleader type accidentally walks in and just stands there and points, yelling, "Gross!"

I haven't told Frank that this is what I'm thinking about. I let him think it's love. I don't think it matters. And, oh yeah, this, too: In Oregon, I don't get my nails done. I do them myself, every so often, but most of the time, I just don't care.

# THE WORD NEBRASKA

The men in Vermont usually thought we were boys when they picked us up. A stone mason stopped for us on Route 5, a two-ton slab of marble in the back of his truck, the big wheels almost as tall as my chest. He was thin and dark, his torso covered by a bulky stained jacket, his hands so huge the steering wheel seemed to disappear between them. His eyes were dark brown, half hidden by heavy brows. I smelled tobacco and sweat when Jake opened the passenger door, but when we climbed into the cab of the truck he yelled, "Jesus fuck! You guys smell like shit; roll down the window!" as I extended my hand to him. The introduction froze on my lips. As the truck accelerated he said, "It's all right. I know what it's like. I started hitchhiking when I was fifteen. I didn't like riding the bus so that's how I got to school. I grew up around here, and after a while people start to get to know you and they don't mind picking you up. Then when I got out of school I didn't stop for a while. I went all the way to the West Coast." He stopped for a moment. "What are you guys doing?"

"We're going out west too," Jake said to him.

"There's nothing much out there. That's why I came back here.

I was tired of being broke, tired of having long hair, tired of being nobody. I guess I was still nobody for a few months even after I came back. I used to terrorize the cops here, come around the curves at seventy miles an hour, and then when one of them would get behind me and flash his lights, I'd speed up even more. I'd race the fucker until I was in New Hampshire and there was nothing he could do to me.

"I came back here because I knew someone who could teach me a trade, and I knew I could make a lot of money at it. I apprenticed for a few months laying brick and restoring old buildings, and then I went off on my own."

He talked about rocks for the next half hour like he was almost crazy. He talked about them like he was in love with them, pointing at old brick farmhouses as we passed by them, telling us how much money each would be worth. "You can charge a dollar apiece for vintage bricks and people will pay it," he said. "That old house over there's got at least a hundred thousand on it." I closed my eyes briefly and saw the building demolished, the burnt orange of the trees rising around nothing.

I noticed him looking at me closely as he talked, as if he were starting to sense that I wasn't a man. Did he notice the absence of a beard or Adam's apple? Was it something in the scent my body gave off, not as spicy and dark as his own? "I wanna pull over for a second and show you part of a wall I restored. I don't want you all getting nervous, it's just off the side of the road here." He pointed to a gravel parking lot and an old brick building. We got out of the truck and walked over to it, close enough so that he could lay his hands on the rough surface of the bricks. "I matched up bricks over here," he said. "Pulled out the old crumbling ones and replaced them. You can hardly tell, can you?" I noticed his fingers were long and thin, the knuckles brushed with hair. He touched the wall gingerly, as if feeling for the pulse of the person who had originally laid the brick.

After the stone mason dropped us off on the side of the road in Massachusetts, Jake and I talked about dragging him off into the woods, looking into his big brown eyes, and forcing him to suck both of our cocks, feeling his white teeth brush up against our pubic hair. It's funny how queerness seems to spread as our lovers take on other genders, how behaviors like sucking cock become desirable and transgressive. We talked about fucking his ass and leaving him in the dry leaves with his pants down around his boots. Maybe we thought about these things because we were terrified of being discovered, terrified of being beaten by small-town boys because we had pussies instead of dicks.

Jake collars me for the first time in a basement in Louisville, Kentucky. I am skeptical. "After I put this on you," he says to me, "I don't want you to make another sound." I face the gray basement wall and he steps behind me, so close that I can feel his broad chest pressing against my shoulder blades. He places the piece of leather across my throat, drawing it so tight against my trachea that it is a little difficult for me to breathe. I close my eyes as he puts it on, trying to process how I feel about it and what I think it means. He grabs my shoulders and turns me around to face him. "I'm going to tie you up now, darlin'," he breathes in my ear. He has a long length of white rope in his hand. He pulls my wrists behind my back and wraps rope around each of them separately, so that my forearms are tightly encased almost to my elbows. He ties a knot to draw my wrists together, and with the same piece of rope ties my feet. "I want to make sure you don't talk," he says, drawing a leather gag through my teeth. "Stand here and wait for me."

He starts walking up the stairs and I feel panic spread in my chest, tightening the ventricles of my heart, shrinking my lungs. My breath turns hot, as if I've inhaled glass. When he reaches the top of the stairs, he flicks off the light switch and I am left in darkness. My feet turn cold and then my shins. I discover that boredom is my greatest fear. I can hear him pacing upstairs and then I hear

the electric pop of the TV being turned on. White-hot anger flares
up in me. The cold spreads to my hands and then stops. I try to
move and I cannot. This is a curious feeling. I strain against the
ropes and they remain tight. I try to expel the gag from my mouth.
I stand for a few moments, long enough to forget that I cannot
walk, and almost fall over when I try. I discover I am terrified of
falling, terrified of what he would do to me if he found me lying on
the dirty concrete of the floor instead of standing.

After a while I feel myself becoming someone else. I am no
longer angry. I want him to come back. That desire shuts everything else up. I stop thinking about getting to the interstate the
next morning and the novel I'm writing. I stop thinking about myself. I think only about whether or not I will be able to do the
things he will demand of me.

Relief mixes with terror when I hear the heavy clunk of his
boots on the stairs again. The light flickers on and I discover I cannot look at him. He is tender when he comes to me, holding my
cheeks, whispering "honey" again and again softly. He removes the
gag and wipes away the drool that is running down my chin. He
kisses me slowly, his tongue filling up my mouth completely, my
face in his hands, his thumbs digging into my cheeks.

He breaks the kiss and sits down in a gray folding chair. He
says, "Come over here, honey." Ashamed, I hop clumsily to where
he sits. "Get down on your knees," he says in the same sweet voice.
He spreads his legs wide and I see the outline of his cock underneath the thick fabric of his work pants. I press my face into his
crotch, the spit from my open mouth staining his pants darker. He
grabs my hair and jerks my head back. "Don't fucking touch me
until I say you're allowed to." He slaps my face hard, the sting of it
spreading to my neck and lips. His gray eyes spark. "You fucking
bitch. If you want my cock so much, I'm gonna make you swallow
it." He unzips his pants and the big black dick he won in a drag
king contest spills out.

I turn into a faggot when I'm sucking his cock. I can envision my eyes closed, my cheeks hollowed out, the perfect curls of my lashes almost disappearing. I look sixteen, dark-haired, some young boy he's picked up off the street. I gag when he puts his dick in my mouth. This makes him impatient. He grabs my head in his big hands and thrusts his hips so that his cock is hitting the back of my throat. It slams into my throat until I finally open up and let it slide in toward my gut. He has his hands squeeze tighter at my temples to let me know I'm not getting away, that I'm not allowed to breathe until he's done. It becomes a meditation: sneaking in bits of air, finding a way to adjust to the thing that is filling up my mouth completely. I suck him off as hard and fast as I can, the muscles in my jaws and neck aching, the ligaments screaming. I lose who I am while I am doing this.

I come back to earth after he has pulled my head away. He zips his pants and stares at me. I'm still on my knees, the collar tight around my throat. "You're so fucking pretty," he says to me and takes out his knife. He bends down and cuts the rope off my ankles. "Get up," he says and leads me closer to one of the cinder block walls. He unbuttons my shirt, the knife clenched in his teeth. He pushes the cloth down to my tied wrists. They tingle with the motion. He rubs his dick against my ass and pushes my naked torso against the wall. My nipples and cheek grind against the rough block. He puts the knife against my throat and whispers again, "Don't make a sound." I feel his other hand loosening my belt and then my jeans drop down to my ankles. He touches my ass and his hand is slippery with grease. The knife presses tighter against my throat so that I am sure there must be a thin line of blood trickling down my throat and across my collarbone.

He presses the big dick against my asshole and I shudder; my body bucks against him. The cinder blocks tear at my nipples. He is rough with me, sliding the first half-inch into me viciously. It stops when it hits the tighter ring of muscle inside my ass. He moves his hips in short strokes against me, thrusting a little harder each time. He does this until he stretches out my asshole. I sense the rest of the dick before he puts it inside me, feel him drawing back before he slams into me. I feel like I am losing consciousness when I am being fucked in the ass, the pleasure so great that all I can do is open my throat and howl. I forget about the knife against my throat. He fucks me until my tits are bloody and I cannot speak.

The clouds in Nebraska almost made me believe in God again. Plains wide and endless, the skeletal bodies of electric windmills, the sky tumultuous and silver. The snow had almost stopped, a few dry flakes snaking across the asphalt. It must be wretched to live in the Midwest during the winter, I thought, cut off from the rest of the world, land fallow, crops plowed under. The clouds were as large as the earth.

Jake and I slept the night before not a hundred yards from the interstate in Des Moines, in a dry ditch covered with leaves. Tall reedy plants grew all around, stalks brown and thin as paper. We stamped out a place to lie down, hard winter stars sparkling above us. We lay half awake and freezing all night, until the sun began to turn the cloudy sky gray. I felt as if I'd never get warm again as we trudged up the on-ramp. Then a woman driving all the way to Denver pulled over and gave us a ride.

After a while landscape becomes conversation. Landscape becomes impetus and reason. It becomes home. Months before, we had stood on a bridge over the Penobscot River in Bangor, Maine, the clear sun creeping up toward noon, the town to the left of us, a conglomeration of church steeples, doorways, and streets. The view from the bridge was enough to justify every step I had taken in my life up to that moment, enough to make up for the hot sun, the highway police, the miles we had walked. New England is mountainous and complicated, Maine filled with people who have gray hands from fishing, from trying to support themselves in small towns with no economy. The silvery timber, Interstate 95 dark and silent but for the occasional roar of a semi, sea water slamming against beaten faces of rocks so hard that the foam surprised us, wet the lenses of our cameras, the cotton of our shirts—these things are a part of me now.

Cutting across these desolate landscapes, I began to remember the desires I had when I was twelve, I began to dig through the dark earth that existed before I became a teenager, before I turned twenty. I used to dream of being cut, of being beaten. I shoved ice cubes into my cunt on summer nights, tied my feet together and dreamt of being left for dead, made molds of my nipples with hot wax.

It was a surprise when these things began surfacing again, when Jake's touch suddenly made me drop to my knees and remember all of the things I used to be. Dreams of stalking through Egyptian tombs, being buried in the hot sand, picking my way through the jagged tops of mountains.

My head is clear when he beats me. Fear supersedes everything else. I sink into myself, dig through layers until I hit bedrock, travel with the rush that is flowing all through me until it emerges, rocket-like, from the side of the mountain. Ancient sediment blasts out over the road, and I remember a thousand things I thought I had forgotten.

Jake calls me from Texas after we stop traveling together. He calls me around midnight, his voice tremulous. "Hello," he says to me, half hoarse. The sound hangs in the air between us, passing over hundreds of miles of dark highway. There is no conversation for us to have. I close my eyes and see his body spread across the floor, breath ragged, hands splayed out against the carpet. Standing over him I feel that I am six and a half feet tall, the muscles in my arms and shoulders huge and full of venom, as if parts of me are ready to explode. I grab him by the scruff of his neck and pull him up on his knees, my forearm a thick bar across his chest, pressing against his collarbone. I take my dick out so that he can feel it between his thighs. He moans and arches toward me more. My arm slides up and presses against his neck. His throat caves in slightly and he goes limp against me, his labored breath becoming so loud that it clogs my hearing. We sink into this silence together; memories flash across our field of vision that we have never had before: ships sailing, the fear of falling off the edge of a flat world, discovery of new lands. I touch a space that exists in his chest only in these moments. It is just as wide as the plains in Nebraska.

When I let him go he falls back to the floor, his arms wrapped around his head and neck. I loosen my belt and fold the soft leather around my fist three times. The first blow is soft, hardly making a noise against his shoulder blades. I am careful to build the intensity of how I hit him, layering the blows to cover every inch of his wide shoulders. He is whining softly now, begging me to hit him harder. I want to hit him until I am hoarse, until my voice disappears, until there is nothing but sensation between us. I raise the belt high above my head and bring it whistling down. He screams and I hit him again and again. I follow the movements of his body and strike him in the places that sting the most. I watch his jaws clench and unclench, his eyes closed tightly. I can tell that he has reached a place of absolute trust, that he has given me the right to do anything to him that I want to with the faith that I will not ask too much. I hit him until I am exhausted, until his back is covered with splotches, until his shoulders are black and blue. I collapse onto him, unable to move.

I do not come to the sound of his voice and the insistent pressure of my finger on my clit. I am left full of desire for him; the thick timbre of his voice is not enough. I think of the places we passed through together, the valleys of Tennessee, the tenement buildings in Manhattan, how our bodies claimed these places and made them a part of our interior. I traced the contours of who I was becoming out of the negative space of what our bodies did. I think of this when I look at my hands, the blue veins raised under the skin and curving like the line of Route 5 across Vermont.

# JOHNNY

I first met Johnny Sisnowski at a transsexual pool party in Hadley, Massachusetts, three months after his surgery, twelve months into the change. I am not transitioning and I've never been what they call gender-ambiguous. I'm just a plain old gay man, born gay and male and no, I am not on a life journey to anything other than gay and male. I've never been fashionable or political, and up until that fated afternoon, the whole transsexual movement had just passed me by. While everybody else was busy rearranging their sexual proclivities or their sexual parts, I was just standing there in my tan Dockers and lace-ups looking for a good man to take me from behind.

When Johnny emerged from the pool that afternoon, his tan shoulders and long tan back glistening in the hot afternoon sun, a slick dome of blond hair dripping pool water across the patio, I just about dropped my spatula. A gorgeous boy with great biceps and a set of mysterious scars on his chest is not what I expected to find that afternoon. Johnny shook the water out of his hair, slipped on a pair of Buddy Holly glasses, pulled a bottle of beer from the cooler, and headed straight toward the grill. He stared down at the sizzling meat. The first thing Johnny said to me was that the sight of raw meat made him queasy.

"I love it," I said and I pressed the juice out of a turkey burger with my spatula. The coals flared and sizzled.

"I'm Greg," I said and I put out my hand.

Johnny shook it, despite the meat. "I'm an F to M," he said.

"A what?"

"A female-to-male." Johnny flashed a winning smile.

He wore the beach version of club-boy clothes: oversized red swim trunks and green goggles that hung loosely around his neck. He held a Corona in his cool, white hand.

"What are you?" he asked.

"Isn't it obvious?"

I stared up at him. His blond hair, slicked back against his scalp, softened as it dried.

"Nothing's obvious," he replied. "Not anymore."

I flicked ash from my Pall Mall into a can on the metal side table and prepared to flip the burgers. Johnny tapped his beer bottle against the side of the grill and stared into the red center of the coals. I was required to lean over him to reach the grill and as I did my face came close to those two scars—young and red—where, I realized, his breasts used to be. They shined up from his broad chest, resting like narrow crescent moons right under his pecs. It made my eyes burn to look at them.

"I'm a fag," I said, "and no offense, but I'm not into girls."

Johnny let out an audible sigh. "I'm not a girl."

"You were," I replied and I lit another cigarette off the burning ash of my last.

"My former gender is a subject we could debate for hours, but right now, here, this minute, I'm a guy. A 'he.' That's the pronoun you're looking for," Johnny said and he took another swig of his Corona.

I remained silent throughout this speech and tended to my

burgers, jogging the spatula up and down in my hand and watching the pink meat turn hard and white. Johnny waited for me to respond. When I didn't he asked me if I would care to see his license.

"It's proof that I'm legally male," Johnny said and he went for
his wallet.

I shook my head. "That won't prove anything. I know a guy
when I meet one; I can tell by the way they smell."

"You don't think I smell like a guy?" Johnny asked and he
stepped up to the grill. "Try me." His voice cracked. He held out
his wrist, nodding toward the upturned arm. "Smell."

I looked down at his arm, the blue veins threading out just under the smooth, tan skin. I turned away from Johnny and stared out
across the patio area. Our hostess, an aging drag queen in a blond
wig and an off-the-shoulder chiffon tea dress, lounged under a
moth-infested rose tree. She was engaged in what appeared to be a
rather deep conversation with a skinny, bearded guy who had huge
breasts. He wore a white shirt that read "boy-girl." It must have
been five in the afternoon. The party was winding down, and I was
late with the burgers.

"Bear with me," I said. "I'm new to this game. I don't even
know what I should call you."

"Why don't you try 'boy.' That's what I've been called all my
life," Johnny said, and he looked away from me.

I followed Johnny's gaze out over the little picket fence by the
garden off into the Holyoke Mountain range. The sun was setting,
and we watched the light fall in soft striations across those green
hills. Just then "boy-girl" handed his glasses to our hostess, pulled
off his T-shirt, stepped up to the pool, and launched into a perfect
dive. As his body cut through the water and disappeared beneath
that cool, aqua surface I turned back to Johnny.

"Kind of nuts, don't you think?" I asked.

"What?"

I gestured with my spatula, sweeping my arm around me. "This
party."

Johnny tilted his head to one side and blond hair fell across his tall forehead.

"Everybody gets all their sexual organs surgically rearranged," I took a long drag on my cigarette, "and then they come here and strip down and show them off all in the name of a good swim."

Johnny paused before answering me. He took a swig of beer. The evening light fell across his tanned shoulders and he looked away from me again.

"Why'd you come, then?" he asked.

"I'm supporting a friend."

"I'd hate to be your friend," he said and laughed a high, soft giggle.

I was not invited to the next transsexual pool party. I can't say that I was surprised, but I must admit that I was oddly disappointed to think that was the end of Johnny, the scarred, beautiful boy in the oversized red bathing trunks. But that was not the end.

Three months later I was in New York for the weekend, trawling the streets of Chelsea in my beat-up Honda Civic looking for a parking space, a futile endeavor. I was double-parked on Twenty-first near the corner of Eighth, and I'd just popped into Bendix for another coffee. When I came back out, there was Johnny in an Armani knockoff, a silver shirt, and matching silver tie, his tight little ass pressed up against my driver's-side door, arms folded across his chest. He looked different. And it was not just the clothes. In those three months he'd grown into his new manhood. He looked less like a petulant boy and more like a man, I thought. But I was damned if I was going to tell him that.

"Hey," I called as I approached the car.

"Don't worry," he said and he stepped toward me. "I know you. I mean, we've met before." He pointed at my Honda. "I recognized the car."

I looked down at his suit. "What happened to club-boy?"

"What?" he asked.

I waved my hand. "Never mind."

"I'm—"

I interrupted him. "Johnny. I remember."

I went to shake his hand and spilled coffee on him. He wiped it away. I said something about his new suit and then I apologized about the coffee, but he put out his hand and stopped me. He said it was nothing. Then we stood there and stared at each other. His hair was close cropped—somebody had been merciless with a razor around the ears and neck. His fingernails were buffed to a luminous shine. He nodded at me, asked what brought me to New York. I said business, which was a lie. Johnny slipped his hands into the pockets of those slim dark dress pants, rocked back on his heels, squinted up into the sun, and said he had best be on his way. He started to walk his brisk, hopping gait across Eighth. I called after him.

"You still a man?"

He stopped dead in the middle of the street, turned around. "You still a fag?"

His voice cracked. A cab rushed past, almost clipped him.

I waved him over. "Get in," I told him.

He practically leapt into the car. "Where we going?" he asked.

I had no idea, but I had been double-parked for half an hour; the cops were circling the block. I knew we had to go somewhere, so I turned over the engine and pulled out into the rush of traffic on Eighth Avenue. I looked over at Johnny, his long legs folded into the front passenger seat of my little Civic. His silver tie, catching the bright afternoon light, glowed along with that absurd silver shirt, as if his chest was made of some precious metal. I told him that it looked like he had got some sun and that it looked good on him. He blushed and even through that ruddy tone I could see the pink rising on his skin.

"I've been out west," he said.

"I see," I said. "Out. West."

We nodded. I glanced over at him as I drove and pressed my

hands into the wheel. A little dip in the center of Johnny's upper lip caused his mouth to look permanently pursed. It lent Johnny a pensive, altogether trusting air. I traced the line of his jaw with my eyes, and something on his chin caught my attention. There, collected on the tip, was a tiny, almost imperceptible patch of silky blond hairs.

"Looks like you missed a spot," I said.

"What?"

"Shaving. If you insist on being a man, you better learn how to use a razor."

Johnny rubbed his chin. "That's my goatee."

I never did find a parking place. In the end we sat in traffic for the entire afternoon. Johnny ducked into Le Gamin on Ninth and ordered us café au lait to go. We drank it and drove around. My hand brushed his thigh every time I downshifted. I don't remember everything Johnny and I talked about that day. I think I finally admitted I had come to town looking for action and he said I didn't seem like the type. But all that is immaterial. It was just a bunch of hot air and empty salutations, leading up to the moment when Johnny showed me the photograph. As we waited at a light in midtown, he pulled it out. I looked down at the small ten-year-old snapshot with beveled edges and a crease down its center, where it lay cupped in the palm of Johnny's hand, and I found myself staring into the face of a sixteen-year-old girl. Slim, busty, her long hair curled into a feathered flip that fell across her cheek and neck. I glanced up at Johnny and saw again the small wisps of hair curled around his narrow chin. Then I looked down into that smooth face, the salt shine on the hairless cheeks, and the slim, gorgeous legs on that California girl. Draping one muscled arm over the rim of her surfboard, she looked out at the camera. I am not a connoisseur of beautiful women, I'm not that kind of fag; but this girl, I knew, was stunning.

"You?" I asked.

"Not exactly."

"But it was you," I said.

Johnny did not reply.

"You were a knockout."

Johnny nodded. "36D."

"Why would you want to go and change?" I asked. "Why mess with perfection?"

Johnny looked out the window, rolled it down further, and pointed at a hot-dog stand. "You want a dog?" he asked. "I could pop out now and get us each one."

"Did I say the wrong thing?"

Johnny ignored me. "The way this light's going we'll be here for a while," he continued.

I knew then that I had just been given some sort of test and that, yet again, I had failed Johnny. The sky had shifted and the sun disappeared behind clouds, but still somehow his shirt glowed and Johnny in that impossible getup glowed right along with it, all silvery and bright.

"You're a beautiful man, too," I said.

Johnny looked out of the car. His long arm was draped over the lip of the door. "Not handsome?" he asked.

"Yeah. You're handsome," I said.

He looked over at me. "Now you're blushing."

I tapped his knee. "Go get us some hot dogs."

Johnny snapped the car door open and unfolded himself out onto the street. He left the photo on the dash. When he returned with two chili dogs I was still staring at it. Chili paste wound its way down his little finger. He held the dog out to me. I took it. The bun was warm and soft. Then I remembered something.

"I thought you were a vegetarian?"

Johnny bit through the skin of the dog. Steam curled out and fogged his glasses. "People change," he said. He grinned at me.

In the photo, an older woman stands on the girl's left, just on the edge of the shot, her hand on her hip, a camera slung over her shoulder. She wears a wide felt hat, patterned with red windmills.

"Who's that?" I asked.

"Her mother."

"She's not your mother, too?"

"Not according to her," Johnny said. He popped the end of his hot dog into his mouth and slapped out a quick, sharp rhythm on top of my glove compartment.

"She's a pretty woman."

"Yeah," Johnny said. "People say we look a lot alike."

Johnny had inherited her eyes. Wide-set, Slavic, with a slight blue cast to the whites, as if the definition between the iris and the white orb around it had been pierced, the boundary broken somehow and that dark, glowing blue melted out.

"They call them watershot, instead of bloodshot," Johnny said and he tucked the photo back into his pocket.

He began to talk about himself and I wanted to tell him that he shouldn't, that he was making a mistake, that I hardly knew him. I clearly didn't understand him, but something made me keep silent and listen. He was from L.A. A transplant, he said. He made a bad attempt at a joke, something about transcontinental and transsexual. It wasn't funny, but I laughed anyway. He grew up in a religious family close to the beach, and no, his parents hadn't accepted "the change." They still called him Jennifer, when they called at all. I put my hand on his wrist.

"Jennifer?" I said.

"Yes. That used to be my name."

He looked down at my hand. I moved it away.

I left him off near Penn Station around four and drove out of the city. I was tired of the traffic and the tall buildings, and somehow I had lost my desire to hook up. On the way home I stopped by Hammonasset State Park, just outside New Haven. I paid for a day-pass, even though the day was almost over, and walked the short path across the boardwalk and down the sand to the water's edge. The sky was shining and dull at the same moment, like hammered pewter. Cupping my hands around my eyes I blocked out the parking lot and the bathhouse and the beach walkers in their neon oranges and greens. All I could see in the round frame of my hands were the marshes, the hibiscus, and the goldenrod, fading down to the line of sand and finally to the dark swirl of ocean water. For a moment, that is all I wanted, just that blindered view of the world with its rosy fruit shuddering in the breeze. It was late in the season for swimming. I hated cold water, but that autumn day, the sun just setting, the wind whipping down the beach, biting into my cheeks, I stripped down to my boxers and walked in. The sand was pebbly and coarse under my feet. Cold flinders of water reached around the backs of my knees. I trembled at the water's edge for a while and then, finally, I dove.

It was not the West Coast. It was the wrong ocean. But I wanted somehow to enter that photo of Jennifer and her mother, to walk into Johnny's past and find him before the change. The worn elastic of my boxer shorts grew soft in the coming tide, and as I swam under the waves I thought of Johnny in the surf on the other shore, across the continent, a lifetime ago when he was more than just a boy; he was a boy in a girl's body. I thought of my own boyhood in that little walk-up apartment with my mother in Cleveland Heights. I had felt out of step with life as a child. Coming out had addressed some of that, but often I was overcome with the feeling that I would always be a castaway, adrift between two shores. That day I felt it again. There in my faded khakis and my pink oxford button-down on the streets of New York, yet again, The Next Big Thing had come along and I had thumbed my nose at it, I had let it pass me by. Under the water at Hammonasset I kept coming back to the moment when Johnny leaned forward and pulled himself out of the car. He turned back toward me for one moment, and touching his finger to his forehead, he saluted me. I wanted to stop him, to keep him there with me, but the only thing I could think to say was Why? Why did you show me the photo? Why trust me, the fool, the wallflower, the one who insulted you at the edge of the pool? I wanted to tell him to be more careful with his past. But he seemed fragile and untouchable at that moment, one eyebrow cocked, the light bouncing off those tan cheeks—as if, should I reach out for him, he would dissolve in my hands. Before I could decide what to do he turned around and walked away—just disappeared into the throng on Thirty-fourth Street. I leaned out of the car and watched his blond head grow smaller and smaller till I could no longer see it. For a second time that year I thought I had lost Johnny for good.

Then, in April, I came across him in a downtown restaurant, in New York—I don't recall the name of the place. This time I made the first move. He had changed again. Gone was the club-boy and the Armani-man. This time I found him in rumpled corduroys and a tweed jacket with elbow patches leaning against the bar, cupping a brandy snifter and chomping down on a pipe. I tiptoed up behind him.

"Professor," I whispered in his ear.

He started. "You must have me confused with someone—"

Then he turned and saw me. He took the pipe out of his mouth—I noticed it was unlit—he called my name and put his arms out for a hug. I walked into them.

"Nice pipe," I said.

"Oh, that," he sighed and slipped it into his pocket.

"How have you been, old man?" he asked and before I had a chance to answer, he flagged down a waiter and was arranging a table for us. "This place is a madhouse on Friday nights, but I know the maitre d'. He'll set us up with something."

A half-hour later he had us seated at a noisy table in the back. We were required to yell over the rattle of pots and the sizzle of oil as the noise of the kitchen wafted into our cramped corner of the dining room. We spent about an hour shouting into each other's ears before we gave up and quit the restaurant. When we got outside, the streets were wet. It had rained during dinner. The sidewalks shined. The air was heavy and sweet, and the smell of exhaust mixed with the scent of sugar-roasted nuts. I looked over at Johnny as he strolled down First Avenue like he had all the time in the world. He slipped his hands into the pockets of those wide-wale corduroys and said, "I've a party that I'm going to tonight. Perhaps you'd like to come along."

"A party?" I asked.

"Yes."

"What sort of party?"

"Come along and you'll find out," Johnny offered.

I agreed to accompany him. Johnny put his hand out and hailed a cab. We hopped in back, and before I knew it we were barreling along over a bridge at breakneck speed.

"It's in Brooklyn," Johnny said.

"I gathered," I replied. I pulled out my pack of cigarettes, then thought better of it and tucked them back into my jacket pocket.

"It's a bit out of the way, but really that's for the best," Johnny said, and I knew he was being cryptic on purpose. I refused to ask any more about this mysterious party. I sunk down into the black vinyl seat, let my head fall back, and stared out at the fog-covered sky.

Twenty minutes later the cab deposited us on a deserted street. It looked to me, from the decorations in the tiny run-down front yards, like a Portuguese neighborhood. The streets were completely dead, and there were no signs of a party. Johnny appeared unfazed by this. He walked up a few blocks, checked the street sign, and ducked down a side street. He waved me over.

"It's just around this corner."

He knocked on the door of a brownstone and a girl in a leather halter top appeared. She wore a pink party hat that frothed over with fuchsia ribbons. Besides that one spot of color, she was clad entirely in black—a half-rubber, half-leather getup with so many

straps and belts and hooks and laces I imagined it took her the better part of the week to get into it.

"Welcome to Chez Alice," she whispered in a low throaty voice
that was decidedly not her natural way of speaking. She took a better look at us, squealed and threw her arms around my companion.
"Johnny! It's you. You dog. Where have you been? We'd half given
up on you." She planted a kiss on his luminous cheek, pulled him
in, and then peered at his outfit. "What's with the Oxford getup?"
she asked. Then she stared down at me. "Who's this?" Her eyes nar-
rowed. "He's not on the guest list."

"It's okay, Paige," Johnny said. "He's with me."

Paige looked me up and down, from my faded Lee jeans to my
Swatch wristwatch. "Is he with you," she asked, looking deep into
Johnny's eyes, "or 'with' you?" As she said this she lifted her gloved
hands and drew quotation marks in the air in front of her bosom.

"We're all free agents here, aren't we, Paige?" Johnny quipped,
and the girl smiled, revealing a charming gap between her front
teeth.

We were ushered into a darkened living room. Every lamp in
the room—and there were many—was draped with scarves in deep
reds and oranges. Someone must have gone wild with a spray bottle
of patchouli, because the room reeked of it. In that half-light I
could just make out the silhouettes of couples, or sometimes
clutches of three or four. A bad, bootlegged copy of a Ziggy Stardust concert played in the background. On the couch writhed three
young things in dominatrix getups who seemed to get as much
pleasure out of the idea of all that moaning and panting as they did
out of each other. Besides Paige, I could not quite place the gender
of anyone in the room. I had figured out enough by now to know
that if you were looking obviously male, you probably hadn't been
for your whole life. The whole scene made me a bit dizzy, and I
leaned over to ask Johnny exactly what he thought he was doing
bringing me to such a place, but he was gone. I accepted a glass of
pink punch from a being in a red leather evening gown, pushed

aside the beaded curtains, and stepped deeper into the apartment, looking for Johnny.

I passed by a game of spin the bottle and stumbled through a room where a woman in a black teddy was fellating a dildoed girl in chaps. Johnny was not there. At this point I was not sure what solace, what island of safety or familiarity Johnny would provide, but I became desperate to find him. Finally, a mustachioed young man pointed his riding crop in the direction of the back stairs by the pantry and nodded. "Up there."

At the top of the stairs I found myself in a badly decorated bedroom. The bedspread, the curtains, the throw rug, the wallpaper— all of it was covered with enormous roses, close-ups of the buds just as they were about to burst open. Pretty tame stuff, but in these circumstances those roses with their overripe blooms, wet and bursting, took on a sinister quality. And in the midst of all this was Johnny, straddling a boy. He must have been about twenty-one, and he was almost as beautiful as Johnny. Dark and slim, he wore a pair of Levi's, red lipstick, and that's all. Johnny had a paddle in his right hand and was smacking this boy's upturned ass. Each time the paddle made contact with his ass, the boy shivered and squirmed. I watched the muscles of his abdomen ripple and shine in that half-light. Johnny grabbed the boy by the hair and pulled him back till his mouth was in reach of the boy's ear. He bent over and whispered something in that exposed ear, something that made the boy whimper and tremble. He kept whispering, and the boy nodded his head in tiny, bird-like bobs.

It was then that Johnny looked up and he saw me. For a moment our eyes met, and I felt the blood rush to my head. The scarf slipped off the lampshade, and suddenly Johnny's face and torso were washed in a dusty and speckled brightness. As he leaned over the boy, looking up at me, I swear he looked like he'd stepped out of a Vermeer painting—that same impassive look of concentration, that same intimate, unself-conscious absorption that makes you feel as if you are witnessing something very intimate, even if it's just water pouring out of a pitcher. Of course the difference was that I happened to be witnessing something genuinely private, or at least I had always thought of sex as a private act. I knew I should walk away, I should just turn tail and leave him, but I could not stop staring. I stumbled further into the room and leaned against a chair. Placing my hands on the back of it, I felt myself stiffen under the soft denim of my jeans. I was glad for the chair, that it hid the bottom half of me. On Johnny's flawless, impassive face, only his eyes moved, taking me in, up and down. He glanced down at the back of the chair and I think he knew what I was hiding, for at that moment the corners of his mouth tipped up, just a flicker. Then he returned to stroking that boy's white skin.

Perhaps it was just the scent of patchouli mixed with hair gel and gin, but the world began to dim for me at that moment, to shimmer and grow fuzzy around the edges. I felt faint. I tried to watch, to stay with it, as I knew Johnny wanted me to. With one arm Johnny shoved the boy down on the bed. His biceps flexed as he reached round, unbuttoned the boy's jeans, and pulled them down. Then he leaned over and kissed that white, upturned ass; and as he did, Johnny moved his hands to his own boxer shorts and unbuttoned them. As Johnny entered that boy, I imagined the long night of sedation when he crossed the ocean from girl to boy. And I thought, This is what Johnny wanted me to see: proof that he had reached the other shore.

As we left that party the next morning, Johnny, glistening with sweat, shivered as the cold air hit his wet skin. He tucked his chin into the collar of his corduroy blazer, and leaned in toward me. Just then I caught the scent of him: patchouli off the lamps had worked its way into his clothes and the tangy chemical-smell of that boy's makeup. But that wasn't what struck me. Under the perfume and the cosmetics I smelled the Pacific Ocean, and burning asphalt and a child running in the orange groves, the sun just setting, girls behind her calling out, *Boy, boy, dirty little boy,* the small hips tightening as Johnny ran and ran. I smelled the scent of dried sweat and fear. Of hiding. Of waiting. Searching for the shore, the sting of alcohol on his skin and, *It's only a pinprick.* I smelled the cool rush of the oxygen, the rubber mask, the scalpel shining in the antiseptic light, pressing in.

"Johnny," I whispered as we walked out into that cold morning, the dawn soaking up the night like a stain. "You smell like a man."

Paula Bomer

# FUCKING HIS WIFE, FOUR MONTHS PREGNANT WITH THEIR THIRD CHILD

After the kids pass out in their bunkbeds downstairs, *Good night, Tom, good night, Mike, sleep well, who loves you? Who loves you the most?* one more kiss, one more kiss, after they finish watching a sitcom on TV, after Sonia drinks that extra glass of wine, after Dick sips his scotch on ice, after they brush their teeth, relieve their bladders, and slide into the clean white, cotton sateen sheets Sonia put on that very morning, Dick leans into Sonia's face and kisses her. First he kisses her on the edge of her cheek, on the part of the cheek that is right next to her mouth. Then he moves in closer to her lips, touching the corner of her mouth with his mouth. She turns her face toward him now, in the dark, her eyes closed, and he leans his upper body over hers and turns his face so his nose won't get in the way and he pushes his mouth against hers and, open-mouthed, they kiss. Their tongues reach out and taste, and damn, if it doesn't taste good. Damn if it doesn't taste like warmth, like booze, and like that familiar flavor that is each other.

This is not a night when Dick will fart obscenely in bed next to her, pretending not to, and Sonia, despising him, will snap her magazine angrily into a perfect tent in front of her face. Nor is it a night, like so many nights just before this night, when Sonia, stinking of sweat from the summer heat, from the sweat of fear and the sharp stink of bile and vomit, is so disgusting, no not disgusting, so terrifying, terrifying in her foreignness, in her stink, in her pale, ugly, possum-in-a-trap look on her face, that Dick just wouldn't look at her. *I'm afraid! I'm afraid! I can't do this again!* her every movement said. She'd be folding laundry and she'd say something, *We're out of milk,* or *Tom skinned his knee today,* or something like that, and he'd look at her, catch her eyes, and her eyes were full of fear and sickness. Her jaw loose and weak. Her face bloated and sickly. Her tone insupportably whiny.

Those first three months are over. Those three months of hell, that first trimester of pregnancy when the only thing Dick could do to survive being in the house with her was to pretend she wasn't there. Gone is that horrible time. Done with it. She'd be there, and he'd pretend, just like he did as a child when his father was yelling, or his mother was yelling, that the person in question was not there. Dick's imagination is so powerful, and has always been so powerful, that he can play this trick very well. He draws a white chalk line around the person, just as if the person were dead, and then "poof!" he can no longer see them. They disappear.

But not tonight. Tonight he can't not see her. He couldn't, if he wanted to, which he doesn't, imagine her gone. Tonight he is mesmerized. Tonight he looked at her on the couch, lazing with him in front of the TV, and he saw a beautiful, young woman. The woman he fell in love with. He saw her as she was fifteen years ago, he saw her as no different than she was when she was barely twenty. And now, in their marriage bed, in her blue nightgown that he lifts over her head, he sees her and loves what he sees. The bones in her face are strong but womanly, her mouth is wet and inviting, her eyes are smart but slightly troubled, definitely knowing. Often thinking of something dirty. His wife is still his dirty-minded college girl. And this, in the dark now, now that she is over that first part of her pregnancy, now that she no longer repulses him, no longer hates him, now that she is resigned to her body and the strange creature inhabiting her, the stranger that neither of them have any idea who it will be, this bud of a person that he planted in her womb, now that this baby isn't torturing his wife anymore, now, now, she is so fuckable. Her skin seems powdered with stardust, it's *moist*, dammit, and sparkling at him he swears, and her eyes are wet like a healthy cat's, glowing at him in the dark, open now, looking at him while their tongues stroke the insides of their mouths like they've never tasted each other before.

How could kissing this woman be anything that ever happened again? After years of marriage, years of just fucking, not that anything's wrong with that, but years really where they would never, ever have kissed, preferring to get straight to the part that matters, kissing having bored them, kissing having been something of the past. Kissing not being on their minds, but they still needed to get off. His balls would fill. There's the nice lady next to him who empties them for him. He always felt gratitude, but he had stopped feeling wonder. Excitement. Urgency. Except during these precious months when she was pregnant with their first son. And their second son. And now, again, this gift. This time, this fleeting moment in their lives.

Here he is, his hands on her breasts which are so swollen, so sensitive she moans and pulls away slightly and he just can't believe these are his wife's tits because these were not his wife's tits a few months ago. His wife's tits a few months again were dried out, tired nipples that lay nearly flat against her ribcage. His wife's breasts, when she's not pregnant, were never as fleshy as her upper arms. It would be jangly arms and flat breasts. Now he can't even see her arms. His wife has breasts! Serious breasts. Not yet full of milk, but swollen and ready for what's to come. He has one in his hand and another in his mouth and she's shaking now, because all those hormones that are making her breasts grow into these beautiful flowers are making them raw with nerves. He has to be gentle. He doesn't want to be gentle, precisely because he must be in the

face of her painful, swollen breasts. He squeezes and sucks them
and she can't stay still, she's just squirming, he can tell it's uncomfortable, hears her breathe out the word *ouch,* and she puts her own
hand on them to protect herself, but also to feel them herself. Because these breasts are a gift from God, the God who gave humans
the ability to reproduce, and to feed their young. These tits are
blessed and she wants to hold them too.

He arches his entire body over her now, he's up on his knees, not
leaning his body on hers, no, he wants to see her, and he locks his
mouth on hers again and fuck, he's kissing his goddamn wife. He
wants to lick out the inside of her fucking throat. And then he puts
his finger in her pussy, just like that, and it's as warm and wet as
melted honey. He nearly comes right then. But he pulls away from
her and takes a deep breath. On his knees now he grabs his dick
hard and pushes at it. Down boy. Not yet. Breathe in, breathe out.
Oh, man. Her skinny legs are splayed out from the bowl of her
small hips, and in the dark he can just make out her glistening pu-
denda. Jesus. He can't look at it. He looks away. If he puts his dick
in there now, he'll just come right away and that is not what he
wants to do. But what else can he do now? He could eat her pussy,
but he doesn't really want to. It's about his dick tonight, about the
effect this bitch that is his wife is having on his dick. He could get
back on those tits, but he'll probably fucking come right away doing that, too. So what he does is turn her over and there's her ass,
which he loves, he loves his wife's ass. But it's calming him a bit, he
loves it but it's familiar, not strange and new like those breasts and
it's not her fucking wet pussy staring at him either, and he feels
calm. But oh God, she's lifting it up at him and there's no hiding
from what's underneath it. And so he leans over her to not look,
and, anyway, his dick has been safely calmed, it's still hard as rock,
but not as near to bursting, and he rubs it on her like a cat in heat
and then she's rubbing her ass back at him, her ass is asking him to
stick it in her, which he does—sticks it into her like a knife in butter—and he leans over her and takes each one of those breasts in his

hands. And then he grabs both breasts in one hand, smashing them together hard, and she lets out a short cry, and with his free hand he grabs her head and twists it around, back toward him, so that he can shove his tongue down her mouth again. Damn. Damn.

Oh, if his wife were always pregnant! Oh, if his wife were always four months, five months, even six months pregnant! Not one or two or three! And not seven or eight or nine! But that middle time, this middle time, how he loves her, how he can't believe it's her, how ripe she is, how womanly, how soft and precious and giving and forgiving she is! Oh, if she could only stay this fleshy, this wet, this ready. If only she were always in a dark room, if only her breasts were always like this in a dark room. Then, then his life would be perfect. His wife, locked away in a dark room, a room which only he had the key to, permanently four months pregnant.

This whole putting things off is not working. Or, rather, it is working and Dick has changed his mind. He turns her over again, and his wife's breasts flop around in a good way, move like Jell-O, loose and real, and there are her hip bones, her splayed legs, and he gently thumbs her clit but she pushes his hand off of her pussy and arches up to him, her own hands on her tits, moaning and he grips her hips and thrusts in there deep and he's just gonna come. It's just gonna happen. Her head is twisted to the side and her own hands smash her breasts together—they touch! They're so big they touch each other!—and he thrusts again but he's going to come and he can come inside her if he wants, she's already pregnant, it's not going to make her more pregnant, and he loves everything about this, the no condom, the no cervical cap which he used to bang up against, the no smelly spermicidal jelly, just the thick, tangy smell of his dick in her pussy and he can come inside her if he wants. But he wants to come on her face is what he wants and he hopes she's up for it, and really he knows she is because that's why he married her. Not because he needed someone to cook him dinner, not because he wanted her to raise his kids, mop his floors, and put his underwear in the dresser drawer. No, he married her because she's the kind of woman who likes to pretend she's a porn star. He wants to lift his dick out and hold it over those breasts and that's exactly what he does, his knees up near her armpits now and one hand is on his pulsing cock, and the other is grasping her round, fleshy breasts together, and he shoots out come all over her tussled, beautiful face, and her round, round breasts, banging his cock against one nipple, then her chin, tap, tap, tap, knocking out every last drop of himself onto her, his wife. And Dick is, in no small way, the happiest man on earth.

Dagoberto Gilb

# From "Snow,"

in *Woodcuts of Women*

She was so tall she looked across at him directly in the eyes and she thumped her big chest right into his. She liked his cowboy boots. Said she liked his worn black jeans and that he was wearing that ordinary sweater. She put her palms against the sweater, pressing. She was drunk. She liked cowboys, or Indians. Or was he Latin? She liked him, she whispered, groping his arms. Her gray eyes were diamonds, her hair a gold fiber, she was as real as a magazine cover girl, a makeup or underwear or negligee ad. If he was not drunk, if he was not stoned, then what? She told him about Memphis. She'd lived in Memphis most of her life except when she'd lived in San Antonio and Germany. She loved San Antonio and missed it. She asked, Do you believe me, dollboy? He felt the heat of the whispered word "dollboy" as it struck his cheeks, lipstick-ad plump lips smearing him until she shoved her tongue into his mouth. Her girlfriends were laughing at her and when she stopped, she laughed overdramatically with them. Come on! she told him, and she held his hand staggering out of Elaine's restaurant and they were in the back of a cab. Her legs were across his lap and she pulled his hand under her coat and blouse and onto the

241

crusty texture of her bra and while both her hands were on top of his, as though she were gasping for breath, she pushed his harder than he would have himself into her soft breasts, then pulled the bra above so that his fingers would strum her nipples.

Outside her apartment, under a darkened overhang at her building doorway, her leg was hooked around his so that she could rub against him, and her hand felt between his legs, tip to base. She was kissing his neck and he ran his hand on the wild curves of her impossibly perfect shape and though he was saying no he wanted to go up with her. How could he not but how could he, how could he, how this, now, her tongue licking his ears and neck, the smallest hairs tingling, him breathless. No, he kept telling himself. A couple of times he said, not very loud, no, he couldn't. He said it to himself and she didn't listen. Not out loud he told her about the pregnancy, love, children, and he was so afraid, and what would happen to him if this too? Not out loud he asked God what to do. Oh Mother of God, he said not out loud, and he saw Her, the Virgin, so beautiful, her eyes downward and shut, hands in prayer, those spikes of peaceful light warming and protecting her. Oh God, he said not out loud. She licked him. On the lips, on his nose, on his eyebrows, on his eyelids, rubbing his, rubbing hers against his thigh, his hand touching the skin of the tightest, smallest waist. Come upstairs and we'll take a bath, she said. Oh God no. No. When she heard him, she stopped, for that moment sober.

And there he was, back, lying on the futon, in the dark of the eighth-floor room. Calm had begun to drizzle like a light rain. He missed his family, a wife and children, as though that were his own childhood, those Christmases, *luminarias* and *tamales dulces* and toys that were so meaningful that morning, Mass and bells and incense, the warmth that is sitting on a porch, seeing Mexico on the horizon, none of it going to be the same again, and then he missed all the land. That grizzly bear standing on his hind legs across a wide river in Glacier. He took himself out to Hueco Tanks, the Apache

land outside El Paso, hiked up the rocks and sat where the always
cooling wind whisked and the clouds drew in the sky. It got so still
and quiet it made him see the plains in Wyoming, a herd of ante-
lope grazing, far enough away from him, not so far. It took him a
while to realize that he wasn't asleep, he wasn't dreaming. It was
quieter than Wyoming. He got up and went to the big window,
the one facing the buildings with column facades and fire-escape
stairs, and he looked down on Broadway. It was white, snow so
thick nothing passed, not a single car, van, or truck. Not even a
taxi. Not a person. Not a sound. Not a bus. She was going to have
a baby. Suddenly he saw a dog, an Irish setter, a leather leash hanging off its collar, leaping through the thick snow, hoops like
stitches in a white cloth, barking joyous, the only sound out there
now, barking, until in the frame, maybe ten feet behind the dog, a
young woman, a cap, a jacket, a sweater, gloves, boots, every color
that made him think of the sun, the West—green, red, yellow, orange, blue—chasing behind, losing ground, happy.

# Tsaurah Litzky

# END-OF-THE-
# WORLD SEX

My friend Carri tells me that since the disaster her Dom won't let her out of bed. The minute he gets home from work he grabs her. It was like a second honeymoon at first, she says, but now she is exhausted, worn out, her Jezebel always sore and aching. I tell her she is free to experiment with my collection of lubes, lately I hadn't had much use for them. She says thanks but she had better get her own.

I am yearning for some end-of-the-world sex but so far I have had no luck. The art dealer I picked up at the New Museum a week after the disaster had nimble, slender toreador hips. He looked like he could maneuver well in tight places but when we went back to his apartment he only wanted to do sixty-nine. I was bloated, swollen with sorrow and rage, all my juices bottled up inside me, and what I wanted was to be pierced, penetrated, and drained. I told him I have some wonderful lube with me, I got it in Amsterdam on the Street of Earthly Sorrows. He looked at me as if I had just told him I had an acrylic womb. "No way!" he says. "I know all about those lubes, they are full of estrogens, I've heard they can give a man breasts." I'm astounded at his ignorance. "You must be kidding," I say. "Very funny, ha, ha, ha." I didn't tell him that I think hermaphrodites are hot. If he had breasts it would make him really exciting to me, a lover for the new millennium. Instead I put my jacket back on and went out the door.

When I got home, I stripped, fell into bed, and slept. I dreamed of men with breasts and hermaphrodite sex. I mated with a hermaphrodite with many sets of arms like a Hindu god and two cocks, one between his legs and one growing from the center of his forehead. Eight, ten, twelve sets of hands caressed me while I held his two purple cocks in my hands and pulled at them rhythmically as if they were teats.

There is a homeless man who lives in a three-sided packing-crate house underneath the BQE overpass. I always see him when I am coming and going to the "A" train. He is heavyset and beneath his tattered sweaters it looks like he has breasts. Maybe he is a hermaphrodite. He often has his prick out and is stroking it with filthy hands. Everyone passes by, pretending not to notice. Since 9/11 I can't stop myself from glancing over. His tool is uncut, huge, the size of my forearm, he could spawn dynasties, propagate thousands. When I look over at his terrible, fleshy baton, I become excited. A warm, liquid lava bubbles between my legs. I wonder if this is my end-of-the-world sex.

The headlines become more bizarre, more sensational. Mayor Giuliani announces they have not found any bodies for five days but they are finding more and more body parts, scam artists try to sell families of the victims dirt from the site, Taliban are infiltrating our colleges, gas mask sales soar. . . . The Mayor says we should get back to normal, eat in our restaurants, take in movies, Broadway shows. When I go to teach my evening classes at the university in Greenwich Village, despite his urging, the restaurants are empty. The once bustling streets nearly deserted.

At night I keep having hermaphrodite dreams. One night there are two hermaphrodites in the dream. They both have long blond hair, obese, fleshy tits, and gray, squiggly cocks like silver corkscrews. One lies beneath me, one on top. I writhe frenzied, sandwiched between breasts and cocks. I come again and again, and when I wake up in the morning the sheets are wet, soaking. First I wonder if this means I will meet hermaphrodite twins, then I wonder if this new obsession is a kind of hysterical reaction to recent events, some kind of post-traumatic stress disorder. I have a dreadful compulsion to read all about the attacks. In the mornings I pull on some clothes right after waking, and go out and get the newspapers. When I open the downstairs door and step out into the streets, there is that now-familiar burnt charcoal smell in the air. Across the river the fire is still burning.

My nocturnal yearnings for a hermaphrodite continue to baffle me. I find myself undressing for bed earlier and earlier. Last night I was under the covers at a quarter past nine. This time I imagine a hermaphrodite who is little more than a boy, a delicate cocoa boy with moccacino skin, golden nappy hair, and eyes the color of honey; his tiny cock, not much bigger than a praline in my mouth, tastes of cinnamon. I had three fingers in the slit below his caramel bon-bons. He was suckling gently at one nipple while with his nimble, wee fingers he pulled playfully at my snatch. The phone rang. I didn't want to leave him so I let the machine take it. The voice of Steve Nicholson, a painter and one of my dearest friends, floats out into the room. He has decided to move back to his family farm in northern California. "My hands are always trembling," he said, "I'm too nervous to paint anymore, I sold my loft to Tony Bambini." I'm shocked, how will I cope without him? Now I jump up and grab the phone.

"Don't go," I say. "Who will I complain to?" "I have to get out of here," he says, "I'm terrified of more suicide bombers, toxic chemicals in the water supply, poison gas in the subway, anthrax. We can talk on the phone, e-mail." He wants to come over and bring me a small lamp I have always admired. He has painted a two-headed moose and a pine tree on the lampshade. "I just don't want you to leave," I say, "and I'm already in bed, but why don't we meet at the Right Bank Bar tomorrow night, I'll buy you a farewell drink, if you change your mind I'll buy you two drinks." "I won't change my mind but I'll meet you at nine o'clock," he says. When I go back to bed I find my little friend is still there waiting for me.

Steve is already sitting at the bar when I arrive. He looks like a lumberjack, a big guy who always wears plaid shirts and Levi's. The exquisite miniature landscapes he paints are a surprise. There is a brown box wrapped and tied with handles under his bar stool, which must be the lamp. His face just lights up when he sees me, there is a halo around his head, the air in the bar seems to be charged with electricity, I can hear it whiz around my head to the beat of "Jumpin' Jack Flash" on the jukebox. The bottles behind the bar are covered with precious gems, rubies, emeralds, sapphires. The mirror is one solid sheet of diamonds. The sudden sense of heightened awareness, this pseudo LSD glow, is what Virginia, the bartender, calls Twin Towers delirium tremens. She says everyone is getting them, they come and go.

"Well, if it's not Miss Dirty Stories of 2001," Steve calls out, his halo doubling in size. I sit down on the bar stool next to his. "Miss Dirty Stories doesn't have anything to write about, she's a fraud," I tell him. I met Steve ten years ago here at the bar. We got drunk on Wild Turkey and went off to his place to write a dirty story of our own. The geometry of his six-foot-five, 300-pound frame and my five-feet-tall frame did not compute. Skewered on his huge tool I felt like a tiny cock ring. I could not encompass him and kept sliding off. In the middle of what might have eventually been the act, we both started to laugh and couldn't stop. Then we decided to dress and go to Chinatown for a very, very early breakfast. Now we are great friends. We commiserate about the vicissitudes of our careers and our love affairs.

He pokes the box below his bar stool with his size fourteen foot.

"Every time you turn on this lamp, I hope you'll remember me," he says. "Yeah, I'll remember that when the going got tough, you ran away." The light goes out of his face and he looks sad. "Come on," he says, "give me a break, a lot of people are leaving. They don't want to raise their kids in the city." "But you don't have kids," I interject. "I am a kid," he answers. "Anyway, weren't you going to buy me a farewell drink?" "Yes," I say, and motion to Virginia. She is wearing a low-cut, red leotard top to show off the tattoo of a butterfly on her chest. "Our usual, two Cuervo Gold margaritas, straight up, no salt. And make them extra strong, I have the Tower tremens." "Who doesn't?" she answers, and then I say, "Can you believe this big oaf is leaving us?" "Yeah, I know, he told me," she answers. When she brings our drinks over and makes change from the twenty I put on the bar, she says, "The next one's on me."

Steve raises his glass and clinks it against mine. "To a better life," he says. "I hope so," I reply. "Besides it's gonzo crazy here," he adds, then he tells me about a big loft party he went to on Saturday night. It was mobbed, everyone was making out, people couldn't keep their hands off each other. "It was like one big, extended daisy chain," he says. "People were screwing on the couches, in the bathtub. There was a woman on her knees in one corner giving men blowjobs. Can you imagine? There was a long line in front of her." I ask him, "Did you go stand in line?" He doesn't answer, he hangs his head, maybe hoping I don't see that he is blushing. He changes the subject. "There was probably Viagra in the punch," he says. "Fear is a more powerful aphrodisiac," I state pompously, as if I'm an aphrodisiac expert. "You must be right," he says. "It's the end of the world, what else is there to do but have sex?"

Then I tell him about my hermaphrodite dreams and we finish our drinks. Steve motions Virginia to bring us another. "Maybe you should go to the Eulenspiegel Society," he says. "Make your dreams become a reality . . . I'll be in town till the end of next week, I'll go with you."

"You look like a CIA agent or an *übermensch* cop," I tell him.

"No one will come near us." "You're wrong," he says. "I'd be a big attraction, they'll be on me like flies on sugar. But right now, I have to see a princess about a frog, excuse me." He gets up and makes his way to the back of the room and the stairs that lead down to the bathrooms. I think about how I will miss him and suddenly feel like I'm going to cry. I pick up my drink and finish it in a great gulp. I make myself smile, I despise looking forlorn in public.

There are more people in the bar now. The tape is playing "Tumbling Tumbleweeds." The couple on the other side of me get up and leave as a little crowd of five or six people come in. They occupy the newly vacated seats next to me and the others stand behind them. It is a group of Virginia's friends. They are all tattooed and pierced. They have shaved heads or long dreadlocks, blue hair or mohawks, many visible piercings. One of the guys has silver studs shaped into a question mark on his cheek. They look like they are in some future world punk band. Actually they go to school with Virginia at the Columbia University School of Economics. The guy sitting right next to me is slim and rangy. His sleeveless leather vest shows off his lean, muscular arms, which are covered with blue tribal tattoos. He has a clean-cut, handsome face, a young Henry Fonda in *Grapes of Wrath*. His dark hair is shaved close to his skull, and there is a Coptic cross tattooed in the center of his forehead. Virginia once introduced us. His name is Hook, and we talked about how he is putting himself through school working for a silkscreen company. I wonder where Steve is and I look around. I see him at the back of the bar. A tall, elongated Giacometti woman with red hair to her waist is holding him by the arm and talking up at him . . . He looks over her head and catches my eye and smiles.

I turn my head and find Hook looking right at me. "Hi, aren't you the writer?" he says. "Yeah," I answer, "Guilty." "Virginia showed me your poetry book," he said. "It's great, not gender based, not that usual snobby feminist glob that goes on and on about the glory of pussy. You're way beyond that." He is obviously a very smart guy. He wants to know when my next poetry book is coming out. I tell him I've been working on a book of erotic stories for a year, that the only poem I have written in the last year was about the bombing.

"How does it go?" he asks. I tell him the first line, it's all I can remember: *Bitter ashes of sunset float down through the sky like dots in a comic* . . . "That's great. When do I get to hear the rest?" he asks, and I realize that he's coming on to me. At least he hasn't given me that terrible line, the one that will make me instantly reject him. He hasn't asked me if I like younger men. He offers to buy me another drink. I look back and see that Steve and the elongated redhead are kissing passionately in one of the booths. I accept the drink and start to flirt with him. We flirt through two more drinks and when he asks me to come home with him, I say yes.

Hook helps me on with my coat. I try to appear cool, nonchalant. I am breaking one of my own rules, one I have broken many times before: never go home with someone the first time they invite you. We walk down Bedford Avenue through a starless, cloudy night to Hook's apartment a few blocks away. I have forgotten the lamp but I don't care. Hook lives right above The Buzzards' Nest Bar, a notorious hangout for the local cops. "At least the building is safe," he says, grinning at me as he unlocks the door. The music from downstairs is so loud it's deafening. Strains of Frank Sinatra singing "New York, New York" float up through the floor. "That's all they play ever since it happened," he says. "It's driving me nuts." He ushers me in before him, shuts the door, and switches on the light. In the stark light of the single bulb, I see how thin he is, supple like a boy. His kitchen consists of an old stove and a table made out of a door and packing crates. On the wall above the table is a large blow-up news photo of the second plane hitting the south tower. Underneath the image, the words END OF THE WORLD OR BEGINNING OF A NEW WORLD ORDER are printed on the photo in red Magic Marker in large block letters. Hook sees me looking at it. "I'm working on a silkscreen of that," he says. There are stacks of

packing crates filled with books everywhere. "My castle," he says
deprecatingly, but I tell him I like it.

We just fall on to each other, start to kiss. Hungry, ravenous, we
suck each other in. Still kissing me, he walks me backwards
through the open door of his other room toward the bed. He puts
his hands inside the waistbands of my skirt and tights, and pulls
them down to my ankles. I step out of them and out of my clogs.
He unbuttons my cardigan sweater and slips it off down my arms.
His lips keep me occupied, his mouth is a loving cup that I am
drinking from. The bedroom window is open. I shiver in my bra
and panties even though a fire is building inside me. With one arm
he shuts the window, with the other he pushes me down almost
roughly on the bed. I watch him take off his boots, his jeans, and
his vest. I love his exotic markings, the blue wings on his back and
on the top of his chest, the many tribal bracelets he wears burned
into his arms. He is not wearing any underwear. His cock is very
long and thin, not pink at all, a startling white. I notice that he has
beautiful, large pink nipples. They look soft, fleshy, like the nipples
on a woman's breast. I want to nurse there. He steps back, mum-
bles something I can barely hear, then I make it out . . . "This is going to be good, I know this is going to be good" is what he seems
to be repeating like a mantra. In an attempt to calm him and reach
out to him, I ask him if he likes my underwear. I am wearing my
favorite matched set, black satin covered with red roses. "Yeah," he
says, barely glancing down. "What kind of flowers are those, carnations?" he asks. "Sure, right, carnations," I say, and I just grab his
hand and pull him down on top of me. His body is so light on
mine. The last time I found myself in bed with a man, he had a big
belly like a sumo wrestler. Hook and I begin to kiss again but now
he is more hesitant. We kiss for a long time. I'm getting wet, wet-
ter, juice running down my legs, but I don't feel his steel pressing
into my belly. I wonder if it's the extra ten pounds I'm wearing on
my thighs but he pulls his head up and says, "You're so beautiful. I
didn't think you would be so beautiful." I realize he is terrified. I

want him to ram his tongue so deep and hard into my mouth that my cervix opens up before it, and he is tonguing my labia from the top side but instead he pulls away . . . He seems to be weeping.

"I'm very sorry," he says. "I can't do this, usually I'm hard right away." "OK, don't feel bad, it's OK," I say. I put my arm around his shoulders. I pull him closer to me. He nuzzles my neck then rolls off of me onto his back. We lie there beside each other like two beached fish at Coney Island. I wonder if this has happened because we are strangers or because we don't love each other. I wonder if the disaster has rendered him impotent or if it was the three beers he drank as he sat with me at the bar. I wonder if it's my old nemesis, tried and true, the luck of the draw.

I glance over at him. His eyes are closed, the wing tattoos on his chest start just above his sternum. It looks as if he is wearing a dainty scarf, a mantilla of blue lace. His large nipples are bubble gum pink. I want to touch them, chew them, suck all the sugar out. First I lean over and kiss him briefly, sweetly on the lips. I stroke his limp cock, cradle it in my hands for a while. I learn the shape of it, stretching it in my hands, then I tuck it between his legs. He starts to mumble something, perhaps a protest, but I shut him up by putting my mouth right over his. I push my tongue deep inside then I pull it out. I push in again, fucking him with it. Then I take his wonderful nipples between my fingers and I tug at them until the tip of each nipple pops out and hardens like a little clit. Finally I put my mouth on his clit-nipple. The surrounding skin is soft and smooth like the skin inside my pussy. Hook must like what I'm doing because he is moving his body beneath me, rocking from side to side. I move my hands down below his hips, squeezing his legs shut tight. He is pinned under me now, pinned with my mouth at his breast, pinned by my two hands below his hips. I take my hands off the sides of his legs and put them together in a V. I press down on his new vulva. I rub it, press it, caress it just the way I like to have my crotch rubbed before I spread my legs wide. Hook is moving under me with such frenetic force that he throws me off but I'm not angry, I have moved into my dreams. He is my hermaphrodite, and he puts a hand out and touches my face. I kiss his wrist, his palm, the tops of his fingers, and then he opens his legs. There it is, in all its splendor, pointing straight up to the skies, white, solid as marble.

As I rise and straddle him, I feel very happy. He is still touching my face. His prick fills me up to the top, hooks me into the center of life. I'm so hot I think I must be burning him but he does not flinch. He moves, thrusting higher and higher into me as I open wider and wider until we are at ground zero. From my position astride him I can see through the bedroom door the picture of the jet hitting the second tower. I hear a distant sound, a great explosion, like worlds colliding. The walls of the room are shaking, the edges of the ceiling beginning to break apart. Just as I am coming, he comes too, exploding into me in a ball of fire, and we are both propelled up through the crumbling roof, up, up into the black skies, our bodies disintegrating, mixing with the clouds like ashes.

# READERS' CHOICE: THE TOP 100 OF THE PAST TEN YEARS

1  The Hit        Steven Saylor,
            writing as Aaron Travis, '96

This particular fantasy started with a movie I saw on late-night TV called *Murder by Contract,* made in 1958 and starring a very young, very hot Vince Edwards (later famous as TV's Ben Casey). A specific scene snagged my imagination, as Edwards's sullen, smoldering hit man verbally abused a cringing room-service waiter. That was the grain of sand that grew into the pearl—the old, frail waiter of the movie became nubile young Kip in my story, and Vince Edwards became Vince Zorio, the mobster—each playing a cat-and-mouse game that led to a conclusion that neither of them saw coming.

2  *The Fermata,* an excerpt   Nicholson Baker, '95

*The Fermata* was fun to write, and I knew as I was writing it that I was probably going to get skewered. That was part of the excitement. When the skewerage is actually going on, though, it can be unpleasant. Critic Michiko Kakutani said the book was "repulsive"—not a positive response—and then Victoria Glendinning ended her review with "Goodbye, Nicholson Baker, goodbye forever," which had a real slap of finality to it. Whatever I'd managed to do, *The Fermata* undid it, apparently. What to write next? A short story about potatoes gone wrong. Stick to what you know.

| | |
|---|---|
| 3  She Gets Her Ass Fucked Good | Rose White and Eric Albert, '97 |

The day my current boss hired me, he said, "Gee, it's not every day you see porn, crosswords, and Phi Beta Kappa on the same résumé!"—Rose White.

| | |
|---|---|
| 4  My Professor | Ivy Topiary, '97 |

| | |
|---|---|
| 5  Two Cars in a Cornfield | William Harrison, '00 |

All genres of mine are liberally peppered with sex. How else does one write about people?

| | |
|---|---|
| 6  Meow? | Shar Rednour, '96 |

| | |
|---|---|
| 7  The Perfect Fit | Katya Andreevna, '96 |

This was the first erotic story I ever wrote. I was sitting in my children's-book publishing office with no compelling work to do and joking around on the phone with [another *BAE* author] Mike Ford. He dared me to write one, and I did.

| | |
|---|---|
| 8  Pearl Diver | Cecilia Tan, '96 |

| | |
|---|---|
| 9  Cinnamon Roses | Renee Charles, '95 |

| | |
|---|---|
| 10  His Little Plan Backfired | Amelia Copeland, '96 |

| | |
|---|---|
| 11  The Case of the Demon Lover | Nancy Kilpatrick, '97 |

My best friends in high school had various bets as to whether I'd
live to be eighteen and then twenty-one. I guess, in a sense, I won
those, but I didn't get a cut of the purse.

Batman wasn't my first superhero crush. In sixth grade I won a bicycle from Kellogg's cereal for drawing a picture of me and Super-
man chowing down on Frosted Flakes.

My mom knew I'd had *something* published and that it was
reprinted in *BAE 1996*. She wanted to see it, but being a good
Southern woman, she didn't dare buy it at the local bookstore. Bear

in mind, this is the woman who convinced me to publish under a
pseudonym "so as not to embarrass the family name." I gave her a
copy on the sly. She disappeared into the boudoir for the rest of the
weekend and would periodically call my step-dad in to read with
her. I thought this was pretty funny, but my brother was thor-
oughly embarrassed.

| | |
|---|---|
| 24 Milk | Michael Dorsey, '93 |
| 25 Lunch | Mark Steurtz, '97 |
| 26 Mer | Francesca Lia Block, '02 |
| 27 *In the Cut*, an excerpt | Susanna Moore, '96 |
| 28 Thief of Cocks | Susannah Indigo, '00 |
| 29 The Man Who Ate Women | Damian Grace, '01 |
| 30 Innocence in Extremis | Debra Boxer, '00 |
| 31 *The Leather Daddy and The Femme*, an excerpt | Carol Queen, '00 |
| 32 How to Come on a Bus | Anne Tourney, '99 |
| 33 Jack | Mike Ford, '99 |

Several books containing my stories have been banned in Canada. I
also have the distinction of being on the American Library Associa-
tion's list of most frequently banned books for my young-adult book
*100 Questions & Answers About AIDS,* which has been banned for,
among other things, "encouraging sex." I understand that my book
*That's Mr. Faggot to You* was mentioned in a newsletter of the Baha'i
faith as being rather subversive, and I have been used by a right-wing

religious group as an example of the rampant spread of homosexuality for an article I wrote years ago for *Publishers Weekly* on the portrayal of gays in books for children. I believe the government is also considering forcing me to have a warning label tattooed on my ass. Other than that, like Eloise, I have never been arrested.

34 For Love or Money                    Mary Malmros, '95

35 Absolution                          John Preston, '94
[I phoned John a few days before he died, asking him if he could fax me permission to run this story. After listening to him barely able to answer the phone, I started crying. "John," I said, "this is so fucked up . . . here you are, dying of AIDS—and I'm calling to get a publishing contract signed. I'm sure you could care less." "On the contrary," he said, "it's really the only thing I do care about."—S.B.]

36 Developer                           Annie Regrets, '95

37 Up for a Nickel                     Thomas Roche, '99

38 Virtue Is Its Own Reward            Tsaurah Litzky, '97

39 Mate                                Lauren P. Burka, '97
When I lost my day job last year (as a UNIX systems administrator) I spent several weeks trying to get jobs in the phone-sex industry. I read many articles pro and con about phone sex before making my decision to go with it. I never managed to connect. The Web sites and e-mail addresses I used to contact businesses disappeared a week or two after I talked to them (not that this was different from dot-com startups). It appears that phone-sex businesses constantly advertise on their sites that they are looking for people whether they are or not. It's quite possible that I've taken myself out of contention by refusing to take jobs that require an up-front investment

(like getting an 800 number) until I was sure I could cope with it. Likewise I was unwilling to promise more than thirty hours a week. Thus my attempts to empower myself by joining the adult entertainment industry came to naught.

40 There's more to that
   state trooper than meets
   the eye                              Estabrook, '96

41 Ten Seconds to Love                  Michelle Tea, '00

42 *Licking Our Wounds,*
   an excerpt                           Elise D'Haene, '99

43 *Glamorama*, an excerpt             Bret Easton Ellis, '00

I pretty much made this sex scene up. It was supposed to be much much shorter, the whole point of it being that Victor—who has been violated spiritually, emotionally, mentally—would now be violated physically—literally—by Bobby. As I started writing I couldn't find a plausible way for it to start happening so I kept writing and writing and repositioning the three of them (and they all had taken Ecstasy!) until . . . finally. I didn't refer to any porn videos in particular when I wrote and rewrote that chapter (which took about a week) but I referred to things I'd seen in porn that I remembered intensely. Since the book was already a satire I didn't necessarily satirize the sex scene itself while writing it. There's nothing sexy about a satirical sex scene. I approached writing it as carefully as possible because there's nothing worse in prose than overwritten porn. The best sex writing is unadorned, direct, straight to the point, and devoid of as many adjectives as possible (except the obvious ones of course). Actually it should be just like sex itself.

44 Sweating in Merida                   Carol Queen, '94

I interviewed at *Screw*, but they didn't hire me. I think I flunked the proofreading test.

I served in the First Cavalry Division in Vietnam and Cambodia, receiving the Combat Medic Badge, the Silver Star, two Bronze Stars for valor, and the Air Medal and the Army Commendation Medal. I cohosted a GI antiwar radio show, and was kicked out of the army on two court-martials for disobeying a variety of lawful orders. At that time no one knew I had tried to kill an army doctor in Vietnam. I tried to frag him. We'd drag in casualties, and he'd be fucked-up drunk. But I had never fragged anyone before and neither had my friend, so we botched the attempt and the man lived. Sometimes I wish he hadn't. That's how real it gets.

56 Night Train                     Martha Garvey,
                                    writing as Nell Carberry, '02

57 Unsafe Sex                      Pat Califia, '94

I think I am the kind of author who only receives literary awards posthumously. There might be a little angst about my acceptance speech.

58 How Coyote Stole the Sun        M. Christian, '97

59 Diane the Courier               Corwin Erickson, '95

60 You Know What?                  Cara Bruce, '01

61 Belonging                       Pat Califia, '93

62 Three Obscene Phone Calls       Marian Phillips, '99

My ambition is to someday write something so offensive that parents use me as a terrible example with which to frighten their children into good behavior.

63 Love Art                        Debra Martens, '94

64 Light                           Bonny Finberg, '96

I was the first totally nude actress on the New York stage in a very bad play about White Imperialism. It was called *The Christmas Turkey* and I played Pauline Peril, symbolizing "white meat" used to tempt the poor starving people of undeveloped nations. I had lines like, "I will turn the other cheek" while shifting over on my haunches from one side to the other, giving the audience a full view of turkey ham. I was reviewed by Dan Sullivan in the *New York Times,* by the *East Village Other,* and by Henry Hewes of the *Saturday Review.* I was photographed one night by a photographer from *Sir* magazine, bathed in red floodlight, looking quite greasy and vulnerable in a 1960s innocent babe way. I got paid two tokens per night, which I saved by walking the twenty-one blocks to the theater.

65 Full Metal Corset                    Anne Tourney, '94

66 Feeding Frenzy                       Ted Blumberg, '97

67 Essence of Rose                      Poppy Z. Brite, '00
There are several bands calling themselves "Lost Souls" who purport to play the music of my fictitious band—but I have nothing to do with any of them.

68 Calcutta                             Bob Vickery, '00

69 Boy Born with Tattoo of Elvis        Robert Olen Butler, '95

70 Bed of Leaves                        Dani Shapiro, '01

71 Backhand                             Ernie Conrick, '02

72 Rubenesque                           Magenta Michaels, '93

73 Big Hungry Woman                     Bill Noble, '00

74 Vox                                  Nicholson Baker, '93
I'm no longer a sex writer (a rauncheur?) because I'm forty-five and I have a lot of gray in my beard and because I don't want to repeat myself. I could say that I'm busy repressing and denying and glossing over now, so that when the time comes I'll burst forth in a hideously glorious filthfest, but that probably won't happen. Who can predict, though?

75 The Wager                            Anna Nymus, '95

76 Why:                     Bob Flanagan, '93

77 30                       Raye Sharpe, '95

78 The Agent                Jess Wells, '00

My first reading in the U.S., from *A Herstory of Prostitution in Western Europe,* was protested by a group of prostitutes who came to the reading with paper bags over their heads; but then they joined in and quite liked it after their initial statement.

79 ReBecca                  Vicki Hendricks, '00

80 PG Diary                 Linda Rosewood Hooper, '94

81 Talk About Sex           Jamie Callan, '02

82 *The Tale of the Body Thief,*
   an excerpt               Anne Rice, '93

83 Sophie's Smoke           Mark Steurtz, '00

84 Temporary Insanity       Thomas Roche, '96

85 Real                     Bill Brent, '97

86 Tell Me What It Is       Edward Falco, '99

87 *Peep Show,* an excerpt  Nathan Englander, '01

88 *The New Kid,* an excerpt Marge Piercy, '01

89 Morning Love             Linda Smukler, '96

90 Midsummer of Love        Simon Sheppard, '00

I was both the school slut and a child prodigy—not always at the same time. I was a geeky hippie weirdo, and most of the boys were too stupid to figure out I was into sex.

The day he died I was sitting in a torture chamber in Berkeley crossing and uncrossing my legs in agony because my golden-shower client was almost twenty minutes late. I reached for the newspaper to distract me from my now almost-uncontrollable urge to run to the bathroom, and there on the front page of the entertainment section was the headline, "Andy Gibb, Dead of Natural Causes at Age 30," along with an airbrushed photo of Andy in his heyday. He really was cute.

Steven Saylor,
writing as Aaron Travis

# THE HIT

The hotel waiter is surprisingly young. And blond. And very, very nervous, all dressed up in his blue monkey suit and black bow tie. Earlier, watching him wheel the breakfast cart into the suite, Vince wondered what the kid would look like naked.

The waiter is pouring his coffee now, holding the china saucer and cup in one hand and the small porcelain pitcher in the other—jangling the cup against the saucer, splattering a few drops onto the deep green spread that covers the serving cart. The kid's lips move soundlessly, forming a curse and then suppressing it. He glances quickly at Vince, then at the hair-matted cleft of muscle exposed between the flaps of Vince's robe, then quickly away. The more nervous he gets, the cuter he looks.

Vince takes a drag off his cigarette and exhales the smoke through his nostrils with an audible rush, letting the kid know he's impatient for the coffee. He spreads his legs beneath the cart and leans back in his chair, letting the robe open another inch or two across his chest. The heavy silk drags sensuously over his thighs, and Vince feels the stirrings of an erection. He bought the robe the week before, during a job in Kansas City, at a fancy high-priced men's shop. In his line of work, at the age of thirty-one, Vincent Zorio can afford to treat himself to the very best.

"You always take this long, kid?" Vince mutters the words softly, but the boy jerks and almost loses the cup.

"No, sir." The kid looks him in the eye for an instant and swallows nervously. He holds out the cup. It jangles in his hand. "Your coffee, sir?"

"Yeah, my coffee. If you're finished spilling it all over the tablecloth."

"I'm sorry, sir. If—"

"Just set it down on the cart."

"Will there be anything else, sir? I mean, if you'll just sign the check . . ."

"Sure." A silver pen lies beside the green-bordered slip of paper, both stamped with the hotel's crest. Vince studies the check for a long moment, feeling the kid's nervousness, feeling his cock growing longer, unfurling warm and thick against the inside of his thigh.

"Is something wrong, sir?"

Vince signs the check and sits back in the chair, holding the pen between his thumb and forefinger, studying it.

"How old are you, kid?"

"Sir?"

"I said, how old are you?"

"Nineteen. Almost twenty."

"Kinda young to be working this job, in a hotel like this. I'd figure you for a bellboy maybe. Or a maid's helper."

Vince glances up. The kid is actually blushing. He'll be biting his lip next. Looking blonder and cuter than ever.

"I've been at this job almost two years, sir, ever since I got out of school. I've never really had any complaints—"

"Shit, they hired you right out of high school? You must have connections."

The kid looks down and shrugs. The uniform jacket stretches

tight across his chest. His body is lean and broad-shouldered, slim hipped, with intimations of smooth muscle inside his tight blue uniform. "Well, yeah, I guess. My uncle Max is head chef—"

"Yeah, figures. What's your name?"

"Kip."

Vince nods. He always likes to know a kid's name before he dicks him. And, in the last two minutes, Vince has made up his mind that the least he'll be getting from cute little Kip is a long and very thorough blowjob.

Vince puts the pen down beside the check. "I guess you expect a tip." He pushes his chair back and stands, walks to the dresser and returns with his wallet. His cock pushes up against the heavy silk, tenting the robe and swaying as he walks. He catches the boy staring, then looking away. Blushing darker than before.

Vince sits. "You have breakfast this morning, Kip?" The kid looks puzzled. "Uncle Max feed you down in the kitchen? Maybe a big juicy sausage, with a couple of eggs?" Kip flinches; Vince has aimed at a nerve and struck it, dead center. He pulls out a fifty and lays it on the cart beside the check. "Still hungry?"

The boy stares at the fifty, uncertain. As green as they come. Vince likes that. He picks up his fork, spears one of the fat link sausages on the gold-rimmed china plate, watches the grease erupt. He says the words again: "You still hungry, Kip? Maybe Uncle Max didn't feed you enough sausage this morning."

The kid looks him straight in the eye. Blushing. Breathing unevenly. Swallowing.

"Push this cart out of the way."

The boy moves to obey automatically. Vince loosens the sash around his waist and pushes aside the flaps of his robe. The boy turns back and sucks in his breath.

Vincent Zorio is a big man. Massive shoulders and chest, huge biceps and thighs, hard muscle without a trace of fat. A big booming voice, intimidating even when he speaks softly. Extra-large feet and hands—a strangler's hands, or a butcher's, meaty and thick.

And a cock to match. It snakes beyond the edge of the chair, heavy and thick, balanced atop the plump cushion of his testicles.

Vince sits back in the chair, sliding his hips forward, spreading his thighs apart. He narrows his eyes. His dick grows into a fat, swollen truncheon of meat, curving outward and up, pointing straight at the boy's face. Kip's eyes are lowered, his lips parted. No longer looking Vince in the face, but staring at the cock. Waiting to be told.

"Go ahead, Kip. Put your mouth on it."

Kip fumbles toward him. Drops to his knees. Stares at the cock for a long moment. Then he looks up at Vince's chest, and his eyes glaze.

Vince smiles. Christ, you got a great body, mister . . . that's what the last kid told him, the cute little brunette with the bubble butt back in Kansas City. But that one Vince picked up on the street—a common little gutter whore, shameless with his mouth. Little Kip is a different story. With Kip, Vince will do all the talking.

Kip's eyes return to the cock. He stares. His chest rises and falls inside the tight blue jacket. He lets out a little moan, then closes his eyes and opens wide, moving forward blindly to take it in his mouth.

Vince butts the palm of his hand against the kid's forehead. "Not so fast, cocksucker." He squeezes his cock at the base and aims it at Kip's mouth, hunching forward until he can feel the boy's warm breath on his dick. Kip stares at it, cross-eyed. "First you kiss it. You look me straight in the eye like a good little cocksucker, and you give my dick a nice, sloppy kiss."

Kip looks up. Eyes hungry, pleading. He seems to hesitate, then presses his lips against the fat bulb of flesh.

The contact electrifies him. Kip shudders and his face burns bright red. The muscles in his neck twist and contract. His Adam's apple twitches; the bow tie does a dance. Vince settles even deeper into the chair. It is all decided now.

"Yeah, kid," Vince croons. "Now wrap your lips around the

head and give my dick a deep, wet French kiss."

Vince stares at the connection: the long, thick shaft leading like
a tube into the boy's mouth, the wide-open lips stretched taut
around the crown, the boy's hollowed cheeks and glittering eyes
staring wildly back at him. His scrutiny is so blatant that Kip finally shuts his eyes tight, embarrassed; but his tongue never stops
squirming against the swollen knob of flesh.

Vince studies the boy attached to the end of his dick. Kip is on
all fours, his butt sticking up behind him, pressing firm and
round against the seat of his pants. Both hands grip the thick
cream-colored carpet—no move to touch himself. Everything
centers on his mouth and the knob inside it, and the nine-tenths
of Vince's cock still waiting to be sucked. A natural submissive.
Vince knows the type, inside and out. Cock-hungry boy. Born to
be dicked. Vince sized him up the moment he walked in the door,
and Vince is never wrong.

"Good boy." He pats Kip's hollowed cheek, at first gently, then
harder, almost slapping him. "Good little cocksucker." Vince grabs
a fistful of silky blond hair. "Now we feed you the whole thing."
Kip's face flashes alarm, and he grunts in protest—and then the
grunt turns to a gurgle as his throat is filled with Vince's cock.

Kip heaves and chokes, spewing a mass of saliva into the pubic
hair against his lips. He struggles to pull his head off the cock, but
Vince holds him tight—then jerks the boy's head back, wrenching
the cock from his mouth. It snaps against Vince's belly, then rico-
chets meaty and wet against the boy's stunned face.

Vince's eyes are heavy-lidded with lust. He purses his lips.
"Mmm. That felt good, cocksucker. Let's do it again."

Before Kip can react, Vince yanks him back onto the cock,
spearing it all the way down his throat. Gagging him with it. Listening to him sputter, feeling him heave. Screwing Kip's face into
the wiry pubic thatch and savoring the deep-throat convulsions.
After a long moment, Vince jerks the boy's head back and empties
his mouth again.

Kip's face is drawn into a long silent howl, like a deep-sea diver breaking surface and gasping for air. Vince grips his cock at the base and spanks his face with it, keeping him off base and dizzy. Kip squeals and tries to say something—but then the cock is lodged deep in his throat again.

This is the way Vince likes it—dominating a kid with his dick. Force-feeding him. Bludgeoning his throat. Punishing him with it and watching him open wide for more. Vince rides the boy's face, holding him by both ears, grinding his head into his lap and screwing it like a cored melon. Yanking his meat out of the kid's mouth and spanking him with it. Rubbing it huge, wet, and slick all over his face, until Kip is drunk with cock.

Vince croons. Beneath him Kip whimpers, gasps, makes strange mewling sounds of desire. The kid is into it now, wanting it bad. Wanting to join in. He balances himself awkwardly on one hand and gropes at the hardness cramped inside his pants. Vince kicks his hand away, and the boy submits, reaching instead with both hands to steady himself against the hard wooden legs of the chair while Vince begins a fresh volley of thrusts down his throat.

Suddenly Vince kicks him away, sending him sprawling against the floor. Kip looks up at him, confused and hurt. Then hungry again, staring up at the huge cock as Vince stands and steps toward him. Then abruptly alarmed, shrinking against the door as the big man looms over him. Vince towers like a giant above him—the broad muscles of his thighs foreshortened, the big cock thrusting upward from his groin, slick and bloated from fucking Kip's throat. His big balls are pulled up tight against the base of the shaft, silky smooth and as swollen as his cock.

Vince smirks. He pinches the base of his cock between his forefinger and thumb and spanks the air with it, watching the boy's eyes as they follow the beat. The kid is his now. He could pull him up off the floor, strip him, run his hands over that smooth, naked boyflesh—see what little Kip looks like bent over the bed naked with a big cock up his ass . . .

Vince glances at the clock on the dresser—a quarter to nine. Already running late. The best will have to wait.

"Up," he growls, beckoning with his cock. "On your knees, kiddo." Kip scrambles to rise. Too slow. Vince grabs him by the hair and pulls his face to crotch level. Kip's eyes are closed, his mouth already open. A natural.

"Cocksucker," Vince whispers, hitting hard on the consonants. He pushes into the waiting hole—between the glistening lips, beyond the clenching sphincter. Deep in Kip's throat, his cock starts to twitch like a snake on hot asphalt.

Kip chokes, caught by surprise. Then his throat begins an automatic undulating caress around the cock, milking it as it empties itself into his belly. Vince throws his head back and growls, twisting Kip's face into his groin, burying his cock another few inches in the boy's neck. His hips shudder and convulse, and Kip's throat spasms in response.

After a long moment, the orgasm peaks, then slowly subsides. Vince keeps his cock lodged deep in the boy's throat, savoring the afterglow and the warm, clenching heat. Finally he pulls himself free.

Below him, Kip squats on folded knees, both hands pressed between his thighs, desperately kneading the bulge in his tight blue trousers. Vince smirks and reaches down, scooping the boy up by his armpits. He brushes Kip's hands away from his crotch. The boy moans in frustration. He clutches Kip's wrists, pins his arms to his sides, and runs his tongue over the boy's face—across cheeks slick with saliva, over lips wet and shiny with semen. He covers the boy's mouth and kisses him—harsh, demanding, sucking Kip's breath away and then forcing it back into his lungs.

Vince breaks the kiss. He pushes Kip against the door and pats him roughly on the cheek, then turns and walks to the chair, stretching his arms above his head, belting his robe before he sits and draws the cart back in front of him.

Kip stands at the door, dazed, breathing hard, reaching up to wipe his mouth with the back of his hand.

Vince looks at him sharply. "Clear out, kid. Uncle Max'll be missing you down in the kitchen."

Kip hesitates, then turns and reaches for the doorknob.

"Hey, kid." Kip turns back, glancing guiltily at Vince for an instant before returning his gaze to the floor.

"Better take the check. And your tip."

Kip bites his lower lip and walks slowly to the cart. He reaches for the tray with trembling fingers, staring at the fifty on top. Vince catches him by the wrist, reaches for his wallet and adds a twenty.

Kip accepts the money in silence. He walks shakily to the door.

"Hey—cocksucker."

Kip freezes. He looks over his shoulder. Vince is sitting back in his chair, smoking a cigarette and smirking at him. "You take it up the ass, pussyboy?" Kip blushes. "Yeah, sure you do. What time you get off work?"

"I—" Kip clears his throat. His neck feels swollen and bruised inside. "Seven."

Vince nods. "Be here at eight sharp. That'll give you time to grab some dinner. Eat light. And don't bother to change—I like the little bow tie. Not that you'll be wearing your monkey suit for long." Vince takes a drag off his cigarette. "I wanna see what you look like naked."

Kip clears his throat again. "I—don't know . . ."

"And keep your hands off your dick. Understand? You just keep that little boner tucked up and twitching inside your pants all day, and think about what I got waiting for you here between my legs."

Kip stares at the doorknob. He grips it tight to keep his hand from shaking. "I don't know," he whispers hoarsely. "I have to go now." Without looking back, he opens the door and slips away.

The coffee is cold, the food lukewarm. Vince doesn't mind. He wolfs down his breakfast in two minutes flat. A blowjob in the morning always makes him hungry.

After breakfast he dresses quickly, choosing his black suit and suede overcoat; the day is hardly chilly enough for it, but the bulk will help conceal the gun strapped across his shoulder. He checks himself in the mirror mounted above the dresser, and glances at the clock. Nine sharp. An instant later, he hears Battaglia's telltale knock at the locked door that joins the separate bedrooms of the suite.

It will all be over by five o'clock. Until then, he and Battaglia will be walking on glass every instant. The job is going to be a bitch. But once it's over, Vince will be twenty grand richer.

Besides, he has an evening with Kip to look forward to. There's always a chance that he's spooked the kid, but Vince remembers the look in Kip's eyes when the boy screwed up his face to kiss the fat knob of his cock. The way he opened his throat for it, like a holster to a gun. Action speaks louder than words, and a big dick speaks loudest of all to a cock-hungry kid like Kip. There isn't a doubt in his mind that the boy will come knocking at his door exactly on time, blushing and biting his lip, looking blonder and cuter than ever.

Vince will have some surprises for him.

Ten till eight: Kip steps into the service elevator off the kitchen and presses the button for the fifteenth floor.

All day long, he has thought of Vince Zorio's cock, and nothing else. The way it filled his mouth. The way it stung his face when the man dredged it shiny and wet from his throat and beat him with it. The taste, overpowering and musky, when Vince packed it all the way home and started shooting.

Big. Big enough to choke him. Bigger than Uncle Max—and Max never uses his cock on Kip the way Vince did. Max never pushes him around, never calls him a cocksucker. Max is always happy to suck Kip off in return. Vince wouldn't even let him touch himself.

Kip has been with relatively few men, despite his looks and his eagerness. A couple of jocks used to let him suck them off in the locker room, but it never amounted to much. Kip is naturally timid about sex and embarrassed by the things he thinks about, naked and alone at night, beating his meat and imagining another man above him—always above, never beneath or beside. Shameful things—like the things Vince Zorio did to him.

Max was the first to fuck him. It was never said outright, but that was one of the conditions of the job: that Kip would do certain favors in return for Uncle Max's help. Kip seldom admits it to himself, but this is what turns him on most about sex with Max—the dirtiness of it, the way it makes him feel soiled and small.

Sometimes he wishes that Max would push harder. Usually it's nothing more than a hurried exchange of blowjobs, or a quick fuck in one of the vacant rooms. But when he lies naked with his fantasies, with his cock in his fist, Kip likes to imagine Max turning mean and ugly . . . calling him names, ordering him around . . . touching him in front of the other employees, letting them all know that he whores for his uncle. But Max will never be the man for that, and Kip is too shy to ever share his fantasies aloud.

Sometimes he has sex with guests at the hotel. They are always older. They always pay. As often as not, they simply want to suck him off. Kip gives them what they want, even though he wants it the other way around. He prefers the ones who want him to do the sucking. Best of all are the men who pay to fuck him. Kip never refuses, even if the man is old or ugly or fat. There is something intoxicating about pulling down his pants and bending over to let a stranger use him. They always rave about his beautiful ass . . .

But in two years of working at the hotel, two years of whoring for Max and the men passing through, Kip has never met a man like Vince Zorio. He first saw him the previous afternoon, checking into the hotel with another man, older and bigger and equally well dressed. Later, Kip sneaked a look at the register: Vincent Zorio, Leo Battaglia, Suite 1505, home addresses in New York. When the breakfast orders arrived that morning, he spotted Zorio's room number and took rounds for the fifteenth floor. It caused an argument with Walter, the headwaiter—the top floor always tipped the best. Max stepped in to settle it, and Walter was out of luck.

As soon as he entered the suite, Kip had gone weak in the knees. The sight of the man wearing nothing but his robe unnerved him; Vince Zorio was darkly handsome, with wavy black hair and strong, blunt features, and an impressive physique that had been obvious even in a business suit. And even before the man showed him his cock and told him to suck it, somehow Kip knew it would be a big one.

But there was something beyond the man's sheer physical appeal that made Kip turn to jelly inside. The sex was like a dream, unreal and out of control, pulling Kip helplessly along; but the fascination went beyond even that. There was something dark inside Vincent Zorio, powerful and frightening. Kip had glimpsed it. He had responded to it; submitted to it; craved it—but exactly what it was escaped him, and he was not sure he wanted to know.

Somehow Kip managed to get through the day. Late in the afternoon there was an echo of excitement from the hotel lobby—a headline two inches tall on the front page of the evening paper, something about two executives shot to death in an office building only a few blocks away. But to Kip, everything was tedium. He worked in a haze, replaying the incident in Zorio's room over and over in his head. His cock stayed so hard inside his pants that it hurt, his balls felt swollen and full; but he did as the man had told him to do, and kept his hands away from the day-long ache between his legs . . .

Now, ascending in the elevator, Kip begins to feel loose and weak between his legs. Vince Zorio intends to fuck him. The man as much as told him so. Vince is going to fuck him, in his room, only minutes from now. Not a quickie, with Kip's pants pushed down around his ankles. I wanna see what you look like naked— that's what the man said. Vince is going to make Kip strip. Vince is going to fuck him naked.

The man will be rough—Kip knows that. Fucking his ass the
way he fucked his face. It will hurt. It always hurts some, at first,
even with smaller men. Kip wonders if Vince will let him touch
himself while he's being fucked. It wouldn't hurt as bad that way;
but it doesn't really matter. Kip liked it, somehow, the way the
man denied him this morning, as if his own big cock was the only
thing that mattered, as if Kip's cock wasn't worth the effort and
didn't deserve to be touched.

Perhaps Vince will let Kip suck it before he fucks him with it.
Or maybe the man will make him wait until afterwards, making
him lick the big cock clean after it's been up his ass, calling him
cocksucker and pussyboy and slapping his face. Maybe he will make
Kip beg for it. Kip will beg. He will crawl on his hands and knees
naked and beg for the privilege of sucking Vince Zorio's dick . . .

Five minutes to eight: Kip knocks at the door to suite 1505. His
hands are sweaty. His mouth is dry. He listens to his heartbeat
pounding in his throat while he waits for Vince to answer the door.

The doorknob turns; the door swings open. The first thing Kip
notices is the heavy shadow of stubble across Vince's jaw, then the
smell of alcohol on his breath.

Vince gives him a cool smile and nods. "Come on in, kid."

Vince walks to the dresser. He still wears the black suit, but the
collar of his shirt is undone, the thin black tie loosened around his
neck. The room is lit softly. On the dresser stands an empty glass,
and beside it a half-empty bottle of expensive bourbon.

Vince lights a cigarette. He reaches for the bourbon and pours
himself a drink. He stares at Kip in the tall, wide mirror above the
dresser. The cigarette hangs from the corner of his mouth.

"What are you waiting for, kid? I'm not paying to watch you
model your monkey suit. Take it off."

Kip hesitates. With the other men there is usually a drink first,
mention of money, some talk to feel him out. But Vince isn't like
the others. That is what had brought him here, after all.

He reaches up to undo his tie.

"The bow tie stays," Vince says sharply. "Take off everything else."

Kip's fingers shake as he unbuttons his jacket and shrugs it off his shoulders. He takes off the stiffly starched white shirt, then peels off his T-shirt, wet with perspiration in the armpits. The refrigerated air is cool against his skin; his nipples turn to gooseflesh, but his face is burning hot.

The patent-leather shoes. The black nylon socks. Then his blue trousers, always hard to get out of. Max ordered them a size too small. Max likes them tight. Kip almost trips stepping out of them. He is naked now, except for a bow tie and black nylon briefs. He hesitates, suddenly self-conscious and uncertain.

"That's far enough," Vince says. He holds the glass of bourbon in one hand. The cigarette hangs from his lips. He stares at Kip in the mirror and motions with the glass. The ice cubes swirl and tinkle softly. "Turn around."

Kip turns and stands rigid. He can feel the man's eyes on his ass, burning hot. He hears the sound of Vince swallowing, then the clink of the glass being placed on the dresser; then Vince's breathing, close behind him.

"Well, well. You dress up special for the occasion—or do all you bellboys wear panties under your outfits?"

Kip flushes. His skin prickles in the cool air. His briefs are sheer black nylon, skimpier than any bathing suit. They ride high in the back, digging into the crack of his ass and exposing the bottom curve of each cheek. In front they narrow to a snug little pouch that cramps his genitals even when they're soft. Max ordered a half-dozen in assorted colors from a mail-order outfit in Hollywood. The catalogue called it the Cupcake Thong—for the young male beauty with his assets in the rear.

"I asked you a question, Kip." Vince's breath is warm and moist in his ear, heavy with booze. "You always wear panties?"

Kip's voice is small and hoarse. "Yes."

"Umm. Cute." Vince cups his hand over one of the boy's firm buns, feeling the smoothness of the nylon against his palm and the even silkier flesh against his fingertips. He slides his middle finger under the hem, over the curve of Kip's ass and into the cleft. He strokes the tightly puckered hole, and Kip sighs in response. "Oh, kid, fucking your hole is gonna be a dream. Yeah. Now be a good little girl and take off your panties for me."

A trickle of sweat runs from Kip's armpit down the side of his chest. Vince is already taking him places he has never been, even in his fantasies. He slides the black panties over his hips and bends to peel them down his thighs.

Vince purses his lips. Sucks in his breath. The kid's ass is flawless. Smooth and white as ivory. Plump but firm, superbly shaped. A real bubble butt, perfect for screwing.

Kip stands, arms at his sides, eyes downcast. Vince slowly circles him, nodding approval. The boy's sturdy little cock stands straight up. The bow tie adds a sluttish touch, like a stripper's prop, flaunting his nudity.

"You work out, kid?"

Kip can hardly speak. "There's a gym in the basement. And a pool . . ."

Vince nods. The kid's body is even better than he had hoped. Lean, muscular limbs, sharply defined under porcelain skin. A flat belly, gently ridged with muscle. Slender hips. A natural posture that pulls his broad shoulders up and keeps the small of his back arched stiffly, making his ass jut out hard and round behind him, lifting his pectorals up for display.

And it's the boy's pecs that Vince can't help staring at. The kid lifted weights to get a pair like that, did a lot of swimming. It shows—big, thick pectorals, pumped-up and round, glazed with a thick sheen of perspiration that makes them shine in the dimly lit room. So big they look lewdly out of place, top-heavy above the sinewy slenderness of his torso, extending a blatant, passive invitation to be cupped and fondled. Capping the smooth mounds are nipples an inch wide, standing out puffy and pink, ripe for plucking.

Vince likes big tits. On his women. On his boys. Twin handfuls of smooth, pliant muscle he can reach around and grab hold of when his cock is buried balls-deep in ass. Nipples he can pull on to make that ass do a grinding dance around his dick.

Vince takes a swig of bourbon. Then he takes an ice cube from the glass. Slowly, watching the boy's reaction, he touches it to the tip of each protruding nipple. Kip flinches and sucks in his breath. The icy contact makes his nipples crinkle and stiffen, erecting them into elongated little nubs of flesh. Vince toys casually with the effect, drawing a gasp from the boy each time he flicks the wedge of ice against the sensitive, swollen tips.

Kip is astonished at the sensation. His tits begin to sting and burn. He closes his eyes and moans. His nipples feel enormous, throbbing with each heartbeat. The frostbite claws into them, filling them like pincushions with sharp needles of pain. His whole body trembles, but Kip keeps his arms at his sides, clenching fistfuls of air. His cock stands up rigid and shiny red.

Then the ice cube is gone, melted away. Vince's forefinger and thumb choose a nipple to pick on, plucking and pulling at the scalded tip.

"You put out for a lot of guys, don't you?"

The question slides into Kip's consciousness, taking a long muddled detour around the ache in his nipples. "No. Not really—"

"Don't bullshit me, kid. I don't like pussies who lie to me. I saw the way you got down on your knees for it this morning. Couldn't wait to get your mouth all over it. You've gone down before, plenty of times."

"A few . . ."

"Oh yeah?" Vince savagely twirls the nipple between his fingernails, making him yelp. "Sucking off the hotel johns for a little cash on the side. You bend over and let those guys stick it up that tight little hole? Or is that just for Uncle Max?" Vince slaps him smartly across the face.

Kip recoils and cringes. "No—I mean, sometimes. But usually, most of them"—he stammers, trying to defend himself—"usually they just . . . want to suck me off."

Vince laughs. "You shitting me, pussyboy? Pay to suck this little weenie?" He runs the chilly surface of his glass against Kip's cock, making him gasp. "Must be a pretty desperate bunch of old toads—paying good money to slobber over your stiff little nub." He raises the glass to his lips and swallows. "You know what I think, Kip? I think you're a cocksucker. And a liar. I thing you're nothing but a cheap little slut, working the hotel johns to get a stiff dick up your pussy."

Kip tries to answer, but his lips and tongue are suddenly shapeless. Instead he only groans. Then yelps, as Vince slaps him across the mouth.

And then Kip is alone again, blushing nude and erect in the center of the room. Vince has returned to the dresser to pour himself another drink.

"Get your pussy over here, slutboy. On your hands and knees."

Kip drops to all fours, suddenly dizzy and glad to be on the floor. He crawls across the carpet, face stinging, nipples throbbing, until he reaches the heels of the man's shiny black shoes. He stares at them for a long moment. Vince turns around. Kip raises his head slowly.

Above him, Vince looks down and smirks. A fresh cigarette hangs from the corner of his mouth. His fly is open. His big, nude cock hovers over Kip's upturned face, softly swollen and impossibly thick. The dizziness returns. Kip clutches the carpet and moans.

Vince takes a long drag on his cigarette and laughs. "See something you like, pussyboy?"

Kip moans louder, and licks his lips. He stares mesmerized at the massive tube of smooth, naked flesh, displayed luridly before his face. So beautiful. So brutally big. Heavy and blunt, corrugated with veins beneath the sleek, taut wrapping of flesh. Pulsing and

growing thicker before his astonished eyes. Suddenly he seems to
see the scene from somewhere else in the room: the nude blond boy
in a bow tie on his hands and knees; the big man in the business
suit above him, lewdly exposing his oversized sex. The man smoking a cigarette casually, taking his time—the boy itchy and hot between his legs, hungry to have it in his mouth. Kip puts on a show
for the voyeur in his mind: wiggling his ass, breathing hard, biting
his lips. Naked pussyboy, craving cock.

Vince finishes his cigarette and snuffs it out. He leans his ass
against the dresser and spreads his feet apart, framing Kip between
his legs. The plump, waxy-looking head of his cock hovers inches
from the boy's parted lips. Kip feels the heat that radiates from the
cockflesh. He watches Vince's heartbeat in the long thick vein that
pulses lazily down one side. His nostrils are filled with the odor of
the man's sex. He can almost taste it on his tongue.

But instead of cock, Vince feeds him liquor. He uncaps the bottle of bourbon and lowers it to Kip's mouth, pushing his head back
and telling him to swallow. He slides the neck of the bottle into the
boy's mouth and pours the booze down his throat in long, burning
draughts, tilting the bottle up and lowering it, listening to Kip
gurgle and cough. Trickles of amber bubble from the corners of
Kip's mouth and run in rivulets down his undulating throat, into
the hollows of his collarbone and over his shiny, pumped-up pecs,
stinging his swollen nipples. Kip's glazed eyes are riveted on the
naked shaft, watching it thicken and slowly grow erect alongside
the bottle, wishing it were the big cock that Vince was emptying
over and over again into his throat.

The bottle is empty. Vince sets it aside and pulls the boy to his
feet. Kip moans, wanting to stay close to the big cock. Then hands
are gliding over his naked flesh, pulling him close, crushing him
against the man's big chest. The hands glide down the small of his
back and onto his ass, pulling his buttocks apart—then a finger
penetrates his hole and slides knuckle-deep into his rectum. He

gasps and looks up into Vince Zorio's smoldering eyes.

"Ummm. Now I think I'm ready to have some fun with you, pussyboy."

Half past nine: Kip kneels on the hard tile floor of the bathroom in Vince Zorio's suite. His trembling body glistens with a sheen of cold sweat. His legs are folded beneath him. His ass rests on his heels. He is naked, except for the bow tie wrapped snugly around his neck, and the black silk tie that binds his hands behind his back. His throat is filled with Vince's cock. His ass is filled with the enema Vince gave him earlier and the cruelly thick buttplug that holds it inside.

Vince sits on the toilet. He has removed his shirt and jacket. Tufts of wiry black hair sprout above the neckline of his undershirt. His pants and boxer shorts are pushed down to his ankles. His bare feet are planted on either side of the toilet, propping his knees wide apart. His dick is buried deep in Kip's throat.

Kip's jaws ache from sucking cock. His shoulders and arms are stiff and sore from being pulled so tightly behind his back. He cannot seem to stop shaking. The enema rumbles in his guts, making his bowels spasm and knot into wicked cramps. His hard-on would have vanished long ago, except for the thin leather cord tied cutting-tight around his cock. Kip is miserable, on the verge of crying.

He pulls his face from Vince's crotch, letting the cock slide free from his throat. It snaps upward from his lips, ramrod stiff and glossy with saliva. It seems to Kip that he has been sucking on Vince's cock for hours. The big dick never goes soft, never shoots. It towers before him like a harsh rebuke, unsatisfied and demanding to be sucked again.

His bowels are knotted with cramps. He shivers uncontrollably. Beads of sweat erupt across his forehead and trickle down his nose. He stares up at Vince's face, looking for relief, but the big man only smirks.

"Please," Kip begs hoarsely. "Please—take it out of me. Out of my ass. Oh, please. I can't hold it anymore."

Vince smiles. And shakes his head. "You know the rules, pussyboy. You blow me till I come. You suck the cream out of my big, fat dick, and then I pull the plug." Vince grabs the base of his dick and waves it like a billy club, cock-proud and horny. He tilts it down, pointing at Kip's mouth, and rubs the head over the boy's pouting lips. "Well, pussyboy?"

Vince is playing a cruel game with him. Kip knows he has sucked the man to the verge of coming several times already—he can tell from the quickening of Vince's breath, the way his body draws taut, the way his cock expands abruptly and throbs in his throat. But every time Vince shoves his mouth away at the last minute and sits gasping on the toilet, letting the orgasm recede, waiting until his twitching dick has cooled before beginning the game all over again.

Kip sobs. Tears well in his eyes. He has promised himself he will not cry, but he can no longer help it. He opens his mouth, whimpering, and leans forward to suck.

Just as his lips make contact, Vince pulls the cock up and out of reach. He looks at Kip thoughtfully. "Uh-uh. I think I want you to suck on my nuts for a while."

Kip groans. Vince pinches his mouth open and stuffs the big balls inside. He sits back on the toilet and spreads his legs wide open. Kip's cheeks are outrageously bloated. The plump, heavy scrotum fills his mouth. The testicles are alive, twitching and jerking inside the sack. Vince laughs. "You look like a little chipmunk, pussyboy. Don't just hold 'em. Use your tongue." Vince strokes his cock slowly and gives himself over to the exquisite sensation . . .

Kip's mind is so jumbled that he can hardly recall a time when he has not been in bondage on his knees, sucking cock and enduring the enema. Vaguely he remembers how it began—in the other room, long ago, when Vince removed his tie and told Kip to cross his wrists behind his back. Kip was slow to respond, partly from the booze, partly out of fear; but as Vince wrapped the silk cord tight around his wrists, placing him in bondage for the first time in his life, he flushed with an excitement that made him shake. To be standing naked and erect and helpless in the man's room, while Vince slowly circled him, pulling on the big, nude cock that jutted from his open fly and appraising Kip like a newly purchased toy— as if a deeply buried fantasy had somehow erupted into the real world and taken on a dangerous life of its own. Kip was excited. Kip was frightened. Kip was a nude, helpless pussyboy with his hands tied behind his back and his cock standing up stiff between his legs, and Vince Zorio was going to fuck him.

Then the man began to humiliate him, gradually escalating the abuse. Vince liked to use his big, meaty hands. Pinching Kip's swollen nipples. Slapping his face. Punching his belly. Squeezing his ass, hard enough to leave bruises. Stinging his sturdy little erection with hard open-handed slaps.

Vince seemed especially to enjoy abusing his cock. Tying it at the base so that it stood up shiny and red. Swatting it with his hand. Raking his fingernails up the length and pinching the tip. Humiliating it—telling Kip he had a little weenie between his legs. Cradling the weenie in his hand and spanking it with his own huge truncheon of meat, driving home the difference between them. Humiliate a boy's hard cock, Vince had once told Battaglia, and just watch the way his hole opens up for anything you wanna put inside.

When it came time to clean the boy out, Vince opened the dresser's middle drawer and pulled out an aluminum briefcase. Kip caught a glimpse of the contents and raised his eyebrows in alarm. A yellow enema bag and a coil of tubing. A huge black rubber buttplug. A confusion of items he couldn't name, made of leather, rubber, chrome. And at the back of the briefcase, buried in the tangle but catching the light with the unmistakable glint of cold black steel, a gun . . .

★

A quarter past ten: Vince has decided to come. It seems a shame. Kip is doing such a fine job on his cock. Hard, relentless, deep-throat cocksucking. Nonstop. No sissy-kissing or tongue-lapping. No idling while the boy stops to catch his breath—getting Vince off is infinitely more important than that.

The dark-headed hustler back in Kansas City sucked with the same enthusiasm. So did the blond bitch in Dallas. So have all the other cocksuckers in all the other towns who have found themselves naked on their knees in a hotel john with Vince Zorio, with an enema up their butts and their hands tied behind their backs. Guaranteed incentive to make certain Vince's cock gets the loving, undivided attention it deserves. A sure ticket to the best blowjob in town—and Vince always treats himself to the best. A UCLA gymnast he picked up at a bar in West Hollywood holds the record—a little over ninety minutes of desperately fucking his face on Vince's big cock before Vince gave him the load he was begging for and pulled the plug from his ass. Of course, the gymnast had the added incentive of the alligator clamps Vince had attached to his nipples and the tip of his penis.

Vince is up for breaking the record. Kip has worked him up stiff as a girder, and Vince could stay that way all night; he is in no hurry to shoot. But little Kip, for all his natural talent, obviously doesn't have that kind of stamina. The boy is covered with sweat, shaking like a leaf. Whimpering and gagging himself nonstop, his head bouncing up and down like a piston about to blow.

At one point the boy even pissed himself—let go with an uncontrollable spray that jetted straight out of his hard, bound cock and spattered against the front of the toilet. Kip flushed cherry red, but never stopped sucking. Vince has seen it happen before.

Remembering excites him. Vince grabs the base of his dick and whips it out of the kid's mouth.

Kip sobs and groans, thinking Vince is teasing him again.

"No," he croaks. "Let me. Put it back—"

"Let you what?"

"Let me suck it." Kip is whining now. Begging. Babbling. "Please—come in my mouth. Oh please, put it back—in my mouth—let me suck." The kid is raving, delirious. "I can't—I can't—Please. Fuck me. Fuck me!" And he opens his mouth almost frighteningly wide, scrunching his features up against his forehead, making his whole face into a gaping, hungry hole.

Vince is impressed. And almost tempted to prolong the torment. Kip looks so desirable that way. Down on his knees, cringing nude in a pool of his own sweat and urine. Big tits heaving out, tight rump sticking up behind. Blond hair plastered against his forehead. Tears running down his cheeks. Every muscle taut and glazed with sweat. Turning his mouth into a pussy that begs for Vince's dick.

The least Vince can do is shove his cock into that hole and come. Instead, he leans back on the toilet and aims his dick at Kip's wide-open mouth. He breathes deep. Two quick strokes and he's there.

It's a hefty load—after so much sucking, Vince's balls hang heavy as a pair of lemons. He thrashes on the toilet seat, shuddering from the force of the climax. His cock is like a hose, spraying semen all over Kip's gaping face and chest.

He takes his time catching his breath, then slowly gets off the toilet, pulls up his pants, tucks in his undershirt. He leaves his fly open. His emptied balls contract to their normal size, but his cock thrusts out the opening as stiff and ready as if he had never come. Finally he pulls Kip to his feet and grabs the base of the buttplug. He has to screw and tug—it's a tight fit. Then he steps aside, laughing, while Kip scurries crablike onto the commode . . .

Midnight: Kip lies on the bed. The sheets are wildly rumpled, soaked with sweat. He is hog-tied, wrist to ankle—arms pulled down alongside his body, legs folded beneath him, knees apart. He began that way at the foot of the bed, with his ass hanging over the edge, an easy target for Vince's dick. Now he is jammed sideways against the headboard, neck bent, face pressed against the wood. Over the past two hours, Vince has ridden him up and down and across the bed a dozen times.

Vince stands at the side of the bed, facing Kip's ass, naked except for his undershirt. The thin, ribbed cotton is almost transparent with sweat, clinging to his broad chest and back. His satisfied, rubbery cock droops heavily from his crotch, coated with shiny mucus and oozing semen from the tip. In his hand he holds a wire coat hanger, untwisted at the top and crudely straightened like a long, thin shepherd's crook.

The wire hanger has done a good job. Vince was lucky to find it. The hotel hangers are all made of wood, but high on a shelf in the closet, left over from a previous guest's dry cleaning, he came across the tool he was looking for.

He would have preferred using his belt. But belts are noisy.

So are boys in the process of having their asses whipped. Which is why the buttplug that earlier held his enema inside is now stuffed into Kip's wide-open mouth, held in place by a bandanna made from his own nylon panties. Kip's face is red from the strain and wet from crying.

Kip's ass is pushed outward and up, taut as a drumhead. So wide open that the deep cleft between his cheeks is flattened and his hole rudely exposed, completely vulnerable. The pale, silky bottom flesh sizzles with thin red welts. The bud of his anus is equally red and chafed, distended and swollen like a bee sting, the tender lips rubbed raw by long, relentless fucking.

Vince reaches for the phone on the bedside table and dials the switchboard. While he waits, he prods Kip's ass with the blunt, hooked end of the coat hanger. Kip's grunt is muffled by the buttplug. Vince snakes the hanger between the boy's thighs and hooks his cock, pulling it backward between his legs. Still hard as a rock.

"Yeah, operator. Suite 1505. I want you to ring the phone in the adjoining bedroom."

Vince pulls the hanger upward and back, seeing how far the stubby shaft will bend. Another inch and it snaps free, slapping up against the kid's belly. Kip moans.

"Leo—I saw the light go on under your door a while back. Getting in kinda late, aren't you? Yeah. So how were the chicks down on pussy boulevard? No such luck, huh? You're a crazy sonofabitch to be out on the streets tonight anyway, not with all the heat. Yeah, tell me about it—always horny as hell after a job. Especially like the bitch we pulled today."

Kip turns his head, realizing only gradually that Vince is speaking to someone else.

"Nah, stayed in all night. Found my piece on the premises. Yeah, you know me. Sure, come on over."

Kip stiffens, suddenly understanding.

Vince is in the bathroom, pissing, when the door to the adjoining bedroom swings open. Pressed against the headboard, Kip can see nothing. But he feels the stranger's presence in the room, somewhere behind him, drawing closer; then hears the toilet flush, and Vince returning.

"Jesus, Vince, you sure did a job on his ass." The voice is deep and detached, faintly sarcastic; delivered from the corner of the mouth, with a more pronounced New York accent than Vince's.

"Yeah." The sound of a striking match—Vince lighting a cigarette.

"And such a pretty ass it is. So what does the rest of him look like?"

Vince seizes Kip by the hair and twists him around.

Above him stands a giant of a man. Thick featured, rumple faced, with a broad, flattened nose. Heavyset and balding. He wears a long purple satin robe and smokes a cigar. A gold necklace hangs from his bull-like neck, almost buried in bristling black hair. Rings glitter on both hands.

Leo Battaglia looks down at the bound boy with the buttplug in his mouth and the bow tie around his throat. He sneers and shakes his head. "Ah, Vincent, you're gonna burn in hell for this kind of shit. You and your boys. But I gotta admit—you know how to pick 'em. Pretty as a girl. And such big titties. You always go for the blonds with big tits, no matter what they got between their legs."

Vince shrugs, smiling faintly. "What they all got between their legs, Leo, is a nice, sweet hole."

Leo snorts. "So where'd you find the little cocksucker—in the hotel, you said?"

"Room-service waiter. Delivered a blowjob with breakfast. Came back for more. Just a hustler, really. Works the hotel johns."

Leo cups the boy's chin. Kip meets his stare for an instant, and shudders. Leo runs his thumb in a circle around the rim of the buttplug, grazing the boy's puffy, swollen lips.

"Good mouth?"

Vince kisses his fingertips. "*Perfetto.* Try it on for size."

"You sure we oughta pull out the gag? What if he starts yelling?"

"No sweat. He's plenty softened up by now. Besides, he's got a sugar daddy on the staff. Uncle Max might just about shit his pants if he could see you now—right, Kip?"

Leo nods. He unties the sash at his waist and lets the robe fall.

The utter corpulence of the man's nudity overwhelms Kip. At one time, Leo Battaglia possessed a magnificent physique; in his youth he must have been godlike. But there is nothing beautiful about his body now. Leo is an awesome wreckage of a man, still muscular but long gone to seed. Enormous slablike shoulders, powerful arms. Big, fleshy tits and a hard, overhanging belly. Swirls of kinky black hair carpet his stomach and chest. His body exudes a crude, intoxicating aura of overpowering maleness; virile, overripe sensuality oozes from every pore. Beside him, Kip feels small and ridiculous, trussed up naked and dribbling saliva around the plug in his mouth.

Kip looks down, between Leo's legs. His eyes widen in alarm. He had hoped Leo might have a small cock, at least smaller than Vince's, easy to accommodate and satisfy. But Kip is out of luck. And the night is just beginning . . .

Five o'clock in the morning: Kip lies on the bed, on his side. His mind and body are exhausted. He can hardly move. But he is no longer bound. He might leave now, escape from the room. But Kip is going nowhere. Because Vince is inside him. The man lies behind him on the bed, pressed against Kip's back, joined by a glue of sweat and semen. His cock is lodged deep in the boy's ass, holding him impaled like a fish on a hook. He nuzzles the back of Kip's neck, grazing it with his lips, nipping gently with his teeth.

They are alone, and the room is dark and quiet, except for the low mewling sounds that Kip occasionally makes, like a puppy whimpering in its sleep. Leo has come and gone. Come twice: once in Kip's ass, once in his mouth.

Kip's mind is neither awake nor asleep, but motionless, running in place. The eternity of the past few hours replays itself over and over in his head. Leo's huge, gnarled cock in his mouth. The wire hanger slashing out of nowhere against his already-punished ass— the memory makes him flinch—and the vibrations of Kip's muffled scream coursing through the man's dick, making it tingle. Leo liked the effect. Vince obliged, wielding the hanger with his strong right arm. They traded places. Leo whipped even harder than Vince.

Then they moved on to another game.

Leo seldom fucked ass. At least not boyass. That's what he said. But Kip was the exception. Vince and Leo double-dicked him like seasoned partners, one of them screwing his mouth, the other his rear, pulling out to trade places again and again, until Kip hardly knew which man fucked him and which man he sucked. His body was a long continuous tube, plugged with thick cock at both ends. Eventually they untied him. Leo said something about getting his gun to make sure the kid didn't bolt. The words hardly registered on Kip's exhausted brain, but Vince snapped at Leo to shut up: "You're gonna really fuck us up one of these days, Battaglia. You're always too fucking careless with your mouth . . ."

But his anger cooled quickly as they returned to using Kip. To satisfy Leo, he retied Kip's hands behind his back. They put him on his knees, then took their places at opposite ends of the room and made him crawl stupefied from cock to cock. When one of them had finished with him for the moment, he would shove the boy away, and Kip would shuffle awkwardly to the other, scraping his knees against the carpet until they were raw. Depending on the hole preferred, he would bow his head to suck, or else turn around and stagger to his feet, squatting back to take the waiting cock up his ass while the man across the room watched and pulled on his own freshly serviced dick.

When Kip suddenly came to a standstill in the middle of the room, unable to go on and begging them to let him rest, Vince reached for the hanger. Kip continued to crawl, miles and miles without ever leaving the room.

At some point, hazy in Kip's memory, Leo finally left, returning to his own room, leaving the taste of his oily semen warm and fresh on Kip's tongue.

Then the evening wound down and contracted to a single spot, concentrated at the point where Vince's cock is now snugly lodged inside the boy's well-worked hole . . .

The cock is deeply rooted—almost motionless—but Kip's ass is so tender that the least movement sends twinges of sensation through his crammed bowels. He can feel each beat of Vince's heart from the veins that throb against his rectal walls.

Vince plays his passive body like an instrument, making him whimper and squirm. His caresses are slow, calculated, tender— but Kip's raw flesh is so acutely tuned that even the most delicate touch courses through him like the crack of a whip. Vince runs his fingertips over Kip's nipples, down the ridges of his belly. The boy quivers in response. He squeezes the swollen head of Kip's cock gently, and strokes the shaft once with his forefinger and thumb. Kip shudders, on the verge of coming. Vince flicks his finger against the boy's balls, seizes a hair, and slowly, slowly plucks it— Kip's rectum convulses around the man's cock. Vince runs his hand over the boy's hip, onto his ass, and plays his fingertips across the welts, like a blind man reading braille. His other hand, circling Kip from below, finds a nipple to twist gently. Kip writhes in the man's embrace and squeezes his ass around the big, inexhaustible cock with a slow, steady rhythm.

For Vince, this is the best of all fucks. The final screw. A tenderized hole that throbs around his dick. A boy who quivers like a bowstring in his arms at the least whisper of a touch. It has taken all night to bring Kip to this point. The effort is always worth it.

A pale blue light shows through the heavy drapes. Dawn, and soon Vince will have to end it. Kip is the best he's had in months. He could easily spend a week working the kid over, or a month, grinding him harder and harder beneath his heel seeing just how deep the boy's hunger dwells. But Vince has an early morning flight to catch; and now that the job is done, there is no reason to stay and every reason to leave.

Soon he will come in the boy's ass, for the final time. And then, to milk the last few drops from his cock, he will finally bring Kip off. The boy's cock is primed to bursting, and has been for hours. A single stroke will do it—a glide of his fingernail down the underbelly of Kip's cock, and the stubby little erection will give a twitch and suddenly explode.

And then—

Vince hears a noise.

In the hallway. Muffled steps. Someone walking up the hall. Not someone—the noise is too complicated to come from a lone walker, or even two. A group of people coming up the hall. Vince goes rigid, wide awake.

A sound at the door. Not the normal jangling of a key in a lock, but quiet, methodical—a stalking, covert sound.

He is off the bed in an instant. He takes Kip with him, keeping his cock in the boy's ass as he bolts toward the dresser and fumbles in the open briefcase for his gun. Kip squeals in protest—the swirling movement dizzies him, the sudden jogging of the cock in his ass threatens to send him over the edge. The gun flashes in the corner of his eye and he stiffens in fear, groggy and confused, but coming rapidly to his senses.

The door to the room bursts open, ripping the chain lock from the wall. Almost instantly the overhead light flashes on, blinding after the darkness, as they rush into the room—a man in plainclothes and behind him uniformed police, at least five of them, more in the hallway, all holding guns.

There is a frozen moment of shock on all sides.

Vince's arm is locked across Kip's chest. His cock is still in the boy's ass, throbbing with a jackrabbit pulse. He holds the gun to Kip's throat.

"My, my." The plainclothesman finally speaks. The room seethes with tension, but the man sounds bored, covering his agitation with studied finesse. He shakes his head. "We knew you was a killer, Zorio. But I had no idea . . ."

Kip's whole body prickles with heat. He cannot escape. There is no way to hide. He feels the eyes of all the men rake over his naked body, hoisted to tiptoes on Vince's cock. He hears them murmur in shock and derision. Pussyboy, caught in the act. His cock juts stiffly from his hips for all to see, quivering and closer than ever to coming.

The plainclothesman speaks slowly, deliberately, getting down to business. "Come on, Zorio. There's no way out of this hole. We got half the department down in the lobby. And the rest are taking a coffee break across the street. Come on. You don't wanna hurt the kid."

Vince stands stock-still, breathing hard. His heartbeat pounds like a fist against Kip's back. And then it happens. Kip cannot stop it. He tries desperately to cover himself with his hands, but his arms are pinned to his sides. His cock twitches and bobs in the air, and then begins to shoot—long, spiraling ribbons of stored-up semen that jet halfway across the room, landing with a dull splat on the carpet before the plainclothesman's feet. He writhes helplessly in Vince's hold, jerking weirdly like a puppet. The ordeal seems to go on forever. The officers stare speechless. One of them mutters, "Holy shit!"

Behind Vince, the door to Battaglia's room bursts open. Vince whirls halfway round. A confusion of sudden movement and shouting—"Watch out!"—then the deafening blast of pistol fire, three times in rapid succession.

With each shot, Vince convulses in a horrible parody of fucking Kip's ass. He staggers forward, his weight bowing Kip's shoulders, then falls back. His softening cock pulls out of Kip's bowels with a loud, liquid fart. His body slams the floor with a thud that reverberates into the soles of Kip's feet.

Kip swings around, his cock still twitching and dribbling. For an instant he sees the motionless hulk of Vince's body, lying flat on his back with a strange surly grimace on his face, his eyes wide open. Then the cops are everywhere, a swirling sea of blue, and the plainclothesman is on him, grabbing Kip by the shoulders and steering him toward the door to Battaglia's room. "No," Kip whispers dully, looking over his shoulder, "no . . ."

There are more cops in the other room, and Leo, standing handcuffed in his purple robe, his big ugly face made even uglier by the unexpected tears gushing over his rumpled jowls. The cops, flushed with triumph, are startled at the sight of Kip, then rally with whistles and jeers. "Can it," the plainclothesman says. He yanks the spread from Leo's bed and wraps it over Kip's shoulders.

With the bedspread folded around him, Kip stands mute and numb as a refugee, shivering uncontrollably. The plainclothesman speaks softly, asking him something, but Kip does not hear. He turns and stares into the other room. Through the narrow frame of the doorway, he can see only Vince's legs and feet. Then a blanket descends, and only the feet are visible. And then, as the policemen swarm, even the feet are lost to sight, obscured by a maze of blue trousers and shiny black boots.

# Nicholson Baker

# FROM *THE FERMATA*

Toward the middle of September, Marian's sexual interest inexplicably abated. She put all her dildi and appliances in the drawer that had once held David's sweaters. The last two toys she had ordered—a tiny vibe, teasingly canine in appearance but molded from an impeccably *comme il faut* piece of pickled okra, and a giant Armande Klockhammer, Jr., Signature Model—she didn't even bother to try out before putting them in storage. She felt a mild snobbish contempt for people who devoted so much of their free time to solo sex-play. Her perennial garden, for example, was far more satisfying than a bunch of pastless, futureless orgasms. She read bulb catalogs avidly. After much study she ordered several hundred tulip bulbs from Mack's. When they arrived, via UPS, she gently deflected the eagerly scrotal leer of her friend John in the brown truck. It felt exciting and strange to be more than a sexual being, to have interests. As she looked over the boxes of bulbs, however, she realized that she would need help cutting the beds and planting them all, so she hired the neighbor kid, Kevin.

Ever since she had been mowing her own lawn, she had lost touch with young Kevin. He seemed to have grown an inch or two.

He had gone out for the high jump, and he had acquired a girl-friend named Sylvie, who he said was "a really special person." For a whole weekend and three cool late afternoons he and Marian worked together preparing the soil in the beds with bags of peat and then setting in the bulbs. The dirt was cool through Marian's gloves. After shyly asking whether she would mind, Kevin brought over his radio. At first she was a little irritated by the sound, which disturbed her bucolic alpha-state—but over time several of the songs separated themselves from the others. In one, a woman sang something about Solitude standing in the doorway. She sang, "Her palm is split with a flower with a flame." Marian kept time to this song, first with her troweling, and then with her chin. When she had heard it the second time, she asked Kevin (feeling a little shy herself), "Who does this song?"

Kevin looked up. "Suzanne Vega."

"Ah," said Marian. "I like it."

"Yeah, it's pretty good," said Kevin. He was impossible to read. He dropped another dark bulb in a hole and gently mounded soil around it. Marian glanced at him several times. He had a gray track-and-field T-shirt over a gray sweatshirt. When he pushed on the earth over one of her bulbs, she imagined the muscle in the side of his arm, as she had seen it when he had had his shirt off that day, long ago, at the beginning of summer, before she had learned to mow. And later, when the song came on again, he looked up at her and smiled and then went back to planting—and Marian noticed that his ears were quite red.

She watered the bulbs in and forgot about them. The ground began to look cold—three long beds of very cold bulbs. As winter hit, Marian became caught up in a battle with a developer who wanted to build another mall outside of town. It was going to be enormous and in its own way wonderful—but there was already a shopping center with a discount chain in it that was working under Chapter Eleven, and the downtown would suffer, as it always did.

She went out on several dates with a man she met at the mall meetings, and while she enjoyed talking to him (he was one of those men who have a passionate interest in some particular writer which at first seems sincere, and then finally ends up seeming almost arbitrary—in his case it was Rilke: he seemed to be getting things from Rilke that he could have gotten from any number of poets, while missing whatever it was that Rilke had uniquely), she nonetheless didn't want to do anything more than kiss him cordially in her driveway.

When spring finally came, she went out every day to her tulip beds to watch for activity. It was an unusually dry hot spring, and she felt that she should water to give her beds a good start, but she despaired at her hose. The faucet still leaked tiresomely. The sprayer was rusty. What would make her bulbs really happy, it suddenly occurred to her, was if she could get a plumber to adapt her own Pollenex showerhead so that it would fit on the end of the hose. She needed a very light, very delicate but insistent spray for her tulips—no garden sprayer could offer that. She also thought that the hose water was much too cold—she felt that the bulbs would do better with warmer water. She realized that she wasn't thinking all that rationally, but her idea nonetheless was: hook up the garden hose to the shower-pipe, run the hose out the bathroom window, and fix the Pollenex showerhead onto the terminal end. Other ideas of interest followed on this one; she called a plumber.

The plumber was a thin derisive man with the usual plumber body-smell who rolled his eyes at her plan, told her she could have done it herself, but agreed, since he was there, to do it for her. He fitted the hose ends and the Pollenex with Gardena quick-clamp adapters so that they could be quickly reconfigured for interior showering or exterior gardening applications. The shower pipe looked exotic when he was done, knobbed with hex nuts and adapters, but the system when tested worked quite well. And the plumber, as he cleaned up, was cheerful, pleased by now that he had built something he had never built before, and that he would be able to tell his partner about the nutty job this lady had gotten him to do. He even showed her how to use Teflon tape and was expansive about its merits over older kinds of sealant. He carried his heavy red toolbox out to his truck and drove away.

Over the next few days Marian took her early-morning shower and then opened the window, hooked up the shower-hose arrangement, and turned on the taps to water her tulips. She used only the fine pulse-mist settings, treating her plants as she would want to be treated herself. The tulips responded with enthusiasm—after a week her beds were popping with color. *They* knew the difference between water from a shower, meant for human use, and water from a crude leaky outdoor faucet. She sat on an aluminum chair with the sun on her legs, reading *The Machine in the Garden.* Every so often she glanced up at her tulips. She felt happy. She had planned this to happen and it had happened: she had delayed gratification and now she was getting the payoff. Young Kevin should see what they had done together, she thought, but when she called, Kevin's sour mother told her that he was at practice. Just as well, just as well, she thought. She began to give some consideration to her drawerful of dildae. But she didn't need any of that; no, she'd moved beyond that.

Just then Kevin's little gray cat with white paws showed up on her lawn, making untoward noises and acting oddly. Quite recently it, she, had been a kitten. Now she was clearly in heat, probably for the first time—and very irresponsible it was of Kevin or Kevin's mother not to have had her fixed! She crawled along with her forepaws very low on the ground, making low desperate mezzo-mewings, her tail jerking back, her little narrow feline hips flaunting and twitching in the air, her rear paws working with quick tiptoe steps. Marian could see her gray-furred opening; wetness gleamed from within. She went over and pressed her finger lightly against the cat's tiny slit; gratefully, the cat returned the pressure and tiptoed ardently in place. This was a cat in the grip of a new idea. Wiping her finger on the grass, Marian found that she had

gotten hot looking at this creature's fluttery haunchings. There was
a purity and seriousness to the cat's simple wish to be fucked immediately that Marian found refreshing. The cat didn't want
love—it wanted cat-cock.

Marian was not a committed zoophile, though—at least she
didn't think of herself as one. True, she and her best friend in sixth
grade had made her friend's black Labrador shoot two quick clear
squirts of come once by gently squeezing his dense buried bulb as
he lay on his back with his legs open and his eyes half closed, but
one swallow doesn't make a summer. Marian was a fan of human
cock, for better or worse. (Dog-dick did still have a certain appeal
to her, in part because when it emerged it had a clitoral, almost
hermaphroditic quality: something bisexual in her was triggered
by the sight of it.) Mentally she again reviewed her dildos—how
could she have (one or two late nights excepted) snubbed them all
winter? The idea of running herself a bath, and then straddling the
cold edge of the tub so that all her weight was on the soft place between her vadge and her ass, began to seem attractive. She could
take one of the middle-sized dildi and swish it around in the bath-
water and shake it off, so that it waggled obscenely, and stick it
down on the edge of the tub and squirt Astroglide all over it. She
could arrange herself over it, supporting herself with her hands on
the edge of the tub, looking down past her hanging breasts at the
slick dildo as it slowly disappeared into her sex-hair and found its
thick way up inside her. She went inside to do just this, but by the
time she had actually drawn the bath and gotten into it, she was
much too aroused to do tame things in her bathroom. She got out
and dried off and slipped on a dress. She had a new plan. She
wanted to have a full-fledged Betty Dodsonian PC-muscled clasm
outside in honor of her tulip garden.

She went out in her bare feet, scouting a location. Kevin's cat
had disappeared. After some pacing and gazing, she picked a place
between two of the tulip beds, near where she had seen Kevin's ears
get red when they had talked about the "Solitude stands in the

doorway" song. The problem was, what could she use as a stable base to affix her dildos to? The grass blades would be a ticklish irritant. Back inside, she tried a rectangular black lacquer tray in the kitchen, but it had a raised edge that, when she put it on a chair and experimentally sat down on it, hurt her butt. She considered a Thanksgiving serving platter but didn't like the idea of its breaking; she pondered a small plastic plate left over from a premium frozen dinner, but it wasn't heavy enough. Finally she went into her dining room and took the tea service off of her grandmother's brass tray. The tea service itself was undistinguished, but the tray was a Viennese beauty, chased with circles of bouquets and thick-scaled fish and pine cones and mythical panthery creatures in high relief. In the middle was a very stylized sun—it looked like a fried egg— and this proved to be the perfect surface on which to fix a dildo's suction cup.

The famed male dancer at the Golden Banana, Armande Klockhammer, Jr., had only once in his distinguished career consented to have a lost-wax mold made of the trilogy-in-flesh that had opened so many doors for him. Along the underside of the slightly upcurved and alarmingly lifelike high-grade silicone cock-stalk, Armande's own signature, taken directly from the licensing contract, ran, in such a way that the two bas-relief *m*'s of his surname appeared right over what would have been, had this been his actual dick, its most sensitive part. Marian arranged her virgin Armande Klockhammer, Jr., Signature Model, along with many of its veteran colleagues, on a linen napkin unfolded on her brass tray and bore them out into the garden. She put the tray down in the thick grass in the chosen spot, leaving room on either side for her to plant her feet. There was a slight haze in the sky, so that it was sunny, but not uncomfortably so. When she moved the napkin aside, the light glinted on the tray's ancient pattern, and, once she had squirted copious Astroglide over its head, on the surface of her chosen dildo as well—which looked opulently nasty poking up from that heirloom.

Then, playing hard-to-get now that she knew she had Armande

where she wanted him, she went for a blithe little walk. She was wearing a jumper printed with big loose flowers and nothing underneath. She went to her mailbox, checked that the mail had been delivered, but left it in there. She nodded to a bicyclist going by—he was wearing a kind of skin-tight black cycling shorts that she normally didn't like, but now she didn't mind seeing his thigh definition. She stood at the end of her driveway for several minutes with her arms crossed, breathing deep breaths of spring air and feeling peaceful and content, or playing at looking like the woman out in the garden breathing deeply and feeling content, while actually part of her was thinking over what dildic wickedness was waiting for her in her backyard. On her way back, she bent and felt a leaf of one of the peonies in the tractor tire in her front yard, very casually, giving the road the chance to appreciate her shape under her dress, and murmured to herself, "Hmm, I think it may be time to do some watering." She went in and got the water temperature just right in her shower, and then drew the hose into the bathroom window and hooked it to the shower spigot. Outside, she turned the stopcock on (the plumber had fixed it so that she could turn the flow of water on and off at the end of the hose) and toured her side yard, sending a frolicsome misty spray from her mobile water-source over the grass and over the mock orange leaves. She hummed "Private Dancer." She heard a truck drive past on the road.

When she rounded the back of the house, she surprised a deer who had wandered by, drawn by the tasty-looking tulip blossoms. It appeared to be licking the pink head of the Armande Klockhammer with its equally pink tongue. "Now, now, enough of that!" Marian called, and the deer sprang away. She glanced around to verify that she was indeed in private, and put her foot up on her lawn chair and hiked up her jumper, holding it in a one-handed bunch just below her breasts, and directed the crown of water-jets on her clit-site. The water was just right. "Oh, nice," she said, watching the flow disappear into the grass. The idea that she could carry her daily shower around with her, outside, pleased her quite a lot. She dropped her dress and began watering again, working up the nodding tulip beds. Her maraschino tingled. She pretended to notice for the first time something alien and fleshy sticking up, pinkly out of place in the general verdancy beyond the near bed of tulips. "What's this now?" She pointed the shower-water at it (making sure to rinse away any deer saliva). "What's this sex organ doing sticking straight up in my garden? Does it need something to fuck?" She pulled up her dress. "Is this what Armande wants?" Again she pointed the showerhead up between her legs, now turning it to PULSE. Big dick-shaped bullets of water thumped against the skin surrounding her clit-pearl, against her vadge, and, as she rocked her hips, tickled against the poor-relation sensitivities of her asshole. "Oh man," she said, loving it. "Listen you, if you liked that Bambi-tongue, you're going to *love* my hot little box." The dildo was unresponsive. She walked closer, confronting it. "Oh? So you're not sure? You're not even sure you want to be in my hot little *ass?* You're shy? Well, I'm sorry, you have no choice now—you're going to have to fuck me in the ass." She took the bottle of Astroglide from her jumper-pocket and slid it between her cheeks and squirted herself with it until it trickled down her leg. Then she put her feet on either side of the brass tray and slowly squatted down until she felt the Klockhammer brushing against her butt-muscle. She directed the showerhead back on her clit. She didn't care if her dress got soaked or not. Her thighs began to tremble with the effort of supporting herself over the dildismic pressure without sliding down on it. Finally she couldn't help herself, and she opened her asshole to its big head and sat all the way down on it, until her cheek touched the cold ornate metal of the tray. She rocked on the feeling of a hefty dickful of pleasure up her ass, adjusting to it. Her drenched dress hung over her thighs. She was fucking Armande Klockhammer's autograph! God, it felt good.

"Hello?" came a voice. Marian looked up to see young Kevin and a girl standing hand in hand a little way off. She supposed the girl was Sylvie, Kevin's new girlfriend. Kevin was looking recently

showered, spruced up, and proud of himself, though momentarily
puzzled. Marian saw his eyes skip down over her exposed, wet legs.
The two of them were wearing matching red-and-white-striped
polo shirts. Marian made a quick attempt to pull her dress down
and over some of the sex toys next to her. She began watering the
tulips with little flips of the showerhead, as if she were conducting
a Sousa march.

"Hi," she said. "Pardon me, I was just doing a little watering.
Come over. Let me turn this off. I had a plumber rig it up for me.
Are you Sylvie?"

"Yes, hi," said Sylvie. Sylvie leaned and shook Marian's hand. She
was a petite, perky, small-breasted girl with long light-brown hair
and a pleasant sly sharp-nosed face. Marian liked her immediately.

Kevin said, "My mom told me you called, so we thought we'd
come over and say hello."

"I just wanted you to see all these tulips," said Marian. "They
turned out well, I think. Thank you for helping me with them."

Kevin nodded. "I like the crinkly ones." He turned to Sylvie.
"Last fall I helped her plant all these."

"They're really really pretty," Sylvie agreed. There was an awkward silence. From a distant part of the yard there came an odd
hissing sound. Kevin's gray cat appeared from behind one of the
mock oranges. A huge golden chewn-eared stray was on top of her.
Kevin's cat crept forward a few inches and then stopped, and the
gold cat, holding Kevin's cat down and biting her neck quite hard,
made tiny jerks of its hindquarters, holding its tail low and fluffed.
The two animals, who didn't seem to like each other much, stared
at nothing at all while they fucked.

"Oh jeepers," said Kevin.

"You really should have taken her to the vet, Kevin," said Marian, though she said it gently.

"I was planning to."

"I can take a kitten if there are some," said Sylvie brightly,
thinking ahead. "Maybe even two."

Marian smiled at her. "That's solved, then. Well!" It was time for them to be off. "I'm really glad you two dropped by. It's very nice to meet you, Sylvie."

"Nice to meet you. But can I ask you something?" said Sylvie. "What are all those?" She pointed to the sex toys laid out on the white linen napkin. Marian's dress didn't really hide them effectively.

"I don't know that we should get into that," said Marian.

"Okay, sorry," said Sylvie. "I kind of know what they are anyway—I mean, it's obvious, but I just want to know what you're doing with them out here. Are you planning on burying them or planting them or something?"

Kevin's ears were changing color. He was readjusting his notion of his employer. Sylvie just looked friendly and sly and curious.

Marian said, "No, I'm not burying them. I just thought it would be exciting to try out a few of them outdoors, and I wasn't sure which ones I would want. It seemed like such a nice setting, my own backyard, with the new parrot tulips."

"Can I look at one?" said Sylvie.

Marian passed her the most decorous dildo—a medium-sized clear lucite thick-veined figurine that the catalog called the Ice Princess. Sylvie handled it carefully, using her fingertips, not, it seemed, out of repugnance, but out of politeness for another's treasures.

"Sylvie," said Kevin in an undertone. "I think she probably wants us to go."

"She's welcome to take a look if she wants," said Marian casually. The Klockhammer deep in her ane was now beginning to reassert itself; it was silencing any objections she might otherwise have had to showing two teenagers wearing matching striped shirts her fuckable toys.

"Can I see that really long one, with the two ends?" said Sylvie.

"Ah yes—this is my Royal Welsh Fusilier. Here."

"Wowsers!" Sylvie held the two dick-ends together, jerking on them so that the movable foreskins wrinkled and stretched in tandem. She offered one end to Kevin, who inspected it with fascination in spite of himself.

"I don't exactly get why you would need something this long with two ends," he said.

Marian hesitated. "Any number of reasons."

"One of which is," said Sylvie to Kevin, "if you misbehave with Karen in any way ever again, I'll put one end right up your fanny and make you jump in your next meet with it in."

"Karen is over," said Kevin. Deferentially he thanked Marian, handing his end directly back to her. "Where did you purchase all these things?" he asked, with an air of serious inquiry.

"Oh, from a place in San Francisco," said Marian. She was using every ounce of willpower she had to keep from announcing to the two of them that she had a massive dildungsroman installed in her butt.

"Maybe sometime you could give us the address," said Kevin, still very serious, very grown up. "We might want to order something or other. Right, Syl?"

"You never know," said Sylvie.

Marian looked at them both and laughed happily. "God, it's nice to see young love," she said. "Are you two lovers, then?"

They both nodded. "We've made love thirty-two times in two months," said Sylvie proudly. "In fact," she continued, putting a fond arm around Kevin's waist, "we were just going out for a little 'drive,' because Kevin's mother doesn't like us going up to his room anymore—which I can understand."

"Ah, a little 'drive,'" said Marian. She looked at Kevin with amused surprise—the employer surprised at the precocity of the employee.

"Yeah," Kevin agreed, gesturing vaguely in the direction of the road. "We'll probably go on over to the fish hatchery."

"Well, terrific," Marian said. "Have a glorious glorious time, you two. I wish I could . . . I mean, I wish you well." She shifted a little on the brass tray and felt the thick steadfast dilderstatesman issuing official pleasure-briefings down her legs and up to the warm unforgotten Fijis of her nipples. It was so fucking *hard*—so hard to keep from saying the things she wanted to say with it deep in there: she wanted to yank up her wet dress for them and say, "Go on and fuck each other silly! Take a good look at this monster cock jammed up my butt! I want you to look right at my asshole crammed with this big fat *dick* and then go out and fuck and suck each other and slam your bodies together!" Her skin prickled with the almost irresistible wish to be obscene. But all she said was, "I must say, I envy you both a little. I'm just sorry I can't get up and see you off . . ."

Sylvie was immediately full of concern. She touched Marian lightly on the arm. "Are you okay? Can we help you up? You know your dress has gotten a little wet."

"I know, I know," said Marian, "I've been watering everywhere."

"Everywhere?" said Sylvie. "Isn't it kind of cold?"

"The water's warm. It's from my shower. Feel." Marian turned the stopcock on and whisked the showerhead spray once over Sylvie's outstretched hand.

"Feels really nice," said Sylvie thoughtfully.

"The tulips love it," said Marian. "In fact, will you two do me a favor and pick some for each other before you go? As my present to you? Pick the ones you like most. The Etruscan Prune variety is my favorite at the moment, but choose whichever ones you want."

Sylvie and Kevin liked this idea a lot and set to work assembling reciprocal bouquets. Now that their eyes were off Marian, she was free to move on the tray again and make pleasure noises in a whispery undertone. She watched them circle her beds. She imagined them all breathless and loving and wide-eyed in a shady spot near the fish hatchery. They were beautiful—fit, healthy, incredibly young—so inexperienced that they thought that their two-digit courtship, or coitship, made them seasoned fuckers. She knew so much more than they did. She lifted the sodden hem of her dress just a little and pointed the showerhead between her legs and let it flood her twat-cleavage. "That's not nearly enough, Kevin—pluck more!" she called gaily, wanting to risk his hearing the irrepressible vulval surges and catches in her voice.

When they stood in front of her again, holding their tulip bunches out to her for her admiration, she pronounced both arrangements equally lovely and told them to give them to each other. This they did with great ceremony.

"Thank you!" said Kevin to Sylvie.

"Thank you!" said Sylvie to Kevin.

They kissed. It appeared that their mouths were a good match. Marian, who normally felt squirmy and put off when she was a witness to heavy public pair-bonding, watched this particular kiss with nothing but good feeling. She *was* the public, after all. There was some tongue-action, but it had the license of youth and looked like it felt better than it looked. They hugged each other hard; Sylvie's heel went behind Kevin's and she used the leverage to press her blue-jeaned mound into him.

When they stopped, Marian said, "What a great kiss! You two are obviously *great* kissers. You must be beautiful when you . . . make love. Your bodies fit together so well. I wish I could—" She shook her head ruefully, her hand on her heart, and let them laugh at the impossibility of what she was thinking, so that they could start to get used to the idea. Then she slapped her hands on her legs and said, "I tell you what. If you would like to borrow any of these toys, feel free. Really. I don't make any great claims for them—I'm sure you can do without them, but who knows, just for fun . . ."

They looked indecisive.

Marian exerted the slightest additional pressure. "Pick one—or a few, even." She felt a trickle of sweat on her back.

"What do you think, Kevin?" said Sylvie.

Kevin shrugged. "Sure, I guess, yeah."

Sylvie and Kevin knelt, not minding apparently that their knees got instantly soaked in the wet grass. Sylvie's face, though averted, was very close to Marian's. "Which one would you recommend?" the girl finally asked, having touched them all lightly.

"Mmm, well—" This was just too much for Marian. She felt her resistance give way completely. "My current favorite is one I just got," she said. "It's called the Armande Klockhammer. As you may know, Armande Klockhammer, Jr., is, or was, a male stripper at the Golden Banana. It's kind of big, actually. Almost too big, depending on where you need it to go."

"Which one is it?" Sylvie asked.

Marian cleared her throat. "I'm afraid I can't show it to you right now."

"Why not?" Sylvie looked at her with innocent curiosity.

"I just can't."

"But why?" Sylvie insisted. "Where is it?"

"It's in use," said Marian. She looked at her two young friends and then down at her wet dress.

Kevin looked surprised. He had finally pieced it together. "You mean that all the time we've been here it's been . . ."

Marian took a deep breath. "Up my ass, yes."

"Up your . . . It's not in your . . . it's in your . . . ?" Sylvie, pointing to parts of herself to clarify her exclamation, looked genuinely surprised.

"It feels super, I must tell you," said Marian. "But that's not the crazy thing. The crazy thing is how badly I want to show it to you. While it's in there, I mean. I'm doing everything I can to keep from hauling this dress up right now and leaning back and showing you how good it feels stuffed up my tight butt. Oh man! Just thinking about it gets me going. Are you repulsed?"

They continued to look a little surprised, but not repulsed.

Marian went on. "I'm afraid you caught me at a particular moment. Kevin, you can attest to the fact that I don't normally talk this way."

"She doesn't at all, no," Kevin agreed.

"It's dildo talk, frankly," Marian went on. "It's the way I talk when I'm sitting on a big fat artificial dick. What can I say? My butt is stretched so damn tight right now—I wish you could see, I really do. I wish I could show you, and I wish when you saw it in my ass you'd take off all your clothes and make love for me right here. Is that so unthinkable? I don't think it's so unthinkable. Kevin, I was so good last summer. Do you realize that? I thought about your cock quite a number of times, I thought about sucking it and jerking it off—I even thought of putting a sprig of parsley in your tiny little cockhole, and yet I never once did *anything!* And now you've found Sylvie, this wonderful friendly open person, who probably sucks your cock beautifully, and it makes me feel so good that you've found her—it makes me want to *see her* suck on your cock. God, I wish I could show you what I have up my ass right now. It feels so fucking hot." She paused. "See, that's a sample of dildo talk."

Sylvie was the first to speak. "You can show it to us," she said. "We won't mind."

"Really?" said Marian. "Well, you take off all your clothes, then, both of you. I'm not going to show you anything until all your clothes are off. Take them off."

Obediently Sylvie and Kevin took off their pants and under-pants and pulled off their matching striped shirts. When the dan-gling and tugging and hopping had ceased and they stood naked in front of her, Marian couldn't help whistling in amazement. Their bodies were so simple and perfect. Sylvie's flattish slanting breasts, with sharp confident little suck-tips, were especially good for the soul. Kevin's white straight penis lobbed and loitered below his tight brown balls; he had a Dennis-the-Menace touch of hair around each of his nipples. Marian had to turn the Pollenex on and point it up her dress in order to recover her seducer's concentration.

"Now show us," said Sylvie challengingly, conscious that her re-vealed beauty gave her power. She ran her fingers over her stomach and brushed the side of her hand casually against Kevin's cock. "Show us what's up your . . ."

"Ah, you're such a beautiful couple," said Marian. "You're made to fuck each other. I'll show you when it's the right time. Right now, I need you to show me how pretty you are together. Show me how you like to suck cock, Sylvie honey. I want to see your pretty lips on that hot cockmeat. Kiss it for me."

Sylvie, compelled by the conviction in Marian's voice, knelt and kissed a path down Kevin's cock until she came to its head, and then she opened her lips and let it fill her mouth. As he watched her and moaned, Kevin's mouth mirrored Sylvie's. He was standing with his hands crossed lightly at the wrists behind his back, his hips pushed forward, looking down at his girlfriend. As he firmed up, Sylvie's jaw was forced open wider and her tongue was pushed down, and Marian was pleased to see her develop a cocksucker's temporary double chin, which, because in reality the girl had nothing approaching a double chin, only made her face look younger and more captivatingly innocent.

"That's so nice, so pretty, that pretty sucking," said Marian, letting her showerhead do the talking for her. Areas of grass near her legs were getting a marshy gleam.

Sylvie turned and looked at her. Her eyes were dreamy with confused arousal. "Please show me and Kev what you have up your fanny," she said again. She added rhetorical weight to her request by stroking three times on Kevin's cock.

Marian pulled her dress up so that it was very high on her thighs, but not so high that anything was revealed. She lifted her weight on her hands for a moment and then swiveled her hips. "It's all slicked up with lubricant. It feels so snazzy in there. I want it in there always. I want to show it to you as it fucks my butt, but I need some inspiration. I need to see your cute little asshole first, Sylvie. That's only fair. Squat right over my feet—I want to see your beautiful back and your open ass and your hot little asshole while you suck your boyfriend's cock."

"But—" said Sylvie.

"You know you want to show me everything about your body.

You're not ashamed of anything, are you? You're proud of your body. You know you want me to look right at your ass while you suck that luscious dick. Don't you?"

"Yes," said Sylvie. "I want you to watch me sucking on Kevin." She planted her feet on either side of Marian's ankles and squatted, her back to the older woman. Marian twisted the showerhead to PULSE and aimed the spray in circles over Sylvie's ass globes.

"Pull your cheeks apart—I can't quite see you, and I need to see you," said Marian. Sylvie got two handfuls of her ass and pulled up, and Marian saw the dark little dot where they met and joined. She pointed the water's pulse straight at it. Sylvie arched her back to get a more direct hit; her breaths began to come harder and more irregularly through her nose. Her hair bobbed as her mouth emptied and filled with cock.

"*That's* what I like to see," said Marian. "Kevin, I wish you could see how beautiful Sylvie is when she sucks on your cock with her sexy ass all open and clean." Kevin looked up at her as she said this, and Marian, as she continued to murmur encouragement, gave him a brief secret show, looking straight at him as she jogged her tits under her dress and pinched her nipples through the fabric. Her fingers were wet, so they left dark marks where they had been. Then, when she knew she had his allegiance, she said, "Kevin, do you mind if I tickle Sylvie's pretty butt with the flowers she gave you? You want her to feel good while she sucks your big dick, don't you?"

"Go ahead," said Kevin thickly.

Marian leaned forward and brushed the tulip heads across Sylvie's shoulders and down her back. She slapped them lightly back and forth on the insides of the girl's fine thighs and up against her popped-out clit. "Ooo, she likes it," she said. Then she turned the tulips in a circle over Sylvie's asshole. "Do you like my flowers tickling your pretty butt? I bet you do."

Sylvie said something affirmative and sucked some more. Then she stopped. She didn't let go of Kevin's shiny cock, but she said, "Could I use your bathroom for a second? I'm dying."

"Sure," said Marian. "But you don't have to. Why lose time? Just let it go. I'll spray it away. Piss it right out on my feet."

"Pee on your feet?" Sylvie exclaimed. "No way! I can't do that."

"Of course you can," Marian said. "What's the harm? Just keep sucking that tasty dick and relax. When I have a big rubber dick up my asshole I like to see everything. I *want* to see it. I want to feel it spray out all over my feet—warm up these lonely toesies." She played the showerhead spray insistently over Sylvie's climb-folds. "Suck and push, honey," she urged. "It'll feel good, believe me. Arch your back so I can see."

Sylvie resumed sucking Kevin's cock.

"Push for me," said Marian. "Push that piss out." But nothing happened.

"I'm really sorry—I can't," said Sylvie. "I'm a little shy about that in front of Kev."

"Ah, I see. Kevin? You don't mind, do you? Of course not. In fact, you know what? I'd love to see a little dribble of piss come out of that big friendly cock. I bet that would help Sylvie relax." Marian moved one of her feet out where Kevin could see it. "Let her hold your cock and jerk on it a little and then point it straight at my feet and push and let go. I bet you can do it."

"Really?" said Kevin. He held his dick for Sylvie to aim it.

"Of course!" said Marian.

"Okay," he said. Sylvie gripped the base of his cock and Kevin's stomach muscles tightened and he pressed his lips together and forced out a curve of hot piss that momentarily reached Marian's foot.

"That's the way!" said Marian. "How did it feel?"

"Felt good," said Kevin. "Kind of burny." He wiped the tip of his dick with his palm.

"Of course it did," Marian said. "Now, Sylvie? You know how badly you need to let it go. You know what's up my ass. How could you possibly be shy?" Again she tapped the flowers against Sylvie's cunt. "Push and piss it out for me."

Sylvie gave it a second try. She pushed very hard. After a moment, her tiny urethra opened and a clear spurt flared out. The flow stopped almost immediately.

"Good!" said Marian. "More!"

"But," Sylvie objected, "I'm pushing so hard I'm afraid something else might happen." She stood up. "I really *need* to use the bathroom—I'm not kidding."

"Oh, but I want to see that, too," said Marian. "I want to see everything you can do."

"Gross, no way!" said Sylvie.

Kevin decided that it was time for him to intercede. "I really don't think she can do that," he said. "I mean, I wouldn't mind at all if she did, but . . ."

Marian pulled off her dress in a quick motion. "Look at this dick up my ass." She leaned back on her hands and lifted her knees back against her body. "See that butthole? See how nice and tight it is? Look at that tight skin. You can look for as long as you want. Look at me rock on it. Can you see it moving in and out? Foo, that's nice! I like to see your eyes on it." She looked at them both and shook her tits for them. "Now, Sylvie, it's your turn. I've showed you, now you show me. Show me that tight little butt of yours again. See, I had no idea you were as full as I am. I want to see that ass open right up, just like mine is. Suck that cock of his and push it out for me. Once you do that, you'll feel free to do anything that feels good, anything you want, and you'll come extra hard, and that's what I want—I want you to come extra hard, because you can be damn sure that's what I'm going to do."

"I really have to go," said Sylvie. "I'm not kidding."

"I know you do! Squat down just like you were and suck that cock. I'll spray you clean, don't worry. Pull up on your cheeks so I can see. Push and let it go."

Sylvie took up her cocksucking squat. She started sucking more Kevin-dick, but faster than before. She pulled one of her cheeks open. Her asshole looked exactly the same—tiny, sexy. Then suddenly her piss gushed out everywhere.

"Ah, that's it!" said Marian, frigging her clit. "Show me how you let it all go. Release it. That's it. Let it all go. Feel it relax." Marian whisked the linen napkin out from under her toys and held it at the ready. "Let that lovely butt open right up for me."

Sylvie made a moan of warning. Her asshole domed out into a doughnut shape and began to open.

"Good!" said Marian. "Now stop! Tighten back up on it."

Sylvie made a straining sound. Her hips rocked, and her asshole slowly closed.

Marian was frigging faster now. She let the spray drive into Sylvie's ass. "That's right, honey," she coached. "Keep sucking that dick. I know you need to let it out. Push on it."

"It's really going to come out this time," said Sylvie, somewhat frantically. "I can't hold it."

"I know you can't hold it. I just want to see your ass open one more time. It's *so* sexy to see it open up. Let it go. Push now. Give it to us. Come on, push."

Sylvie moaned again. Her asshole domed and opened wider, and a big dark hard dickshape began to push its way straight out. Marian held the napkin underneath. "Oh yeah. Keep pushing, baby. Push it all out." She felt the weight drop in her hand and immediately folded the napkin over it and sprayed Sylvie clean. "*Now* we're ready!" she said. "We're ready to fuck, kids. Come on, Sylvie, get on your hands and knees over me. Open that cunt for Kevin's cock. I want to see Kevin's hard dick up your cunt while I pinch your nipples. Come on. I want to see some good hard fucking!"

But Sylvie didn't obey immediately. She had rights now. She was free to do anything she wanted. Boldly she lifted one of Marian's juggy tits and bent to slap it around with her tongue. Then, bringing her blond cunt-site close, she brushed Marian's nipple-tip over her neglected clit. "Could you hold those tits tight and point them right at my pussy?" she requested, with the zeal of a convert. "I think I've got a little pee left over for them." Sylvie pushed and let a brief spurt spray over Marian's mildly surprised breasts. "Let

me hose it off," she said, and she took the showerhead from Marian
and sprayed her mentor off.

"See?" said Marian, recovering quickly. "You can do anything
now."

"Yeah, and *now* I'm ready for some cock. I need to be fucked
good, Kev. Give it to me good."

She arranged herself on her elbows and knees over Marian's legs.
Marian grabbed the girl's asscheeks and spread her open. Kevin got
behind Sylvie; he stared at his girlfriend's impish twat as if he'd
never seen it before and pumped his dick in his fast fist. It was a
handsome dick, no question; watching him, Marian felt she needed
to hold that purple stanchion for herself at least once. "Sylvie?" she
asked. "You won't mind if I make sure your lover is good and stiff
for you, will you?"

"No, just do it fast and get him in there!" said Sylvie, kissing
her own biceps muscle. "Either that or shove one of those big
dildo-dicks up my cunt and jerk him off onto my asshole. Your
choice. But get something big up my cunt now!"

"I'll get him nice and fat for your cunt," said Marian. She surrounded Kevin's cock with her right hand and registered its
warmth and livingly resisted rigidity. It felt, she found herself ob-
serving, extremely realistic. She steered its head toward the opening of Sylvie's pink slot and jerked its stem fairly hard in place a
few times. "Feel the big head?" she said. "Wiggle a little for him.
He's almost ready." She looked up at Kevin and mimed a licking
mouth to show him how she would lick his dick if given the opportunity. He was aroused and slit-eyed, and, she noticed, he was
gazing fixedly at her breasts.

"Could you please put him in now?" urged Sylvie.

"He's going to push it in now," Marian said, giving his dick a
few last jerks. "Push that cock in her, baby." She held his shaft for
as long as she could until it disappeared into Sylvie's cunt; Sylvie
was very tight but equally wet, and the dick's length slid in without bending.

"Oh, fuck, that's good," said Sylvie, sighing with relief. Immediately she and Kevin started slapping fast against each other.

"Oh yeah! I like to see that dick slapping in there!" said Marian, turning the showerhead on her clit. "I can feel it in my cunt just looking at it! Yeah! My cunt is so empty and yours is so full of that sweet hot dickmeat!"

As they fucked, Sylvie focused on the dildos, which lay tumbled on the grass. The girl turned so that her face was close to Marian's. Her hair was in her eyes. In an uneven whisper, she said, "I need one of those. Pick one and put it in my ass, will you? Please?"

Marian brushed the tulips down Sylvie's back and tapped them against her asshole. Then she replaced the flowers with her middle finger, resting it lightly on the opening. "Is that where you want something? Right in there?"

"Oh," moaned Sylvie, "I want what's in your ass."

"Honey, I've got something much better than that for you," said Marian. "Kevin, look where my finger is. Isn't that a pretty little asshole? Has your cock ever been in there?"

Kevin shook his head no. His hands were on Sylvie's hips, and he was pushing with a circling motion of his hips, making gravelly grunts.

"I want to see that dick up that gorgeous little butt. That okay with you, Sylvie? You want your honey's big burning dick up your ass? Believe me, it'll feel good. You know you want it, don't you."

"Yeah I want it, I want it," said Sylvie.

"You want it straight up your ass, don't you," Marian repeated.

"I *need* it up my ass," Sylvie pleaded. "Kev, I need it up my ass!"

Marian grabbed the four-foot-long Welsh Fusilier and turned it on. She whispered to Sylvie, "Slide this up my cunt." Sylvie fumblingly obliged. "That's good. I want our slutty cunts to be connected while you get fucked up the ass for the first time," Marian said. She handed her end of it to Kevin. "Pull out of her, baby. Push this in instead." Kevin's long glossy dick emerged from behind the horizon of Sylvie's ass-curve and with evident reluctance he fed the end of the double-vibe where he had just been. Sylvie made a surprised shout and arched her back and started fucking against it.

As soon as Marian saw Kevin's cock reappear, she knew she had to suck it. This was her one chance. "Oh, God, that's a pretty cock," she said. "I need a real dick in my mouth for a second, just for a *second*. Come over here for a second, baby. Sylvie, he needs to be super stiff for your tight little butt. You don't mind if I get his dick good and stiff for you with my tongue, do you? I'm sorry, but I just have to suck on this dick."

"Suck him!" said Sylvie. "Ooh, God, suck him stiff for me. Just hurry and get something big up my ass. I'm so hot for it." She circled Marian's clit with her end of the Fusilier, gazing at the base of the Klockhammer buried in the older woman's ass. Marian, her mouth stuffed with purple cock, groaned and opened her legs for the pleasure. As Sylvie felt Kevin jabbing the other Welsh-head in and out of her own buzzing cunt-lips, she reached back and spread her asscheeks open and said, "That's enough. Stop sucking my boyfriend's dick and get it in my ass!"

Marian pulled her mouth off of Kevin's dick. "Okay, sweetie, it's ready for you." She squirted lube on Sylvie's asshole. The squirt bottle made rude noises, but nobody cared. She pulled Kevin into position by his cock and tapped the head of his dick on Sylvie's now-sloppy ass-crack, circling it over the opening. Then she pointed it and held it still. "Okay, push in slow, Kevin. Open up for him, Sylvie. He's going in."

"Push it in me! Fuck this ass!" cried Sylvie.

Marian held Kevin's cockshaft while it began to drive slowly in. It bent a little as he put his weight behind it; then, as Sylvie relaxed for him, it straightened out and filled her.

"There he goes," said Marian.

"Fuck me with that dick, oooooooo!" said Sylvie. Kevin began making very slow long strokes.

"That's it, Kevin—fuck straight into her perfect ass—you're getting it." Marian took hold of the end of the vibrator in her cunt and started pulling it in and out in rhythm with Kevin's steady dick-thrusts. Its length curved up and disappeared into Sylvie's clim. She kissed Sylvie on the shoulder. "God, I like being con- nected to your sexy pussy, sweetie!" she said. Sylvie was looking straight ahead, taking little breaths as she pushed back on Kevin's thickness. "You like him in your ass, don't you?" Marian asked her.

"I like him to fuck me hard!" said Sylvie. "Fuck my hot ass, Kev. I'm getting closer to the smiley face!" She looked at Marian. "That's what we say when we're going to come soon," she breath- lessly explained.

Marian sprang into action. "Hold on, though—one last thing." She picked up the little okra-sized dildo and slipped it over her middle finger and squirted some Astroglide on it. "Can I put this in Kevin's ass?" she whispered. "I want to feel him fucking you when you come. Can I?"

Sylvie blew up on her bangs and nodded. "Just hurry." Marian flicked the okra-dick over Sylvie's nipples and then dragged it down Kevin's ribs and slid around to the base of his back and gripped the near cheek of his ass, so that her four fingers were near his asshole.

"What are you doing?" Kevin said, freezing suddenly.

"I'm putting some okra up your ass so you won't feel left out," said Marian. "I want to help you fuck Sylvie. I want to feel you fucking her ass, and I want your asshole to feel you fucking *her* ass- hole. Don't trouble yourself—just let it in and keep fucking."

"Let her do it, Kev!" Sylvie called earnestly.

Kevin overcame his uncertainty and resumed his slow, deliber- ate ass-fucking. But now, each time he pulled out for the next thrust, Marian drove the okra-dick a little farther into his reluctant male hole. He seemed to like it more after a minute or two, and as he began to get his own butt in gear, Marian started urging and guiding his movements, making him go a little faster, getting him to angle his thrusts, the way she knew Sylvie wanted it. Every push he made made his high-jumper's maximums-muscles bunch memorably under Marian's cupping hand. "See how she likes it faster?" Marian said. "Fuck her like this." She controlled his pumping torso with the okra-plug like a puppet-master and he said, "Oh, jeepers! Get it up there!"

"Pinch my nipples hard!" Sylvie ordered Marian in an urgent whisper. "I'm right *at* the smiley face," she called to Kevin.

"Let's get off together," said Marian, pinching as she was told. "Come on. Come on, come on. Fuck her, Kevin! Shoot that come in her. Look at this cock up my butt, Sylvie. Come over me. Oh! Oh fuck!" She let go of Sylvie's nipples and held the Welsh-head tight to her love-bean as her orgasm gathered the necessary signatures. The autographed Armande had been in her ass for so long that she felt the biggest climax of her life had to be well on its way. But she wasn't quite ready for it. She pushed her breasts forward and said, "Suck my tit-bags for a second, Sylvie. Suck them hard, bite them, bite them. Oh shit! Now come for me. Come around that hot dick-meat."

"Oh, God!" said Sylvie. She tried to suck Marian's nipples but couldn't concentrate on them and arched her neck, staring forward at the invisible pleasure in her head.

"That's okay—come for me, baby. She's starting to come, Kevin! Shoot that hot juice up her ass for her! Fill her ass with that burning come!" Marian finger-fucked the okra-dick faster in and out of Kevin's asshole, and he leaned forward to take it and then straightened up, lifting Sylvie by the hips right off the ground and pulling her back against his cock. "Now, Sylvie?" he said.

"Oh, fuck me good, Kev! Fill my fucking fanny!" Sylvie shouted, looking in Marian's eyes and then down at her toy-filled fuckholes. "Harder! Oh yes! Fuck me real good, darling! SHOOT THAT HOT DICK UP MY FANNY-HOLE! OH! OH!"

With an astonished expression, Kevin made one last long lurching shuddering push and started to come.

"OH YES!" said Sylvie, feeling Kevin's cock empty ounce after ounce of boiling scream-cream into her ass. "AH! I'M COMII-

INNNG!!!!!" As pagan pleasures wracked her body, she did indeed make a huge grimacing smiley face.

It was Marian's turn now. She allowed the idea of Kevin's squirting dick in Sylvie's ass to merge with the sensation of Armande Klockhammer, Jr.'s in her own. She conjured up the sight of the dollar bills stuffed in his asscheeks as he danced with his back to the audience. She thought of the shouting women; the whomping music; the sight of him turning on the stage and tossing his heavy live meat around inside its black silk pouch as he looked out at all his women. All these memories were *up her ass.* She opened her eyes and said evenly, "Please watch me come, now, you two. Watch my asshole and cunt come around these huge horny cocks!" Then she threw herself back on the wet grass and lifted her legs and rested her feet on Sylvie's back; she let them watch whatever they wanted while the brutish, hunky orgasm ennobled her body. "Oh nice . . . so nice . . . so nice . . ." she sighed as the clit-twitching ebbed.

When the three of them had recovered a little, Marian rinsed off Kevin's softening cock and lifted herself off the Klockhammer and sprayed it fresh.

"Can we pick some more of your tulips sometime?" said Sylvie sweetly before she and Kevin, dressed once again in their matching outfits, left for the fish hatchery.

"Anytime you want," said Marian. "I love young love." Naked, replete, she put her toys and her abandoned book on the tray and went indoors. Over the next year, with Kevin and Sylvie's weekend help weeding and planting and mowing, her backyard became the envy of her neighbors.

Rose White and Eric Albert

# SHE GETS HER ASS FUCKED GOOD

When she wakes up, he's in her ass.

"Isn't this your second time tonight?"

"I'm not the only guy who's had another turn."

So that explains the ache there, the raw, tender, exhilaratingly sensitive feeling in her ass. Her ass is all relaxed, his cock glides in and out, like all the other cocks have done. Her ass has been used for hours and she's loved it.

More awake, she pushes back against him, grinds her ass into his crotch, makes sure his cock is in as far as it can go. She's sore, but she still loves feeling his cock up her, loves feeling it get harder while he thrusts, loves feeling his crotch hit her ass, and hit her again, his balls slapping against her gently even though the fucking is hard.

She's on her hands and knees now, butt tilted up to get the best of his cock, to get his cock against the sweet spot in her ass. She puts her hand between her legs and starts to play with her pussy. She fingers her clit and he moans, he tells her how tight that makes her ass. She puts her finger in her cunt and feels his cock through the wall of her cunt. She presses against his cock and makes him moan again. She's really worked up now. She wants to come with a hard cock up her ass, to feel her ass contract around a hard cock. Like all the other times tonight.

She can't count anymore how many times she's come, come just like this, with a man behind her, with a cock up her ass. She can't count anymore how many men. She's completely lost track, lying there on the bed, with the blindfold on. Sometimes she knows them, knows them by how they touch her, how they fuck her, how they moan. When they're quiet, though, when they don't make noise and they don't touch her, she doesn't know them, she only knows their cocks. For long stretches tonight, that is all she has known.

She gets serious about coming. He's thrusting steadily and that makes it easier for her. She fucks back against him as she fingers herself. First she plays with her clit, touching and teasing it, feeling it rise. Then she starts in on it, pressing against it hard, rubbing it with her fingertips. The warmth spreads so not just her clit but her whole cunt feels hot and wet and heavy.

"Put it in my pussy."

He pauses. Then he's moving in her ass again.

"Why."

"I need it there."

He fucks her some more, sliding in smooth and fast and banging her, hard, each time his cock hits bottom, taking her breath away, keeping her from doing anything but moaning. Finally he slows down.

"Why."

"Because it's hard. Because it's dirty."

"You sure?"

"Yes, I'm sure. Fuck my pussy."

He pulls completely out of her and she feels his cock hard and straining in the cool night air behind her cunt.

"You sure?"

"Yes. Yes."

He slams back into her ass, there's no resistance as the head of his cock enters her, she's instantly full with him.

"Your asshole's so loose, might as well be your cunt."

"Please."

"Why."

"My pussy needs your prick."

"You tell me why."

"You know why. Stuff it up my cunt, then in my ass then in my cunt then in my ass till I can't tell what you're fucking anymore."

"You say that to all the guys."

She gasps.

"That right?"

She's shaking. His prick moves in her tender ass.

"You put your butt up in the air and wait and anyone comes along can stick his thing in your holes, that right?"

". . . that's right." She's whispering.

"Asshole, cunt, you don't care, long as someone's fucking you."

"Yes."

"Tell me."

"Anyone. Anyone can stick it in."

"Three guys, one after the other."

"Yes."

"Ten guys."

"Oh. Yes." Her clit jumps. She stops rubbing, starts tapping lightly, holding the orgasm back.

"Tell me."

"Ten hard pricks sound good to me. Ten guys using me."

He jerks out of her. She moans. He slaps her ass with his prick, she feels the sticky mark he leaves.

"Put it in my pussy. Please."

"Suck me clean first."

She opens her mouth without a thought. Behind the blindfold she sees herself: crouching, ass up, nipples hard, mouth open, everything open. Bitch in heat, she thinks.

He slips back up her ass.

"You'll do anything to get me in your cunt. Won't you."

"Yes."

"Say it."

"I'll do anything you want. Uhh." He's rammed her. He pulls back out.

"Tell me."

"I'll take your prick down my throat."

"You do that anyway."

"You can hit me. Hard as you want."

"Don't feel like hitting you."

"Anything. You tell me what."

"You going to piss all over this bed?"

"Jesus." She yanks her hand off her clit, too close to coming. "Just put it in. I'll soak your prick. I'll soak the sheets."

"All to get my dirty cock inside your pretty cunt. That the thought that's got you wet?"

"God, yes. I've never been so goddamn hot!"

"Good."

And—wham—he's in her ass again, fucking the hell out of her, forcing her to the edge of coming. She gasps, she's touching her clit, she's losing it.

He moves in her, light and quick, working her ass so sweetly she wants to scream. She's going to come. She stays there for a while, riding the knowledge, her clit full and her cunt dripping and her ass on fire. It's so dark with the blindfold on and all she can think about is how good it will be when she comes, how good it will feel, how it doesn't matter about her ass being sore, how nothing at all matters but this orgasm.

Suddenly he reaches forward and grabs her breasts. He rubs her nipples hard between his fingers, pinches them, and that's it, that starts her coming. She's touching herself and he's fucking her and she's fucking back, rocking on his cock, and he's pinching her. She's coming and it's the hardest she's come all night. She comes hard because he's the best fuck, he knows what she likes best and he gives it to her. She keeps coming and he's yelling at her. He stops pinching her and he's slapping her ass, yelling, "You can come harder than that, I know you can!"

"Then fuck, you just keep fucking me, fuck me harder, fuck me, you fuck me!"

He stops slapping her, he stops touching her, he's kneeling straight up, connected only by his cock, fucking her ass as hard as he can, hard as she's ever been fucked. She's yelling. She's coming so hard she thinks she'll pass out. She knows it feels good to him, she knows he loves to fuck hard, and that excites her even more. She feels him slow down a little. She feels his fucking get steadier and she knows he's close. He thrusts, and he thrusts, and when he thrusts again he moans just a little and he hesitates and then he buries himself in her ass and she feels him coming, his cock pulsing and his body shaking, and she screams, she's so happy. He fucks her some more, keeps coming for a little while. He slows down. He fucks her some more. He stops.

They collapse on the bed, he covers her with his body pressed against her length. They roll onto their sides, spoon to spoon. Time disappears.

She takes off the blindfold and lets the world explode in the sudden brilliance of the bedroom light. Behind her, he pulls out, wincing from the long night's loving. Stars dance in her eyes as she reaches across the bed and twists the switch. Darkness covers them, they rest in peace, they fall asleep, his cock against her ass, where it belongs.

Ivy Topiary

# MY PROFESSOR

My dear reader, understand that I scarcely know how I came to be here. I—young, lovely—have been cruelly transported from the wilds of my sylvan Northwest to this East Coast horror-school, a college made up of, God forbid, all girls.

I, so skilled at being all things to all people in secondary school: piano recitals, straight A's, literary magazine, secret mistress to my hoodlum beaux, wild nights, things I cannot here recount. What irony to find myself here, at eighteen and one-half, amongst these rotting, moneyed virgins, and the only men available more rotting, moneyed virgins at the men's college nearby. What have I done to deserve this purgatory, this wanting, waiting?

To be fair, there is my roommate Sophie, a rich, patrician beauty from Connecticut, blue-eyed, innocent, just my age. Besides her loveliness, I felt she had little to recommend her until I witnessed her practicing her cello; she played with the most intriguing mixture of concentration and wild euphoria on her face as she sawed the bow back and forth. There was that, and there was the way she watched me covertly when I undressed.

I surprised her upon my return from the library one night, as she was changing her clothes. It was raining an autumn downpour, and in I came, rivulets running down my face. Here was Sophie, feigning modesty, clutching her L.L. Bean flannel nightgown to her breasts.

"Sorry, Soph," I said, approaching her slowly. "I didn't mean to startle you," closer and closer now, and I licked my lips and kissed her fully, insinuating my tongue into her mouth to graze her orthodontically perfected teeth. I pulled her nightgown away and cupped her breast, rubbing the nipple against my wet rain slicker.

"I don't think we should be doing this," she whispered, pulling her mouth away, but arching her back to bring her body against mine.

"You don't think?" I breathed into her ear, kissing my way down her cheek, stopping to suck on her neck, and bending quickly to take her nipple into my mouth. Licking, sucking like a baby, I unzipped my raincoat and dropped it to the floor. I began unbuttoning my blouse one-handed.

I reluctantly let her go, but only to pull my blouse open and my black lace bra down. "You don't think?" I asked again, quietly, looking at her eyes, her body. Her breasts were full, mine smaller; but our nipples were spaced precisely the same distance apart, I noted as I circled the tips of mine against hers. She looked down and watched, breathing hard. "What *do* you think, Sophie?" I said, as her arms went around me.

"You're all wet," she said. And I was. I leaned back against her bureau as her hands slid down to my hips, lower still to my thighs, then back up under my plaid skirt. I made a resolution to stop wearing underwear as she cupped my ass through the black lace overlay.

My hand went down between us, between two flat, flawless stomachs, to reach her blond nether hair. My index finger opened her pussy and found wet softness, then riding back up, fingered her clit. I rubbed myself, through the lace, with the back of my hand. "Do you think you'd like to take those off?" I asked as she felt my ass through the underwear, and obediently she slid them down, her hands trailing fire on my bare flesh. She bent her head, moaning, as I pushed another finger into her cunt, and began licking just the tip of my nipple. I watched her tongue flickering between her even, white teeth, my nipple getting hard, and I felt a spreading hot wetness of desire between my legs. I increased the pace of my moving hand, and she responded, sucking my tit with force, her hips rotating, her fingers finding my snatch, pushing recklessly inside me.

Sophie threw her head back and I beheld the look of strangely focused abandon, her eyes almost closed, the muscles in her neck straining. I wondered what music she was hearing. I held her around her waist, pressuring her clit the way I like to do my own, sawing my hand back and forth inside of her. She convulsed and bit her lip with one pearl tooth till it bled. She faltered in my arms and I trailed my hand up from her cunt to her mouth to wipe away the red drop; but she took my finger in, tasting herself, her blood.

After one still, singing moment, she slid down to her knees, spreading my legs and pulling up my skirt. Shyly she kissed my inner thigh, her eyes watching my face. I looked down at her, smiled, and she trailed her mouth across the fur. My knees went weak, and I leaned on the dresser as she licked and sucked and ate me. She traced my ass with her fingers and finally put one, two, then three up inside me, moving them gently, then fiercely, until my mind was gone and there was only me, burning bright, coming to the extinguishing, the measureless brief throbbing bliss of nothing.

So there is Sophie. We climb in bed with each other now and then, which is nice as the winter grows closer. We love each other like sisters, one of us turning around under the covers and fitting mouth to cunt, cunt to mouth, so we can come at the same time. Even so, it is never quite like the first time, and Sophie, well, as I say, I love her like a sister.

So, to the library to study. Ninety-nine percent of time spent "studying" is actually spent thinking about sex. I think, as I gaze at

Manet's *Olympia* in my art history text—o! that cool fire, that forth-right look of desire. I want to be her, a whore laid out for viewing, to view, full breasts, the object of lust. My hand finds its way inside my sweater, fingers squeeze and rub my nipple; I creep my other hand up under my skirt, pushing my underwear aside (it grows too cold here, I have found, to go without), pressing my fingers against my clit. I look around, finally; no one is near, stacks of books, an iso-lated desk: let the mewling maidens find me here, anyway, plea-sured, who cares? I flip through the book with one hand, fondling myself, stopping at Michelangelo's *David*. Ah, that cock, beautiful inside me, alive, yes—*but what ugly hair!* a little voice in my head mocks, as I come, sighing. After a moment I turn, reluctantly, to the poems of Wordsworth. He's pretty dry, and maybe that will take my mind off fucking, I think; plus, the old bag who teaches Romantic Poetry is giving a quiz tomorrow. Hellfire and damnation.

But lo and behold, the next day the old bag is gone, dead of a heart attack. The entire class is horrified, devastated, and secretly pleased, none more than me as I look upon her replacement. Our new professor is virile, young, handsome. He is saying he regularly teaches upper-division classes, but in the event of this tragedy, here he is, to try to help us go on. *Help me go on,* I think, staring wide-eyed at him. He meets my gaze, briefly, looks for one instant un-nerved, quickly looks away. My professor.

I watch him, his crotch, undress him with my eyes for fifty-five minutes; then at the end he says he has read over our Coleridge pa-pers in an effort to get to know us (*Get to know me!* I think) and would like to see the following students during office hours this af-ternoon, *Me,* I think, *me,* and miraculously, my name is called, and I cannot believe it. "Did he call me?" I ask the girl next to me. Yes, she nods, and the look in her eye says, *You lucky bitch.*

I run to my room after the bell. I know just what to wear: white—virginal white—garter belt, white stockings, white cotton underwear (over, not under the garters), short plaid skirt, soft white button-up sweater (not buttoned up very far, and no bra, so my nipples will show through), and my reading glasses. Hair in a bun, red red lipstick. I grab a pen and whirl around: Sophie is sitting on her bed, reading, "Oh, hi Soph, gotta go," I say, and run out.

Outside the door to his office I breathe, pinch my nipples hard through my sweater, and, glancing up and down the hall, quickly reach up under my skirt and pull off my skivvies. Can only get in the way, I think, stuffing them in his mailbox that hangs by the door. I knock. "Come in," his voice answers.

I open the door, step in. "Well," he says, "Miss . . ." As I turn to shut the door I drop my pen, bending deep from the waist to pick it up. I know he can see the tops of my stockings, maybe more, I hope. I straighten up and turn around. "Pardon me," I say, looking at him sitting in his big leather chair, a tent already being pitched in his pants. I want to laugh. The walls are lined with books; his desk is massive; a radiator clanks under the window. Dusk is falling. He coughs. "Miss?"

"Forester," I say. "Miss Forester, but you may call me Emily."

"Please have a seat, Emily," he says, swallowing, and I sit, subtly hike my skirt up, and lean forward.

"Ah, Miss Forester," he says, shuffling papers, "your paper had a most, well, interesting, how shall we say, slant, hmm . . ." He flushes red, looking at it. "Very sophisticated, very . . . complex." He puts the paper down and stares at me. "I see in your file that you are from Portland, Oregon, and a freshman, and this paper is just, well, very engrossing, well written, and, eh, sophisticated, yes . . ." He is breaking a sweat. I spread my legs so he can see, darkly, my fur, my lips, which begin to burn at the thought.

"We are not completely bereft of culture, or of stimulation, out west, Professor," I reply. "What is the point you are trying to get across?" I ask, toying with the pen.

"Well, yes, I see . . ." he says. "Well, I suppose the point, er, the thrust, well, it is an interpretation of 'Kubla Khan' that is very well sexualized, yes, interestingly so . . ." he says. He leans back in his chair; sweat shows on his shirt in his armpits, and the bulge in his crotch has grown to interesting proportions.

"Well, Professor," I say, "what really could that 'deep romantic chasm' with its 'cedarn cover' represent but the woman wailing for her demon-lover's deep, wet cunt?"

He stammers.

"Professor," I continue, "that mighty fountain exploding, the writer's desire, the sexual impulse, the milk of Paradise, it's all hot come out of a hard cock to me."

My professor chokes a bit. I look him straight in the eye and stand up. "Ah," I say, glancing at the wall, "Blake's illustrations of the *Inferno*; beautiful, aren't they?" I turn to them to give him a moment to compose himself. "And here is my favorite, Canto Five, the poor hellish lovers . . . her words are so poignant . . ." I hear him come up behind me.

He breathes in my ear, "'. . . and when we read of the longed-for smile that was kissed by so great a lover, he who never shall be parted from me, all trembling, kissed my mouth.'" My professor presses against me; I can feel him, the specific pressure against my lower back; I turn my head and he roughly kisses my mouth.

I whirl around and push him away. "Professor!" I say, shocked. He retreats, quickly, in disbelief, behind his desk. "I am so very sorry," he says, "I must have misunderstood . . ." His voice falters, but as he sits I can see the bulge in his pants is unaltered but for a tiny stain.

I follow him back behind his desk.

"You could at least quote the Italian. And don't you know, with the climate as it is in academia nowadays, that this type of so-called misunderstanding could ruin your career? Don't you know what could become of your reputation?" I say, coming around and leaning on his desk in front of him. I ease up my skirt and unbutton my sweater, pulling it down to reveal faultless shoulders, firm breasts.

I cannot quite make out his answer as he clamps his mouth on my nipple: "I don't care"? "I have tenure"? He pulls me down to sit astride his lap, and I reach out to tease his cock through his pants. It is rock hard, and he moans. I undo his belt, unzip his zipper, open his fly—aha! no underwear!—and run my finger down his shaft.

"Oh," he moans into my nipple, pushing his fingers into my wet, wet pussy, " 'light of my life, fire of my—' "

"Quiet, Professor," I say, pulling myself further onto him, moving my cunt in a warm stain up his leg to the base of his cock, riding up and down the length of it, before sitting up on it, pushing myself down, gradually, taking it all in, slowing to tease him. He feels good, he feels good, and he is burying his face in my breasts, and moaning, and I ride him, and we come, together: o, the ascent to the heavenly, the descent into hell.

# William Harrison

# Two Cars in a Cornfield

There were eight of us, and we all worked hard in our high school classes, played on the teams and kept things normal with outsiders, including our parents, so our secret stayed intact.

The girls were Dana, Sylvie, Joanna, and Tibby. The guys were Brad, Chase, Tim, and me. They called me Kipper in those days, a name that came out of the baseball squad, who knows what it meant. Even my father called me that after a while.

My father also seemed concerned about who my steady girl might be. One night at supper he started again, saying, "Okay, I think Dana's your best gal, am I right?"

"We're all just good friends," I explained. "You know, for all the movies and ball games. We don't want to get serious."

"That's perfectly smart of you," my mother put in.

"True, you don't want anything complicated," my father admitted, drawing on his heavier baritone, the voice he sometimes used at town meetings.

"Real friendship is wonderful," said my mother. "You're all intelligent kids. Romantic love is probably a silly idea to you."

I nodded with relief. The roast beef that night was cooked rare, the best cut. We ate well at our house because my father owned the big market and butcher shop in our little Missouri town. He was putting on weight that year, moving toward the heart attack that took him away.

"Can I use the delivery car again this weekend?" I asked that night.

"One accident or one ticket and you don't use it anymore," he reminded me, as always. I delivered groceries for my father's store, but we went through this ritual every weekend. Most of our group had driven farm tractors or pickup trucks from the time we were thirteen years old, driving illegally, covering the whole county and beyond, and our parents gave us permission—because of our good grades, our mainstream lives, our innocence.

At school the eight of us agreed there would be no meaningful glances between us, no touching, no bragging, no confessions if caught, and no falling in love with just one of the partners. Looking back, wondering how it all happened, I remember all the guys as slender and muscular. Both Dana and Joanna would become school queens, although Sylvie and Tibby in their separate ways were even more stunning.

Things began the night we drove over to Nevada, a nearby town. Afterward, driving back from the movie, Chase and Tibby started undressing each other in the backseat. I gripped the wheel of the old Chevy, stunned, as Dana kept peering over at them and breaking into nervous laughter.

"You keep doing that," she warned them, "and I'm going to keep watching." She nudged me, jerking her head toward them and trying to get her giggling under control.

"They're in a trance!" Dana squealed, and she clawed at my shirt, urging me to stop the car and to become a spectator with her. After another mile I pulled in to a roadside picnic area, stopped, turned off the headlights, and turned around. By this time Tibby had shed the rest of her clothes, and I found myself addled with the sight of nakedness. Dana began to gently stroke my backside. Dumbstruck, empty of thought or language, I didn't know what more to do until Dana moved against me, making her own signals clear, then as I started unbuttoning her denim shirt I thought, hey, this is it, we're all virgins but this is it. This is ignition. The endowment inside her bra filled up my puny imagination.

Chase made deep groaning noises.

It was a moonless April evening: the hawks silent in the new leaves of the trees, the fields alive with the smells of earth and honeysuckle.

"Go ahead, touch me there," Dana whispered, and the car became hot with movement and starglow. We opened the car doors that faced the nearby woods. As Dana and I started our awkward contortions, Chase and Tib reached a loud crescendo. Moments later they leaned forward, looking over the seat to become our grinning audience. We became exhibitionists in our first coupling, oblivious, proud of our bodies, part of the wonder of the night, mysterious and reckless.

As I emptied myself into Dana's clumsy thrusts, she arched herself, reaching up, her heavy breasts flattened, stretching out as if in a delicious yawn, and found Chase in her arms. They kissed in a long, delirious, wanton hello as I found Tibby's eyes fixed in mine. A capricious tick of the psychological clock in us all: Tibby held out her hand and I took it. The girls passed one another as they climbed over the car seat, then we all groaned and started again. Tibby's slender body became a new intoxicant and she came to me like an oiled, experienced woman.

Half an hour later we stood and sat outside the car, naked, cooling ourselves, our thoughts obliterated. Chase, our quarterback, our first baseman, the friend who worked in my father's grocery store at my side, leaned against the old Chevy with his muscular arms folded across his chest, a two-hundred-pound god, serene, as if the night belonged to him. I sat on the fender with my arms around both girls, listening: I could hear the wheeling of the stars overhead, the cosmic winds, mortal voices from other planets, and I felt both drained and wise.

Occasionally, a car passed on the highway below us. Tibby addressed us in that throaty voice of hers. She was our intellectual, the debate squad member, a writer of notebooks that no one was ever allowed to read, and she was musing on what had just happened, yet in that special way of hers. "Now I'm sixteen years and one hour old," she sighed, and I loved her voice.

Then a car cruised up beside us in the darkness and stopped. It happened with Tibby's sighing observation covering the soft sound of the approaching tires. Arriving with its headlights off, it was there with us before we had a chance to be startled, so we were naked, philosophical, and caught.

"Kipper?" asked a voice, and it was Brad. The old Dodge had entered the roadside park in darkness, its occupants looking for a spot to make out, and they had recognized my mottled white Chevy—the one I made grocery deliveries in, its license plate forever tilted.

"Chase?" came the soft whisper of a girl's awed voice.

The faces of Brad, Tim, Sylvie, and Joanna peered at us and we heard our names repeated in sudden amusement. Looking back, though, it was Chase who made the difference. He stood as indifferent as a marble statue, beautiful and muscular, his penis still swollen, arms crossed, and only later did Joanna and Sylvie admit to what desire, jealousy, and yearning they suddenly felt. I wanted to cover myself, but Tib and Dana stood their ground, so there I was: trapped in the naked tableau, seeing the gesture through, taking my unspoken instructions to stay cool. In any case, Sylvie decided that we wouldn't outdo her. She slid out of the car, raised her arms, and pushed her fingers into her dark red hair. For a moment she struck a dancer's pose, legs slightly apart in an arrogant stance. Then she somehow reached back and drew her cotton dress straight up over her head. She wasn't wearing a bra and she came out of her panties in a neat, liquid movement. No one said anything.

★

Twenty years ago, all this.

Our town was small then and now, with a population of less than two thousand, and our families lived in the snug values of times maybe thirty years before that time, in years that hardly seemed touched by assassinations, Vietnam, or any part of the sexual revolution. Middle America: we grew up on church suppers, sports, fair play, and honest labor. Each house around the square stood up white and pious, part of a stubborn theology of a time that had long ago passed away.

What set the eight of us apart in those strange days? We experimented with a little booze, sure, but found it ineffective and stupid compared to the inebriations of the flesh. None of us were radicals. We liked each other because we were all psychologically straight without annoying tics or dark corners. Tibby, later, in one of her more psychological moments, offered that it was just all the movies we went to see. Into our consciousness came Michael Corleone, Sally Bowles, James Bond, the shark from *Jaws,* Woody Allen, Peter Sellers, and a hundred couples who talked dirty and did it onscreen. Locked in the middle of the continent, we were hooked on movies, and our parents often relented and let us drive over to Nevada—and, later, places like Fort Scott or Joplin that they didn't know about—to see movies. We became free, Tibby suggested, because life was out there to be seen. Maybe so: made wild and sophisticated by the celluloid stories that flickered through our heads.

"You want to drive all the way to Fort Scott for what? For an Australian movie? I didn't know they made Australian movies," said my father one evening. "And I can't believe the parents of all those girls put up with your late hours, either."

"We just go to movies, get burgers, and talk, that's all we ever do," I argued. "Nobody drinks. We drive slow. All the other parents trust us."

That won my mother to my side again. "We trust you, too," she insisted. "But do try to get home a little earlier."

After the ball game with Jericho Springs—I played shortstop, got a hit, and Chase whacked a homer—we drove to the hillside at the far end of Brad's farm. We could see for miles from that little hillside, so could easily spot the headlights of an approaching car. This was soon after our first meeting, but already our inhibitions had vanished in a barrage of dirty language and sexual acrobatics. We watched each other and had contests. We even gave each other anatomy lessons, huddling together as a group once or twice to pay elaborate attention to demonstrations. We howled with laughter or groaned in unison. Blankets and pillows appeared. Hygiene and the use of the Pill became topics and it became a frenzied class, weekend-night class, we called it, and there were no rules for those who participated or watched.

One night we played hide and seek, but that proved uncomfortable—the young corn stalks raking our thighs and butts. Tim, who was loudest among us, soon settled down, and after the sex we soon started settling into one car, crowding together, to talk. The subjects ranged from life on other planets to the dreary lives of our parents. Dracula. Mick Jagger. Religion. Bums who took drugs.

I was the astronomy freak and out there beneath the stars where the heavens opened up to us we talked about the speed of light, the formation of the galaxies, and the nature of infinity—the concept beyond concepts. It was all teenage excitement and speculation: only a few random facts, but intense.

"Black holes suck," Tim offered wistfully, like a line of melancholy wisdom, and we broke out in laughter.

"Men are just these tiny lost sperm, swimming along in the cosmos," Tibby later offered.

"That's for sure," Joanna agreed.

In the midst of these celestial discussions, Brad wanted to know if any of us could get another erection by just thinking about sex. This was after we had all exhausted ourselves. We sat in two naked clusters, front and back in the Chevy, trying to talk our way back into the rational life that would move us back toward our separate houses before dawn.

"No visual aids," Brad said. "Without looking at the girls. Just close your eyes, concentrate, and get it up."

"I can only do that in study hall," Chase muttered, and we howled again with laughter.

"I've been laid four times tonight, but I think I can do it," Tim asserted.

"None of you can do it," Sylvie added, challenging us.

Standing with our backs to the parallel cars, shutting our eyes tight, the girls acting as judges, we tried to get our lewdest thoughts collected. It was a short contest that we all lost. After that the girls sat in the Dodge discussing Warren Beatty and the guys slumped in the Chevy talking sports.

At the end of the school year we decided who would take whom to the prom. I asked for Tibby because I figured she'd keep up the conversation all evening. Other classmates invited various ones of us to get drunk, to drag race, to go skinny dipping, and to meet at the mill in Bolivar for breakfast, but we all knew where we'd spend the night when the official fun ended: back in the cornfield, folding silken dresses and rented tuxedoes into the trunks of the cars, going at each other again.

On prom night we had the first of our several fantasy sessions. In time, we played nurses and interns, bosses and secretaries, and models and photographers.

That summer all the boys and two of the girls worked at part-time jobs while Chase and I played summer-league baseball, yet we all managed to keep up the rendezvous in the cornfield. With summer came the first few small complications, too. Two yeast infections. Then Sylvie was grounded for yelling at her mother, though her parents forgave her in six days. The carburetor in the Dodge went out and Tim's parents promised to fix it, but didn't. All of us found a rebuilt one and struggled to install it.

One day Tibby, who worked mornings at our dinky little town library, brought me a book on astronomy. Telescope photos, mostly, and a few artist's conceptions that are now long outdated. The birth of the stars, all that. I was loading up cardboard boxes for my noon delivery when she stopped off with the book. We stood beside the meat locker as Chase, sweeping the floor, gave us a knowing glance, raising an eyebrow as if to say, hey, no flirting.

Tibby asked if I wanted her to make deliveries with me.

"What for?" I asked, being dumb.

"Just to do it, okay?"

"Sure, I guess so," I answered, and I looked over to see if Chase was watching us.

"Then I'll wait in the Chevy," she said lightly, and she went off toward the front of the store with a nice sway, waving at my father before she went out the door. She would circle back to the car in the alley, I knew, and the deception gave me a charge.

"You two got something up?" Chase asked, coming over with his broom. He wasn't smiling.

"Nah, everything's cool," I told him, and I showed him the book and explained why she stopped by, lying to my best friend, yet it was a lie in the future tense, a lie of possibilities and uncertainties.

Tibby and I made three deliveries in town, then took the back road out toward the Grandy farm, a gravel road that still winds along the curves of the Osage River. Tibby pulled up her knees and hugged them as we drove. She talked about how in two years she'd be at the University of Missouri, then how in two years after that she'd take a junior year abroad, traveling around Europe, and how she planned to be a journalism major, then a writer different from a journalist, not that she knew exactly what sort. As I drove I glanced over at her long legs, the most perfect long legs. She was like a movie librarian, one of those who suddenly takes off her glasses and lets down her hair to reveal that she's really the most beautiful girl in the movie, not just some dog librarian. Seriously good looking,

Tim once said about her, but also seriously and unfortunately smart.

Driving along as she talked, I thought how I watched her that first night at the roadside park. In a corner of my thoughts, she was Chase's girl because they started it all. So why did she ask to come with me today? And what was I feeling?

The summer grew suddenly more complicated.

She helped me carry the two boxes of groceries onto the porch of the farmhouse where Mrs. Grandy met us. We were led inside where the old man sat drooling in his wheelchair in a room filled with bric-a-brac, doilies, musty rugs, and creaky furniture. We accepted a sugar cookie warm from the oven. Small talk. Tibby asked all the right questions about the old man's condition and said all the appropriate things. Meanwhile, I felt my chest tighten so I couldn't breathe.

We waved good-bye and drove away. Near the river we found a bower of trees. A curtain of lush July foliage blocked the view from the road, hiding us, and the strong midsummer fragrance of the river filled the car.

"Let's do oral," Tibby said, grinning wickedly. As I turned off the engine, I could only look ahead at the river and nod. It was something the eight of us had never done and I wasn't sure, for my part, how to go about it.

She kissed me, later, with my own taste in her mouth, a kiss like nothing I had ever known, possessive and softly fierce. She was breathing hard and laughing, saying, "Oh god, that's a first, oh my," and I felt unusually successful in my performance, joining her in her laughter.

Afterward, she started talking again. I suggested that we should maybe put our clothes on and I had the overpowering desire to get out of there, but she went on about writing and traveling the world.

"I mean it," I urged her. "Some fishermen might come along. It's the middle of the day."

She might become a novelist, she told me, or a foreign correspondent.

While I buttoned up my shirt, she fixed those dark eyes in mine. "But you'll always be my first love," she told me. "Always."

"Who, me? How could I be? You did it with Chase first."

This reply, I realized later, was wildly inappropriate.

"Chase?"

"Sure, at the roadside park that first night."

"What are you talking about?"

"Well, isn't he, technically, your first love?"

"Only my first lay," she corrected me. "Besides, Chase will always have three or four girls wherever he goes. And, believe me, he won't go far. But you will. You're different."

"How's that?" I asked, and I really wanted to know.

"Because you're sensitive. The most sensitive boy I've ever known."

"Sensitive?" It was a word I wasn't sure of, but certainly more in fashion in those days than now.

"Kipper, you're on a completely different wavelength from all the rest of us, don't you know that?"

I didn't know it, yet I quickly wanted to believe it. I only knew that my name was Kipper Jones, and that until this moment I had been a shortstop, a pal, a good son, a sex machine, a movie addict, and a part-time delivery boy for my father's store.

"You're capable of real love, Kipper, don't you even know that? And I need love, as it turns out. A true heart. I mean, god, we have another whole year of high school before we can get out of this town. And if we don't take love where we find it, god, well, I think I'd just break in half."

Mesmerized by Tibby's husky voice and the strangeness of her words, I just looked at her. Clearly, she was the most beautiful naked object in the world. How could I want more? Yet I wanted to speak about the eight of us, the rules, the magic of the last three months.

Then she addressed all that.

"The eight of us won't last the summer," she predicted.

I made some slight gesture with my hand as if I knew that, too, but I didn't.

"There are lots of little signs, Kipper. I mean, Brad smells a lot like manure these days, and not all of us are happy with him. And Dana, well, she's fragile. She might go goofy on us. And Chase is already looking around. I think he wants to bang every female in school, including Miss Reinhardt in gym class."

Who among us, I wanted to say, doesn't?

"Don't get dressed," she said, sighing. "Come here." She pulled me close and opened herself to me again. "Besides, I don't want to share you with anybody. And now we can do it all the time. Twice a day all summer. Think about it. Three times, if that's what you want, then every day during next school year."

She made a strong argument for love.

"Also, we can talk. I mean you really listen to me, but you also have lots to say, that's why you're special. And maybe we can sleep together. God, I'd love to sleep with you all night. Let me think about it, I'll plan something. Wait, that hurts. Hold it. There, now that's better."

As she talked on, I once again managed to turn myself into molten lava.

We drove back from the Osage River as a couple.

When I saw Chase back at the store, I worried he suspected. That night in the game against Carthage I made my first two errors of the season, booting one easy grounder that I took on the chin. Distractions. The whole team became sullen after the loss and I felt guilty. Still, Chase didn't say anything.

To my amazement we went back to the cornfield that next Friday night, having told our parents that we were driving to Fort Scott to see a Jack Nicholson movie. That whole evening I kept watching Tibby for a signal, expecting her to make an announcement, but she seemed equally wild for all of us. Then, afterward, we all talked music: Tower of Power, Lynyrd Skynyrd, ZZ Top, Stevie Wonder, Aerosmith, Cat Stevens, and all the others. Everybody had a different favorite, so minor arguments broke out, then at last I was alone with Tibby in the front seat of the Dodge while Tim and Dana rutted away in the backseat with their usual noisiness.

"What's going on?" I asked Tib. "What were we talking about there at the river? You said you didn't want to share me."

"Ssh, not now," she replied. "Let's just do it."

While we made out, the title of an album kept buzzing in my head, a Doobie Brothers title: *What Once Were Vices Are Now Habits.* Was there a song by that title, too? Half a moon rose up over the horizon, giving us its lunatic light. Later on I stretched out on top of the Chevy, confused, and nobody even bothered to say anything to me. The music deep inside me was definitely funk.

In the days that followed I suspected Tibby might be giving all the guys special treatment on the side. A clever girl and not an impossible thought. I also decided that Tibby, not my friend Chase, had caused all this to happen, and that what occurred that first night in the roadside park she had orchestrated. She was the one who drove Chase crazy, the one who took off her clothes first, and maybe now, I decided, she manipulated all of us.

Then she phoned to explain.

"Joanna's parents are making her go with them to the Grand Canyon for a whole month. A big summer camping trip. Can you believe it? So that'll break up the group, but also Chase is going to be on the all-star team which means he'll go away for that. What do you call it?"

"The All-State Tour," I answered sadly, wishing that I was better than a .256 hitter with a good glove.

"So why should we take the blame for breaking things up? It's happening anyway. That's what I needed to tell you, but couldn't."

"It seemed to me you were just jacking my emotions around," I complained.

"I meant what I said about this summer. Three times a day if you want me, Kip. We can go back to our spot by the river. There's also a little room in the library I want to show you. And I can get the key to my folks' cabin. By the time everybody gets back at the end of the summer, we'll be together. Just the two of us. It'll be natural. Just one of the things that happened."

"You seemed to enjoy yourself the other night," I accused her.

"I tried to be a good sport," she countered. "Don't be jealous. Oh, god, Kip, I can't wait to get you alone, I really can't."

When I finally got off the phone I passed my mother in the hallway. She might have been listening in, and asked me who I was talking to.

"Tibby," I said with a sigh. "I guess we're in love."

Tibby's predictions came true. Chase was voted onto the All-Star squad that finally played a big game in Kansas City. Joanna, crying and begging to be let off, went with her parents. "The goddamned Grand Canyon," she wailed. "Isn't there a movie about it? Can't they just go to a movie and see it?"

We had a last Saturday night together. It was the night I sort of fell for Sylvie. In the backseat of the Dodge she held me close, breathing in my ear, and said quietly, "Kipper, you're the best. Not like anybody else. Gentle and—" Sensitive, I almost said to help her out. She began to cry.

"It's out there, so huge," she whimpered, growing small in my arms. "Life. It's going to gobble us up, isn't it?"

Sylvie was pure feeling. Years later she would be a dancer, dazzling, and that night I kissed her slender neck, watching the tears edge down her cheeks in graceful rivulets. She was soft in a way, I knew, that Tibby would never be.

That night a sadness befell us, a sexual melancholy—although none of us were capable of naming it. We spread out blankets and piled on, all eight of us, our bodies moving over one another in a slow adagio of touching. Only Tibby and I knew it was good-bye, that idyll, that last long kiss of summer, and we didn't tell what we knew, just as none of us would ever tell others in that little town or the strangers who couldn't understand out there in that huge world of which Sylvie spoke.

As I grew older and read some of the books that awaited me, I learned of naked children in the far islands who embraced their sexual lives far sooner than we did—short, happy interludes of abandon before the little girls became pregnant and the brief cycles of romance ended. It was true in many places—along the frozen tundra of the Arctic circle and in the deepest thickets of Africa— children thrusting themselves into nature where lust, unchecked, becomes curiously innocent. If the eight of us were out of step with the normalcies of a small town in the midcontinent, the larger questions remain: what is right, what is natural, what is true, and who speaks with authority about any of it?

Anyway, the ironies overtook us. I became the writer, not Tibby. She became a lawyer in Chicago, married with three children. Brad and Dana were once engaged, then married others. Everyone finally married, except for Chase, who kicked around the minor leagues for a few years, then joined the Marines and was killed in the skirmish we now call Desert Storm. Friendly fire brought him down.

A dozen years after we left high school I took Sylvie out to dinner in San Francisco. She was the lead dancer in a West Coast ballet troupe, and I was on a political assignment for my magazine, when I saw her photo in a newspaper and managed to get her phone number at the theater.

We sat in an open restaurant on the wharf, the one that serves such good abalone, and we talked about everybody. She asked about Chase.

"You didn't hear?"

She read my face and tears pooled in her eyes. I told her the few facts I knew. "Oh, Kipper," she said softly, and she looked out over the bay. No one had called me that for years.

We sat there holding hands after the meal. I was newly married and she was engaged, and we ached for each other.

"Was it terrible what we did?" she asked me.

"No, I believe it was good for us all," I answered truthfully, though perhaps she didn't quite believe this.

"We were so young," she said, managing a smile. "Sometimes I think nobody was ever that young."

Still holding hands we strolled the wharf while the gulls circled and cried above us. It occurred to me once more that I might have missed Sylvie, missed the great love of my life, but sex, after all, is a mystery; we can possibly be honest about everything except sex, we can know ourselves and not understand it, we can be completely worldly, yet innocent in its wake and impulse.

Sylvie was beautiful and elegant as we walked in silence and I was proud to be at her side. I brought her fingers to my lips and kissed them. In our thoughts, I know, we were in a long-ago time, in that strange American twilight before so many of the brutal vulgarities, hidden in the cornstalks, moving from the old Dodge to the old Chevy, back and forth in a burning game that somehow never burned us out, eight of us, four couples, our sixteen-year-old bodies aglow, far away.

# Contributors' Notes

**Dorothy Allison** is the best-selling author of *Bastard Out of Carolina, Cavedweller,* and a memoir, *Two or Three Things I Know.* She is also the author of *The Women Who Hate Me,* a collection of poetry, and *Skin: Talking About Sex, Class, and Literature,* a collection of essays. Her collection of short stories, *Trash,* was reissued in 2002 with new material. Born in Greenville, South Carolina, she currently lives with her partner and her son in northern California.

**Bertice Berry** is a sociologist, award-winning lecturer, comedian, and the best-selling author of *Redemption Song: The Haunting of Hip Hop* and three works of nonfiction. She lives in San Diego where she raises her sister's four children and is involved with community outreach.

**Paula Bomer** grew up in South Bend, Indiana, and now lives in Brooklyn, New York. This is her second consecutive appearance in *BAE.* Her work has appeared in *Open City, Nerve, Global City Review,* and other magazines. She has also made appearances in the books *The Mother's Guide to Sex* and *Gig: Americans Talking About Their Jobs at the End of the Millennium.* "Fucking His Wife, Four Months Pregnant with Their Third Child" is a chapter from a novel-in-progress titled *Nine Months.*

**Greta Christina** has been writing about sex since 1989. Her writing has appeared in *Ms., Penthouse,* and *On Our Backs* (a cross-section that she finds hilarious), as well as several anthologies. For her day job, she is the video and toy buyer for Blowfish, the mail-order sex products catalog. Her hobbies include long sword dancing, attending historical costume balls, watching *Buffy the Vampire Slayer,* and otherwise reveling in her nerdiness. She lives in San Francisco.

Since she was a teenage walking installation piece, **Vaginal Davis** (www.VaginalDavis.com) has been known as a performing and visual arts treasure. Her medium is the indefinite nature of her own whimsy. Whether tweaking the notion of an art-rock concept band ("Black Fag," "The Afro Sisters," "¡Cholita!—the female Menudo," and "Pedro, Muriel, & Esther") or deconstructing show-biz shtick via her experimental film oeuvre, Davis has been at the forefront of a new breed of art mavericks who take the Warhol adage of "everyone will be famous for fifteen minutes" one step further, by creating new movements every fifteen minutes. Ms. Davis's critically acclaimed concept album, *The White to Be Angry,* was nominated for a Grammy in 1997. She is a regular contributor to the *LA Weekly, Index, Purple, Lingua Franca, New Musical Express,* and the influential French fashion magazine *Dutch.* A book of photos, text, and drawings called *Magnificent Product* will be released next year by Plug-In Editions Press. Currently Davis is writing a semi-autobiographical novel called *Mary Magdalene.*

**Jack Fritscher** is the author of sixteen books, including the erotic memoir of his bicoastal lover, *Mapplethorpe: Assault with a Deadly Camera;* his signature novel of 1970s sex, *Some Dance to Remember;* and *Rainbow County,* winner of the "Best Erotic Book" award in 1998. His X-rated magazine cover/centerfold photography book was published in the U.K. as *Jack Fritscher's American Men.* Fritscher is the writer, director, and photographer of 152 gay features as released by PalmDriveVideo.com. His work and erotic history can be seen at www.JackFritscher.com.

**Dagoberto Gilb** made his living as a construction worker for sixteen years, twelve of them as a high-rise carpenter and member of the United Brotherhood of Carpenters. He is the author, most recently, of *Woodcuts of Women.* His previous books are *The Magic of Blood* and *The Last Known Residence of Mickey Acuña,* and a collection of his nonfiction essays, *Gritos,* is due out this year. His fiction and nonfiction has appeared in magazines such as *The New Yorker, Harper's,* and *The Threepenny Review,* as well as many anthologies.

**Myriam Gurba's** fiction has appeared in *Tough Girls, Bedroom Eyes, Electric 2,* and *Best Fetish Erotica.* Her writing has also been featured in a range of magazines from *On Our Backs* to *Garage.* Her muses include Lupe Velez, Maria Montez, and Dolores Del Rio.

**Robert Irwin** studied Modern History at Oxford and taught Medieval History at the University of St. Andrew's. In addition to *Prayer-Cushions of the Flesh* and *The Arabian Nightmare,* he has written four other novels and is the editor of *Night and Horses and the Desert: An Anthology of Classic Arabic Literature.*

**Tennessee Jones** is an excommunicated Southerner currently living in New York City. She has spent the last six years moving through anarchist culture, sleeping on couches, living in collective houses, and riding in the cabs of eighteen-wheelers. Her goal for her writing is to blend politics and thoughtfulness in a way that reminds the reader of the deepest part of their humanity and how their existence relates to the rest of the world. Her work has appeared in *On Our Backs, Best Lesbian Erotica, Slug & Lettuce,* and *Clamor* magazines. Her first book, tentatively titled *The Slave Ship That Never Moves: A History of Prisons in Pictures,* is out from Soft Skull Press this spring.

**Susanna Kaysen** is the author of the novels *Far Afield* and *Asa, As I Knew Him,* as well as the memoirs *The Camera My Mother Gave Me* and *Girl, Interrupted.* She lives in Cambridge, Massachusetts.

A pilgrim in the all-night cafeteria of reckless lust, this is **Tsaurah Litzky's** sixth appearance in *BAE.* Her work has appeared in over fifty other publications. She commutes from her Brooklyn waterfront apartment to Manhattan where she teaches erotic writing and erotic literature at The New School.

**Martha Miller** is the midwestern author of *Skin to Skin: Erotic Lesbian Love Stories, Nine Nights on the Windy Tree: A Mystery,* and *Dispatch to Death: A Mystery,* published by New Victoria Press. Like all of her female characters, she finds that rapture has a double edge.

**Chuck Palahniuk** is the author of *Fight Club* (which was made into a film by director David Fincher), *Survivor, Invisible Monsters,* and, most recently, *Lullaby.* His nonfiction work has been published by *Gear, Black Book, The Stranger,* and the *Los Angeles Times.* A collection of nonfiction and essays, *Stranger Than Fiction,* is forthcoming.

**Scott** served in a Ranger Battalion of the U.S. Army and was honorably discharged in 1992. He lives outside West Point, New York. "Semen in a Bullet" is Scott's first published story.

**Alison L. Smith** lives in Northampton, Massachusetts, where she is often found at local animal shelters visiting with the dogs. Her work has previously appeared in *Best Lesbian Erotica 1999, 2001,* and *2002.* She has just completed a memoir. She can be reached at alisons@rcn.com.

**Mel Smith** is a single mom, lives in a motor home, and writes gay porn. Her stories have appeared or will appear in *In Touch* magazine, *Best Gay Erotica 2002, Friction Vol. 5: Best Gay Erotic Fiction, Best of Friction, Full Body Contact,* and online at www.VelvetMafia.com and www.PeacockBlue.com.

This is **Jill Soloway**'s first published work of fiction. Jill lives in Los Angeles and works as a television writer on HBO's *Six Feet Under.* She is also currently adapting David Sedaris's *Me Talk Pretty One Day* into a screenplay for director Wayne Wang.

**Susan St. Aubin** lives in northern California with three attendant spirits (one human and two feline). Her erotic fiction has been published in many journals and anthologies, most recently in *Clean Sheets,* the *Herotica* series, *Best Women's Erotica* (2000 and 2002), *Best Lesbian Erotica* (2001), and *BAE* (1995 and 2000). She is currently finding her way to new worlds and universes.

**Susan Volchok** is a New York City writer whose short fiction has appeared in a wide variety of literary journals, 'zines, and anthologies: "How We Did It" will serve as the final story of her first collection—which is not, itself, entirely (ecstatically) about sex.

**James Williams**'s stories have been published in *Advocate Men, Attitude, Black Sheets, Blue Food, International Leatherman, Sandmutopia Guardian, Spectator,* and other magazines; online in www.MindCaviar.com and www.Suspect-Thoughts.com; and in anthologies such as *BAE 1995* and *2001, Best Gay Erotica 2002, Best SM Erotica, Bitch Goddess, Doing It for Daddy, My Biggest O, Rough Stuff 2,* and *SM Futures and SM Visions.* He was the subject of profile interviews in *Different Loving* and *Sex: An Oral History.* He lives in the San Francisco Bay Area.

**Lisa Wolfe** lives and writes in the San Francisco Bay Area. Her work has been published in www.ScarletLetters.com and in the anthology *Best Women's Erotica 2002.* Writing erotica is the most fun she's ever had with a laptop.

**Zane** is the national best-selling author of *Addicted, The Sex Chronicles: Shattering the Myth, Shame on It All,* and *The Heat Seekers.* She is also a contributor to *Brown Sugar II: Great One Night Stands, Herotica 7, Best Black Women's Erotica,* and www.BlackGentlemen.com. She is the webmistress of www.EroticaNoir.com.

# Credits

# Reader Survey

*Please return this survey or any other* BAE *correspondence to: Susie Bright,* BAE *Feedback, P.O. Box 8377, Santa Cruz, CA 95061. Or, e-mail your reply to: BAE@susiebright.com.*

1. What are your favorite stories in this year's collection?

2. Have you read previous years' editions of *The Best American Erotica*?

3. If yes, do you have any favorite stories from those previous collections?

4. Do you have any recommendations for next year's *The Best American Erotica 2004*? (Nominated stories must have been published in North America, in any form—book, periodical, Internet—between March 1, 2003, and March 1, 2004.)

5. How old are you?

6. Male or female?

7. Where do you live?
❑ West Coast    ❑ South    ❑ Midwest    ❑ Other    ❑ East Coast

8. What made you interested in *The Best American Erotica 2002*? (check as many as apply)
❑ enjoyed other *Best American Erotica* collections
❑ authors' reputations
❑ enjoy short stories in general
❑ read book review
❑ editor's reputation
❑ enjoy "Best of" type anthologies
❑ word-of-mouth recommendation
❑ erotica fan

9. Any other suggestions for the series?

*Thanks so much, your comments are truly appreciated. If you send me your e-mail address, I will reply to you when I receive your feedback.*